O9-BTJ-701

## Praise for
# KINDNESS GOES UNPUNISHED

"Johnson deftly integrates country and city sensibilities; makes Walt's love and fear for Cady palpable; and casts a droll eye on Walt and romance. . . . A must-read for both the tough and the tenderhearted."

—*Kirkus Reviews* (starred review)

"Johnson crafts great, imaginative mysteries with lots of twists, turns, and misdirections. Even in this big-city setting, a sense of the West and its values overlays the action . . . (and) the author skillfully seasons his books with humor too often missing in his genre."

—*The Billings Gazette*

"The quick pace and tangled web of interconnected crimes will keep readers turning pages." —*Publishers Weekly*

"Johnson's love for his main characters—including Longmire's fiercely devoted partner (and Philly native) Victoria Moretti and his friend Henry—also extends to the many side characters and villains that populate the novel's urban wastelands. There's genuine emotion and care in these pages, with humor and humanity to balance its undertone of imminent violence." —*Mystery Scene Magazine*

"Craig Johnson's third installment in his Sheriff Walt Longmire series, *Kindness Goes Unpunished*, solidifies this author's stature as a mystery storyteller at the level of Michael Connelly, Tony Hillerman, and James Sallis. Craig Johnson's eye for drawing upon his deeply developed characters' personalities and their realistic emotional and physical reactions to tragic events is what makes this author stand out with these icons of the mystery genre."

—I Love a Mystery

## Praise for
## Craig Johnson's Walt Longmire Mysteries

"*The Cold Dish* is my top pick for the first novel Edgar Award. It's that good!"

—Tony Hillerman

"Johnson delivers a story you can wrap your arms around. . . . We in the West have a major new talent on our hands."

—*The Denver Post*

"A winning piece of work, and a convincing feel to the whole package."

—*The Washington Post*

"The characters shoot from the hip and the Wyoming landscape is its own kind of eloquence."

—*The New York Times*

"Johnson delivers great storytelling in an intelligent mystery packed with terrific characters and an engulfing sense of place . . . capturing life in a breathtaking, unyielding landscape."

—*The Oregonian*

"Johnson knows the territory, both fictive and geographical, and tells us about it in prose that crackles."

—Robert B. Parker

"*Death Without Company* moves swiftly and the dialogue shines, but it's the Western mood and sensibility that set Johnson apart."                    —*Rocky Mountain News*

"Pile on thermal underwear, fire up the four-wheel drive, and head for Durant. Walt and his idiosyncratic crew are terrific company—droll, sassy, and surprisingly tender-hearted."                    —*Kirkus Reviews* (starred review)

"*Death Without Company* is a vivid ride through the modern American West. Great characters and storytelling make this well worth your time."
                    —Christopher Moore, author of *Lamb* and *A Dirty Job*

"*Death Without Company* exudes Johnson's bone-deep knowledge of the harsh, sometimes desperate side of the American West. . . . No pretty ponies or slick cowboys here—this is the real thing."
                    —Neil McMahon, author of *Revolution No. 9* and *To the Bone*

A PENGUIN MYSTERY

# KINDNESS GOES UNPUNISHED

Craig Johnson is the *New York Times* bestselling author of the Longmire mysteries, the basis for the hit Netflix original series *Longmire*. He is the recipient of the Western Writers of America Spur Award for fiction, the Mountains and Plains Booksellers Award for fiction, the Nouvel Observateur Prix du Roman Noir, and the 2015 SNCF Prix du Polar. His novella, *Spirit of Steamboat*, was the first One Book Wyoming selection. He lives in Ucross, Wyoming, population twenty-five.

Look for the Penguin Readers Guide in the back of this book. To access Penguin Readers Guides online, visit penguinrandomhouse.com.

# BY CRAIG JOHNSON

### THE LONGMIRE SERIES

### ALSO BY CRAIG JOHNSON

### STAND-ALONE E-STORIES
(also available in *Wait for Signs*)

# CRAIG JOHNSON

# KINDNESS GOES UNPUNISHED

PENGUIN BOOKS

PENGUIN BOOKS
An imprint of Penguin Random House LLC
penguinrandomhouse.com

First published in the United States of America by Viking Penguin,
a member of Penguin Group (USA) Inc., 2007
Published in Penguin Books 2008
This edition published 2020

Copyright © 2007 by Craig Johnson
Penguin supports copyright. Copyright fuels creativity, encourages diverse
voices, promotes free speech, and creates a vibrant culture. Thank you for
buying an authorized edition of this book and for complying with copyright
laws by not reproducing, scanning, or distributing any part of it in any form
without permission. You are supporting writers and allowing Penguin
to continue to publish books for every reader.

Netflix is a registered trademark of Netflix, Inc. All rights reserved.
The series *Longmire*™ is copyrighted by Warner Bros. Entertainment Inc.,
which also has a trademark in the series title.

ISBN 9780670031573 (hardcover)
ISBN 9780143113133 (paperback)
ISBN 9780143134855 (mass market)

Printed in the United States of America
1   3   5   7   9   10   8   6   4   2

Set in Dante MT Std

This is a work of fiction. Names, characters, places, and incidents either
are the product of the author's imagination or are used fictitiously,
and any resemblance to actual persons, living or dead, businesses,
companies, events, or locales is entirely coincidental.

For the Donut, who started it all . . .

# ACKNOWLEDGMENTS

A writer, like a sheriff, is the embodiment of a group of people and, without their support, both are in a tight spot. I have been blessed with a close order of family, friends, and associates who have made this book possible.

I have the usual posse to thank, and a few new deputies that came along for the ride. Thanks to Gail Hochman for pulling out the jail bars. Kathryn Court, Ali Bothwell Mancini, Clare Ferraro, and Sonya Cheuse at Viking/ Penguin for having the horses saddled, Susan Fain, Joel Katz, and Richard Rhoades for the cover fire, and to all the Troiano's for the spaghetti westerns.

Thanks to Mandy Smoker Broaddus for use of her poetry from her book *Another Attempt at Rescue* (Hanging Loose Press), and to Marcus Red Thunder and Henry Standing Bear for cutting the telegraph lines. Eric Boss for selling the snake oil, Neil McMahon, Bill Fitzhugh, and Christopher Moore for baking the cake with the file, Margaret Coel for the Derringer in her garter belt, and to Tony Hillerman for the pardon from the governor.

Thanks to Jim Pauley and the City of Philadelphia Police Department Public Affairs Office, the Trauma Center at the Hospital of the University of Pennsylvania, Opera-Delaware and the Grand Opera House of Wilmington, Delaware. Thanks to the Pennsylvania Academy of the Fine Arts and to Judy, my favorite masterpiece.

Philadelphia, where no good deed goes unpunished . . .

—STEVE LOPEZ
*The Philadelphia Inquirer*
January 15, 1995

# KINDNESS
## GOES
# UNPUNISHED

# 1

I didn't wear my gun. They had said that it was going to be easy and, like the fool I am, I believed them. They said that if things got rough to make sure I showed the pictures, of which there were only twenty-three; I had already shown all of them twice. "'Long, long ago, there lived a king and queen . . .'"

I looked around the room for a little backup, but there wasn't anyone there. They had said that I didn't have to worry, that they wouldn't leave me alone, but they had. "'. . . who didn't have any children. One day, the queen was visited by a wise fairy, who told her, "You will have a lovely baby girl." The king was so overjoyed when he heard the news that he immediately made plans for a great feast. He invited not only his relatives, but also the twelve fairies who lived in the kingdom.'"

"Where's your gun?"

My thought exactly. "I didn't think I was going to need it." They all nodded, but I wasn't particularly sure they agreed.

"How long have you been a sheriff?"

"Twenty-three years." It just seemed like a million.

"Do you know Buffalo Bill?"

Maybe it was a million. "No, he was a little before my time."

"My daddy says you're a butt hole."

I looked down at the battered book in my hands. "Okay, maybe we should concentrate on today's story . . ."

"He says you used to drive around drunk all the time . . ."

The instigator in the front row looked like a little angel but had a mouth like a stevedore. He was getting ready to say something else, so I cut him off by holding up *Grimm's Fairy Tales* open to the page where the young princess had been enchanted and put to sleep for a hundred years. "Why do you think the fairy visited the queen?" A dark-haired girl with enormous eyes who sat in the third row slowly raised her hand. "You?"

She cocked her head in disgust. "I told you, my name is Anne."

I nodded mine in contrition. "Right. Anne, why do you think the fairy visited the queen?"

"Because their daughter is going to fall asleep." She said it slowly, with the hearty contempt even young people have for civil servants who can't get it right.

"Well, yep, but that happens later on because one of the fairies gets angry, right?" Anne raised her hand again, but I ignored her for a slight redheaded boy in the back. His name was Rusty, and I quietly thanked the powers that be for word association. "Rusty?"

"My dad says that my uncle Paul is a fairy."

I'm not sure when it was that my storytelling abilities began to atrophy, but it must have been somewhere between *Sesame Street* and *The Electric Company*. I think I used to be pretty good at it, but that was a long time ago. I was going to have to ask my daughter if that really was the case; she was now "The Greatest Legal Mind of Our Time" and a Philadelphia lawyer. When I had spoken to Cady last night, she had still been at the office library in the basement. I felt sorry for her till she told me the basement was on the twenty-eighth floor. My friend Henry Standing Bear said that the law library was where all the lawyers went to sleep at about $250 an hour.

"You are the worstest storyteller we ever had."

I looked down at another would-be literary critic who had been silent up till now and wondered if maybe I had made a mistake with "Brier Rose." Cady had loved the story dearly at an earlier age, but the current enrollment appeared to be a little sophisticated for the material.

"My daddy hides his medicine whenever anybody knocks on our door."

I tried not to concentrate on this child's name. I propped the book back up on my knee and looked at all of them, the future of Absaroka County, Wyoming.

"He says he doesn't have a prescription."

I was supposed to make the drive to Philadelphia tomorrow with Henry. He had received an invitation to lecture at the Pennsylvania Academy of the Fine Arts with his Mennonite photograph collection in tow. I thought it would be an opportunity to visit my daughter and meet the lawyer who was the latest of her conquests. The relationship had lasted about four months, a personal record for her, so I decided that it was time I met the prospective son-in-law.

"His medicine makes him fall down."

Henry was planning on driving Lola. I had tried to talk him into flying, but it had been a while since he had driven across the country and he said he wanted to check things out. The real reason was he wanted to make an entrance with the powder blue 1959 Thunderbird convertible; the Bear was big on entrances.

"He smokes his medicine."

We were going for only a week, but Cady was very

excited about introducing us to Devon Conliffe, who sounded like a character from *The Philadelphia Story*. I had warned her that lawyers shouldn't marry other lawyers, that it only led to imbecile paralegals.

"My mommy says the only thing his medicine does is keep him from getting a job."

Patti with an "i," my daughter's secretary, agreed with me about lawyer interbreeding. We had talked about the relationship, and I could just make out a little reservation in Patti's voice when she mentioned him.

"He's my third daddy."

We were supposed to have dinner with the elder Conliffes at their palatial home in Bryn Mawr, an event I was looking forward to like a subcutaneous wound.

"I liked my second daddy best."

It would be interesting to see their response to the Indian and his faithful sidekick, the sheriff of Absaroka County. They probably wouldn't open the gate.

"I don't remember my first daddy."

I looked up at the kid and reopened the book. "'Long, long ago, there lived a king and queen who didn't have any children . . .'"

Dorothy Caldwell turned toward the patties on the griddle behind her, lifted the press, and turned them. "What'd you read?"

I pulled Cady's personal copy from the stool beside me and sat it on the counter. *Grimm's Fairy Tales*. "Brier Rose"— "Sleeping Beauty" before Hollywood got hold of it.

She gave me a sideways look and then leaned over to glance at the love-worn cover. "Kindergarten?" She shrugged a shoulder as she placed the meat press aside. "Kids have gotten a little jaded since Cady's generation, Walter."

I set my glass down. "Well, I don't have to do it again until after the election." She slipped the hamburger, lettuce, tomato, and bacon onto a toasted bun and slid the plate toward me. "The usual?"

She nodded at the old joke, sipped at her own tea, and peeked at me over the rim. "I hear Kyle Straub is going to run."

I nodded and put mayonnaise on my burger, a practice she hated. "Yep, I've seen the signs." The prosecuting attorney had jumped the gun this morning and placed his red-white-and-blue signs in all the strategic spots around town before finding out for sure if I was really going to run again. So far, it had been the strongest motivation that I had had to continue my tenure.

"Prosecuting attorney/sheriff." She paused for effect. "Kind of gives you an indication as to what his administration would be like."

I thought about my original plan, to run for sheriff, put in half a term, and then hand the reins over to Vic, allowing her to prove herself for two years before having to face a general election. I chewed a chunk of burger. "You think Vic would make a good sheriff?"

Dorothy slipped a wayward lock behind her ear and looked past me. Her hair was getting longer, and I wondered if she was growing it out. The answer to my question about Vic, like everything else about Dorothy, was definitive. "Why don't we ask her?"

I fought the urge to turn and look out onto Main Street, where I'm sure a handsome, dark-haired woman was parking a ten-year-old unit in front of the Busy Bee Cafe. Wyoming had never elected a female sheriff and the chances of their electing an Italian from Philadelphia with a mouth like a saltwater crocodile were relatively slim.

"She's got the Basquo with her." There was a pause as I continued eating my lunch. "Those two are quite the pair."

Santiago Saizarbitoria had joined our little contingency three months ago and, with the exception of trying to put out a chimney fire single-handedly on an ice-slicked roof, had proven himself indispensable. I listened as the door opened and closed, the laden April air drifting through the brief opening. They sat on the stools beside me and threw their elbows onto the counter. In identical uniforms and service jackets, they could have been twins, except that the Basquo was bigger, with wrists like bundled cables, and had a goatee, and he didn't have the tarnished gold eyes that Vic had.

I kept eating as Dorothy pulled two mugs from under the counter, poured them full, and pushed the cream dispenser and the sugar toward the old world pair. They both drank coffee all day. Vic slipped her finger through the handle of her cup. "How was this afternoon's premiere at Durant Elementary?"

I took another sip of my iced tea. "I don't think we'll make the long run."

She tore open five sugars and dumped them in her mug. "I been here two years. How come they never fucking asked me?"

I set my glass back down. "It's hard to read nursery rhymes with a tape delay."

She stirred the coffee into the sugar and spoke into the mug. "That monkey pud Kyle Straub's got signs up all over town."

"Yep, I heard."

Saizarbitoria leaned in and joined the conversation. "Vern Selby was talking very highly about Mr. Straub in the paper yesterday."

"Yep, I read it."

All our radios blared for a second. Static. "Unit two, 10-54 at 16, mile marker four."

We looked at one another. Ruby had made a crusade of using the ten code in the last few weeks, and it was turning out to be a royal pain in the ass for all of us. I was the first one to guess. "Intoxicated driver?"

Vic was next. "Road blocked . . ."

Saizarbitoria took one last sip of his coffee and slipped off his stool; he knew the chain of command. He clicked the mic on his radio. "Ten fifty-four, roger." He looked at the two of us and shook his head. "Livestock on the road."

Vic and I shrugged at each other as she tossed him the keys. She sipped her sugar as he hurried out. "Do let us know."

Vic hitched a ride with me. As we walked up the steps of the old Carnegie Library that housed the Absaroka County jail and offices, I could smell her shampoo and the crab apple blossoms. We were about halfway up the steps when she stopped me with a hand on my arm. I turned to look at her as she leaned against the iron railing and slid that same hand up the black-painted steel bar. I waited, but she just looked off toward Clear Creek, where the cottonwoods were already starting to leaf. She glanced back at me, irritated. "You still planning on leaving tomorrow morning?"

I adjusted the book of fairy tales under my arm. "That's the plan, at least mine."

She nodded. "I have a favor to ask."

"Okay."

She sniffed, and I watched as the wrinkles receded from the sides of her nose like cat whiskers. "My mother wants to have lunch with you and Cady."

I waited a moment, thinking there must be more. "Okay."

She continued to look off toward the creek. "Super Cop might be too busy, but my mother is feeling negligent in her attentions toward your daughter." I watched as the muscles of her jaw flexed like they always did when she mentioned her father.

"Okay."

"I mean . . . It's not a big deal. She just wants to have lunch."

I nodded again. "Okay."

"You can go to my Uncle Alphonse's pizzeria—it's nothing special."

I smiled and dipped my head to block her view. "I said okay."

She looked at me. "It's a family thing, and like most of the family things concerning my family, it's fucked up." She sighed. "I mean . . . they should have gotten in touch with her a long time before this, but in their usual, fucked-up way . . ."

"We'll have lunch." I watched as she studied her Browning tactical boots. Her dark hair stood up in tufts of dissatisfaction. "I would love to meet any of your family."

"Uh huh." Nothing was ever easy with Vic; it was one of her charms. She started up the steps without me. "Just don't expect too much."

I shook my head, followed her, and caught the beveled-glass door as it swung back into my face. I gently closed it and walked by the photographs of the five previous Absaroka County sheriffs. I saluted the painting of Andrew Carnegie as I mounted the final steps to the dispatcher's desk where Ruby sat reading the last series of updates from the Division of Criminal Investigation down in Cheyenne. "What the hell is a 10-54?"

She raised her blue eyes and gazed at me through her salt-with-no-pepper bangs. "Ferg says that he's 10-6 today if he's got to work the next week and a half solid, and I'm 10-42 as of five forty-five for my church's ice-cream social."

I decided to ignore the flurry of tens. "Did he go up to Tongue River Canyon?" She nodded. The Ferg was my part-time deputy who made a full-time habit of harassing the local aquatic life with his hand-tied flies. He was going to have to take up some of the slack while I was gone, so I didn't begrudge him a day casting bits of fur and feather upon the waters. "Any Post-its?"

"Two, and that young man who is supposed to come in this afternoon."

"What young man?"

She shook her head. "The young man from Sheridan who applied for the other deputy position in Powder Junction. He said he'd be here before five."

I sat on the corner of her desk, looked at the time on her computer, and reached down to pet Dog. "Then he's got twenty minutes."

The beast's head rose, and Ruby examined the scar that a bullet had left near his ear; a tongue the size of a dish-washing rag lapped my hand. "Lucian called to see if you'd forgotten it's chess night."

"Damn." I was going to have to go over to the Durant Home for Assisted Living to see the old sheriff.

"Cady called."

"She's changed her mind and doesn't want us to come after all?"

Ruby wadded up the second Post-it and dispatched it

with the first. "Not likely. She says for you to bring along your gun because she wants to take you to her shooting club on Thursday." We looked at each other for a moment, and then she raised an eyebrow. "Shooting club?"

I scratched the corner of my eye, where the scar tissue had healed. "It's this thing that Devon Conliffe's got her involved with."

She smiled. "Devon Conliffe again?"

"Yep . . ." I didn't sound all that thrilled, even to myself.

"This kid's got you worried."

She watched me scratch my eye for a moment longer, then reached up and pulled my hand away. I thought about it. "Methinks she doth protest too much."

Ruby shook her head. "She's scared you're not going to like him." She carefully released my hand. "He's young, handsome, accomplished, and makes about six times what you do on an annual basis. He has wooed and infatuated the most beautiful, intelligent, and precious woman that you know." She watched me with a smile. "It's perfectly reasonable for you to hate him." She batted her eyelashes. "Ten twenty-four?"

I looked at her for a moment, then trailed off to my office and wondered if anybody would notice if I slipped out the back. I sat at my desk and thought about calling the Bear to see if he didn't want to get going early. He wouldn't. I hit the second automatic dial button and listened as the phone rang at Henry's going concern at the edge of the Northern Cheyenne Reservation—free parking, no minimum.

He snatched it up on the second ring; it was his signature. "It's another beautiful day at the Red Pony Bar and continual soiree."

"Can we leave early?"

"No."

I hung up. There wasn't any reason to argue; I'd lose. I stared at the old Seth Thomas clock on the wall, thought of my packed bags by the door of my cabin, and sighed.

I punched the first number on my automatic dialing system and listened to the phone ring one thousand nine hundred thirty-six and one quarter miles away, to the place where my heart was on sabbatical.

"Schomberg, Calder, Dallin, and Rhind. Cady Longmire's office; can I help you?"

Patti with an "i." "Hi, Patti, you guys are working late."

"Yo, Sheriff. We've got a brief that has to be filed by tomorrow. How's things out in the Wild West?"

I leaned back in my chair and set my hat on my desk. "Uninteresting." I threw my feet up, something I rarely did, and almost flipped over backward. I grabbed the edge of the desk to steady myself. "Is 'The Greatest Legal Mind of Our Time' available?"

There was a clicking noise and the phone rang half a ring before she picked up. Near as I could figure, Schomberg, Calder, Dallin, and Rhind were getting their collective money's worth. "Cady Longmire."

I smiled in spite of myself; she sounded so grown up. "You're a punk."

There was silence on the line for a moment, then a slightly plaintive voice. "Have you left yet?"

"No, the Indian isn't packed."

Another short silence. "Is he still carrying the photographic find of the century around in hatboxes?"

"Probably. What's this stuff about bringing my sidearm?"

A quick sigh of exasperation. "I told you about it. Devon and I go to this shooting club over on Spring Garden on Thursday nights."

I was bored and decided to use up a little time arguing. "Why?"

Another, longer, silence. "It's something to do, Daddy. Don't start making judgments."

"I'm not. I just don't understand why you and a bunch of lawyers feel compelled to go out and shoot things on Thursday nights."

"We don't 'feel compelled' and we don't 'shoot things.' We go to a registered firing range, where we take out our secured weapons from the locked trunks of our cars, apply for our assigned ammunition, and shoot paper targets under the careful eye of a licensed instructor. He's an old fart, an Army guy like you."

"Marines."

"Whatever." She sniffed and got soft again. "I just thought you could meet him. It would be nice."

"Is this a Devon thing?"

Her voice turned sharp. "Bring your gun or don't. You're being impossible, and I have to go."

I looked at the phone. "I'll bring it."

"Whatever."

The phone went dead in my hand. I put my feet back down, placed the receiver on the cradle, and thought about how I was making friends and influencing people. I thought about closing my door and taking a nap but, when I looked up, a tall, slim young man with sandy hair was looking at me through the doorway. "Sheriff Longmire?"

"Yep."

"I'm Chuck Frymyer." I stared at him. "About the job in Powder Junction?"

I motioned for him to sit down and pulled his file from the pile on my desk. Only a month earlier, we couldn't get two deputies to rub together, but now we'd had over a dozen applications for the job. Frymyer had the most experience, with two years in Sheridan County.

I looked at the young man's application; he was way overqualified. I glanced back up at him. "You do realize that this job is our equivalent of the French Foreign Legion?"

"Sir?"

I tossed the file back on my desk. "You're going to be out in the middle of nowhere. Have you ever been to Powder Junction?"

"I've driven through it, on the highway."

"Under the best of weather conditions, it takes me forty-five minutes to get down there, so I need deputies who can take care of themselves and the southern part of this county."

"Yes, sir."

"Don't call me sir." I looked at him a while longer and figured that, like "Beau" Geste, he must have his own reasons for wanting to go off to the end of the world; it probably had to do with a woman, but maybe that was the romantic in me. With his two years of patrol duty, he'd be a nice addition to Double Tough, the other deputy I had down there. "You're sure you want to do this?"

He smiled. "Yes."

I stood up and stuck out a hand. "You may curse me for it later, but you've got the job. Get your stuff together and report here on Monday morning, eight o'clock, and we'll get you sworn in. Sheridan's uniforms aren't that much different from ours, but you can wear blue jeans in Absaroka County. Get a badge and a patch set from Ruby at the front desk; we'll order up the rest. No black hats—we're the good guys."

I leaned back in my chair as he smiled. Ruby appeared in the doorway and cleared her throat. "I have some bad news."

I leaned forward and rested my chin on my fingers, which spread across the surface of my desk. "I'm on my way out."

"It's Omar and Myra. They're shooting at each other again." I raised my head and looked at her. "It's a 10-16, technically." She smiled. "I'm going to my ice-cream social. Have a good time in Philadelphia and give Cady a kiss for me."

And she, too, was gone.

I yelled after her. "Who called it in?"

I heard her stop in the hallway. She came back and picked up my hat, carefully dusting it off and placing it on my head. "Go out there, make sure they don't kill each other, then go over to the Home for Assisted Living and play chess." I looked up at her. "I'll take Dog with me, and if you decide to take him with you, just stop by on your way out of town."

I drafted Vic before she could get out of the office and told her it was a chance for us to say goodbye before I left; of course, we could also be shot by the matching set of .308s with which Omar and Myra usually held their domestic disputes.

Omar Rhoades was the big dog of international outfitters; if you wanted to kill anything, anywhere, Omar was your man. He led big-game hunts on all seven continents, but the most dangerous game he had ever faced was his ex-wife, Myra. They had been divorced for about a year now, but Myra had left her belongings at the Rhoades ancestral manse, and it was like a ticking time bomb as to when Myra was going to be back. The home they had built together was on the northern border of our county, about halfway up the mountain; if they were serious about killing each other, then they were already dead.

I banked the next turn and gunned the Bullet into the long straightaway.

Vic unlocked the Remington 12-gauge from the center hump. "The gate's open."

It was about a hundred-yard shot to the circular turnaround at the main entrance, and I missed the fountain by less than a foot. We slid to a stop, and I jammed the truck into park and unbuckled my seatbelt. Vic was already up the front steps before I could get out. "Hold up! It's one thing if Omar wants to shoot us, but I'll be damned if I'm going to be shot by accident."

I pulled my .45 and looked across the heavy, cherry-paneled door that hung open. Vic jacked a shell into the Wingmaster and looked at me. You could hear music, and I'm pretty sure it was Edith Piaf.

I took a deep breath and, after a second, stepped over the threshold.

Vic's voice lashed at me from behind. "Well?"

It was dark in the main hall, the gallery windows affording only a flat, yellow light from the dying afternoon. There was no one on the landing and no one in the entryway. "C'mon." I aimed at the stairway to the left, following the wall with a foot along the baseboard and kicked a broken bottle of Absolut raspberry vodka. There was no liquor on the floor, so the bottle had been empty when it hit. Great.

I looked past the mounted heads that led down the main hall toward the kitchen and passed under the cape mount of a particularly large buffalo. "Omar!"

Omar was a friend, having gone so far as to haul my ass

up onto the mountain in a blizzard and fly my daughter, who had been caught in another, from Denver for Christmas, but drunk and full of rage he was capable of accidentally shooting either of us.

Vic moved along the wall next to me. "You want me to check the back?"

"No, we'll go upstairs; that's where the music is coming from." I took another deep breath and peered over the foot of the landing. "Omar?"

The furniture was toppled into the middle of the passage like a makeshift barricade. There were holes in the sideboard and the Chippendale chair, with splintered wood and upholstery stuffing scattered on the oriental runner. I slumped against the wall and looked at my deputy. "Either they're dead, or they can't hear us over Edith Piaf."

I started back up the steps; at least the barricade afforded some defense. At the top railing, I made the turn, thought about the layout of the second floor, and remembered that the master bedroom was at the end of the hallway. It was about forty feet to the door, which was closed, but even at this distance I could see where match-grade loads had traveled through it; ten rounds, maybe, at three thousand feet per second. Since Myra was the one who had been in Paris for the better part of the last year and since the music was French, I assumed it was she who was in the bedroom.

I was looking at the door when I ran my leg into the edge of the sideboard, causing the mirror to flip on its pivot and crash to the floor. Even with Piaf, it was a loud noise. I looked at the shards of mirror scattered across the expensive Turkish rug and thought about seven years of bad luck. Edith took a breath, and I made out the distinctive sound of a modular bolt action slamming home.

I dove behind the barricade and flattened myself against the floor as the first round splintered through the wood of the upturned edge of the sideboard. Less than two seconds later, the next round caromed off the door facing and dug into the floor just short of my outstretched right hand. I was attempting to scramble toward the stairway when Vic leaned out from the railing and snapped off two 12-gauge rounds into the ceiling, the salvo allowing me a rather ignoble retreat. I ran into Vic, and we both fell down the remaining steps.

I was lucky enough to have landed on the bottom; she was sprawled across my chest. We looked at each other, and she grinned. "That was close." We stayed like that for a moment, then she rolled off me and I slid against the wall. We were sitting there on the landing a full ten seconds before we saw Omar. He was standing in the foyer and was eating a ham and cheese sandwich and drinking a bottle of beer.

"What the hell?" He lowered the longneck bottle and cocked his head. "What're you guys doing? You could get killed up there." He started up the steps, and I noticed he had a .44 hunting sidearm in a holster at his leg. "I brought you guys a beer." We continued to look at him. "If you want a sandwich, the stuff's still out." He took another sip, and I thought about throwing him over the railing. He motioned for Vic to take the bottle, which she did after shuttling the shotgun under her arm.

"What's the story?"

He rolled his eyes and pushed his 50X silver-belly hat back from his forehead, the long curls of gold reaching to the collar of his white dress shirt. "She started drinking this morning, after we had a little talk." He took another bite of his sandwich—I have to admit, it was looking pretty good. "She said she had traded me in on two twenty-year-olds, and I told her she wasn't wired for 220. The conversation kind of deteriorated from there." He finished off the beer and threw the bottle so that it shattered against the hand-patterned drywall. He put his hand to the side of his mouth to direct the volume: "Bitch!"

Two more .308s slammed through the door above. Vic and I simultaneously ducked as the rounds sped harmlessly down the empty hallway above us.

Omar took both of the beers from Vic, opened them on his belt buckle, handed her one back, and took a swig from the other as the cap fell to the carpeted landing and rolled down the stairs. "You didn't, by chance, happen to count how many holes were in the door?" He continued to look after the bottle cap. "There's only one box of shells for that thing, sixteen in a box . . ."

I knew that there was an abundance of weapons in the Rhoades household. "What about all the other guns in the safe?"

"No ammunition. I moved it all downstairs."

They both took sips and looked at me. "Twelve." I nodded back to the landing. "And two more makes fourteen."

Omar nodded. "She's got two left." We all nodded, as he casually drew the big .44 from his holster, aimed it straight up, and fired two shots; the long-barreled Smith and Wesson bucked in his hand. A few pieces of the entryway, elk horn chandelier, and plaster ceiling fell down on us. "Cunt!" The .308 thundered in response, but this time only once. Omar took another swallow. "Wisin' up, conserving ammo."

I looked at Vic, who looked at Omar. "Any chance of talking to her?"

Omar laughed, and I looked at him. "Is there a phone in the bedroom?"

"Yeah." We traipsed down to the entryway table where an old-fashioned Belgian dial phone sat. Omar picked up the receiver, dialed the number for the bedroom, and handed the phone to me. "She's not going to talk to me."

The phone rang three times before Myra answered. "Bastard!"

"Myra, it's Walter . . ." She slammed the receiver down with an ear-shattering crack. I asked Omar to dial the number again. She didn't answer this time, but the thunderous report of the .308 and the brief squall and whine of the line informed us that Myra had shot the bedroom phone.

I hung up and looked at the two of them. Vic looked back at the landing. "She's out?"

Omar agreed. "Yeah."

I wasn't convinced. "How drunk is she?"

"Pretty damn, but she hasn't missed the door yet."

I crossed the landing, staying to the right, where I knew I could dive into the guest bedroom if she had ammunition left after all. The problem was that the closed door seemed a very dangerous twenty feet away. Credit the carpenters that built the Rhoades mansion—the floor didn't creak as I carefully made my way around the barricade.

I had holstered my .45; I had no intention of shooting Myra.

With the volume of the music, it was impossible to hear any movement in the bedroom. As Edith Piaf continued singing, I looked at what the 150-grain softpoints had done to three inches of solid wood and felt that familiar weightlessness in the trunk of my body.

I counted the holes in the door again, but the damage caused by the large-caliber rifle made it difficult to be sure how many shots had really been fired. I wasn't betting the farm. It did look as if the shot closest to the knob had taken most of the mechanism with it, and the door itself stood ajar about a quarter of an inch, so I opted for nudging the base of it with my boot; it opened four inches. I waited, but nothing happened. I nudged further, gently sweeping it back about halfway before my leverage gave out.

I took a deep breath to clear my head and stepped through the doorway into the outstretched barrel of the big .308. She had been waiting, but my left arm was still to my right so, with a sweeping gesture, I carried the barrel down and away from me in a backhanded pull that exploded a round into the floor. The sound in the room was just short of deafening.

I was going to kill Omar.

I made a grab for the front stock but missed as she stepped back, and the seemingly endless length of the bolt action swung up.

I had forgotten how good-looking Myra was, and the yearlong sabbatical in France with close to forty-eight million dollars had done her no harm. She had long, blond hair, the kind you see on the covers of magazines, and perfectly tanned skin that I'm sure had been kissed by the French Riviera. She was wearing a pink mohair cowl-neck sweater that barely reached the top of her thighs, and that was all. She was tall and lean, with strong, capable hands. The honking diamond that Omar had married her with was still on the left hand that pointed the rifle at my face. Above the scope was the palest blue eye, and as my lungs froze, the barrel dipped a little, and the sweater-matching pink lips smiled as slowly as glacial encroachment. I listened to Piaf singing "Le Chevalier de Paris" or "Mon Legionnaire," I wasn't sure which, and thought about how this wasn't the worst way to go.

The powder blue blinked, and I settled on "Le Chevalier de Paris" as the little bird trilled and softly breathed out her lovingly aching words.

Myra sagged a little, almost as if someone had punched her, and tossed the rifle aside. She stepped forward, her arms outstretched around my neck as the sharp fragrance of raspberry vodka scoured the inside of my nose and her sweater bottom rose higher. "Walter . . ."

"Good thing she likes ya." He brought his queen out. It was the second game, and my plans for an early evening had gone the way of my three pawns, two rooks, and a knight. I went with the other knight and felt a shadow of impending doom as his bishop slithered along diagonally. The stem of his pipe swung around and pointed at me like the barrel of a gun, the second of the evening. "You get 'er outta the house?" The pipe returned to his mouth.

I leaned back in the horsehide wingback chair and placed my hat on my knee. The old sheriff wasn't ready to end the evening and skimmed the other bishop across the board for a completely different attack on my king. "She's at the End of the Trail Motel over in Sheridan; flies out tomorrow."

It was quiet in the room as the old sheriff looked at me. Lucian's mahogany eyes flickered in the half-light of the kitchenette behind us. He shook his head. "Well, ya know how my marriage experience ended."

I did, and we sat there in silence for a while before I admitted a prejudice. "I hate the domestic stuff."

He nodded and watched me. "Like the third man in a

hockey fight, ya get the blame and get the shit kicked out of you for yer troubles." He waited as I made another inane move. "I hear Kyle Straub's got signs up all over town."

I took a sip and crunched one of the cubes. "I heard that, too."

"You gonna stand?"

"I don't think I've got any choice if I want to get Vic in."

He shrugged. "I'd vote for her, but I've got the weakness." Lucian was referring to his habit of addressing Vic's chest as if it had an identity of its own. "The rest of Absaroka County is another question. Now, you can make sure she's the next sheriff, but it's gonna cost you a year or two of your life." I made a face. "But then, I didn't know yer life in office was so damn bad." His gaze dropped back to the board. "Check."

I looked at the assembly of courtly pieces and placed a finger on my king, casually toppling him over to premature death. "Yep, well . . . no act of kindness goes unpunished."

# 2

It took five days to get the three of us to Philadelphia. He didn't let me drive. He drove only during daylight hours, and he went fifty-five the whole way. I read the AAA books as we drove across the country, even though I had an inkling that the Cheyenne Nation had not appreciated my oratory since Iowa, and I decided that the majority of the United States consists of gently rolling hills with light industry. I was still reading as we loped across the Schuylkill Expressway with the top down, eased off the 15th Street exit, took a left on Race and a stately right on Broad. "'It was a gentleman's agreement in 1894 that no skyscraper built would be taller than Penn's hat, but in 1986 all bets had been called off, and now the majority of the fifth largest city in the country looks down on Billy Penn and City Hall.'"

Henry carefully parked the big convertible in front of a high-Victorian gothic building and cut the engine. "You can stop reading now. We have arrived."

"I've still got the Philadelphia section to . . ." He gave me a dirty look. We figured we had best check in at the Pennsylvania Academy of the Fine Arts, since they were expecting the Bear a day earlier. I unclipped my seat belt, tossed the guide into the cavernous backseat, and scratched behind Dog's ear. "I hope you're not in trouble."

His expression didn't change as he pulled the handle and swung the four-foot door onto greater Broad Street, causing a taxi to swerve and blare its horn. He stepped out of Lola and stood, stretching his back and flipping his ponytail over his shoulder. He pulled a half-beaded, fully fringed leather jacket from behind the seat and slipped it on, instantly going native. "I am never in trouble."

I watched as the cars continued to swerve around him. "Thinking you're not in trouble and not being in trouble are two different things."

His face remained immobile as he shut the door and walked back against the traffic. "No, they are not."

Dog immediately jumped into the driver's seat, another gentleman's agreement broken, and we both watched as the big Indian casually crossed the sidewalk past the federal-style lampposts, mounted the steps, and disappeared behind the dark oak doors. People who were walking by stared at Henry, then at Lola, Dog, and me. I waved, but they didn't wave back; so much for the City of Brotherly Love.

I looked south, then west to Market, and then up thirty-two imaginary floors to where the next-in-from-the-corner window of a particularly dark, glass-clad building would be if not for the building in front of it. I had asked Cady why she hadn't gotten the corner office, to which she had replied, "I will."

I glanced back to the courthouse clock: 6:20. She'd still be at work; she never got home until at least eight. I looked around for Henry's cell phone, finally locating it at the end of the power cord under Dog's appropriated seat. I wasn't very good with the things, but I pushed one of the little buttons that had a tiny phone image on it, was rewarded with a chirp and an illuminated display of the Bighorn Mountains, and was immediately homesick. I got over it, and selected CONTACTS, working my way through about twenty women's names just to get to the Cs. I scrolled down to CADY/WORK and pushed the phone button again. It rang only once. "Hello, Bear, are you finally here?"

Evidently, I was in trouble. "If you could look out your window, up Broad Street, you would see a powder blue convertible with a seasoned, yet ruggedly handsome, sheriff and his trusty companion, Dog."

There was a pause. "You brought the dog?"

Evidently, I was in a lot of trouble. "Is that a problem?"

Another pause, this one no shorter than the last. "Devon's allergic to dogs."

I looked over at my buddy, who looked back at me with his big, brown eyes. "You have hurt Dog's feelings."

"Daddy . . ."

I reached over and scratched under his chin, which was his favorite spot. "Well, I can see if Henry can take him." There was even another pause, and I started getting a little miffed. "We wouldn't want to inconvenience Devon . . ."

"Dad."

It was a short word, but it had a lot behind it.

I watched as an elegant woman of about thirty rushed across the sidewalk and quickly made her way up the stairs, her charcoal trench coat billowing after her. She wore heels and had very nice legs. A set of keys hung from a lanyard in her hand along with a collection of IDs. Probably something to do with Henry.

I was still looking after her when a black, basket-weave Sam Browne belt with a Glock 19 blocked my view. I looked up at a young, blonde policewoman with a name tag that read OFFICER SHARPE, and spoke into the phone. "Let me call you back."

"Dad? Wait a . . ."

I pushed the red button, and the tiny phone chirped again. Dog growled, and I hushed him with a quick glance. I tipped my head back to look at myself in the cop's sunglasses; she gestured with her pen, which was already out.

"He didn't drive the whole way, did he?"

I tossed the cell phone onto the center console and smiled. "No, we switched off in Cleveland."

She didn't smile back. "Ya need'a move the vehicle."

I looked over the steering column at the empty switch. I had never seen Henry Standing Bear take the keys out of anything in thirty years. I glanced back up. "I don't have the keys."

"That's okay, I'll get it moved for ya." She snapped the button on her two-way and held it toward her mouth. "Unit 43, 10-92 at the corner of Cherry and Broad." She paused. "Roger that, 10-51. I need a hook."

I thought of my luggage, of Henry's, and of the Northern Cheyenne photographic find of the century that was in three hatboxes in the trunk. "Patrolman Sharpe, I think my friend just ran inside to find out where we could unload some things."

She smiled for the first time, maybe because I noticed her name and rank, or not. "That's okay, we let'ya get ya stuff out, before we take the car. I'll even let'ya keep the dog." She was talking into the mic again. "Long as ya got a leash for him."

I thought about all the things Dog didn't have, including a leash, as the cell phone began ringing. "Can't you just write a ticket?"

She pulled out her docket and flipped it open. "I'm gonna do that, too."

I picked up the phone and read Cady's work number. "Make it an expensive one, will you?"

I pushed the talk button again. "Hello?"

"Did you just hang up on me?!"

I was distracted by a movement to the officer's side; the woman I had seen disappear up the stairs was back. "Hi, Kathy."

Officer Sharpe lowered her pen as she half-turned. "Michelle?"

I looked up at the window on Market, and I swear I could feel Cady looking down on me. "I didn't hang up on you . . ."

The woman indicated the car in which I was sitting. "This is one of ours."

The officer sighed. "Is it movin' soon?"

The voice on the cell phone was insistent. "Are you still there?"

I tried to speak quietly. "I've got a little situation here."

Michelle nodded and stepped back to trail an arm toward Henry, who was now standing at her side. "This is Henry Standing Bear. He's here in conjunction with the Museum of the American Indian and the Smithsonian to . . ."

"Look, Dad, I've got to work late tonight so you're on your own. I probably won't make it home till after ten. All right."

It wasn't a question. "All right."

"You remember where I told you I hide the key?"

"Yep."

"You and the Bear can find the place?"

I nodded at the phone, like I always do when I'm trying to get it to like me. "I think so."

"See if Henry can take the dog, please? Devon is deathly allergic." I stared at the receiver for a while. "Dad?" It was quiet on the phone. "It's been a long day, and it looks like it's going to get longer."

I nodded some more. "Anything I can do, like bring you dinner?"

"No, Patti went out already. Dad . . ." The irritation was returning to her voice. "That Moretti woman called twice to set up lunch with us. I spoke with her earlier today, when I thought you were going to be here, and she wanted to stop by tonight." The irritation was now back in full. "Do you know why this has suddenly become so important to this woman? I mean . . . I've been here for a while."

I remembered the conversation on the jail steps. "Vic said something about how her mother was feeling guilty about not getting in touch with you."

"Well . . . If you would, her number is on the notepad by the phone at my place. Can you call and set something up with her for some other time? Tonight just isn't good."

"I'm getting that." The longest silence since I hadn't hung up on her.

By the time I'd closed the phone and rejoined the outside world, Dog had jumped into the back, Henry was fastening his seat belt, and the women were gone. He watched my face. "Trouble?"

"Always." I studied the windshield. "Where we headed?"

He watched me for a moment longer and then slipped the big bird into gear. "I can drop you off, then come back here and unload the stuff."

"You wanna get something to eat?"

He cleared his throat very quietly. "I think I have a date."

I had to smile and shake my head. "Already?"

His turn to look out the windshield. "The corner of Quarry and Bread, over in Old City?"

I thought about how there were more than nine times as many people in Philadelphia than there were in the entire state of Wyoming and how it seemed that none of them wanted to have dinner with me. We circled around City Hall and headed east on Market. I wanted to reconnoiter a little before being left on foot; I had never been to Philadelphia before and was planning on spending the next day as a tourist, so we took a brief detour around Independence Square, taking in Independence Hall and the Liberty Bell Center and Pavilion. There were more trees on this side of town, and I was comforted by the park rangers in their dark green uniforms and Smokey-the-Bear lids. At least I wouldn't be the only one in town wearing a cowboy hat. "Where have they got you staying?"

He shrugged, checked the rearview mirror, and took a right on Race, between the National Constitution Center and the Mint. I could see why Cady had chosen this part of town, with its narrow, tree-lined streets, its access to the Delaware River, and the overarching view of the Benjamin Franklin Bridge. It felt like a neighborhood. I guess it had always been one; the AAA book said that Old Ben was buried here, at Christ Church.

A year ago, when Cady had bought her building with the trust money bequeathed to her by her maternal grandmother, Old City had again been an up and coming area. As I looked around at the boutiques, coffee shops, and trendy bars, it looked like Old City had arrived. Henry slowed the convertible and waited for traffic to move so that we could turn at Bread Street and Paddy O'Neil's Tavern, a little Irish bar on the corner that Cady had told me about. She went almost every Saturday night to hear the live music and stayed until the musicians were subdued by the local Yuengling beer. Cady always brought me a six-pack of the longnecks in her carry-on.

I looked at the blue and gold lights of Ben's bridge shooting into the darkness, the suspension cables only half-lit in the fading umber of twilight. The stacked stone buttresses looked like castled pavilions along the Delaware River, with the arch lights illuminating the stone with a yellowish-green tint. I could hear the clatter of the light rail banging along on the tracks below the bridge's walking paths. Cady didn't have a car and generally walked the thirty-two blocks back and forth to work. I wondered if she ever had the time to see this picture-postcard view of her neighborhood. I worried about her walking home at night, but I worried about her brushing her teeth and breathing. Like most parents, I just worried.

"You can drink your dinner."

It sounded appealing; they probably had food, and it was within easy crawling distance of home. I glanced in the windows of the bar as we passed. It was a Thursday night, which meant I wouldn't be assaulted by live music or a crowd; I'd just pay for the privilege of my own company.

I had seen pictures of the little tannery building she had bought, and there it was, a strangely squat, one-and-a-half-story commercial-looking structure with a forged-iron atrium. The large carriage opening was still there along the street, but there was also a side entrance with a covered entryway. The Bear eased the car to a stop along the curb. The only light was on the corner about fifty feet and another building down. We sat there for a moment, and I broached the subject of Dog. "If it's going to be too big of a pain in the ass, just say so."

"It is going to be too big of a pain in the ass."

I nodded, and we got out and retrieved my bags from the trunk. I wheeled everything across the cobblestones to the door. "Breakfast?"

"How about lunch?" I nodded and shook my head as he climbed in and started the T-bird. Leave it to Henry to have already arranged a tryst.

"Dog." The big brute had been waiting for the word and lithely slipped over the side of the car. He joined me on the sidewalk as we watched the twin-turbine's brake lights disappear down the cobblestone street.

I scratched his bulky head, and he looked up at me. "Piss on the bunch of 'em, huh?" He wagged in response: two orphans in a town without pity.

The key didn't work.

I tried it the way she said; I jiggled it and struggled to get it to turn in the other direction, but no go. I walked back to the carriage entrance and tried moving these doors, but they didn't budge. I thought about abandoning my bags and heading for O'Neil's, but I wasn't sure how they'd receive Dog, and we were in it together. There was a narrow walkway of broken flagstone and weeds to my right, so I decided to see what the back of the building held in way of ingress. I stuffed my suitcases in the entryway in hopes that they would still be there when I got back, picked up the sidearm case, patted my leg for Dog to follow, and turned sideways for the two-step between the brick walls. The brim of my hat proved to be cumbersome, so I removed it and held it in the hand with the small locked case. The wall behind me was solid, but Cady's building had windows set high, about six feet up, and I could see the suspended walkways that made up the mezzanine. Dog was looking as well and cocking his head at what might have been singing.

I was almost to the end of the path when I fully heard it. It was "La donna è mobile" from Verdi's *Rigoletto*, sotto voce and melodic without trying, but there was no instrumental accompaniment. I couldn't help but wonder where you would get such a recording.

I thought the sound might be coming from the building behind me but, when I got to the end and a chain-link fence, I realized it was coming from Cady's overgrown terrace. If Verdi had been with me, he would have folded his arms across the top of the gate, placed his chin on his arms, and gazed at what I'm sure he would have perceived as the Gilda of his dreams.

At the center of the patio, in the perfect light of dusk, I could make out a fine-featured, dark-haired woman seated at a round bistro table, her legs stretched out before her and crossed at the ankles, with one elbow resting on the table's pockmarked surface. She wore black Capri pants and a stylish white blouse open at the throat; one arm was relaxed over the iron chair and the other was holding a short-stemmed wine glass, to which she sang like a child.

Woman is fickle, indeed. It's a tenor part for the Duke, but she sang it effortlessly with a husky soprano that would have had Verdi rethinking his libretto, if not his libido. She paused at one of the breaks in the music and, with perfect timing, raised the wine glass to her lips. Even from this distance, I could see the hint of ginger in her almond-shaped eyes.

I slipped my hat back on for identification purposes and softly applauded as her face turned toward me. *"Brava! Bellissima, bella . . . bella!"*

She saluted ever so slightly with her glass and downed the wine in one smooth swig like a longshoreman. "Howdy, Sheriff."

She opened the door without any problem. I dropped my bags, and we reoccupied the small terrace. Lena Moretti had raided the pantries of a dozen specialty shops in the Italian Market, and we were currently munching on small slices of stiff bread, prosciutto, mozzarella, and basil, all of which had been smothered in olive oil, first-pressed. We were about to finish the bottle of Chianti Classico, and she still wouldn't admit she could sing.

"I heard you."

She pulled her fingers through a thick tress of almost-black hair, touched with just a bit of silver, and then allowed her hand to collapse against her shoulder, the arm crooked like a broken wing. "I think hunger has affected your hearing."

"I'm tone-deaf; it gives me an advantage."

She laughed a slow laugh and brought the broken wing down to caress Dog, fingering the bullet scar. "Victor is the real talent in the family."

"Victor."

There was only a momentary pause. "My husband." She looked like Vic did whenever he was mentioned. "They're doing *Rigoletto* at the Grand Opera House in Wilmington, and Victor is playing Monterone."

I thought about it. "A considerable role."

"Not as considerable as Rigoletto, the role he thought he should have received."

"He's that good?"

"Yes."

I took a sip of my wine. "Wow, the Singing Detective."

"Chief Inspector, Field Division North." She said it as if she'd been corrected herself, numerous times.

The night didn't seem dark on the little terrace, almost as if the sky was charcoal rather than black. I took a moment to study her as she looked up and revealed a beautiful throat, and I was glad we were discussing her husband.

"It's still his first love." There was a lot in that statement.

I waited a moment before responding. "I'd imagine it's difficult to sing professionally."

Her face turned to me, and it was unsettling to see the resemblance to Vic. "Victor came from a working-class family, one that didn't see the arts as a respectable career choice."

"First generation?"

"Yes."

"You?"

"I was born in Positano; my parents had a small hotel there after the war." She took a sip of her Chianti and continued to study me. "You have to understand the chronology of the Moretti family, with Vic the father, Vic the son, and Vic the Holy Terror."

I had to laugh. "That would be my Vic?"

She blinked a slow blink in response. "That would be your Vic."

"Four boys?"

"Victor Jr., Alphonse, Tony, and Michael."

"Alphonse?"

She shrugged. "He was named after Victor's brother. Not my idea. We call him Al."

"Michael's the baby?"

"Yes." She smiled with just the corners of her mouth. "You try to not have favorites, but . . ."

"They're all police officers?"

"All but Al, who owns half a pizza parlor with the Alphonse who is Victor's brother." She nodded. "Also not my idea."

I took a sip of my wine. "Hard, raising boys?"

"At first, but then it gets easier. Unlike with girls, you only have to worry about one prick." She immediately blushed, and I got a clearer idea from whom Vic's linguistic patterns had developed. "Oh my God . . ."

I laughed, and Dog looked at both of us.

She set her glass back on the table. "I've had too much wine." She glanced around the terrace and desperately tried to find another subject. "Yours seems to have done well."

I set my own glass down. "Yep, I just wish she was closer. I worry about her a lot."

She grew quiet, and I waited. "When they're little, you wonder what they're going to be, and when they grow up you just want them to be happy." She nudged her glass with her fingertips. "Only child?"

"Yep."

Her hand was still. "It's probably better that the Terror and I have some space."

"Two thousand miles?"

"Her idea, not mine."

I looked at her. "I thought it was the ex-husband's."

"Yet another one that wasn't my idea." She looked back up to me and shrugged again, this time with an eyebrow. "One would think I didn't have many ideas. I guess that's what happens when you second-guess for a living."

My lungs forced out a little air in response. "How did those two end up together?"

She picked up her glass in spite of herself. "We all hated him, so of course she married him." She took a sip. "Reaction has always been Victoria's trademark." She swirled the wine in the glass, regarded it, and I hoped she would sing again. "I never thought it would last; he was such a straight arrow, so . . . normal."

I nodded. "We call it mugging. Out where I'm from, if you've got a horse with too much spirit, you just tie it to a mule for the night. When you come back the next morning, you'll have a different horse."

She studied me. "I guess the mule always wins?"

"Pretty much." It wasn't the response she wanted.

She continued to study me, and I was starting to feel uncomfortable. "How come you haven't gotten remarried, Sheriff?"

I was seeing even more of Vic. "I, umm . . ."

"I guess that was a little forward of me, huh?" She waited. "I guess it was, since you're not talking."

"No, I was just thinking. I do that, sometimes, before I talk."

Lena smiled, this time with her entire mouth. "Not me, robs the evening of all its spontaneity. A little wine, a little truth, and pretty soon you've got a real conversation on your hands." She took a last sip.

I started to pour us both some more. It seemed like the conversation was getting interesting, and I wasn't quite ready to leave it. "Did you drive here?"

The smile lingered. "Cab. I lost my license two years ago, and Victor made sure I never got another one." She watched as I poured with abandon. "You haven't answered my question."

I set the empty bottle back down, allowed the muscles in my neck to relax, and peered from under the brim of my hat. "I'm not so sure there is an answer." I thought about it, as promised, and stared up through the trees at the back of the little tannery. "I was . . . I don't know, depressed for quite a while, and I'm not sure I'm out of the habit."

"Of being depressed or of marriage?"

"Both."

The smile at her mouth faded, but it stayed with her eyes. "Funny, that's exactly what Vic says."

"She knows me pretty well."

"She says that, too."

I laughed and widened my eyes, letting them drop back to her. After a moment she stood, and I thought the evening was over. "You want to take a walk?"

We strolled left on Quarry and went toward the river, having left Dog curled on the leather sectional sofa in Cady's living area. As we walked down the cobblestone street in the amber glow of the city's lights, she broached the subject that must have been on her mind for a while. "What's in the case on the kitchen counter?"

"Sidearm."

She was silent for a moment. "Have gun, will travel?"

"Something like that."

We walked past Fireman's Hall and down to Elfreth's Alley which, by the sign, was the oldest continuously inhabited street in America. By the time we got to the end, we could see the municipal pier stretching out into the black distance of the river. The surface of the water reflected the lights of the boulevard, and the rumble of traffic thumped away on the concrete surface of I-95 above. It was a beautiful night, and the humidity-laden air of the river made rings around the gumdrop-shaped lampposts. It was odd, seeing that much water just floating in the close air; it was something that only happened with a hunter's moon on the high plains.

There was sporadic traffic, so we crossed halfway down the block and looked back up at the western buttress of the bridge. "So, what are you going to do in Philly?"

"I'm supposed to meet the potential prospective parents-in-law in Bryn Mawr. You know where that is?"

"Main Line; just follow the smell of money." She smiled. "Serious then?"

I looked at the flat expanse of the buttress, which stretched up to the illuminated cap above. "No ring, but it's the longest relationship she's had so far."

She watched me. "You don't like him?"

"I've never met him."

"That's not what I asked."

I shrugged. "All right, you got me. It's why I brought the .45 . . ." She laughed and then laughed again. "I don't know. I never thought I would be one of those fathers that think no one's good enough . . ."

"But?"

"No one's good enough." Another laugh. "All of yours married?"

She turned and looked at the water. "No, the Terror's the only one who has tried it. Vic Jr.'s got a hairdresser he knocked up, so I figure it's only a question of time. Al's been dating the same girl for four years but refuses to buy the cow, Tony's a ladies man, and Michael . . ." She continued to look at the water with her lips compressed.

"Michael . . .?"

She didn't move. "No one's good enough."

It was getting late and I wanted to be there when Cady got home, so we started back from the marine center, where we had been watching the boats gently rock in the current of the big river.

"So, what else have you got planned?"

I tucked my hands into the front pockets of my jeans and listened as my boots made more noise than her shoes on the sidewalk. "I don't know if Vic's told you about Henry's photography exhibit?"

"The Native American photographs?"

"Yep." I nodded at the political correctness. "The reception is Friday, but that's about it as far as formalities." We walked along in silence. "I think I was looking for an excuse to come here, and I think Henry was, too."

"It's good to keep tabs." Her turn to nod. "I don't worry about Victoria out there. I know it's foolish, but I figure the odds are better."

"They are." I slowed down a little, deciding it was time to comfort my undersheriff's mother. "There are inherent risks with the job, but county-wise we have one of the lowest crime rates in a state with one of the lowest crime rates in the country."

I was blowing sunshine her way, but she didn't seem to mind. "I hear you're going to retire soon?"

Kyle Straub's signs had made an impression all the way to Philadelphia. "It's a strong possibility."

"What then?"

I thought about it. "Maybe I'll be your daughter's deputy."

It was amazing to me how many people were still on the streets. There were couples walking arm in arm, people in suits swinging briefcases in a desperate pursuit of momentum, and a homeless guy who put the touch on me at Race and 2nd. He was an older gentleman and rocked gently on dirty tennis shoes with a sign teetering in his right hand that read VETERAN, HOMELESS, PLEASE HELP.

Lena watched as I pulled a five from my front pocket and palmed it into the palsied hand. "Thank you, sir."

His voice was remarkably cultured, and I looked at him for a second more—at the surprising blue of his eyes—and then continued on with Lena.

"You keep that up, and you won't have any money by the time you get out of here."

I nodded.

"He'll just use it to get something to drink."

"I would."

She shook her head and smiled at me some more. "You were in the military?"

I raised a weak fist. "Remember the *Maine*."

"You don't want to talk about it?"

I smiled at her. "I'll make you a deal; I don't have to talk about Vietnam, and you don't have to sing."

"Deal."

We crossed at Paddy O'Neil's Tavern and looked down Bread, where there was a Philadelphia City Police cruiser idling with its parking lights on. I couldn't be sure, but it looked as if it sat at Cady's front door. I glanced at Lena, but she was frowning at the car. "Anybody looking for you?"

"Always."

We walked down the narrow street; she was hurrying and was just a little ahead of me. By the time I got to the driver's side of the unit, I could see that the young man behind the wheel looked remarkably like Lena and could only surmise that he was a Moretti. She was the first to speak. "What are you doing here, Tony?"

The patrolman looked up at her, but he didn't smile. "Hey, Ma." He looked past her to me and at my hat. "Are you Walter Longmire?"

Whatever smile I had drained away. "Yes."

"There's been an accident."

# 3

The Trauma Center at the Hospital of the University of Pennsylvania was on the other side of town and the Schuylkill River, but it took Officer Anthony Moretti only twelve minutes to get there. It took me half that to get to the Surgical ICU on the fifth floor, and numerous lifetimes to think about the nature of trauma and how it takes more lives than cancer and heart disease combined. He wouldn't give me details, only that my daughter had been involved in some sort of accident, that she was being treated at HUP, and that, as a professional courtesy, he would drive me there.

Lena Moretti had accompanied us, stating flatly that she could just as easily get a cab from Penn as from Bread Street. She had stayed with Tony while I found myself looking into the very tired eyes of a trauma physician who explained that Cady had sustained a depressed skull fracture and that she was currently unresponsive. A CAT scan had confirmed the damage, and there was a neurosurgeon battling a subdural hematoma.

There really wasn't anything I could do but sit there with a Styrofoam cup of coffee and wait. There wasn't a lot of room in the ICU, so I dragged one of the gray upholstered chairs into the hallway, where I had a clear view of the red doors of the emergency elevator. I watched it for the next ten minutes. It was creeping up on midnight and, with the lights on all the time and the sounds of the machines, it was like a casino—only the stakes were higher.

Nobody speaks to you in these situations—it's like you're a pitcher throwing a no-hitter—they don't look at you, and you don't want them to. I thought about all the people I should call, but it was only Henry who could do anything. I pulled out my wallet; the business card from Fred Ray's Durant Sinclair Service had Henry's cell phone number scrawled across the back. I didn't call him on his mobile very often and could never remember the number. I went to the nurse's desk and asked if I could use the phone. I dialed and watched the elevator as the phone rang and a prissy little voice informed me that the person I was attempting to call was unavailable but that I could leave a message after the tone, which I did.

"Henry, it's Walt. Cady's been hurt, and I'm in the ICU at the Hospital of the University of Pennsylvania." I gave him the number of the phone I was speaking into, along with the extension. As I hung up, Lena Moretti and another young police officer who was carrying a plastic basket and Cady's briefcase turned the corner at the end of the hall. I stood there and waited for them; they stopped a full step away, like you would approach a large wounded animal.

Lena's hand trailed out to me; she was the brave one. "How is she?"

I took two fingers of the hand and looked at the eyes that were so much like Vic's. I felt my knees buckle a little. The next thing I knew, the cup of coffee from my other hand was on the polished surface of the speckled tile floor, and I was sitting in my chair trying to catch my breath. Lena and the young man kneeled beside me; he had placed the basket beside my chair, and I saw a small purse, a holstered electronic device I didn't recognize, a cell phone, a wristwatch, and her grandmother's engagement ring.

"Take it easy there, big fella." He had one hand on my shoulder and the other at my back and was holding me there.

I took a deep breath. Lena's hands were cool on my face. "Walter?"

I continued to breathe and leaned back in the chair. "I'm okay."

She looked at me, not sure. "Do you want me to get a doctor?" She glanced around for comic effect. "I mean, there seem to be plenty around."

I tried to laugh, but I think all I accomplished was a funny face. "I'm okay, really." I thought I was but, when I looked at the young officer to thank him, he looked like Lena, too; everybody had started looking alike. I dipped my head back down and blinked to clear my vision; I looked back up at the guy, but he still looked like Lena, although not exactly like Tony. I felt slightly better when I glanced at his name tag. "Michael Moretti?"

He smiled. "How ya doin'?"

Michael was a handsome kid; somehow the features I had grown used to on females worked on him as well. The eyes were a true dark brown, and his chin was a little stronger, with a cleft that neither Lena nor Vic had. He was a little shorter than six feet, but his shoulders and arms were very large. I nodded to him. "I'm okay."

He continued to smile. "Yeah, that's what you keep sayin'."

I looked at Lena, at the parchment lines at her eyes. "You called in the cavalry?"

She nodded. "It's in his district, the Wild West. Tony's the sixth."

Lena got some paper towels from the nurse's station and cleaned up the coffee as I signed the personal property list. Michael had heard through unofficial channels that Cady was stabilized and would be moved from surgery to the ICU soon. I looked at the favored son and listened as his almost new gun belt creaked in the silence of the hallway. "Mr. Longmire, do you mind if I ask you a few questions?"

"Walt, just call me Walt."

"You sure you're up to this?"

"Yep."

He nodded. "Your daughter is an associate at Schomberg, Calder, Dallin, and Rhind?"

"Yep, she was working late."

He wrote on his notepad and looked back at me. "Working late?"

"Yep. I spoke with her earlier, and she was supposed to have dinner with your mother and me, but she had some work to do."

His lip stiffened, just a little. "The firm is located on the 1500 block of Market?"

"Yes." I waited.

"Then do you have any idea why she would have been assaulted at the Franklin Institute?"

"Assaulted?"

"Look, I could tell you that it was an innocent accident . . ." He paused and then inclined his head a little. "But the attending officer said he spoke with the security guard, and he said there was an altercation between the young lady and another individual: male, Caucasian, approximately mid-thirties."

"Where?"

"Franklin Institute, across from Logan Circle, near the art museum." He continued to look at me. "The security guard said he heard voices, and then the next thing he knows the guy is beating on the door and asking for help. By the time he got the door unlocked and got out there, your daughter was lying on the steps and the man was gone. When you spoke with her, did she say anything about another engagement this evening?"

"No, she just said she'd be late."

"Does the description of the individual sound familiar?"

"Well . . . she's dating a young man."

"And that man's name?"

I paused a second before I said it. "Devon Conliffe."

He wrote it down. "Do you have an address?"

"No, but he's another lawyer . . . I'm sure Cady has it."

He looked at the basket. "Would you mind if I looked at her PDA?"

I'm sure he was aware I was staring at him. "If I knew what it was, probably not."

He reached down and plucked the unknown device from the basket and pulled it from the leather holster. "Is he an attorney with the same firm?"

"No, a different one, but I don't know the name."

It looked like a calculator, but evidently it had other abilities. He scribbled Devon Conliffe's address and phone number on his notepad, put the device back, stood, and looked down at me. "Look, it's probably nothing, but I'm gonna follow up on this and, if there's anything, I'll let you know." There was an easy quality that overrode how brand-new his uniform looked; I was betting he had been in for less than a year.

He kissed his mother and turned to summon the elevator, but the door was opening, and an entourage of attendants, nurses, and physicians wheeled out machinery and a gurney on which Cady lay. I stood, and we all moved against the wall to allow them to pass. It was good that I had the wall to stand against, because I was feeling a little shaky again. They had shaved the side of her head, where there was a U-shaped incision, and a breathing tube ran into her throat. Her eyes were closed, and she didn't move. I trailed along behind the group and watched as they installed her in the corner room; the ironic sadness of that was not lost on me.

They parked her carefully like you would a new and expensive car. I watched as the electrocardiogram was attached to the wall monitor, and it began the familiar line and spike.

The same physician who had spoken to me before separated himself and came to the doorway. His ID said Rissman. He looked at the floor, looked at the wall, and finally settled on my left shoulder as a focus. He talked about seizures sweeping across Cady's brain like electrical storms, flashing from the horizon and disappearing. He explained that Cady's Glasgow coma score was a seven and that she was only responding to painful stimuli in an involuntary manner. I guess I understood the rest, but the word that hung in my head was coma. How she responded within the next twenty-four hours would determine whether she would join the 53 percent that die or remain in a vegetative state, or the 34 percent that will have a moderate disability and/or good recovery. I wasn't sure about the other 13 percent, but I knew about head trauma, and I knew about coma; what I didn't know about was the next twenty-four hours.

He said that she was in excellent physical health otherwise and that youth was on her side, that she had had normal pupil reflex upon arrival, and that the entire team was hopeful. I had heard this speech before, because I had made it; I knew what it was worth.

Dr. Rissman said he would be back in an hour to check on things and then introduced me to the primary nurse, a solid woman in her forties; she said nothing but squeezed my hand before moving away. I sat in the chair beside the bed, and Lena Moretti was the only one left in the doorway of the glass-partitioned area. She came to the bedside and stood beside me, placing a hand on my shoulder and, thankfully, offering no advice. She stood like that long enough for me to start feeling guilty. "You should go home."

Her voice was very quiet. "You're sure?" I didn't say anything; evidently that was okay, because she patted my shoulder and assured me that she'd be back in the morning with breakfast. And she was gone.

I listened as the machines breathed for my daughter, monitored her heart, and fed her intravenously, but I kept looking at the incision where they had removed a portion of the skull to allow her swollen brain enough room to survive. A small piece of Cady was now in a freezer on the fourth floor and, when I thought about it, the weakness threatened to overwhelm me again; so I looked at her face. It was lovely, and every time I looked at it, I had a hard time convincing myself that I had had any hand in it. I always loved the finished quality of her features; she was like her mother in that respect. Mine were more blocked, as if nature had started with a pretty good idea but had gotten bored with the effort. Cady was different. She was beautiful.

I thought about the two photographs that were on my desk at the office in Wyoming. One was a preteen shot. She was tossing her hair back, exposing the large hoop earrings that she had favored until her sixteenth birthday, when she exchanged them for the tiny ones I gave her. She was smiling. If pressed, I'd have to say that I don't remember her smiling during this period—she mostly frowned in disapproval of my very existence—but she must have, because there was photographic evidence.

The other photo was from the summer of bum, as it later became known. Between law school at the University of Washington and the subsequent bar exams and her current stint at Schomberg, Calder, Dallin, and Rhind, she had spent a perfectly glorious summer along the Bighorn Mountains sleeping, sunbathing, and shopping. The photograph was taken near the end of August, and she was seated on the deck at Henry's house, her oversized feet in flip-flops. A battered pair of jeans and a stunningly studded Double D leather jacket that had cost me a half-week's pay completed the outfit. She was smiling again—Tuesday's child, full of grace.

My eyes started tearing. I looked toward the doorway and tried to clear the heat from my face and the wild thoughts that swooped through my mind like barn swallows under a dark bridge.

The plastic basket along with Cady's briefcase had been carefully placed on another chair. I went over, pulled her cell phone from the bin, and returned to my seat. I looked at her some more, then flipped open the phone, which was a much fancier version than Henry's. I scrolled down, and it didn't take long to find BEAR/CELL. I pushed the green button, and the prissy voice told me that the person I was calling was unavailable; I left yet another message, this time with the caveat that I was calling from Cady's cell phone. I hit the red button and looked at the other functions on the tiny screen, one of which read RECEIVED CALLS.

I stared at the phone a while longer and then pushed the button: DEVON 10:03 PM. I scrolled down, and it read DEVON 10:01 PM.

DEVON 09:47 PM.

DEVON 09:32 PM.

DEVON 09:10 PM.

DEVON 08:48 PM.

I ran through all the calls: Twenty-six, and all from Devon. All unanswered.

I remembered to breathe and felt the wingtip feathers of vendetta scouring the insides of my lungs. I swallowed, watched my hands shake for a moment, and then hit the function button that indicated that, in all those calls, there was only one message, and it was from the last call.

There was the little voice that said don't do it, but every other voice was screaming at me to listen. It was what I would do for anybody else; it was my sworn duty. I took a guess and punched in BEAR as the security code.

"You have one message." I had none, but I was listening.

For the next two minutes, I listened to Devon Conliffe. He was in a spitting rage and referred to Cady as everything but a child of God; the language he used to describe her actions and person would have paled Vic. He threatened to do things to her that I hadn't heard in a four-year stint with the Marines and close to a quarter century of law enforcement. Toward the end, he had become breathless but no less vitriolic, closing with one last salvo that promised a savage retribution if she did not appear within the next minute. The line went dead.

I closed the tiny cell phone; soundings from a very dark place began working their way to the surface. I knew the timber and the danger of these thoughts. My face cooled where a healthy heat had been, and a stillness crept over my hands.

I placed the cell phone in the front pocket of my jacket

and hung it on the back of my chair. I pushed my hat back a little, crossed my arms, and looked directly at Cady; the smooth, steady movement of my actions raised a sliver of panic in the rational man who was abandoning me.

I wondered what in the hell she had been doing on the other side of town. Why would she be at the Franklin Institute instead of with me at her house in Old City? Had what happened been an accident and, if she and Devon had had an argument and he had pushed her, why hadn't he called someone? Why wasn't he here?

I pulled the phone from my pocket and listened to the message again.

I now knew some answers. The next questions would most likely be asked by the fifth largest police force in the country. I had no jurisdiction in Philadelphia. I listened as the sliver attempted to gain a little leverage and force some light into the emotional dusk, but darkness can be stubborn.

I sat there in the glare of the ICU and the murmuring of the machines and watched my child as all the shadowy things loosened themselves and began their steady ascent to open air where they could do the most damage. I suppose an hour had gone by when Dr. Rissman came back and checked her vitals.

He closed her eye and again looked past my shoulder. I felt like punching him for not looking at me directly but, instead, shook my head and cleared my throat. "No movement."

"It's still early."

"I know."

He gave a perfunctory nod and went out to the nurse's station, and I was alone again.

It was approaching dawn, and the trauma physician had checked in five more times with the same results. The faint glow of the sun crept against the adjoining buildings, and it felt like I was in the turret of an unending castle. My eyes must have grown tired because, when I blinked, somebody else was in the room. I tried to focus, but the strain of the night made it feel like I was dragging 600-grit sandpaper over my eyeballs. I closed them and opened them again, but the image of the man kneeling by the bed remained blurred.

A small panic sparked, and I shifted in my chair, but he put out a hand and stilled me. It was only when the image shifted and I heard the intricate melody of the Cheyenne song that I knew it was Henry.

Epigrammatic whispers escaped from him as from a man possessed, and maybe it was the voices of ancestors winging their way onto the tongues of the living. I watched the broadness of his back drawing in the air of the room and swallowing the damage that had been done to Cady. There was a momentary stillness, and the song began again with a wailing tremble and ended with a final gasp.

After a moment, he turned to look at me, and I could see that he had been crying and that he must have been singing for some time. He wore a faded denim shirt that I had seen many times, and the collar was darkened with the tears that still streamed down his face. He didn't stand but pivoted on one foot and sat on the floor by the bed. He didn't wipe the tears away and gave me a tight-lipped smile as he folded his hands in his lap. "What has happened?"

I explained the medical situation as best I could.

His eyes stayed very steady. "How did this happen?"

I told him what Michael had told me.

His eyes still did not move. "Who has done this?"

I pulled the phone from my jacket pocket and tossed it to him. "There are twenty-six received calls on her phone, but only one message." I stood as he pushed buttons. "The security code is BEAR." I walked around to the other side of the bed to stand over Cady and looked for some sign that would give me hope that she would be in the 34 percent that made it back. I waited and watched, feeling the heat return to my face, the quiver to my hands.

He closed the phone with a distinct snap and sat there. His movements were deliberate as he stood and turned and studied me from across the bed. His voice was strained. "Do not do this."

"Do what?"

"Do not do this thing." He waited, but I didn't say anything. "Do not do this thing, because I cannot save you from the man you would become, if you do this thing."

I took a deep breath and could feel the rattle all the way down to my boots. "I guess it'll all depend on what happens next."

He leaned in, trying to get within my line of sight. "That is not what it depends upon."

I looked at him, but his eyes were drawn to something behind me. I turned to look at the uniform, badge, gun, and Moretti standing in the doorway. "How ya doin'?"

"We'll see." I turned back to Cady as Henry made his way around the bed and extended his hand, quietly palming the cell phone into his left.

"Henry Standing Bear."

They shook hands. "Michael Moretti."

Henry held on to his hand and took a closer look. "I assumed Vic had eaten any brothers or sisters."

He smiled. "Some of us made it." The Bear followed the

young man as he stepped to the foot of the bed. "Any improvement?"

"Not really." We all stood there for a moment, and I'm sure I wasn't the only one that could hear my heartbeat. "They say it's still early . . ." I knew which question I was going to have to ask next, so I thought I'd get it over with. "Did you get a statement from Devon Conliffe?"

Every trace of the smile vanished. "Didn't see her last night."

I turned and looked at him. "What?"

He pulled out a thin black notepad and consulted his own writing. "I spoke with Mr. Conliffe this morning, and he stated that he had not met with Miss Longmire."

I listened to my heart. "You spoke with him this morning?"

"Yeah."

The thumping was like the traffic on I-95. "What about last night?"

"I tried his residence about a half-dozen times."

I nodded. "Did he say where he was?"

"Phillies game and then his parents'."

"A baseball game."

"Yeah . . ." He glanced back at the notebook. "I've got two witnesses, and his parents corroborated. His firm's got a box, and he said he's got it today at 12:30 for the businessman's special."

I thought about it. "He lives here in the city?"

"Yeah."

"Any word on why it is he would have gone to his parents' house to sleep?"

"No."

Henry was watching the two of us, finally speaking when the silence got to be too much. "He went from the ballpark in South Philadelphia to his parents' home on the Main Line and then back in this morning to go to work?"

"That's what everybody's saying."

"He did a lot of driving around last night." I'm sure the pounding in my chest was causing my shirt to jump. "Did he seem concerned that his girlfriend was lying at the University of Pennsylvania Hospital in a coma?"

The young man closed his notebook and watched me for a moment. "Mr. Conliffe conveyed to me that the relationship between himself and your daughter was not of the serious nature you might have believed it to be." He pushed the notebook into the inside breast pocket of his jacket. "He stated that he had been out on a couple of dates with her but that he had ended the relationship because it was far too serious on her part."

I looked at Henry, who was watching me closely. Devon had lied and, if his parents and two other people had corroborated, then they had lied, too. I nodded, and Henry tossed the phone to me. I punched the necessary buttons and handed it to Michael. He glanced at the two of us and then held the phone to his ear. The young man stared at Cady's feet, covered with a sheet and a polyester blanket, for the full two minutes. His expression didn't change; he pushed the disconnect button and closed the phone.

I watched him and then spoke very slowly. "There are twenty-six received phone calls from Devon Conliffe from 5:11 P.M. through 10:03 P.M. last night, ending with the message you just heard." I took a breath, pointed to the cell phone, and continued. "To me, that doesn't sound like a man involved in a relationship he doesn't take seriously." I could barely talk. "And I didn't hear any baseball game in the background of that message."

He held the phone close to his chest. "Do you mind if I take this?"

"I think I'll insist."

His smile was grim, and I was liking him more and more. He nodded and placed the phone with his notepad. "I may not be the one who talks to you about this next."

I looked at my daughter. "That's all right, as long as somebody does, and damn soon."

After Michael left, we sat in chairs on either side of the bed and watched Cady. "It was the right thing to do."

I had been listening to him think it for so long, I wasn't sure if I needed to reply. "Yep."

He glanced over to me. "Why am I not so sure that you believe that?"

"Maybe it was the halfhearted response you just got."

"Maybe." He waited. "Is there anybody you want to call?"

"Not yet."

He nodded, his eyes returning to her. "You should get some sleep."

"No."

"You are not doing anybody any good falling asleep in a chair." I looked at him. "You might as well lie down."

"No."

"How about something to eat then."

"I'm not hungry."

He sighed a large sigh. "Then go take a walk, anything, but do not just sit here brooding."

"I'm not brooding."

"Planning then." I looked at him, the man who knew me better than I knew myself. "Concentrate on walking, breathing, eating, drinking, anything but this." I could still see the streaks on his face. "I will watch her. Go."

I didn't make it very far, but I made it outside and, with the number of hallways, elevators, and stairwells I had to use, that was a miracle in itself. I walked through the revolving doors and onto the University of Pennsylvania campus. It was spring, even in the winter of my discontent, and all the freshmen were hurrying to their eight o'clock classes. They looked as asleep as I felt.

There were a few roach-coaches across the street, and I figured I could get a cup of coffee from one of the food carts without contracting a disease. As I stood in line, I noticed people looking at me, and I figured I'd strangle the first one that made a smart remark about my hat. I stepped up to the counter and asked for a large one, which cost me two bucks.

"Here ya go, Tex."

I let him live.

I wandered back across and sat on one of the low cement walls that had flowering shrubs planted behind them. My back hurt and my shoulders ached. I took off my hat; even Atlas shrugged. It was a gorgeous day, and the apple and cherry trees were exploding in a riot of effusive color. I pulled in a deep breath. As a westerner, I'm always amazed at the balm of eastern air, the coursing, life-giving humidity. Even on the busy street, I could feel the trees, the river, and maybe just a little bit of the ocean off the coast of New Jersey, not so far away.

I took the top off to allow the coffee to cool when someone moved my hat and sat on the wall beside me.

Lena Moretti looked a lot better than I did. She was wearing a simple floral-print sundress and was carrying two small bags that she set on the concrete. She placed my hat on her head, and it dropped down over her ears so that

I could barely see her eyes. "Didn't trust me to bring breakfast, huh?"

"I forgot."

She tipped my hat back and pointed to the cup in my hand. "Is that coffee?"

I looked at the cup. "I'm just waiting for it to cool."

She reached out a hand. "Here, I'll show you what to do with that." I handed her the cup, and she poured it out on the sidewalk. A young woman, slouched over with the weight of her backpack, was walking past and gave her a dirty look.

"That was my coffee."

"No, this is your coffee." She handed me another lidded cup from one of the bags, and I held it with both hands. She opened her own and took a sip. "I took your dog for a walk this morning."

"Thank you." I had forgotten about him. "Where did you find a leash?"

"I used an electric cord." She crossed her legs at the ankle. I was beginning to think that she was capable of just about everything.

I opened my coffee and looked at the decisively dark brew. "This looks strong."

"Espresso, tall, double-shot. I thought you could use it." She looked at me. "How's she doing?"

I took a sip and swallowed most of the enamel from my teeth. "I figured one of your troopers would have reported in by now."

"He did, but that was almost half an hour ago."

I nodded. "No change."

We sat and drank our coffee in silence. "The Indian up there now?"

"Henry. He ran me out."

She smiled. "Here, I brought you something to eat." She dug into the other bag and handed me a collection of biscuits and a tiny paper napkin. "Biscotti. I didn't think you would be very hungry."

"You're right."

She chewed on one herself, and I watched as she unconsciously began swinging her intertwined legs. "Almond, Michael's favorite." The biscuits were good, and the only sound for a while was the munching of our communal breakfast. I noticed she was looking up at the brim of my hat that was still barely above her eyes. "Does the Terror wear a hat like this?"

"No, she says they're goofy."

She munched some more. "How disappointing." She glanced down at my feet. "She wear boots?"

"She has one pair she wears on special occasions."

She watched me for a long while. I took another breath and looked above the buildings to the clear blue sky. I could feel the thumping in my chest as the temptation to turn and count the floors up to five tugged at my jaw. A few fat pigeons ambled over from across the quad and positioned themselves in front of us. I broke off a little biscotti and tossed it their way. They grabbed the pieces and looked at me some more, giving up on Lena as a native.

"Dr. Rissman said the damage was blunt trauma from a fall?"

I nodded. "Concrete steps."

She didn't say anything for a while. "She's going to be okay."

I looked at her, still wearing my hat like a child. "How do you know?"

She ignored my ridiculous question, smiled, and looked back into the bag. "I've got a coffee for Henry, too."

I had been about to apologize, but took another deep breath instead; the darkness was there as we made small talk. "You got cream and sugar?"

"Yes."

I tossed the pigeons more biscotti. "He's particular."

She smiled. "I've heard that." She sipped her coffee and watched as I continued to feed the birds. "We may have to toughen you both up a little while you're here."

The pigeons stood next to the blunt toes of my boots. The darkness was with me again, and a plan was unfolding like a crisp linen tablecloth, snapping across the expanse of a long table and floating down to cover everything. "Lena, I may need a favor later today."

She turned at my tone of voice. "Anything."

The pigeons were now standing on the wide part of my boots, happily taking the crumbs from my fingers. "I may need you to take a shift with Cady."

"Anytime. I'm a woman of leisure." She sipped, and her ginger eyes stayed steady. There were too many cops in her life to fool her for long. "You got plans for the afternoon?"

I handed the remainder of the biscotti to Mutt and Jeff and looked across the street toward the river. "I thought I'd take in a baseball game."

# 4

"This is a really bad idea."

I looked around at the thousands of Philadelphia Phillies fans walking along Pattison Avenue toward Citizens Bank Park. "Seventy degrees and sunny. It's a beautiful day for a ball game."

"And a lousy one for aggravated assault." He looked at me and shook his head. "Where do you want to hide the body?"

"I just want to talk to him."

The Bear pursed his lips. "How about behind third; the Phillies have not shown any signs of life there in years."

I bought some upper-tier tickets from a guy standing behind an abandoned magazine stand on the corner of 11th and Pattison. I handed Henry a ticket and stuffed the rest of my money back in my wallet.

We were undercover. The Cheyenne Nation was resplendent in jeans, his weathered chambray shirt, and a pair of running shoes. He had bought a Phillies hat as we'd gotten off the subway at Broad and had tucked his substantial ponytail over the adjustable strap in the back. He could have been from Philadelphia; he could have been a very large Indian from Philadelphia, but he could have been from Philadelphia. I was blending in even better. I had left my hat at the hospital on Lena Moretti's head, had purchased a natty fitted cap and a vast red-satin jacket from the Broad Street vendor, and now approached the major league ballpark looking like a British phone booth.

"What if he is not here?"

"Then we watch a ball game." The tiny terror was creeping in on me again, even though we had checked with Lena no more than ten minutes earlier. She said that eleven lawyers from Cady's firm had stopped in, that even David Calder—the Calder of Schomberg, Calder, Dallin, and Rhind—had been to visit. Lena said she had recognized him from *Philadelphia Inquirer* society page photographs, that he was ancient but that he liked my cowboy hat. She also said that Cady was resting comfortably but had shown no signs of change.

We gave our tickets to the lady at the turnstile and walked into the broad interior thoroughfare of the ballpark. Under different circumstances, I might have enjoyed the environs, with the Kentucky bluegrass below-street-level playing field, giant scoreboard, and a capacity approximately one-tenth that of Wyoming's entire population, but I had other things on my mind.

I bought a scorecard and a stubby pencil from a vendor and stepped onto the metal treads of the escalator for the ride up. Henry lingered behind me. "Do we know which luxury suite?"

I shrugged. "How many can there be?"

There were seventy-three, to be exact. This we discovered from a kindly octogenarian in a red straw hat and vest. The Bear also asked what we should do if we were invited to stop by one of the luxury boxes but had no tickets? He said we should call our friends and have them meet us at the back of the secured area at the rear of that level.

We went up. Henry paused at a railing and looked

across center field toward the skyline of the city. "Do all the larger law firms have sky boxes?"

"I'm not sure. Why?"

"Do Schomberg, Calder, Dallin, and Rhind have a box?"

It's thinking like this that kicked Custer's ass.

I held out my hand for his cell phone, a device at which I had become a past master. I only slightly felt the twinge at seeing CADY/WORK just before I pushed the button. "Schomberg, Calder, Dallin, and Rhind, Cady Longmire's office, can I help you?"

"Patti, it's Walt."

There was no pause, and her voice lowered. "The police were here, asking questions."

"Was the name Moretti?"

"No, a detective by the name of Katz. He left his card."

"Patti . . .?"

"There was a black guy with him. He didn't leave a card, but I think he was a detective, too."

"Patti?"

"They asked a lot of questions about her and Devon . . ."

I let her wind down. "Patti, I need some help."

It was quiet. "What do you need?"

I explained that we were on a little investigative junket of our own and was wondering if the firm had a luxury suite at the ballpark. She assured me that they did and, after a brief consultation, reported that it was being used by a couple of city council people today but that there were seats still available. I asked her how we could get in, and she said to check the Phillies community relations office in five minutes.

The older lady at the double glass doors smiled as she tore our tickets and handed us the stubs. "Enjoy the game."

The gallery that provided entrance to the luxury suites was a carpeted hallway that arched around the balcony from foul pole to foul pole. We were in suite 38, and as luck would have none of it, we were right there. When I glanced into the box, I could see two brassy-looking older women drinking beer out of plastic cups that would have looked more at home strapped to a horse's nose.

One turned and looked at me, nudging her friend with the frizzy orange hair. "Franny, look, boys!"

I stood with my head in the doorway, not sure of what to say, finally settling on a western favorite: "Howdy." In retrospect, it probably sounded a little odd coming from someone who looked like the assistant carbohydrate coach of the Phils.

I left Henry to entertain as I excused myself to get something to drink. Bernice said that they had waitresses, but I told her I didn't want to wait that long.

There were small nameplates beside the doors of each suite, so it was just a question of finding the right firm. I was relying on a distant phone conversation I had had with Cady months earlier when she mentioned where Devon was employed. I remembered it was Somebody and Somebody, as opposed to the Somebody, Somebody, Somebody, and Somebody of Cady's firm. I remembered that they were not particularly memorable names and, about a third of the way around, I read HUNT AND DRISCOLL.

I slipped my scorecard from my back pocket and pulled the pencil from behind my ear when I heard the announcer roar through the starting lineups. I was, after all, undercover. I leaned against the far railing, which gave me a decent view of suite 51. A few people passed by, but I feigned concentration and raised my head only after they had all passed.

I could make out the backs of three young men sitting on the arm rails of their luxury box chairs. They were talking, but I couldn't hear the conversation clearly. Having never met Devon was putting me at a disadvantage, but fortune took a hand in the form of a young woman in short pants and an abbreviated, torso-baring Phillies T-shirt. "Miss?"

She was another south Philly gem, with mall-chick hair, blue eye shadow, and rounded vowels. "Yeah?"

"Could I get you to do me a favor?"

"Prolly."

I took this for probably, tucked the scorecard under my arm along with the pencil, and pulled a crisp twenty from my wallet by way of the Durant State Bank ATM. "Could I get you to take the largest beer you've got in to a young man in that suite by the name of Devon Conliffe?" She took the twenty, which was a lot even by ballpark standards. "It's important that he not know who it's from."

"Wa's goin' on?"

I duly translated and responded. "It's a surprise."

She looked at me for a moment more and then looked at the twenty in her hand. "Awright."

"When you get done, I'll be over there, and there's another twenty in it if you tell me his response." She practically left skid marks.

Henry met me in the stairwell. "I am not going back in there."

"Okay."

He looked around, and I noticed that his eyes were dark searchlights scanning the distance and calculating all the odds. "Is he here?"

"I'm about to find out." We waited as the young woman entered the suite; there was a loud cry of drunken insouciance, and she rapidly reappeared without the beer. I pulled another twenty and handed it to her as she tucked her serving tray under her arm. "Success?"

"Friends a youse?"

"Not exactly."

She glanced at Henry and then glanced again; I was used to it. "I did like you said an' tole him it was a secret admirer."

"Tall kid, brown hair?"

She looked at me. "More blond."

"Right." I nodded my head. "Wearing the blue shirt?"

She continued to look at me. "White."

I nodded some more. "And the red tie?" It was a chance, but he seemed like the red-tie type.

"Yeah."

I handed her another twenty. "Wait about ten minutes and give him another one, okay?"

She shrugged and was off. I watched Henry watch the hot pants. "Restroom?"

I took a deep breath. "Looks like the best shot we have at getting him alone."

"Before or after?"

I stared at the doorway to suite 51. "Before. Nobody's tough when they have to pee."

The Phils blew a double play at first, allowing the Small Red Machine two runs, and it was a brand new ball game. Personally, I was beginning to think that Devon Conliffe had a bladder like a sea lion's. I had paid sixty dollars for the three most expensive beers in Philly and, so far, *nada*.

Henry had walked to the area that overlooked an

atrium to the concourse below. He was watching the game or appeared to be watching the game. He looked back at me, and I shrugged. I was about to order the two of us a couple of beers when Devon came out of the suite. He was pretty easy to spot; it was the smirk. Tall and thin, white dress shirt and a patterned red tie. He had blondish hair parted at the side, classic Waspish good looks, and all I could think of was the phone call I had listened to very early that morning. I said "yo," and he actually nodded to me as he passed.

"Yo."

It was the same voice as the one on the cell phone, and I signaled the Bear and disappeared into the restroom.

I had cased the place; there was one row of sinks and mirrors along one side and urinals and toilet stalls along the other. He was just getting ready to unzip his pants and get down to business when I came around the corner. "Devon Conliffe?"

He turned and looked at me, the smirk still firmly in place. "Yeah?" He said it like I should know. "Do I know you?" I kept coming toward him. He was looking a little closer now, but it was only when he saw the cowboy boots that he started to turn. I caught him with a hand to the closest shoulder, which propelled him to the far wall. "What the fuck! Who the hell are you?"

I kept coming, and he tried to go to the right, so I caught him and pushed him back into the corner against the toilet-stall partition and the tiled wall. "My name is Walter Longmire." He didn't move, but his eyes flicked around the contained space. I stopped about two feet away. "You know who I am."

Maybe he was buying time, but I was fresh out. His face stiffened, and he tried to look around me again, thinking that somebody should be coming to his rescue by now, but I knew that when the Cheyenne Nation shut a door, it stayed shut.

I inclined my head a little, wanting to see him up close; I saw the muscles tense in his upper body. I supposed he thought I was going to hit him, but I was wrong; he punched a quick jab and popped my nose.

I'm sure I looked surprised. I've been punched in the face numerous times, sometimes on purpose and sometimes not. Henry had had the best shot when he popped me one in grade school but, other than that, a blow to my face has never been anything more than an irritation and a nuisance. Whatever it was that he had been expecting, it wasn't me leaning in closer and whispering. "You do that again, and I'm going to pinch your head off."

Physical force having failed, he went back to negotiation. "Your daughter's crazy."

"Bad conversation." I could feel wetness on my face, and I guessed my nose was bleeding. "I haven't really touched you, yet. You and I are going to have a chat, and we're going to keep it civil so I won't have to. Clear?"

Some of the smirk came back. "Yeah?"

"Yeah." I took a breath to clear the urge to grab him by the throat. "Tell me about last night."

"I don't have to . . ." He was probably used to having his way, of simply changing his tone to obtain the upper hand, but he was in a different league now. He lurched from the wall in an attempt to get clear. I stuck my left arm out to stop him and watched his left retract for another shot at my face. I grabbed his wrist with my right and brought my left up and around his throat, effectively blocking his right arm against the wall with my side. He was almost as tall as me, but the extra seventy pounds I had on him flattened him against the tile. He tried to kick me, but I had prepared for that by turning my body a little away.

"Don't move." He struggled some more and started to yell, but I closed my grip on his windpipe and the only thing that came out was a wheezy yelp. His eyes bulged, and I thought about how the thumb fits so well over the larynx, and with one good squeeze . . . I could feel the nausea in the back of my throat, rising up to tell me that what I was doing was wrong. I stood there swallowing the bile that kept reminding me who I was and of what I could forgive myself. It took a few seconds, but I lessened my grip and allowed him a little more air. His eyes stayed wide, but they didn't bug quite as much as before. "Tell me about last night."

"Look, I didn't do anything!"

"Anything like what?"

I let him swallow. "Anything to her."

"I don't believe you." He looked around wildly, thinking there must be some way out. "Tell me the truth."

His eyes began to well. "Look . . ."

"The truth."

The first tears fell down his well-structured face, and I was feeling worse and worse. "It was an accident . . . We had a fight."

"Tell me about it."

He looked directly at me, and in some frantic, twisted way, I think he believed what he said next. "I love her."

"You have a funny way of showing it."

He started to move his arm, probably to wipe away the tears, but I wouldn't let him move. "She fell! We were having an argument, and I tried to grab her arm . . ." I watched him as he took a breath. "She yanked her arm away . . . And then she fell." I tried to concentrate on what he was saying.

"I haven't even been home! I've been wearing the same clothes for two days now."

My head was starting to hurt. "Why didn't you stay with her."

He half howled. "I was scared!"

I felt tired all over, and I released my grip, but he started to slide down the wall. He was openly weeping. I was too weak to hold him up, so I allowed him to slide to the floor where I joined him and sat down, my hands dropping to my lap. We sat there looking at each other.

"Didn't you care what happened to her?"

He could hardly speak, he was crying so hard. "I was scared. I didn't know what to do . . . I mean, she was just lying there."

"Did you even check to see if she was alive?"

He wiped his face with a sleeve and stared at the floor. "I heard somebody coming, another guy, so I just ran." He looked back up at me, and I wasn't so sure I believed him. "I've never done anything like that before. I was scared."

I nodded and took a deep breath. My head hurt, and I was tired of talking, especially of talking to Devon Conliffe. I rolled to my side and stood up slowly; my left leg was still worrying me from a gunshot wound that I had gotten over four months earlier. I put my hand out and against the toilet partition, steadied myself, and took another breath. "Tell the police."

It took a second for him to respond. "What?"

I looked at him. "Tell the police." I watched him, not so sure he would, especially once he was out of the restroom. "You call the police and you tell them everything you told me. Understand?" He looked back at the floor, and I waited for a response. "Did you hear me?"

He inhaled. "Yes." He glanced up at me again, and there was a strange look to his face. "That's it?"

I nodded. "That's it."

I pushed off the partition and stood there. "You call the police and you tell them everything that was said between us." I started to walk out but paused for a moment. "You tell them . . . Or you'll see me again. You'll see me again just out of the corner of your eye, and I will be the last thing you ever see."

The Bear appropriated a bar towel from the waitress as she passed. She stopped and peered at my face. "He didn' like the beer?"

I shrugged as I wiped my nose. "Some guys just can't hold their liquor."

As Henry and I walked toward the escalators, he put a hand out and pulled the towel away. He tilted my head back and looked up my nostrils. "So, what does the other guy look like?"

"I punched him in the fist with my nose, but I think he'll live." I pinched the towel over my nose and leaned against the escalator's moving rubber railing, glad that something else was providing the locomotion. I looked back up at Henry. "I didn't kill him."

The wide face nodded, inscrutable to the end. "Good."

As we were riding down, two men were riding up. The one in the front was silver-haired and was sharply dressed in a charcoal suit with a maroon tie and a black trench coat; behind him was a man with a tightly cropped haircut and a suit, tie, and overcoat all the same shade of dark tan. It was difficult to see where the clothes began and the man stopped. They stared at us as we rode closer; by the time we passed each other, I could see that the first man's designer glasses had small, red dots on the frames that emphasized his large brown eyes. The second man smiled a very becoming smile, and I noticed the bulge of a shoulder holster at his left armpit. "Foul ball?"

I rolled my eyes and nodded.

We quickly made our way from the ballpark and walked toward Broad and the subway. Henry didn't say anything, which gave me plenty of time to think, mostly about whether I believed Devon Conliffe.

At some level, just about everybody lies to you when you're a cop, whether they have a reason to or not—some little portion of the truth that they feel would be best omitted in their dealings with you. The only good thing about it is that you start being able to tell when people are doing it, and I was sure that Devon was. The kid obviously had a lot of emotional and mental issues to deal with, but I was having a hard time working up any empathy.

I watched Henry pull out his cell phone before we got to the subway entrance and call Lena Moretti. I looked south at the big highway overpass that with a few right turns would take me back to Wyoming. I wondered when that would be, if ever. When I looked back, he was closing the phone. "No change."

I nodded, and we continued down the stairwell toward the thundering clatter of the Broad Street SEPTA line. We chose an almost empty car and sat across from each other on the orange fiberglass seats at the end. I finished with the bar towel and carefully folded it on my knee. My head was still pounding, and it was good to sit down.

"Lena says she can stay as long as you would like and, if she has to leave, Michael can take over." I didn't respond. "She sounds very nice."

"Yep."

He watched me. "Are you okay?"

I looked at the floor. "My daughter is in a coma, I think my nose is broken, and I'm about to have every policeman in Philadelphia after me. How could it be any better?"

The train stopped at the next station, and a few more people drifted on and sat down. He looked at me but didn't say anything until a few stops later. There were a lot of other people on the car now, and his voice was low. "I need to go to the museum and help with the installation this evening."

"I understand."

He waited a moment. "I can cancel the whole thing."

"No." I smiled, but there was no joy in it. "One of us should be doing something constructive, don't you think?"

He smiled back, but at least his had some warmth.

I abandoned him at City Hall and took a regional rail line over to University City and the hospital. It was getting late in the afternoon, and all I could think about were the hours that had been ticking by with no improvement, lowering our odds with every passing minute.

It was clouding up to the west, and it looked like there might be a few showers in the evening. There was another street person at Convention Avenue, and I gave him the jacket. There were a few blood spots on it and it fit like a blanket, but he seemed happy. I thought about giving him the hat, but it was growing on me.

When I got to the fifth floor, Lena and Dr. Rissman were waiting for me in Cady's room; Lena was the first to speak. "She moved."

I couldn't trust my ears. "What?"

"She moved her leg."

Rissman was next. "She reacts to environmental stimuli. There's still no eye response, but this is very, very good."

All the heat came back to my face, making my nose throb even more, and I looked around for a place to sit. I collapsed on the nearest chair and looked at Cady. Lena was crying by the bed and trailed a hand down to my daughter's foot. Her leg moved, and the sounds erupted from my throat. "When?"

Rissman was kneeling by my chair, and he looked at the wall and the floor before again finally settling on my left shoulder. "About five minutes ago. What happened to your nose?"

I leaned back. "I get nosebleeds." I looked at Cady. "She's going to make it."

"Let's not get too carried away; she's moving, and that gives us a lot better odds than before . . ."

I looked at him, at the silver bristles of his hair, even if he wouldn't look at me. "Hell, yes."

He nodded. "I just don't want you to jump to any conclusions; this is a long road, and at any given time it could just stop."

I took a deep breath. "I like the odds better now."

He patted my shoulder as he stood. "Well, they are certainly better than before." He smiled a shy smile at Lena's shoulder. "I'm going to run another series of tests in about an hour, which means the two of you will be looking at an empty bed for the majority of the evening." He glanced back to me, making eye contact for only a second. "I think you should go home and get some rest."

We shared a taxi to Old City, where she dropped me off at Cady's place. I tried to give her some money, but she wouldn't take it. She handed me my hat, and I popped it on over the Phillies cap. I'm sure I was a pretty sight. Before the cab pulled away, I remembered to ask. "Did you call Henry?"

"I left a message."

"Thank you."

"Speaking of messages, you've got a lot of them on her answering machine. I hope you don't mind that I listened to them, but I thought it would help if I copied them all down for you on a notepad. It's by the phone."

"I guess I need to call Wyoming."

I stood on the Bread Street cobblestones where we had taken our walk. It seemed like decades ago. Night and the city—I found myself wanting to ask her in but realized that the poor woman had a life of her own. "Thank you again."

She leaned forward, looking up through the half-light of the cab. "It wasn't anything." She ran her fingers through her hair, and I was still amazed at the bluish gloss.

"Yes, it was. I don't know if I could've gotten through last night without your help, let alone today." I could see her eyes half closed in pleasure, like a cat being stroked. The smile was there, a soft and easy smile. I didn't want her to leave without some arrangement to meet again. "How about lunch tomorrow?"

"Deal. I'll meet you at the hospital?"

I nodded and closed the door. The driver was doing some of his paperwork, so we waited for a moment on either side of the window, and I had a strange twinge of something as she looked at me again. I extended my hand; she sat there watching me as the taxi started off down Bread, took a left on Quarry, and disappeared.

The skies were looking more threatening, and I wasn't sure if it was thunder I was hearing in the distance or the train on the bridge. I turned and walked to Cady's door, reached above the junction box, and pulled down a note with the key. Lena had filed it so that it would now operate smoothly in the lock. I opened the door and was immediately mauled by Dog.

I gave him the ham that had been left over from Lena's picnic basket and figured I could always get a couple of hamburgers from Paddy O'Neil's—me too, for that matter. There was a menu, which gave me the luxury of phoning in my order. I opened the fridge and there was a six-pack of Yuengling, so I popped a bottle out and drank it while I looked for the bathroom. I took a shower and got out some clean clothes from my duffle, which I'd left next to the sofa. There was a clock on the microwave that told me I still had three and a half hours before Cady would be back in the ICU, so I got the pad from beside the phone and read the numerous and assorted messages from practically everybody in the Cowboy State. Most of them were from Ruby and Vic, but there were also ones from the Ferg, Lucian, Sancho, Double Tough, Vern Selby, Dorothy, Lonnie Little Bird, Brandon White Buffalo, Dena Many Camps, Omar, Isaac Bloomfield, and Lana Baroja.

There were no messages from Devon Conliffe.

I shuttled the dark thoughts toward the back of my mind and placed the notebook on the glass coffee table. I had been here two days and hadn't called anybody. I wasn't sure if word had gotten back to Absaroka County through the Moretti network, the University of Pennsylvania Hospital, or the Philadelphia Police Department, but I had a lot of explaining to do. I suppose I had been waiting till I could give some sort of hopeful prognosis and, now that Cady had given even an involuntary response, I should call.

I looked at the phone but just didn't have the energy. I

took a deep breath, lay back against the pillows on the sofa, and placed my cowboy hat over my eyes. Dog jumped on the couch uninvited and, after what seemed like a long time, we were both asleep.

I'd been dreaming a lot lately, and there were always Indians in my dreams, so it wasn't surprising when I could see them from the corners of my eyes. I could feel the wind, the kind we get on the high plains that's only a notch or two below hurricane force. I was leaning into the gale at the edge of some bluffs near Cat Creek. It was hard to focus; my eyes were thin slits with tears streaming from the sides. I turned my head a little and could see a Cheyenne brave who instructed me to lift my arms by raising his own. He wore a fringed and beaded war shirt with the bands of blue and white seed beads running up the arms, and I could make out a parfleche medicine bag painted red and black with the geometric wind symbol.

The old Indian half smiled, brushing an arm toward my face and forcing me to concentrate on what was in front of me. I glanced at the horizon as the lightning flashed like the seizures in Cady's brain and swept across the sky in a silent electrical storm. I looked down into the canyon, and a chill shot from my spine like a fuse; there was nothing below us for at least three hundred feet.

The phone rang, and I lifted my hat to look at the greenish numbers on the microwave that told me that I'd been asleep for about an hour. A pang hit me as I listened to Cady's recorded voice on the answering machine and heard the beep. "Walt, it's Ruby. I hope you're getting these messages . . . Vic said she got a phone call from her mother saying that there had been an improvement in

Cady's condition. I just wanted to check in and see if there's anything any of us can do here. We've been trying to call Henry, but he doesn't answer his phone either." There was silence on the line as I sat there with my guilt and listened. "Vic is threatening to fly back there, so you better call us." Another pause, and I would almost swear she knew I was listening. "Please call us. We're worried about Cady, and we're worried about you." I was about to reach for the phone when the line went dead.

I sighed. If Cady's situation stayed the same, there would be no going back; it was as simple as that.

I looked at Dog, and he looked back at me. "You want a hamburger?" He wagged, and I took it for a yes. I ordered us up four cheeseburgers to go from the leprechaun at the end of the block.

I went to the terrace doors and listened to the sporadic drops hit the leaves of the crab apple tree. It was a gentle rainfall that unfocused the hard edges of the city night, making all the surfaces glisten. It was only about fifty yards to the side entrance of Paddy O'Neil's, so I figured I could get there and back without getting soaked. I watched the drops fall slowly past the yellow of the streetlights and into the widening pools on the cobblestone street. I looked up at the span of the bridge arching into Old City and listened to the steady thrum of the traffic.

Even over the blare of the Celtic band and the raucous crowd, the brogue wasn't a generation removed. Black Irish; a handsome kid about Cady's age with a wayward eye that kept tracking left. "Yore Cady's fatha', the sheriff?"

I looked up at the brim of my cowboy hat. "Yep." He was like one of those bundles of baling wire that I had seen in Vietnam, the ones that went into the Vietcong tunnels with .45s and the balls of a cat burglar. "You O'Neil?"

He smiled a grin. "Hisself. Took the place over from me Uncle Paddy, the original O'Neil." He handed me the bag full of cheeseburgers, and I noticed the tattoos up and down his arms. I paid him, with a little extra for his trouble. "Where's ya daughter?"

I waited a moment, the hubbub of the bar swirling around me. "She's not feeling well." I leaned in and cleared my throat. "O'Neil, can I ask you a question?"

He wiped his hands on a dish towel. "Ya?"

"You ever met her boyfriend, Devon Conliffe?"

His hands stopped working the towel. "Ya, I met 'im a couple'a times."

I nodded, my face only a foot from his. "Nice guy?"

He worked his jaw for only a second. "Ya."

"O'Neil?" He leaned in a little closer with the question. "You're a liar." He watched me for a second, then laughed and walked down to the other end of the bar to help the overworked waitresses. He glanced back at me only when I left.

Dog ate his cheeseburgers faster than I ate mine, so I gave him the last bite of my second one and tried to fade into another nap, but I suppose I was worried that I might oversleep and, as a result, didn't sleep at all.

I finally gave up after an hour and called a cab. I looked at Dog from the door; he was watching me with his big, brown eyes. "They don't allow dogs in the ICU." He continued to look at me, and I was sure he understood every word. "There's nothing I can do." He sat. "I'll take you for a long walk tomorrow." He lay down, still watching me. "Honest."

It was raining a little harder when I stepped out and, just before jumping into the taxi, I noticed the throb of blue tracer emergency lights that seemed to spring from the support cables of the Benjamin Franklin Bridge; in the darkness, it looked like the body of the bridge was hanging in the saturated air. There must have been a wreck. I stood there for a second more, then decided it was somebody else's problem and climbed in the cab.

There wasn't that much traffic this late at night, so we made good time, and twelve minutes later I was sitting at Cady's bedside. She had just been brought back from testing, and the nurse at the desk said that there wasn't any substantial change but that the stimulus response was a very positive sign.

The gentle spring showers had gradually given way to sheets of rain splattering against the windows like waves in some fifth-floor tide. I sat there for a couple of hours before falling asleep to the sound, my chin resting on my chest.

When I woke up it was still raining, but there was someone else in the room. I blinked and looked at the man standing on the other side of Cady's bed. His black trench coat and umbrella were still dripping, so he couldn't have been there long and, when I glanced back at the doorway, I saw wet tracks leading to where he now stood. On the other side of the glass partition, the black man with the close-cropped haircut was talking to the nurse who had assured me earlier.

When I looked back to the man beside the bed, he was watching me with the brown eyes through the designer frames with the little red dots. "Hello."

"Hello."

He looked back at Cady. "You have a beautiful daughter."

"Thank you."

His eyes stayed on her. "I don't suppose you remember . . ."

"Yes, I do."

He nodded and turned to look at me. "Good. You know why I'm here?"

"I'd imagine it has something to do with Devon Conliffe?"

He came around to the foot of the bed. "You'd be right." The detective pursed his lips and stuffed a hand in his pocket, the umbrella's handle still over his wrist. "What can you tell me?"

I thought about it and about what Devon had probably told them. "I was a little angry . . ." I yawned, covering my face with my hand. "So I went down to the baseball game and tried to get the truth out of him."

"And?"

"I'm not so sure there's any truth in him." I reached up and rubbed my nose. "I think he roughed me up more than I did him."

He nodded. "That the last time you saw him?"

"Yep. Why?"

"Because . . ." He studied me closely. "About three hours ago, somebody threw him off the Benjamin Franklin Bridge."

# 5

They didn't take me downtown. I've always wanted to be taken downtown, but I guess they didn't think it was necessary, so we made an appointment for 9:30 in the morning. Henry showed up at 9:00 and handed me a cup of coffee. I told him about my conversation with the detectives.

I took the lid off, but the cup looked suspiciously like the one Lena had poured out on the sidewalk the day before. "I didn't do it; did you?"

"No, but it certainly makes things inconvenient." He took the chair on the other side of the bed.

"For whom?"

He sipped his coffee. "Devon, for a start."

I grabbed a cab in front of HUP and headed across town to the police administration building; it was about four-and-a-half blocks from Cady's. It looked a lot like two beehives and had a statue on the newly grown grass of a patrolman holding a child in his arms. They called it the Roundhouse, and it was all very impressive until I had to walk around the block to find a way in.

There was a bulletproof window with a sign in seven languages that said translators were available. I told the patrolman I was here to see Detectives Katz and Gowder and that I might need a translator. He didn't have much of a sense of humor. There weren't any chairs, so I stood along the wall and waited and read about Philadelphia's most wanted. It looked like they had a lot more activity than we did in Absaroka County. I thought about Vic working here and figured her five years' experience easily surpassed my twenty-three. After seven minutes, both Gowder and Katz appeared.

The coffee that I had bought from the vending machine was worthy of the Lena Moretti treatment, but I sipped it anyway and looked around at the floor-to-ceiling windows and at the benches and indoor trees. "Don't you guys have a room with a chair and a single lightbulb hanging from the ceiling?"

"Budget cuts." Gowder was doing most of the talking this morning. His suit, shirt, tie, and shoes once again matched his skin; I bet his socks did, too. "That nose looks like it hurts."

"I've had worse."

Katz wasn't saying anything; interested cop, indifferent cop.

"Why don't you tell us about the ball game?"

I sat down on one of the benches and tipped my hat back. "I just went down to talk to him about a phone message he left for my daughter and to get a clearer idea of the relationship between them."

"And did you get a clearer idea of that relationship?"

"I think so." I thought about it. "On his end, not a remarkably healthy one."

He leaned forward and crossed his arms. "Well, we'll have to take your word on that, since neither party is available for comment."

I set my coffee on the table in front of me and let a long

moment pass. "Maybe you'd better speed this up. I'm starting to lose interest."

Gowder smiled and looked down at my hand that had just relinquished the paper cup. "Big hands." I waited. "The late Devon Conliffe had marks on his neck indicating that he might have been strangled by somebody with big hands."

"That the cause of death? I thought it might have had something to do with falling off the bridge."

"Deceleration trauma." It was the first time Katz had spoken.

I didn't have anything to hide, so I went ahead and told them everything. "I put him up against the wall in the restroom, and my hand was around his throat because he was trying to kick me in the groin." I looked at the two of them. "Look, if you guys liked me for this you would have arrested me last night. I realize that taking a nap is not the best alibi in the history of the western world but, if we can figure out when I bought the cheeseburgers from O'Neil's and check that against your time of death, then you guys can get started on catching whoever really did this."

"Where were you after the baseball game and before the nap?"

I turned back to Gowder. "The hospital." I shook my head. "I can appreciate what you're up against, but when would I have tracked him and how would I have gotten him up there?"

Gowder smiled some more. "Like I said, you're a big guy."

Katz set his own coffee down. "What Detective Gowder is alluding to is that the killer would have had to have thrown Mr. Conliffe over the railing and across the PATCO lines. That, without Devon's participation, would have been quite a physical feat."

I leaned back against the bench. "What about suicide?"

"What about it?"

I made a face. "I only spent five minutes with the kid, and I could tell he had problems, plus what happened the night before last."

Katz leaned in this time. "And what did happen night before last?"

I told them what Devon had told me, including his promise to tell the police. "What'd he say to you?"

"He said that you had gotten rough with him and that he had to kick your ass." I sighed and looked down at the surface of the table. Gowder chuckled. "We thought it sounded a little funny, too."

"What did he say about the relationship?"

The one detective glanced at the other. "Same thing he told Patrolman . . . umm . . ."

Katz finished for him. "Moretti."

The smile was back, and he looked at Katz longer than necessary. "Moretti. How could I forget?"

"I'm assuming you've listened to the phone messages?"

Katz pulled Cady's cell phone from his breast pocket and handed it to me. "We have. We also checked his cell phone, his home phone, and as much correspondence as we could find at his residence, all of it confirming that the relationship was indeed of a serious nature." He adjusted his glasses and looked at me between the red dots. "Mr. Longmire, I want you to know how sorry we are for what has happened to your daughter, but there are going to be a lot of questions concerning this young man's death."

Gowder raised his eyebrows. "His father is a judge with

criminal appeals, and he has a lot of ties with the city's current administration. Read: shitstorm."

I thought about it. "What leads you to believe it wasn't a suicide?"

"No note and, more important, even with the history of emotional problems, there's no track record of attempts." He looked at Katz, who shrugged.

"Look, Sheriff, you're right, we don't like you for this, but you had an altercation with the young man. He's killed eight hours later a block and a half from where your daughter lives, and there you are without a strong alibi." He laced his fingers together and looked at me from over the top of them. "We've done a little research and know everything there is to know about you. Marine investigator, one silver, one bronze star, Navy Cross . . . You're a regular Audie Murphy."

"Don't forget my merit badge in macramé."

He studied me for a moment and then continued. "More than a quarter century in law enforcement with backing from the state attorney general's office, the Wyoming Division of Criminal Investigation, and the governor of Wyoming, all of whom seem to think you walk on rarified air."

I watched the two of them. "So, what do you want from me?"

Gowder smiled again; I was trying to get sick of it, but it was a great smile. "We both have a half-dozen homicides in a caseload . . ."

They needed an ally. The things you can always count on in law enforcement are that you'll be underpaid, overworked, and looking for somebody to jump in the foxhole with you. "You guys hiring?"

Katz raised his head, and he was smiling, too. "We thought you might be able to assist us in that you have an advantageous position in connection with the case."

I'd never get away with a statement like that in Wyoming. "You bet."

We agreed to meet again in wind or rain, fair or foul, but mostly tomorrow at breakfast. They told me to keep Cady's phone. I asked if I got a Junior G-Man ring, but they reminded me of the budget cuts.

When I got to Cady's, Dog was happy to see me and was even happier when I found the extension cord that hung on the hook by the door. Clouds continued to threaten but nothing fell. I walked him up Race and took a left on Independence; there was a locked gate on the north side of the bridge. I looked at the open south-side walkway and decided to at least give it a try. There were two cruisers and a van from the crime lab unit still there.

I could see what Gowder had meant. There was a substantial railing and a light-rail track's width across the high-speed train line, and only then the street below. Would have taken quite a throw; I figured Devon must have been moving about forty miles an hour when he hit the alley. The walkways looked to be twenty feet across, so there had been plenty of space to launch him, but who would he have trusted to join him that late at night?

There was a patrolman from the other side yelling at me to move on; he must not have gotten the memo. I waved and took Dog back down the walkway. At the bottom, we found a quirky subterranean passageway to the other side. We emerged just past the locked gate on the north and continued to street level, cut back on New

Street, passed Saint George's United Methodist Church, crossed 2nd, and stopped where the police barricade blocked the alley.

There was a chubby cop eating an honest-to-God do-nut. His collar insignia said UNIT 6, which I had learned was Cady's district. He seemed like the friendly type, so I asked him what had happened.

He looked at Dog, the extension cord, and me. "You're not from aroun' here, are ya?"

I was going to have to lose the cowboy hat and get Dog a leash. "Visiting my daughter."

"She live aroun' here?"

"Over on Bread."

"Well, if the jumper had been so inclined, she could've had a hole for a skylight." He fed the last part of his donut to Dog. "Some society kid from out on tha . . ." He clinched his jaw for the imitative effect. "Main Line." He licked his fingers after feeding Dog, and I liked him.

"Seems like an odd place to jump."

He looked back. "Yeah, they usually go out over the water. Who knows, maybe he couldn't swim." He scratched Dog's head as the beast looked around for more donut. "What's your daughter's name?"

"Cady Longmire. She bought the little tannery behind Paddy O'Neil's."

He nodded. "O'Neil's I know." His name plate read O'CONNOR. "Ian got it from his uncle 'bout a year ago. He runs a clean place, jus' don' talk politics."

"IRA?"

"With a vengeance. You Irish?"

"Isn't everybody?" I looked past him toward the crime lab truck parked in the alley. "You guys stuck here long?"

"Nah, we'll be outta here this afternoon." I made a

mental note and walked Dog on down the street. "I'll keep an eye out for your daughter."

I half turned. "Thanks."

By the time we got back down Race, O'Neil's was ready for business. I stood at the propped-open side entrance with Dog and heard noise from behind the bar. "Anybody home?"

Almost immediately, hisself popped up. "'Ello."

I gestured toward Dog. "You mind if we come in?"

He paused for a moment. "It's against city laws, but there's n'body 'ere. C'mon in." I sat on the stool nearest the side entrance, and Dog curled up in the doorway. "What'll ye have?"

"How about an Irish coffee minus the Irish?"

He smiled. "One American coffee comin' up." He poured two and joined me, leaning on an elbow and extending his other hand. I noticed scars on his forearm along with the rows of Celtic snake tattoos coiling up and into his black T-shirt. "We waren't properly introduced las' night. Ian O'Neil."

I shook the proffered hand. "Walt Longmire."

He leaned over to get a look at Dog. "Who's the beastie?"

"His name is Dog." He looked at me. "Honest."

"How's ya daughter doin'?"

"A little better." I changed the subject just to see if he'd trail along and looked behind me toward the bridge. "Looks like they've got some business?"

When I looked back, he was still looking at me. "Aye, somethin' ta do wi' tha boy that fell."

"What do you know about that?"

He reached down the bar for a copy of the *Daily News* and tossed it in front of me. "Only what I read in tha newspapers." There was a portrait photograph of Devon Conliffe and another of the Benjamin Franklin Bridge; the headline read JUDGE'S SON DIES IN BRIDGE FALL. The brawny young Irishman leaned in the way I had last night. "Sheriff, if ye wanna drink or a bite ta eat, yer more then welcome, but if yer in 'ere playin' policeman, I'd just as soon ye go somewhere else." He smiled to show me there were no hard feelings.

I smiled back, feeling like a complete ass. "Sorry."

He reached behind for a bottle of Jamison's and poured a dollop into his coffee. "I don' see how ye can drink tha' stuff without assistance." He held the bottle out to me, but I shook my head. "So, yer tryin' to find out who killed yer daughter's boyo?"

"Something like that." I took a sip of my coffee. "What makes you think it wasn't suicide?"

He snorted. "He was a prick. If nobody killed 'im, they should've." He set his coffee cup down and looked at it. "Look, Sheriff . . . I don't need any trouble. I've had me share between Ireland for the Irish an' Ireland for the Catholics. Now is jus' an Irish bar, know wha' I mean?"

When I got back to Cady's place, I began my investigation by going through the mail I had been dumping on the kitchen counter. There were the usual bills and junk but nothing pertinent. There was a calendar on the side of the refrigerator; I had forgotten about the shooting club until I saw that Thursdays had been marked. I tried to think of the street that Cady had mentioned on the phone and finally came up with Spring-something. I fished around in her desk drawer and pulled out five inches of Philadelphia Yellow Pages, flipped to GUNS, and found the subheading

"Safety & Markmanship." There were a half-dozen, but only one was on Spring Garden Street. It was listed as Tactical Training Specialists.

I copied the address and number onto the notepad on which Lena had written all my messages and looked at the phone. It was too early to call anybody in Wyoming except Ruby, who was always on duty early.

"Absaroka County Sheriff's Office."

"It's me."

It was quiet on the line. "How is she?"

"Oh, as good as can be expected, responding to external stimuli but still no eye movement."

The silence again. "Oh, Walter . . ."

"Yep."

I could hear the choking in her throat. "What are you going to do?"

"Wait." The silence again, and I thought I could hear sniffing on the other end, so I changed the subject. "How are things back home?"

She tried to laugh. "You want your Post-its?"

"Sure."

Her voice strengthened, and she cleared her throat. "Chuck Frymyer came in and got his uniform."

"Who?"

"The young man you hired for Powder Junction." There was a pause. "Somebody stole all the pool balls at the Euskadi Bar."

"Look under the table where they keep the rack; folks think it's funny to hide them there."

"Bessie Peterson reported that somebody dumped garbage over her back fence."

"Talk to Larry Stricker. He's the one that's got the

barking dog that she complained about last week." Dog, thinking he heard his name, came over and put his head on my knee.

"A woman reported that an elderly man was walking down the middle of Route 16 wearing coveralls and a hunting cap. He sticks his thumb out and, when you drive by, he raises both arms."

"That's Catherine Bishop's brother; he gets confused and goes out for unscheduled walks."

"A caller requested an officer's assistance, then hung up. Officers were dispatched and found a couple in a verbal argument. The telephone was found ripped out of the wall. An open bottle of whiskey was found on the kitchen counter."

"What brand?"

"The report doesn't mention."

I petted Dog's head, and it was silent on the line. "You know all this stuff."

"Yes."

"So this was all for my benefit?"

"Yes."

The heat in my face was returning. "Thank you."

She breathed on the phone for a while. "People are asking, so the prognosis is guarded but hopeful?"

The heat was on high. "Yep."

"Vic was threatening to jump a flight to Philadelphia or call Omar and commandeer the Lear.

"Tell her I'm okay."

"You don't sound okay."

"I better go."

"Walt?"

"I'll talk to you later."

I hung up the phone and stared at the glass surface of

the coffee table that reflected the clouds passing over the skylight. It seemed like everything in the world was moving.

I petted Dog again, then went over to the work area and looked at Cady's desk. There wasn't a piece of paper on it, but there was an expensive-looking laptop. I could call Ruby back and ask her to help me with the computer, or I could wait and let Henry have a shot at it. There were some framed photographs on the desk: one that I had taken of her at the Absaroka County Rodeo when she was about eight; another of Cady with a young woman I didn't know on some sort of cruise ship; and one of Henry looking at the camera with an eyebrow pulled like a bowstring.

There were no pictures of me.

I opened the desk drawers and found supplies but no work. I looked up at the metal-framed atrium and the walkways above. I knew there were two bedrooms up there, but so far I hadn't made it to either one.

At the top of the spiral staircase, the master bedroom wasn't very large, but it had a balcony overlooking the terrace in the back. It must have been the offices of the tannery when it had been a commercial venture, but now it contained a large four-poster bed and a French country bureau that her mother had bequeathed to her. I stood at the end of the bed and was flooded with Cady's scent. I hung there like an impending avalanche, thinking about her, about Jo Malone grapefruit shampoo, about a partially shaved head and a U-shaped scar.

I sat down and stared at myself in the simple cherry mirror. It reflected me and a small, metal case that sat on the surface of the dresser. I went over and tried to open it, but it was locked. I put in Cady's birth year and the small clasps popped open; I shook my head at her predictability.

Sig Sauer P226, 9 mm. It was a pricey version with plated controls and 24-kt-gold engraving; leave it to my daughter to get a designer handgun. There were two fully loaded clips in the case, and I made a mental note to discuss gun safety with her, if I ever got to talk to her again.

I pulled the ammo, placing it in the bottom drawer, closed the case, turned, and walked out of the room to the small landing above the kitchen. Dog watched me from the sofa below and then lowered his head to continue his nap.

I stood there for a while, holding on to the railing, and tried to think of what Cady would want me to do. Like me, she couldn't abide mystery. Even as a young child, she asked questions—questions as statements, questions as answers, and questions as endless inquiry. She wanted to know everything and, if you told her to go look it up, she would and then come back with even more questions. Even then, she could interview a stump.

I turned and walked into the other bedroom. There was an old Pronghorn skull we had found on the backside of the ranch when she was six. It had probably been shot in the dirty thirties, dehorned, and left to bleach in the high plains sun. Cady had asked me what had happened to the antelope, and I told her the truth, like I always tried to do. She had taken it to Henry and, with his help, had decorated it with beads and feathers. It had hung in her room at the house in town; had hung at her assorted apartments in Berkeley, San Francisco, and Seattle; and now hung over the guest bed in Philadelphia. There was also an elaborately framed but rusted sign that read "Department of the Interior—Indian Affairs, Boundary Indian Reservation" that Lucian had given her, and more photographs, but still none of me.

I glanced down at the bed at what had caught my eye from the landing. It was an ivory vellum envelope that read DADDY. I picked it up and saw an After Eight mint on the pillow beneath it. I opened the tiny envelope and read the three words, then carefully closed it and placed it in my breast pocket over my heart.

I had called Lena Moretti to tell her that there had been a change of plans and that we'd be having lunch at the Franklin Institute. She said that she'd never eaten there and probably for good reason, so we opted for Philadelphia-style pretzels. It was my first and was slathered with brownish spicy mustard. I had spoken with the head of security, and he said he'd send Esteban Cordero, who had been the security manager on duty at the time of Cady's fall, down to speak with me as soon as he got in.

Lena was wearing jeans and a white snap-button blouse I was sure Vic had sent her. I figured she was trying to make me feel more at home. We sat munching and drinking cherry cream soda as children raced up and down the steps from the buses to the entryway of the museum. "What was she like as a child?"

I readjusted my Phillies hat. "We had the two-cheek rule. Cady always sat about halfway on a chair whenever we were trying to have dinner, so we instituted the two-cheek rule." I sipped my soda. "What was the Terror like?"

Lena shrugged. "Disapproving." She watched the children, who were making noises like birds—indiscriminate, bright sounds that made you happy to hear them. "She was a thirty-year-old trapped in a child's body. She and her grandmother Nona always got along in their mutual dissatisfaction with me."

"You? What's not to like?" It was an innocent question,

but it hit something along the way, glancing off and taking a lot with it.

She licked a spot of mustard from the corner of her mouth. "I had a rough period a while back." She took a sip of her pop and looked at me. "I had an affair eight years ago. I'm surprised you didn't notice the red *A* on my blouse."

I was about to reply when a shadow crossed over me from the other side. I looked up and an elderly Latino in a blue blazer was looking at me with concern.

"Are you the man whose daughter was hurt?"

I stood and introduced Lena. We followed him up the steps and to the right as he told us about the police interview. "They asked a lot of questions the night it happened, and then another patrolman came and asked again."

I finished my pretzel and pop on the way up the stairs, where a handicapped-access ramp ran along the side of the building, then changed direction and returned to the sidewalk below. He pointed to the flat area. "She landed there."

I looked at the cement sidewalk. I tried to see the evening as Devon had described it; he had grabbed her arm, she had jerked it back and had fallen. It made sense as I looked at it. He was upset, she had gone to meet him, and there had been an argument.

I looked back at the entrance to the museum, but I couldn't see the doorway from where we stood. "You saw her fall?"

"No."

I turned and looked at him. "Then how did you know this had happened?"

"The kid banged on the door."

"He came to the door?" He nodded, and I thought

about what Devon had said at the ballpark, how he had said that he had run away. "Devon Conliffe came to the door of the museum?"

He nodded some more. "Yeah, I was in the main lobby when this kid ran up to the door and started pounding and screaming."

"What'd he look like?"

He thought. "Tall, suit, blue tie, raincoat . . ." He watched me. "He said his name, pointed to what had happened, and yelled for me call 911."

"He told you his name?"

"Yes."

"Then what?"

"I called the police, got another one of the guys to come up to the lobby, and came out here."

"How long did that take?"

He took a breath. "A minute, maybe two."

"Then what?"

"When I got out here, he was gone."

"When did the police arrive?"

"A couple of minutes later." I stared at the concrete, and I looked back up at him. "What'd he look like?"

"The cop?"

"No, Devon Conliffe. You said he was tall and how he was dressed, but what did his face look like?"

"I don't know. White kid, dark hair parted on the side . . ."

"Do you have this morning's *Daily News*?"

He looked at me for a second and then nodded. "Yeah, I've got it up at the front counter, but I haven't had a chance to read it yet."

"Would you mind if we take a look?"

We passed the statue of Benjamin Franklin, who was

seated contentedly in the warm glow of the science museum.

My attention was drawn back to the security desk. Cordero had slapped the newspaper onto the counter. I looked at it for a second and then spun it around so that it faced him. "Look carefully. Is that the kid who pounded on the door?"

He stared at the front page for a minute and then looked back up at me. "You know . . . I don't think it is."

# 6

"Three things. Devon said that he had run away as soon as another person had arrived. I assumed it was the guard he was talking about but, when I noticed that you couldn't see the museum entrance from where Cady had been hurt, I started wondering." I took a bite of my ice-cream bar and watched as Lena did the same. What would lunch have been without dessert?

"Second, Cordero said that Devon had dark hair, but it was blond."

"And third?"

"The blue tie. When I spoke with Devon, he said that he hadn't been home and that he was still wearing the same clothes. At the ballpark, his tie was red." We were sitting on a bench in Logan Circle watching the fish and swans blow water twenty feet in the air, as if the humidity needed any help. "Individually, it's not much, but all together . . . Of course, now that Devon's picture is plastered across every newspaper in town, it'll probably be harder to find the mystery man. Whoever he is, if he's smart, he'll fold up the tents and head home."

"What if he was just some passerby? I mean, it is a big city."

"I don't think so. There weren't any functions at the Institute that night, so why would anyone be hanging around the museum steps? How would he know Devon's name, and why did he identify himself as Devon Conliffe?"

I leaned back on the bench and took another bite of my ice cream. I thought about it as I looked at the nearest Indian in the Fountain of Three Rivers; he was representative of the Delaware River and had more than a passing resemblance to Henry. "Maybe, after Devon ran, the other fellow decided to pin him to the incident."

"Then disappeared himself?"

"Evidently he had something to hide, too." I finished my ice cream and was chewing on the stick. "We are looking for a Caucasian male, approximately thirty years of age, dark hair, and at least six feet tall."

"You think the mystery man had something to do with Devon's death?"

I could feel the wood beginning to splinter between my teeth. "It makes sense. Somebody cares enough about Cady to follow her, cares enough to chance revealing himself after she's hurt, and cares enough to possibly toss Devon off the bridge."

She finished hers. "That's a lot of caring."

"Yep."

"Are you still hungry?"

"Hmm?"

She smiled. "You're chewing the stick, and I thought you might want something else to eat."

I dropped it in the nearest trash can. Henry was with Cady this morning, and I wanted to get back to the hospital before he had to leave for the museum, but Lena was doing so much. I took a deep breath. "You want to tell me about this affair?"

She laughed and then looked at me through the corner of an almond-shaped eye. "I wasn't sure if you remembered that part of the conversation."

"I'm pretty good with details, especially those involving domestic disturbances."

She looked at the Indian maiden leaning modestly on her side against an excited swan. I had read the plaque after we had crossed the street and knew that the young girl represented Wissahickon Creek, but in Lena Moretti's mind she was possibly emblematic of something more. "It was eight years ago. Victor had made inspector and just started working with the Mayor's Task Force on Organized Crime. He wasn't home a lot, and I guess I got bored."

I waited, but she didn't say anything else. "It sounds like there's more to this story."

She continued to watch the fountain. "There is, but that's probably all you need to know."

I waited a respectful moment before replying. "Okay." I watched the people around the fountain, and it was only after a moment that I realized I was looking for a thirty-year-old male with dark hair and a darker reflection.

When I looked back, she had turned toward me and was smiling. "Who's got the afternoon shift?"

"I do, but if you could check on Dog and cover for me for a little while this evening I'd really appreciate it."

The smile held. "Buy me dinner?"

I looked back at the Indians. "Sure."

She tossed her stick into the trash can as well and stood; she looked exactly like Vic. "My pick."

I put Lena in a cab and grabbed one going in the opposite direction for myself. It didn't take long to get to Spring Garden, and I felt a release doing something to track down some answers.

Tactical Training Specialists was the only going concern

on the block, with gratings over the windows and a door that would have been more appropriate back home at Fort Fetterman; it didn't look like the best part of town. The sign on the glass read RETAIL HANDGUN SALES— NEW AND USED, HOME DEFENSE CLASSES, IN- DOOR SHOOTING RANGE, AND BASIC THROUGH ADVANCED TRAINING. There was an adjacent parking lot with a side entrance that probably led to the range. I tried to remember what Cady had said about the instructor but could only come up with him being ex-army and a pretty good shot. I wondered casually how he handled throwing bodies over bridges.

I pushed the door open and an entry bell sounded. There was every gun I'd ever seen lined against the walls all the way to the back of the place. Glass-topped counters held the handguns, while the rifles and shotguns stood at attention, chained to the racks behind the counters. There were displays of body armor and home security sensors with locks and alarms at the center of the shop along with three-dimensional targets and gun safes.

"Can I help you?"

Jimmie Tomko was a little younger than I was, of average height and build with a light complexion and pattern balding that did nothing to hide the fact that he was missing his left ear; it also looked like he had a glass eye. He was sitting on a stool behind the counter and to my right, where he could see whoever walked in before they could see him. I noticed he was wearing a shoulder holster with a Kimber .45 and was reading the *Daily News,* which was folded back to the second page and the continuation of the Devon Conliffe saga.

I extended my hand. "Walt Longmire. My daughter is Cady Longmire."

He smiled without parting his lips. "Hello, Sheriff."

We went to his office, which overlooked the firing range, and he told me about his experiences in Quang Tri Province, which ended with a pressure-detonated mine made from one of our duds, a 105-millimeter round that had been booby-trapped. "Roughly two platoons had walked right by the damn thing, and I was next to last when the guy beside me stepped on something, and I turned." He gestured toward his left eye. "Poached my eye just like an egg. They say the sand was probably the only thing that saved me and the guy in front of us." I didn't ask about the fellow who had stepped on it.

Not for the first time, I was anxious to get out of Vietnam, so I changed the subject. "Jimmie, how long have you had this place?"

"Since '77." He gestured toward the shooting gallery. "Put the firing range in about ten years ago, and it's been the only thing that saved my butt."

"That many people want to learn how to shoot?"

"There's that, but it's also the permits." I looked at him questioningly. "A lot of these yuppies want concealed permits, but the chances of getting one in the city, even with training, are about as likely as Wilson Goode joining the Strategic Air Command."

I vaguely remembered an instance in the city involving the ex-mayor, a helicopter, a bomb, and a housing project, and deduced that getting a concealed weapon permit in Philadelphia was nigh on impossible. "So, can they get limited permits through you?"

"Yeah, that way they get to transport the weapon to and from the premises within a locked case in the trunk of their car, ammo separate."

"I gather that some of them have been abusing the privilege?"

He sighed. "I had been making good money until we had a prominent assistant district attorney who unloaded on a Toyota station wagon on Roosevelt Boulevard. He said a couple of guys had chased him at speeds in excess of a hundred miles an hour."

I thought about it. "I wasn't aware that Toyota station wagons could go a hundred miles an hour."

"He said it was drug dealers."

I thought about it some more. "Is the Toyota station wagon the vehicle of choice for Philadelphia drug dealers?"

"No. So then he said it could have been the KKK, except that in the earlier statement he said the two occupants were not white." Tomko watched me with the one eye. "Now, there could be two nonwhite members of the KKK cruising around Philly in a Japanese station wagon, but . . ."

"There's just as much a chance of Wilson Goode joining the Strategic Air Command?"

"Exactly." I was getting the hang of it. "Now, you are probably wondering why it is that I have told you this story." He angled the front page of the paper toward me.

I stared at him. "Devon Conliffe?"

He nodded. "He was in the car with ADA Vince Osgood, a buddy of his."

"What were they doing being chased by drug dealers?"

"There were a lot of questions along those lines." He dropped the corner of the paper back on his desk. "Surprise, surprise, the charges were dropped. I think it might have been because Devon's father, the judge, had pull with the court."

"His father?" Tomko nodded. "And Devon still came here?"

"Lawyer League. They all come in on Thursdays." He

sat back in his chair and leaned a scarred chin on his fist. "They didn't cancel his permit and, like I said, all the charges were dropped."

I thought about the judge's son. "So he might have been involved in some things he shouldn't have been."

"It's likely."

"Can you think of anybody who might've wanted to kill him?" The one eye stared at me for a while. "Besides me."

"About half of Philadelphia." He looked away for a second. "Look, I know your daughter was dating the guy, but he was a piece of shit. Did you ever see the two of 'em together?"

"No."

"Not for nothin', but it was like she was his personal servant." His eye came back to me. "Why don't you ask your daughter?"

I studied him but could tell nothing. "I'm saving that as a last resort."

He nodded. "I'm not so sure why it is you're concerned; best thing that could've happened to her." He cleared his throat and shrugged. "Sheriff, in case you hadn't noticed, your daughter is quite a looker, intelligent, and possibly one of the best shots I've ever had the pleasure of not teaching." He folded his hands in his lap. "It's none of my business, but I think she's a lot better off."

I withheld comment. "You mind if I come in tomorrow night?"

"Nah, but there's a guest fee, thirty bucks plus ammo. What d'ya shoot?"

"A .45 ACP."

He nodded; the caliber probably reminded him of Quang Tri, land mines, and poached eggs.

———

It was close to one o'clock when I got back to the hospital. "When do I get to meet the mother?"

I ignored Henry and watched Cady. "Anything?"

"No, but I sang to her all morning."

I sat down. "Thank you."

His eyes stayed on Cady. "She hears us."

I had thought about it a great deal, but I wasn't sure. "You think?"

"Yes." He exhaled a short laugh. "This may be your only chance to get the first, middle, and last word." He looked at me now, his eyes steady. "She must hear our voices so that she can return to us."

I thought what a wonder it was that this individual should be with me, here, now. Even as a child, he had always known something the rest of us didn't. I thought about the book I'd brought from Wyoming, the love-worn collection of Grimm's Fairy Tales. Maybe I could read her that. "Well, I don't sing. Any suggestions on what I should say?"

He smiled. "Tell her how much you love her; everything after that is small talk."

I talked to Cady for the next four hours, and then the nurses ran me off so that they could bathe her. I took my chair and sat in the hallway. The *Daily News* was at the nurse's desk, so I appropriated it.

JUDGE'S SON DIES IN BRIDGE FALL. I studied the photo of Devon Conliffe; it was most likely a publicity shot from his firm. There was no denying that he was a handsome kid, but there was a wayward quality to the eyes, something that said the young man was looking for a way out. I guess he found it, or it found him.

I looked at the picture of the bridge that had a superimposed dotted line of his fall and an arrow showing where he had landed. I thought about the alley where I had spoken to the cop with the donut and made a mental note to return there in the morning when the police and the crime lab people had cleared out.

". . . 10 P.M. as the traffic grew sparse on the Benjamin Franklin Bridge, Devon Conliffe, son of judge Robert Conliffe, fell to his death." The article was pretty straightforward, concentrating on Devon's career in the law and on the assorted community services he was involved with, only mentioning the episode that Jimmie Tomko had described as "the incident on Roosevelt Boulevard." Robert Conliffe was quoted as saying that his son was a good man and an excellent lawyer who would be sadly missed in society.

There was no mention of Cady. I figured the Conliffes and I were off for dinner. The Roosevelt Boulevard thing bothered me; I needed to find out more about Devon's background. I knew two detectives who might help me out. I dug Cady's cell phone from my jacket, but the battery was dead. I put it back in my pocket and settled on brooding, something at which I was pretty good.

It was possible that what had happened to Devon had been triggered by what had happened to Cady, but not exclusively. It appeared that the young man could have been involved in any number of situations that could have led to his violent end.

The nurses had finished. I folded the paper, placed it back on the counter, and leaned my elbows on the ICU desk. Nancy Lyford, the head nurse, the one who had held my hand when we had first arrived, came over and stood by me. "Your friend has a beautiful voice."

"Yep, he does."

"He's Native American?"

I smiled. "Indian. Yes."

"Isn't Native American the correct term?"

"I suppose, but most of the Indians I know would laugh at you if you used it." I figured I'd better explain. "Most Indians don't identify themselves as American particularly, but as members of nations unto themselves." She looked at me blankly. "A nation, like a tribe."

She thought about it. "He said he was Cheyenne?"

"Northern Cheyenne and Lakota."

"Sioux?"

I shook my head. "You start calling Lakota the Sioux, and you're going to get in real trouble."

She laughed. "Sounds more complicated than Native American."

I gestured toward my daughter. "How's she doing?"

She glanced over her shoulder. "The bilateral constriction subsided to a normal reaction of the pupils, which gives her a much better opportunity of recovery. The involuntary response to external stimuli is also a very good sign."

It was basically the same speech I'd gotten from Rissman the day before, and I wasn't sure if that was good or bad. "Still a wait-and-see situation?"

She nodded her head and looked a little sad. "It's not like television. It's a long process that takes a lot of effort, even if things go well." I nodded, and she looked back at Cady. "I'm not sure if now is the time to mention it, but the things that people have been sending and bringing are beginning to pile up." I guess I still looked blank. "Cards, stuffed animals, flowers, and things like that." She smiled. "She's a very popular young woman."

I had the flowers donated to other units and started to put the rest into a large shopping bag the head nurse thoughtfully provided. I was still talking to Cady. "I've half a mind to leave all this stuff here and have you lug it all home yourself." There were stuffed animals, mostly indicative of the West—buffalo, horses, and a bear. There were assortments of candy and a stack of cards, most of which had her name on them, except for one that had mine. I held the little envelope up for her to see. "There, I'm popular, too."

It was the usual size of a thank you note, with a mechanical, typewritten print that read SHERIFF. I nudged my thumb under the flap and opened the sealed envelope. Inside was a plain white card that looked like the ones used for names at a place setting; it read, in the same type, YOU HAVE BEEN DONE A FAVOR, NOW DROP IT.

I looked at it for a long time. I finally noticed that my finger and thumb were holding the card like a life preserver; I guess I thought that if I let go, the card might disappear. I studied the envelope. There was nothing to indicate where the note had come from or whom it was from. I held it up to the fluorescent light and could see the indentation of the mechanical typewriter's strike, worn, with a small dropout at the bottom of the O. A typewriter? No one used one of those anymore.

I stood and walked out to the nurse's station. I held up the envelope. "Excuse me, but do you have any idea where this one might have come from?"

She shook her head. "No, I really can't say."

"Can you check with the rest of the staff and see if any of them remember anyone bringing this particular envelope?"

She reached out for it. "Certainly."

I held on. "I need to keep this, but there aren't any others that are typewritten. Do you think you could bring them here or describe it to them?" She looked uncertain. "It just says SHERIFF in capital letters."

"Yes." She continued to sit and look at me.

"I mean now."

The other three staff members who were on the floor had never seen the note and, after a few phone calls, it was ascertained that the others hadn't either. I plucked a card from my wallet, looked at the great seal of the City of Philadelphia, and thought about the deep-set eyes that had watched me so carefully this morning. Asa Katz, Detective, Homicide Unit, 8th and Race. There were four different phone numbers, and I didn't call any of them.

I was standing with the head nurse in Cady's room when Lena Moretti arrived.

The sun had set, but the last of its golden light reflected off the other sides of the building in a burnished brilliance of dying illumination, peaking and then dimming like a thought having passed.

"No, I didn't write it."

I reached out and held Cady's foot; I felt the momentary reflex of response and the heat in my face as I looked at hers. "Well, I just wanted to give you the chance to give yourself up." I heard her exhale with a smile.

"What are you going to do?"

I gave a little laugh myself. "You know, your daughter asks me that a lot." The hot spots of the sun were reflecting back to my mountains in Wyoming, and I thought about how deceptively simple life seemed there. "I figure I'll give the detectives a full report in the morning."

"Yeah, but what are you going to do tonight?" She was

holding the card and stood in the golden light with her other hand propped at the small of her back.

"That note seems to indicate that Devon Conliffe's death is a direct result of Cady's accident." I smiled at the floor tile some more and didn't answer.

I stood there with the Cheyenne Nation, looking up at the tall building and the night sky. "Are you going to tell me that this is a bad idea, too?"

He considered the streetlights running down Market. "Nah, this is a good idea."

Now I was worried.

The clouds hadn't given way to the moon and were still skimming along the tops of the buildings and reflecting the city's light. It was a warm, balmy evening and, with the cloud cover, everything felt close.

I looked at my pocket watch and glanced down both sides of the city street. Patti-with-an-i was to have met us at nine o'clock, but it was creeping up on a quarter past. "You think she changed her mind?" He didn't say anything, just looked off toward City Hall. He looked remarkably like the Indian at Logan Circle.

"For what, exactly, are we searching?"

"I don't know. That's why we have to look for ourselves."

His eyes turned to me. "You do not think the police have already done this?"

"I'm sure they asked some questions, but that's probably all. It's hard to deal with lawyers without a warrant."

He looked back at the building. "Which is why we are breaking and entering?"

"Just entering; I'm not planning on breaking anything." He nodded but didn't look particularly convinced.

It was just then that the woman I assumed was Patti turned the corner and approached from the plaza on Broad. She was looking around as she crossed the street. "I'm sorry, I had trouble getting a babysitter . . ." She stopped talking and looked at Henry. The Indian had that kind of an effect on people east of the Mississippi River.

"Patti-with-an-i, I'm Walt and this is Henry Standing Bear."

He inclined his head, extended a hand, and smiled while she melted into the cracks of the sidewalk. "Patti-with-an-i, I have heard a great deal about you."

I rolled my eyes and converted it into a glance through the revolving doors of the lobby, where a couple of security guards sat at a centrally located desk between the banks of elevators. I wondered mildly if we might have been better off leaving the Cheyenne Nation out of the equation.

Once inside, Patti just waved at the men; I noticed one of them was reading the *Philadelphia Inquirer,* which had a more demure take on the Devon Conliffe saga. The other looked at us a little quizzically but made nothing more of it.

We watched as Patti punched the up button, and we got on the elevator as she slipped a security card into the panel and hit a red one marked thirty-two. We got off and followed her to a set of opaque glass doors where she inserted the card again. The doors buzzed. I pushed one only partly open. "This is as far as you go."

She looked up at me. "I thought . . ."

I shook my head. "It's bad enough that the guards have seen you with us. If we get caught, I don't want you anywhere near."

"You're not going to know what to look for."

I glanced over at Henry. "We'll have to take that chance."

She sighed. "Her office is straight down the hall past

the library, then take a right and go to the corner; she's the next to last door on the left."

I saluted, and we waited till she was gone. I turned to look at Henry. "I like to ask myself, what would Gerry Spence do in a situation like this?"

"Gerry Spence would not be in a situation like this."

The main hall was a straight shot to a conference room. The lights were all on, and I expected somebody to cross at any second and turn to look at us. I waited a moment, then stepped into the entryway and looked both left and right down the first intersecting hallway. There seemed to be three more before the end. We listened, but the only sound was the heating/cooling air handlers.

I watched as Henry took his rightful place at the front, always the scout. He advanced to the next intersection and motioned for me to follow, never taking his eyes off the area ahead. I moved out and up behind him as he crossed and continued.

We were at the doorway of the library when he stopped and angled his head in the direction of the opening. I expected to hear the shriek of lawyers, aware that they were being attacked by a war party, but it was silent. I waited as Henry held up a fist, then a single finger, and then the fist again.

Hold, one person, stay there.

I waited as he crossed and peered into the room from the opposite angle. I watched as the dark eyes flicked around. He froze for a second, then slowly turned away and placed himself flat against the far wall; I did the same. I listened more carefully as someone rustled some papers and walked through the room about twenty feet from the door.

After a moment and more than most white men would

wait, the Bear inclined his head and looked into the library. He glanced back and gestured for me to come along. I crossed and followed him to the far corner, where he stopped and once again looked both ways.

Every light in this part of the damn place was on as well, and I started wondering how much Schomberg, Calder, Dallin, and Rhind could shave off their billing by turning them out. Paintings on the walls in the corridor that led to Cady's office were abstracts of what I took to be Indians. When I turned to look at Henry, he was studying the nearest one, looked at me, and shrugged.

To my relief, most of the doorways leading to the right were either dark or closed. Seeing the lights from the other tall buildings glide past as we worked our way down the hall was making me dizzy, so I was glad when we got to the door that read CADY LONGMIRE on a little brass plaque. The door that was three before Cady's was open with the light on. The plaque on it read JOANNE FITZPATRICK; the name sounded familiar. Henry turned the knob to Cady's office and closed the door behind us after I followed him in.

It was a small room, and we stood there for a moment to let our eyes adjust to the darkness. I could feel some of Cady's clothes hanging on the back of her door and steadied their swinging with my hand. Henry stood slightly to the left, looking out the floor-to-ceiling glass wall ahead of us. William Penn and City Hall were to our right, and the yellow glow of the clock below Penn told us it was a time when all good lawyers should be home and in bed. The bluish light of the building across Market reflected the streetlights below and the image of the building we were now in.

Henry reached across the shadow of a desk and clicked

on a green tortoiseshell lamp. The illumination was ample but not so much that it reached the space under the doorway. I breathed the first deep breath since entering the offices. "Somebody was in the library?"

The Bear nodded. "Yes. Pretty girl, about Cady's age with long, dark hair."

I thought about it as I looked around. "I don't know anybody she works with by sight." He nodded.

There wasn't much room to move; there were file boxes lined up against the wall, so I crossed behind the desk where there were more piles of folders and a computer. There were even more boxes at the foot of the windows, with another wall of file cabinets to the right.

I sat in her chair and looked around. There was a large map of Wyoming from the turn of the century in a heavy gilded frame. There were four ledger drawings that Henry had acquired for her flanking both sides, and an etching Joel Ostlind had done of Cloud Peak. I looked at the elegant simplicity of the etching and could feel the air and the cold wind of the west ridge.

On the desk, there was an old photograph of Cady with Martha after the chemotherapy had begun taking its toll. I studied the beautiful bone structure of the two women, mother and daughter, the brightness of their eyes, and the languid relaxation of their hands as they lay draped over each other's shoulders. There was another of Henry standing with Dena Many Camps in traditional dress at the Little Bighorn reenactment. There was even one of Dog.

I suppose my disappointment was evident. "What is wrong?"

I waited a moment and then responded. "I know it's stupid . . . but there aren't any pictures of me." I cleared my throat, hoping that maybe I wouldn't sound so stupid and pathetic when I continued. "There aren't any photographs of me at her house or here." He was silent as he watched, watched the guilt of my misplaced emotions blunder forward like those of a wounded animal. "I just thought I was important enough in her life to support one or two photographs."

He quietly reached across the desk and hit the space bar on the computer.

I raised my eyes, and the wave that hit me was like a wall of sentiment: wet, deep, and ancient. I sat there as the swell subsided, but the saltwater stayed in my eyes and blurred my vision.

It was a full-screen wallpaper of me with my head crushed against Cady's, and it was obvious from the angle that she had taken the photo at arms length. We were both smiling, and her nose was stuck in my ear.

# 7

We had made it through only one box. The one thing we were able to discern was that Cady was involved with an awful lot of cases and that we knew little actual law.

Henry rubbed his eyes. "What time is it?"

I glanced back over my shoulder at City Hall. "Coming up on ten."

He closed his folder. "We are looking for some personal connection in one of her cases?"

"Yep."

"Someone who thinks that killing Devon Conliffe would help Cady?"

"Yep."

"May I see the note again?" I pulled it from my pocket and handed it to him.

I waited, but he didn't speak. I gestured toward the card. "We can deduce through this that the killer knows Cady, that the killer knew of Devon, and that the killer knows us."

He was looking at a photograph of Cady and a young woman with long, dark hair. They were on horseback, and there was a sign that read Gladwyne Stables in the background. "A warning?"

"A threat?"

His eyes came back to mine. "And you think it is someone connected to her through work?"

"It's the only criminal element that she has any contact

with." I shrugged. "When I'm looking for candy, I go to a candy store." We looked at the boxes. He stood, moved toward the door, and stretched his back. "What are you doing?"

"I am going to go get two cups of coffee . . ." He turned the knob, opened the door, and slipped into the hallway. "And a lawyer." Like a fool, I figured he would come back with only the coffee.

I leaned back in Cady's chair and looked at the city stretching out along the Delaware River, the only dark band in what seemed like an ocean of diamonds on a velvet pad. It was easy to make out the Benjamin Franklin Bridge, with its blue cables and yellow buttresses stretching over to New Jersey, where I doubted life was any easier.

Who could have gotten him up there? The signs on the walkway said that the gates were closed and locked at 7 P.M., so it wasn't a casual meeting. Somebody had wanted Devon Conliffe on that bridge, somebody who had wanted him dead.

I thought about the people I'd talked to earlier. Jimmie Tomko obviously held no great love for Devon, but in our brief interview he didn't strike me as the type to toss people off bridges. It would be interesting to go to the firing range the next night to broaden the suspect pool. Ian O'Neil was intriguing—a young man with a past—and I figured he had a thing for Cady, but that's about as far as that went as well.

I closed my eyes and listened to the skyscraper, to the elevators rattling up and down their shafts, to the retreating surf of the air conditioning, and to the building itself, sighing and shifting with the breeze like some colossal ship at dock.

I leaned back and felt as if I too were coming unmoored. Out of my element, it was possible that the deductive process I had always relied on was now leading me astray, or maybe it was just that I couldn't stop thinking about Cady. I thought about walking over to the other side of the building to look out one of the windows so that I could find her. It felt like up here, with our ships anchored in the sky, I might be able to catch a glimpse of her as she used to be.

I could hear more than one pair of footsteps padding along the carpet. The door opened, and Henry stood there holding a bassinette; beside him stood a young woman with long, dark hair. She wore jeans, sneakers, and a western-style rhinestone belt; her hair was pulled back into a ponytail, but she was the same woman as the one who was in the photograph.

"I got us a lawyer." I stood up as he handed me a cup of coffee. He looked at the baby. "This is Riley Elizabeth Fitzpatrick, and this is Joanne Fitzpatrick, an associate of Cady's."

I noticed the way he used the word associate, like it was a friendship rather than being at the bottom of the firm's food chain. Cady would have noticed, too. I took off my baseball cap and held out my hand. "Walt Longmire. I'm Cady's father and potential felon."

She laughed, then put her hand to her mouth and looked out the partially open doorway. She glanced at her daughter, Henry, and then me. "I understand you need some help."

The current case on Cady's agenda was one that involved the SEC and didn't seem personal enough to get anybody thrown off a bridge. The only criminal case we had stumbled across so far was a pro bono one that concerned an inmate of Graterford Prison, a maximum-security facility in eastern Pennsylvania. He had a religious grievance, and Cady had named the file WHITE EYES. Henry was the first to ask. "How many Indian cases does the firm handle?"

She shook her head and looked a little nervous, the way Easterners do when talking about Indians to an Indian. "Hardly any, but Cady's the one who would get the pro bono stuff concerning Native Americans. The plaintiff is one of those cell block lawyers with about forty-seven grievances."

Henry looked up from the file. "If this William White Eyes is Indian, why is his vita marked Caucasian?"

Joanne shrugged, still looking slightly anxious. "White Indians. It's really big in the prison system."

"You're kidding." I rubbed my nose, which had started itching. I peeked in the bassinette, but Riley Elizabeth continued to sleep peacefully.

"No, I guess their experiences with our society didn't work out so they decided to go over to the other side." She glanced at Henry. "No offense."

He smiled. "None taken."

"He's even got a 1983 filed with the DOC for not having a sweat lodge available to him in pursuance of the right to freely practice his religion according to PRP Act 71 P. S. 2402."

Whatever that meant. "What are the pendings on this William White Eyes?"

"It looks like he's been released, but he's just a cook; no violent crimes."

"Cook?"

"Designer drugs. Looks like William is a pretty smart

kid with chemicals, but I doubt he'd know which end of a gun to point."

Everybody tossed the files into the open box on Cady's desk. "Jo, do you ever go shooting with Cady and that bunch?"

She looked at me, then shook her head. "Thursday nights? No, that was more of a Devon thing." She thought for a moment and then glanced away. "There's a guy from the district attorney's office who used to go with them. Vince Osgood."

"Vince Osgood's the assistant district attorney who was suspended in the Roosevelt Boulevard incident?" She nodded. "Can you think of anybody who might want to protect Cady, to the point of going after Devon?" She looked at the Bear and me a little too long. "Besides us."

She thought about it. "Not really. I mean, everybody loves Cady, and nobody was really crazy about Devon, but strongly enough to push him off the BFB? I don't know."

"Can I ask you another thing?"

"Sure."

I glanced over at Henry, looking for a little backup. "Why was she dating him?" He smiled and shook his head, but I thought it was a pretty good question.

She paused for a second. "He wasn't that bad of a guy, and I think he was a reclamation project." She looked at me. "I don't have to tell you; she was like that." I stayed silent. "I mean, she knew about his problems . . ."

"And what were those?"

"I'm not sure how much of this I should really be telling you."

"Please?" Begging, I have found, can be a very persuasive tool in law enforcement, not to mention with women.

She looked from me to Henry and then went ahead. "There was a drug problem a while back . . ."

"Does that include the Roosevelt Boulevard incident?"

She nodded her head. "Yeah, it was about then that they booted him out of the firm."

"This firm?"

"Yes." She crossed her arms, and I thought she might stop talking, but she didn't. "Booted is probably too strong of a term. He was a recreational cocaine user that let the stuff get the better of him. His work was suffering and, when his yearly review came around, it was considered best that he pursue his career as counsel elsewhere."

"Where did he go?"

"Hunt and Driscoll." We tried to look blank. "It's a very good firm." She went on. "That's how they met. Devon still had a few acquaintances here, and he and Cady went out to lunch with a mutual friend."

"Who was that?"

She sighed and looked at the filing cabinets. Her eyes came back to mine. "I introduced them, but I didn't tell them to start dating." She took a deep breath. "I'm sorry. I'm just feeling bad about the way that things turned out."

I smiled, just to let her know that I didn't consider her responsible. "I think everybody is." I picked up my coffee from the desk and took a sip; I wasn't drinking it because I was thirsty. "So, you knew him pretty well?"

She looked at me, Henry, and then back at me. "He was very kind to me in a period when I needed it." Unconsciously, her hand went out and touched the bassinette. "I dated him a couple of times before Cady. Nothing serious."

"What was he like?"

She bit her lip. "I think he wanted people to like him; he just didn't know how to get them to. I think he was already chemically imbalanced, and once you added the cocaine . . ."

"Where did he get the stuff?"

Her eyes sharpened. "I really wouldn't know."

"Who would?" I was pushing, but it was part of the job.

She watched me for a moment and then sighed. "There was the guy I mentioned, Vince Osgood, Oz. There was a story on WCAU about him where he said he liked to go out with the boys and kick some butt. Word has it he was trying to get himself appointed by the new governor as assistant attorney general, but he's still under suspension for being involved in the Roosevelt Boulevard thing."

"Was anybody prosecuted in that case?"

"One of the guys in the other car."

"Do you know any details, like their names, and whether they were convicted?"

"I'm really not sure." I made a face. "You don't believe me?"

I cleared my throat, trying to soften the tone of what I said next. "I find it odd that you were dating but that you don't know any more."

She stiffened a little in her chair. "Like I said, Oz and I weren't dating; he was just helping me out." Her hand was still on the bassinette.

I glanced up at the photo of her on horseback and then back to mother and daughter. There were parts here, but I wasn't quite sure how to put them together yet. "Do you mind if I ask who your baby's father is?"

Her eyes looked directly at mine. "Yes, I do."

When we got downstairs, two cops were standing in the middle of the lobby. "Hello, Michael."

"How you guys doin'?"

"We're all right." I glanced back at the two security guards. "They call you?"

"Yeah, they thought it was suspicious that you went in with the lady, and then she came out without you."

I waved at the security guards, but they didn't wave back. I was beginning to think that Philly was just not a waving kind of town. "Who's your friend?"

Michael gestured toward his partner. The young man beside him was roughly the same size as Michael and in very good shape. He looked like he was enjoying himself, too, and I figured we'd have to fight them because we'd never outrun them. "This is Malcolm Chavez. Malcolm, this is Sheriff Walt Longmire and his Native American sidekick, Henry Standing Bear."

"Actually, I'm his sidekick." Henry didn't seem to care one way or the other. "Aren't you guys out of your district?"

"Yeah, we heard about the wild west show on the radio and called it in ourselves."

I looked at the Bear's fringed jacket. "It's your fault." He didn't seem to care about that either. "Are we in trouble?"

"Well, we have to file a report even if you didn't do anything."

"We didn't do anything."

"Yeah, well, we have to file a report which means you're probably going to hear from Vic the Father."

"Our Vic and this one's dad." Henry nodded, continuing to give the cops the wooden Indian treatment. I put my hands in my pockets and looked at my boots. "Do Katz and Gowder work for him?"

"Yes, they're Homicide North, but I heard that Katz had switched over to Internal Affairs." He glanced at Chavez, who nodded. "I'm not sure why he's back with Gowder in homicide, but it must've been some real juice from upstairs. I'm sure Vic Senior ain't happy about it."

I looked back up. "I got a question for you. Does Vic the Father get along with anybody?"

It was the first time I'd seen him smile without any warmth in it. "I gotta feeling you're gonna find out."

We filed through the revolving doors and back onto the street. Chavez opened the back door of the cruiser for us. "You guys are just giving us a ride, right?" He nodded, and we got in.

It was the beginning of the late watch, so they dropped Henry off at the Academy and drove me over the bridge into their own district. The lights on the Schuylkill River reflected the buildings along the west side of the city, and I got a quick glimpse of the Philadelphia Museum of Art and the stairs that Sylvester Stallone ran up in *Rocky*. Just past the museum, the eerie outline of Boathouse Row gave the empty impression of haunted houses, and I tried to think about something other than how the back seat of the cruiser smelled.

I watched the back of the two patrolmen's heads through the screening, the high and tight haircuts and the perfect uniforms; they even wore their hats in the car. Most of my stuff was pretty threadbare, like me. I couldn't even remember the last time I'd requisitioned a duty shirt.

Chavez responded to a call on the radio as we drove past 30th Street Station on the way to the hospital. Michael leaned back, laid his arm across the seat, and looked at me through the rearview as we waited at a stoplight. "We have to make a little detour."

"As long as your mother doesn't mind staying with Cady a little longer."

Michael looked at Chavez, who smiled back at me. "Hey, man, did he just say something about your mother?"

They both exhaled a laugh and then turned on the light bar and sirens. We turned up 34th and turned left on Lancaster Avenue. I called Lena. She said to take my time, that there was no change, and that she was reading a Margaret Coel and was fine. The neighborhood began changing from the late-night bustle of Market and the colleges as we headed west; the buildings became smaller, rundown, and dirty. People began disappearing, and the streetlights grew farther apart. We were in a place like the Indian reservations back home, a place where dreams would die unquestioned, a place for the quick and, more than likely, the dead.

We traveled a ways up Lancaster before Michael responded to another call and slowed the cruiser to a stop, turning off the lights and siren. We parked in a deserted gas station. There was a wig shop across the street at the end of the block with only one unbroken window. Michael switched off the headlights and let his eyes adjust to the dark. He peered past the corner, but I had to lean forward to see where he was looking.

It was an abandoned lot, unwanted and unoccupied except for the usual urban detritus. There had probably been more than one building there at one time, but they had collapsed or burned. Only a three-story row house was still standing. I could tell that it had been something in its day, but the years of neglect and abuse had left it looking decrepit and dangerous. There were no lights in the building, only the mirrored illumination in the broken windows, which reflected the glow of the one streetlight left lit half a block away and the close shine of the low-flying clouds. There was garbage everywhere, and a barricade of dumpsters overflowed across the street.

Chavez turned his head to look at me, putting his palm out flat to introduce the scene. "May I present Toy Diaz's Fort, the Wanamaker's of crack houses." I could make out patterns of movement in the shadows as he spoke. "The seller takes the money from the buyer, the seller goes into the building to give the money to the holder, the holder gives the stuff to the seller, and the seller comes back out and gives the stuff to the buyer. Pretty slick, and according to the letter of the law, at no time is the seller on the street with the money and the stuff . . ."

I finished the statement for him. "Which means possession, but not possession with intent to distribute."

Chavez laughed. "There's a new sheriff in town."

I watched as Michael's jaw clenched like Vic's. "Some scumbag realtor in the Northeast owns the building, and he gets a monster kickback from the whole deal."

"Who is Toy Diaz?"

"Salvadoran refugee, truly a grade-A asshole. His brother caught some time a few years back, but we're still trying to get the devil himself."

Chavez pointed. "With all the open space around the building, we can't get near the place without somebody giving the high sign. We come roarin' up and they just pitch the stuff and the guns." They were silent for a moment. "There's a lot of guns in there."

"Tell 'em about the 32s."

"That's what we were just responding to on the radio. Business gets good, and they just call in a 10-32 on the other side of the district to keep us distracted." Even with my limited knowledge of the city ten code, I knew a 10-32 was a man with gun and a priority call. "They keep about twenty vials out on the street, hidden all over the place. I found one in an empty potato chip bag one time. They sell those out, then they go back in and get more, usually during a shift change."

Michael shook his head. "They don't even walk away when we roll on 'em anymore. We've hit that damn place a dozen times now; we hit 'em twice this evening. Nothing."

We watched as the shadowy figures went about their business. I wanted to get back to Cady but started thinking about what the Cheyenne would do in this situation. "Do you think they count?"

Both of the young officers turned to look at me. "What?"

"Do you think they count how many cops go in during a bust, and how many cops come out?"

They called a point-to-point for some of their buddies so that the radio signal wouldn't reach Central. The eleven officers who showed up were like Moretti and Chavez—young, hopeful, and pissed off. Michael started to describe the plan.

Three cruisers would make their standard run at the place, with the fourth parked close but not within view. Nine of the eleven officers would rush the Fort, and the two men in the fourth car would call in a 10-32, pretending they'd gotten the call from the district. The cops would race out of the place, jumping in their units to respond to the fake point-to-point that no one else in the district would hear besides them and the drug dealers monitoring the police radio. The trick was that four officers would remain on the roof of the building and wait about five minutes for the dealers to reacquire their weapons and restock from inside.

Malcolm Chavez wanted to be on the roof squad, but Michael convinced him that he could go better undetected by the dealers since all white guys look alike. Chavez and another officer by the name of Johnston would do the fourth car position and call in the thirty-two at the appropriate time. Only the radios in the immediate vicinity would receive the call, but that would include the spotter the drug dealers were using, who would watch as the cops all piled out of the house, jumped in their cruisers, and sped off. At least all the cops he knew about. Then the ones on the roof would rush the building from behind. My job was to sit in the back of the cruiser on my hands and try not to think of why I was here and not with my daughter.

"So, when you were planning your trip to Philadelphia, did you ever think you'd be sittin' in the ghetto with two brothers?"

"You bet."

Rayfield Johnston was a likable sort, a little older than the others. He had been an elementary school teacher but had grown restless and decided to switch careers. I told him about my experiences reading to Durant Elementary School students. He thought it was pretty funny.

Johnston shook his head and compared notes. "We got the Police Athletic League, and I umpire up north of Belmont . . ."

Chavez blew air out. "Shit . . ."

Johnston laughed. "Combat pay, man. Combat pay."

The radio broke in with Michael's voice. Static. "Unit 18, 10-34, Lancaster and Pauley." We listened through the open windows as the sirens of the associated units sped toward the Fort about two blocks away. You could actually make out the blush of the surrounding buildings as the flicking red lights caromed off the uneven surfaces of the derelict row houses.

I thought about the people in the little buildings, dwarfed by the towers of Center City only a short distance away. You could see the tops of the skyscrapers from here, hovering over the moat of the Schuylkill like some magical kingdom. I wondered what they thought about the activity just outside their doors. Would they be happy that this little cottage industry of poison was being interrupted, or were we just another event in a constant cycle of tired desperation and civic stupidity? I looked at the heads of the two men in the front seat and thought about Johnston being screamed at by overenthusiastic parents and coaches, and about Chavez returning to a place he had fought so hard to escape. Hope is what it always comes down to, whether it's a trailer home on the other side of the tracks in Durant, Wyoming, or a tiny row house in the Wild West of Philadelphia. I smiled to myself and hoped my thoughts wouldn't carry to the patrolmen up front—they would laugh. Far beyond the badges and the guns, hope and laughter were their most powerful weapons.

Chavez started the car, and it seemed like he was in slow motion as he lifted the mic to his lips. "Unit 41, I've got a 10-32 at 52nd and Market." We listened as the sirens fired up again and the light show increased its intensity. The cavalry had made its charge and now appeared to be retreating.

Chavez hung the mic back on the dash and slipped the cruiser into gear. "Here we go."

We slipped through the remaining blocks to another corner, made a left, and were looking straight at the back of the row house. There were partial balconies at the rear of the building all the way up to the third floor, with a flight of stairs winding their way from the right-hand side. The remnants of aluminum awnings cast shadows across the back of the structure, making it difficult to see where anyone might be stationed. There was an abandoned car with its wheels removed and what looked like the remnants of an old chain-link fence stretching across the backyard. It was like a demilitarized zone, and all I could think of was the amount of guns that were about to converge there.

When Chavez slid the cruiser behind a derelict van, he and Johnston got out of the vehicle; the young officer reached back and lifted the handle to allow me to join them on the street.

"Lose your batons and hats."

Johnston turned and looked at me, neither of them having heard a word I said. "What?"

"Lose the batons and hats; they're going to fall off anyway. Turn your jackets inside out so that none of the metal reflects." They both looked at me for a moment more and then did as I told them. They looked so young.

Chavez, having prepared himself, studied Johnston. "You still look like a cop, man."

Johnston smiled. "Yeah? Well, you do, too." They both turned to look at me. "He doesn't." I smiled and took off my Phillies cap, placing it on Chavez's head.

He pulled it off at an angle, gangsta style. "You gonna be all right while we're gone?"

I looked up and down the street, where there was only one light on in a second-story window at the end of the block. "Looks pretty quiet in my part of the neighborhood."

"That could change." He reached back in the open window and unlocked a black Mossberg 590 DA 12-gauge and handed it to me. "You know how to use that?"

I checked the breech and safety. "Yep."

He smiled. "I bet you do."

The requisite amount of time had passed, and in the next few minutes Michael and his team would begin a very noisy descent from the roof. We were counting on it.

I watched as Chavez and Johnston moved around the discarded van and started working their way across the street and over the sagging fence. They stayed apart, and I didn't hear any warning sounds coming from the Fort as they slowly covered the fifty yards to the abandoned car.

I draped the Mossberg down along my leg after re-checking the safety, resting the end of the barrel on the toe of my boot. I figured if anybody were looking out the window, it would be prudent to not advertise the shotgun. I moved along the side of the van for a better vantage point and watched as the squad cars returned after pulling a quick U-turn. Michael and his group should now be descending the stairwell inside the building.

I could hear the thud of the back door being kicked in and watched as Chavez and Johnston disappeared into the darkness. People were yelling all over the place, and I could make out someone from inside shouting that they were the police and that whomever they were talking to should freeze. There was more yelling, and I watched as the beams from the cops' Maglites flashed inside the row house, some on the third floor and some on the second.

There were people running everywhere; the patrolmen coming from around the front tackled a few. Some of the more lithe individuals were able to slip by and disappeared into the streets and alleys beyond.

It was then that I heard the first shot, that cattle-prod reaction to the sharp sound of gunfire. It doesn't sound like in the movies; it is more like a quick smacking sound that makes you second-guess. I heard the sound again and was pretty sure it was coming from the second floor. I looked down at the 12-gauge in my hands, noticing that I had already clicked off the safety.

I moved across the street and was approaching the sagging fence when I saw some commotion at the second-story window and heard the report of a handgun. I sped up.

An uneven image crowded the window, and I watched in horror as what looked like two men scrambled and then tumbled from the second story. They crashed through the partial aluminum awning of the first floor and slid onto the back porch. There were more shots with a lot of screaming and yelling before one of the figures stood and leapt from the stoop, clearing the back of the collapsed porch in one leap. He turned as other people crowded the doorway and reached for something at his waistband. He tripped but converted the fall into a lope that brought him back up on a course for where I now stood.

It appeared as if his eyes were right on me as I stood there at the fence with the shotgun trained at his middle. I could make out Chavez's voice screaming for him to stop and prayed that they wouldn't open fire with me directly in line, but no bullets came whizzing from the Fort, only a half-naked man who still seemed to be fussing with something in the low-hanging pants at his midriff.

The police behind him screamed again, but he wasn't listening, intent only on his line of escape. As he got closer, I could see the well-defined muscles that covered his body and figured he was roughly my size, but in a lot better shape.

I looked over the shotgun and then thought about what I was doing and where I was. I clicked the safety back on.

As he got closer, I could see the tattoos that seemed to cover his body. He was a monster. I stayed alongside the abandoned car for a moment and then took two steps, catching him halfway over the fence.

There were two things they taught me when I was an offensive lineman at USC back in the Dark Ages. One: after a holding call, grab anything that moves because they're not going to make two holding calls in a row. Second: never underestimate the power of a good clothesline tackle. I felt the liquid thump of a body giving way as my right arm came up and caught him in the middle of the chest, forcing the air out of him,

He didn't make it over the fence, but what was in his waistband did; a small 9 mm semiautomatic pistol that struck the sidewalk and skittered over the curb and into the street, next to a sewer grating.

I watched as he gurgled for a moment, then breathed in an unsteady motion, clutching his abdomen and rolling from side to side; I noticed in a moment of irony that he was wearing black alligator cowboy boots. As one of the cops made it to the fence, I slipped the shotgun under my arm and walked into the street to look for the automatic, but I was pretty sure it'd dropped into the sewer.

There was a gaggle of police vehicles and EMTs, all with their gumballs going, at the front of the Fort, so before anybody with more authority could get back to where we were, I handed the shotgun to a patrolman named Fraser. His partner rolled the already complaining man over and cuffed him.

"This one had an automatic, but I think it dropped into the sewer grate."

Fraser smiled. "We'll light it up and take a look."

"Everybody okay over there?"

"Moretti stepped on a nail, so the big pussy's going to have to get a tetanus shot."

The large man in the cuffs cocked his head and stopped groaning long enough to yell toward me. "Hey, motherfucker, my ribs are broken!"

I looked back at Fraser. "What was all the gunfire?"

"Hey, motherfucker, who are you?!"

He motioned to the drug dealer. "One of his buddies threw a few into the stairwell before shooting himself in the leg."

"Motherfucker, I asked you a question!"

The other cop yanked him a little to the side. "Shut the fuck up, DuVall!"

"Who went out the window with this guy?"

The patrolman looked serious for a moment. "Johnston."

Two of the EMTs were working on Rayfield by the time I got there. He had dislocated his shoulder and broken a collarbone, but he was smiling when I leaned against the porch, eye to eye with him. They were stabilizing his arm and preparing a gurney to transport. "How you feeling?"

He groaned. "Like shit. How'd we do?"

I looked around at the assembled cops, spotting Chavez and some of the others smiling like guys who had gotten away with something. "I think pretty good."

My nostrils flared, and my nose hurt. I rubbed it cautiously and looked at Cady. I thanked Lena and apologized for being late, but I didn't ask the usual changing-of-the-guard question, whether there had been any improvement, and Lena hadn't volunteered any information. I wondered if that was the first phase in giving up, if I had passed over some threshold of hope. I didn't want to start saying Cady as I had said Martha, with a level of such misery and despair that I just couldn't say it without people looking away.

I sat in the chair by Cady's bed and remembered a game we used to play when she was around eight. If I would get home late, later than her bedtime, I would carefully make my way down the creaking hallway of our rented house, softly push apart the painted surfaces of the door and jamb, and stand in the backlight of the doorway. She was supposed to be long asleep, and she was a very good actress, but I could tell. If I thought it was a performance, I'd walk over to the bed and place my face only inches from hers, say the magic word, and be rewarded with an explosion of giggles.

I scooted my chair over and rested my chin on the sore arm that I had carefully placed on Sleeping Beauty's bed. I leaned in very close to her face and whispered. "Faker."

She didn't move.

This time I got the ride downtown; as a matter of fact, I got a ride to another state.

The big Crown Vic took the Broad Street entrance ramp onto I-95 southbound. There were ducks on a lake off to the right; I felt like joining them.

By the time the PPD had gotten its investigative ducks in a row and been fully informed about what I'd been up to, it was late in the afternoon. Katz and Gowder had picked me up from Cady's, where I had retreated for a shower, and hadn't mentioned anything about missing our breakfast. Henry had taken the afternoon shift at the hospital and had called to warn me of the detectives' impending arrival. I had taken Dog for a walk, and they had been waiting when I returned.

I studied the small red dots on the frames of Katz's designer glasses and wondered where he had gotten them. "So, you guys are going to drive me back to Wyoming?"

He sighed deeply as Gowder changed lanes, took the unmarked car into the far lefthand one, and leveled off at an even ninety; evidently, wherever we were going, we were in a hurry.

Katz cleared his throat. "I'm trying to figure out if I have made a terrible mistake."

I could feel my face redden a little. "No, you haven't . . ."

He continued as if I hadn't spoken. "I'm trying to figure out if you are going to be an asset or a detriment."

Gowder was watching me in the rearview mirror as I answered. "An asset. Cross my heart."

Katz blinked for the first time. "We have about 350 homicides per annum here in Philadelphia, and we try to keep the number of police officers on that list to a minimum." He glanced at Gowder, who might have smiled. His eyes returned to me. "Do you have any idea how lucky you were last night?"

"Probably not."

He nodded. "Personally, I don't think you have any idea, but since the Chief Inspector's son was injured . . ."

"He stepped on a nail." It was the first time Gowder had spoken, and Katz looked at him like he was a potted plant with blight. He stared at the side of Gowder's head until Gowder leaned an elbow on the window ledge and covered the smile with his index finger.

After a moment, Katz looked at me again. "So, do you mind telling me how your adventures last night are going to aid in our investigation?"

"They're not."

He compressed his lips. "You can't do things like that anymore."

We rode along in silence, Katz studying me a while longer before handing me a manila envelope with more than a few files inside. I looked back up at the two of them as we rocketed down I-95. "Devon Conliffe?"

Katz spoke over his shoulder. "You've got thirty minutes."

I opened the envelope. "Do you guys mind if I ask where we're going?"

"The opera." Gowder smiled, and the mole under his eye kicked up in the rearview mirror.

The Grand Opera House in Wilmington, Delaware, incorporated the same wedding-cake characteristics as Philadelphia's City Hall but with slightly less drama, inside or out. French Second Empire with a cast-iron façade, it was lit from below with floodlights that highlighted the detail.

A grumpy, elderly gentleman was sitting on a stool in the lobby and ushered us into the main auditorium, where Gowder and I sat just below the balcony. Katz continued on into the dark of the theater to a large soundboard that straddled two rows at house center and tapped the stage manager on the shoulder.

The young woman pulled her earphones aside and spoke with him. He waited as she returned to her headset, prefacing and ending her conversation into it with the word "Maestro." The seats were comfortable; I watched as Gowder propped his feet over the back of the next row, and I noticed that his socks did, indeed, match today's ensemble. He whispered, with his head inclined toward me. "Where in the world did you get the idea for the crack house?"

I also whispered. "OIT."

"What's that?"

"Old Indian Trick."

He smiled the becoming smile, and we watched the rehearsal. It was the end of Act II, where Monterone confronts the hunchback, reaffirming the curse he had placed on Rigoletto and the Duke. The irony of the father/daughter opera was not lost on me, and I could only hope that Cady and I would have a happier ending.

The scenery and costumes were brilliant, with the Duke's salon and adjoining apartments drifting to the sixteenth-century Mantuan skyline. It was night, and the jester was watching as the tortured father was dragged away. Inspector Victor Moretti cut a bold figure as Monterone, in a torn robe stripped aside to reveal his lashed back. He was tall and lean like a Doberman, and even from this distance I could feel his eyes. Lena was right about his voice; Victor could sing his baritone ass off.

I watched and thought about the manila folder the two detectives had shared with me. The chain holding the gate to the north-side entrance of the bridge closed had been cut with a substantial pair of bolt-cutters, and there had been a scuff mark on the sidewalk next to the railing of the bridge that indicated that the perpetrator had worn leather-soled shoes or boots. There were no fingerprints at either location, and it was surmised that the killer had also worn gloves.

The decedent had been propelled over the railing and across the PATCO rail lines before landing in the alley below. Somebody had thrown Devon in an arch close to twenty feet before he fell. I would have suspected me, too.

The topper was Devon's blood sample, which indicated that he was loaded with ketamine hydrochloride, otherwise known as Special K, a club drug that he had snorted in powder form. A chemical cousin to the animal tranquilizer PCP, ketamine creates a dreamlike state by binding the serotonin transmitters in the brain, consequently destroying the user's ability to regulate mood, appetite, sleep, and temperature, but it supposedly feels good.

That was probably how Devon had been coerced onto the BFB late that night, in search of another hit; he'd got it, all right, and then had been thrown off the bridge. I was working on a Rasputin-like scenario when I noticed Detective Katz standing in the aisle with Verdi's Monterone. They were talking sharply, but sotto voce, and I was pretty sure it wasn't in English. I looked at Gowder. "Are they speaking Italian?"

He nodded. "Asa does it to piss Victor off. His Italian is better." He chuckled to himself. "He does everything he can to piss Victor off, including fuck his wife."

I sat there for a moment and then turned in my seat. "What?" He didn't have time to answer because the next thing we both knew, Chief Inspector Moretti was standing with his arms folded in the aisle in front of us. It could have been the stage makeup, but he seemed like the most intense person I'd met in quite a while. His hair flourished in a sweeping mane with eyebrows to match, and he wore a silvered goatee. With the torn robe and lacerated back, it was like meeting the returning Jesus Christ; a pissed-off, returning-like-a-lion Jesus Christ.

I smiled, but he didn't. "Sheriff Longmire?"

I stuck my hand out. "Walt."

He looked at my hand, then back at me, his voice flat and emotionless. "Sheriff, I'm terribly sorry about what has happened to your daughter."

I let the hand drop. "Thank you."

"But you must realize that you have no jurisdiction here in the city of Philadelphia or the state of Pennsylvania."

"I am aware of that." I was also aware that we were in Wilmington, Delaware, but figured now was a bad time to argue geographic discrepancies.

He glanced at both Gowder and Katz. "We have a number of very fine detectives assigned to the incident that concerns your daughter and to the one concerning Mr. Conliffe." He paused for a moment. "You need to listen to this next part very carefully." He unfolded his arms and placed his hands on the seat in front of me. "If I find that you have involved yourself in this case, in any way, I will have you in the Roundhouse so fast your eyes won't have time to water." He leaned in with his exposed and stage-makeupped chest. "Do you understand me?"

I nodded. "Yep, but before you get yourself all worked up, you better take a look at this." I pulled the card from my shirt pocket and handed it to him.

He took the envelope and, to my unseen amusement, Katz lent him the designer glasses. He looked back up at me as the detectives gave me worried looks. "Where did this come from?"

"It was left in my daughter's room. None of the staff had any idea who could have left it or when."

He lowered the glasses and handed them back. "Did you know about this?"

I interrupted. "I asked them to let me tell you."

He held the card a little higher. "So, from this, we are to assume that you are already involved."

"It kind of looks that way."

"Let's make sure it stays in an unofficial capacity."

"You bet." I waited a moment. "But can I give you a piece of advice?" He didn't move. "Monterone wouldn't wear the Rolex."

"I think that went well, don't you?"

They weren't talking to me.

"Guys, I'm sorry . . ."

Katz didn't turn this time when he spoke. "We have just given you access to some of the most sensitive evidence in this case, and you withhold something like this?" He held the note, now safely encased in a ziplock bag.

"I was going to tell you about it."

"When?"

I looked out the window and into the velvety darkness of the Delaware River toward the New Jersey Pine Barrens. "After you showed me the reports."

Katz finally turned and looked at me. "This is not a poker game where we call and see; this is a murder investigation, and if you don't start coming clean with us, then all bets are off, and you can take the next flight back to cowtown."

We sat there for a little longer. "I've got more." They looked at each other. "I questioned the security guard at the Franklin Institute, Esteban Cordero, in a little more detail." I had to be careful how I did this, so that none of the blame would fall back on the inexperienced Michael Moretti. "He remembered that a young man had banged on the door after Cady's fall, but I don't think it was Devon Conliffe." I had the detectives' full attention as I explained about the incongruities of the man's appearance and the red tie. "After we looked at the picture on the cover of the *Daily News*, he positively stated that it wasn't Devon who knocked on the door."

Katz turned to look at me again. "So someone else was there."

"Someone who identified himself as Devon Conliffe and was gone by the time the guard got outside." As they absorbed that, I asked them a question. "What can you guys tell me about Devon's Roosevelt Boulevard incident?"

It was Katz's turn to sigh. "That was yours, Tony. You tell it."

"It was before Thanksgiving." Gowder made eye contact with me in the rearview. "Assistant district attorney with the Special Narcotics Prosecution Unit . . ."

"Vince Osgood."

"You've heard of him?"

I paused a moment, not wanting to get anyone else in trouble. "He sounds important."

He laughed. "Important enough to get charged by a federal grand jury for violating the Racketeer Influenced and Corrupt Organizations Act; about a half-dozen counts for racketeering, possession with intent, conspiracy to extort money, conspiracy to manufacture drugs, witness tampering, and retaliation against a witness."

"This guy's on our side?"

"Wait, it gets better," Katz interrupted. "Tell him about the retaliation."

"Tim Gomez, writer for the *Daily News*, investigates and writes about Osgood's activities with the Special Narcotics. Being a good reporter, he catches wonderboy Vince outside 13th and Samsom, where he asks the assistant DA about property seized by the drug task force. Oz loses his mind, has to be forcibly restrained after kicking Gomez and screaming about how he's going to bitch-slap him all the way to Camden if he doesn't lay off."

"Always good to have positive relations with the fourth estate."

Gowder laughed. "Some of the extortion charges dealt with sums over $100,000."

I shook my head and looked out the window. "What about the possession/distribution charges?"

Gowder shook his own head and concentrated on the road. "Oz was reported to have watched another man cook about 118 grams of designer stuff and then accepted half in June of last year for distribution. Local kingpin Toy Diaz is picked up on a traffic stop by Osgood's buddies in the drug task force and relieved of about two million dollars worth."

"Must've been a big car." I thought about it. "Toy Diaz is the operator of the house we took out last night."

"Could be. He's got his fingers in a lot of pies."

"In the aforementioned transaction, all the evidence disappeared from the holding unit, and that under Vince Osgood's supervision."

"What about Roosevelt Boulevard?"

I saw the mole kick up again, and I was sure he was smiling. "Easter Sunday, and Oz leaves the office with good friend and fellow attorney . . ."

"Devon Conliffe."

"You got it."

I glanced at Katz. "Easter morning?"

Gowder went on. "As they pull away, they notice that they are being followed by a Toyota station wagon occupied by two nonwhite males, approximately thirty years of age. Osgood pulls a sawed-off shotgun from under the seat and rests it in his lap. Then he instructs Conliffe to take the 9 mm, which he keeps for insurance, from the glove box and be prepared for what happens next." He took a deep breath, glanced at Katz, and continued. "Being a concerned citizen and aware that gunfire may result, Oz takes the exit at 5th and pulls up at an abandoned lot in Fentonville . . ." His voice slowed for effect. "Three congested city miles from where they started. Oz's initial statement was that they had decided to confront the individuals in a neutral area."

I cleared my throat. "Going to a police station didn't occur to them?"

"Evidently not." Gowder eased his way around a slowpoke, and I noticed we were approaching ninety again. "Oz states that, after a brief but heated discussion punctuated by rapid small-arms fire, he saw the passenger's head thrown back on impact and then the Toyota sped away."

I had to ask. "What was Oz . . .?"

"A Hummer."

I nodded. "I heard that Osgood also stated that they might have been KKK?"

"Yeah, his statements were a little confusing. Then Toy Diaz showed up at Temple University Hospital with numerous shotgun pellet wounds and a wounded Ramon Diaz, who had just done a three spot at Graterford."

"Ramon any relation to Toy?"

He inclined his head to indicate I was a good student. "Brothers."

"So it was revenge?"

Katz answered. "Well, that was the tack the U.S. District Court took, but Toy Diaz continued to state, with a great deal of emphasis, that it was an independent capitalistic venture that took a surprising turn."

"Osgood didn't want to pay for the drugs?"

"That was Diaz's story, but since he is from El Salvador, and a four-time loser on assorted drug charges, his statements were taken with the proverbial grain of judicial salt."

"Where is Toy Diaz?"

"Good question."

"What'd Devon Conliffe say?"

Gowder laughed. "He said whatever Osgood said, and whenever Oz's story changed, he said that, too."

Katz studied me. I glanced up and watched the lights of Penn's Landing reflect from his glasses. "So, Osgood was suspended?"

It was quiet in the Crown Vic as we took the off-ramp just past the Benjamin Franklin Bridge. "Yes, but he has a lot of friends in the city." There was a moment's pause as we stopped at a red light. "I assume we're taking you to your daughter's place, but if you need to go to the hospital we can drop you there."

"Actually, as much as I'd rather go to the hospital, I need to go to a gun shop up on Spring Garden."

They were both looking at me now.

When we got to Tactical Training Specialists, I had Gowder pull into the secured and packed parking lot and waited as he released the locks. There were no handles on the inside, so I waited for them to let me out. "Graterford."

Gowder was looking at me, and it was a relief to see his entire face. "What?"

"It might be nothing, but there was a pro bono case that Cady was working on when we went through the papers at her office; something about Graterford. A white Indian." I thought about it for a moment. "William White Eyes."

They both looked at me blankly, Gowder cocking his head in disbelief. "A white Indian?"

"I've been told that it's not that unusual."

"By who?"

I folded my hands in my lap. "This guy White Eyes was trying to arrange for a sweat lodge in Graterford through the freedom of religious expression legislation. It was a pro bono case Cady had worked on, the only criminal case I could find."

Katz shook his head. "There are four thousand guys up in Graterford . . ."

"It could be nothing, but I thought I should mention it."

"William White Eyes?" I nodded. Katz wrote the name in a small notepad. "We'll check it out."

I stepped out, and Katz closed my door. "Thank you."

"Hey, you're doing us a favor." He noticed the bright yellow Hummer parked alongside the building. "Want company?"

I looked back, thought about what Gowder had intimated about Lena Moretti, and looked at Katz with new eyes. "No, I think I'll get better responses in my official unofficial capacity."

Gowder's voice caught me as I approached the wire-mesh, steel security door. "Hey, Sheriff?" I stopped and half-turned to look at the detective, still seated in the cruiser. "Is that a government-issue Colt .45 I see in a pancake holster at the small of your back?"

I stood there for a moment. "Why? Does it make me look fat?"

The party was in full swing. I was in a side hallway with Jimmie Tomko, and I could hear music playing and the excited sound of young people's voices, younger than me at least. I held up a finger, pulled out Cady's cell phone, and called Lena. She said there was no change but that she wanted dinner at the end of her shift. I told her it was still her pick and that Henry had promised to be there in an hour. I told her I'd met Vic the Father, and she said she was sorry. I left out the part about who had introduced us.

I've spent a lot of time in gun ranges but never one like this. The entire shooters' area was carpeted, and the walls were paneled with black walnut and decorated with green-matted Currier and Ives hunting scenes illuminated by turtleshell sconces. There was a bar, but all I saw were water bottles and nonalcoholic beer. The back wall was lined with tufted leather sectionals that gave spectators an unobstructed view of the seven firing ranges in front of them.

The place was crowded, and I stepped back as a diminutive blonde with a 9 mm Beretta approached. I looked at the congestion and then at Tomko. "Are they all lawyers?" He nodded, the glass eye drifting off. "Good time to spray for 'em."

I tried to find a familiar face, finally recognizing a striking, dark-haired woman at the bar. As the blonde half-pointed the Beretta at our feet, I released Jimmie Tomko to his appointed rounds. "Greta, you need to not point the weapon toward . . ."

I turned sideways and made my way past the staging table, all the while trying to spot someone who could be Vince Osgood. They were an attractive crowd, well-dressed and coiffed, but they were lawyers, not paupers, so it was to be expected.

There was a tall man holding forth at the center firing range, his voice probably sounding normal to his muffed ears and in competition to the hip-hop music. There was a small man standing with him, and I was starting to think it odd that no one was firing when the blonde who had aimed at my feet let rip with a scattered salvo, only two rounds out of fourteen striking the paper silhouette. Jimmie Tomko raised an eyebrow at me; just in case, I kept my front toward the range to keep from being shot.

I watched as the short Latino peeled away from the tall guy so that he would intersect with me about halfway across the crowded floor. I tried to step to one side, but he countered, and we were nose to sternum. I nodded an apology and stepped to the right, just as he did. I was struck by the precision of his appearance, how defined his hair and clothes seemed. As he looked up, I noticed that his pupils were very large and that they gave his face a lifeless quality.

His voice was soft and cultured. "Pardon."

"No, my fault." He slipped to the side before I could continue the conversation and watched me as I made my way across the room.

Joanne Fitzpatrick's eyes locked with mine as I lumbered up to her. "Hey, Jo." I looked around for effect. "What're you doing here?"

She smiled. "I thought you would be happy to see a friendly face."

She didn't have one of the cases that most of the people in the room carried. "You don't shoot?"

"No."

"Me either." She laughed, and the smile was an exact replica of the one that was in the horseback photo in Cady's office. I took one of the bottled waters from the bar and glanced back over my shoulder, but the tiny man was gone. "Do you know that guy I was just dancing with?"

"Who?"

"The little guy?"

"No."

I nodded my head at the tall man at center. "Is that Osgood?" She nodded slightly. "He doesn't seem real broke up about his buddy Devon."

She leaned in. "No, he doesn't."

About that time, Osgood unloaded his 9 mm into the paper target at the center of the firing range. The kid was pretty good. There was a smattering of applause as he turned and took a perfunctory bow, taking just an extra moment to glance at me.

I turned back to Jo. "C'mon, I'll teach you how to shoot."

Tomko handed me a tray with a box of .45 ACPs and a questioning look until I patted the small of my back. By the time I made my way to the other side of the room, Osgood was openly watching me. I gave him a tight-lipped smile and a nod, but he didn't respond.

I set Jo up at range 7 along the wall in hopes that numerology would be on our side. "I've never done this before."

I unsnapped the thumb strap from the Colt at my back, pulled it, and placed it on the counter with the slide group locked in the open position and the magazine removed. "That's what they all say." I palmed the seven-shot clip in my hand, dropped it to my side, and told her to pick up the .45.

"It looks old."

"Older than you." After getting her acquainted with the particularities of the weapon, she adopted a wide stance with her arms extended; we both now wore the hearing protectors that had been hanging in the stall.

She squeezed the trigger as instructed, and the big Colt jumped in her hands; it was pointed at the ceiling, but I caught her shoulder. She peered at the paper target but could see no effect, unaware that the gun hadn't fired. I pulled one of her ear cups back. "You flinched."

"No, I didn't."

I cocked the empty .45. "Try it again, but make sure you keep your eyes open this time." I put her ear cup back, and she imitated the exact same motion, but this time the automatic stayed steady.

She turned and looked at me. "It didn't fire."

"It didn't last time either." I showed her the clip in my hand. "The involuntary response is pretty common. You think the gun's going to jump, so you make it jump." I took the Colt, popped the mag into place, cocked the slide, and placed her hands around the gun, aimed toward the target. "Don't worry about blinking; a lot of people do it."

She spoke out of the side of her mouth. "Do you?"

I looked at the target. "No."

She doubled her attentions on the silhouette and squeezed, all her efforts going into not blinking. The .45 blew her back and, from her expression, there was no doubt in her mind that it had fired this time. We both peered at the target; there was a perforation at his left kidney on the line between the four and five score. "Much better."

She smiled and pulled the ear cup back again. "Do they all kick like that?"

I smiled back. "No. This one's just an antique, heavy, hard to aim, slow rate of fire . . ." Her smile faded quickly as she looked over my right shoulder, past the barrier, and I figured I had accomplished what I'd set out to do.

She handed me the automatic and pulled her ear protectors all the way off. "Hello, Oz."

I didn't turn but lowered the hammer on the Colt and pushed the safety. His voice wasn't what I'd expected; it was higher pitched and discordant.

"I thought I'd come over here and see who was shooting the howitzer." It was silent, except for the music and a few conversations that were still going on a little ways away. "Who's your friend?"

Her face remained still. "This is Walt Longmire, Cady's father."

"Oh, my God." He was as tall as me, mid-thirties, with an athletic build, a receding hairline, and the ubiquitous goatee. "I am so sorry about your daughter."

I placed the Colt on the counter. "Thank you."

He switched the Glock to his other hand, and I noticed the clip was in and the safety was off. He extended his right. "Vince Osgood. They call me Oz." I nodded, and he continued. "I was a friend of Cady's."

I noticed he used the past tense, which made me want to grab his throat. "You were also a friend of Devon Con-liffe?"

His eyes were steady. "I was . . . Did you know Devon?"

I pointed at the Glock in his left hand. "Would you mind securing that weapon before we talk?"

He froze up for a second. "It's got a safe-action feature . . ."

I did my best ol' boy routine. "I'm just a little nervous around unsecured firearms."

He reached down and pushed the button, the image of allocated grace. "Sure. I'm around these things so much that they just become second nature."

"I was able to meet Devon just before the accident."

"Yeah, I heard about that." He leaned against the stall, and I could smell his aftershave. "You and I should talk."

I nodded and glanced at Joanne. "I agree. You might be in a position to give me a better insight as to what's going on."

He puckered his lips and looked down at his four-hundred-dollar shoes, the picture of the all-knowing assis-tant DA, if suspended, there to assist his rustic cousin. "I think I can do that." His head came back up. "Where will you be later tonight?"

I thought about Lena. "I've got a dinner date this eve-ning, but I could meet you after for a beer. You know a place called Paddy O'Neil's on Race?"

He watched me for just a second too long. "Near the bridge?"

I pulled out my pocket watch. "Ten thirty?" He nodded, and I gestured toward the Glock 34. "You're pretty good with that thing."

"Goes with the job."

I wondered about lawyering in Philadelphia and picked up my Colt. "You gonna shoot again?"

"Oh, yeah, how about you?"

I let him watch as I reloaded and replaced the .45 in the pancake holster at my back. "No, thanks."

He smiled and bobbed his head. "I guess you're pretty good, too, huh?"

Good enough to know I was cocked and locked with a full clip and one in the pipe; good enough to know he was empty.

# 9

"Alphonse, if you don't turn the tourist music down, we're going somewhere else."

The restaurant had been closed, but Lena had unlocked and marched through the back door as if she owned the place. She deposited me in a small booth by the kitchen and called up the steps to Alphonse, threatening him with brimstone if he didn't come down and fix us dinner.

Alphonse, the uncle, was Victor Moretti's brother, and his restaurant was quintessential Italian Market, from the red-and-white-checkered tablecloths to the battered, raffia-covered Chianti bottle with a tapered candle flickering in its throat. The booths were high-backed and worn, with the many layers of varnish making their surfaces glisten, but it was Alphonse who made Alphonse's. Alphonse Moretti must have weighed as much as I did, no mean feat since he only stood about five foot six.

"You want me to create, I have to have music." He blew through the kitchen door with a fresh bottle of wine and an assortment of water glasses, pulled the cork with his hands, and slid onto the bench with me, singing along with Frank Sinatra in a soulful duet of "The Lady Is a Tramp." He wore glasses but, like everything else on his face, they looked as if they were being swallowed by flesh. The only part that seemed up to the fight was his mustache, a salt and pepper affair that drooped past the corners of his mouth. It would have looked dour on any other man, but it gave Alphonse the look of a painter who had stuffed a brush in his mouth and had forgotten about it. "She is beautiful, isn't she?"

Lena rested her chin in the palm of her hand and looked at him. "Alphonse . . ."

He poured the wine into the water glasses and slid one toward me. "A race of *principessas*, not like us peasants." Lena slouched against the wooden back of the booth and looked at me; I was sure this was a repeat performance. "You know the island of Capri?" He extended a chubby finger toward Lena and spilled a little wine on the table. "This one, she will tell you she is from Positano, but this is not true."

She picked up her glass and retreated from the candlelight. "Al, you don't have any wine glasses?"

He gestured toward her again. "You see—*principessa*." "Al . . ."

"*Un pezzo di cielo caduto in terra* they call it; a piece of heaven fallen to earth. They say Lucifer stole the place and brought it to Italy, and if you want to know about beautiful women, you ask the devil." Lena blew air from her lips in dismissal. He continued. "You know Tiberius, the emperor that threw people off cliffs?" I nodded. "He had palaces built across the entire island, even moving the imperial capital to Capri."

Her voice was soft. "Jesus, Al . . ."

He crossed himself. "She is a bad woman, but so delicious." I felt Lena kick at him under the table. "Tiberius has all these palaces scattered across Capri, now he needs women with whom to debauch. The word goes out across the empire that all the most voluptuous and desirable women should be brought from all Italy. Villa Jovis is the palace of palaces, so it must have the woman of all women.

Tiberius has all the *principessas* brought to the palace and disrobed, one by one." He gestured toward Lena. "This one's ancestor, Dona Allora, is last, and when she drops her robe, the court is silent. They have never seen a woman until they have seen this woman. The emperor must have her at once, so he takes her on the floor of the palace with the entire court in attendance."

In the silence, I thought I should say something. "Romantic devil."

Lena shook her head. "Bullshit."

"Allora had her revenge." Alphonse took a drink of his wine. "They say Tiberius was suffocated by a rival, but . . ." He pointed the sausage-like finger at Lena. "You cannot love a women as beautiful as this; she will twist your heart."

"I wish I could twist hearts the way you twist the truth."

He was looking at me. "I chased after this woman for three months before she took my ugly brother who is not as smart as me." He touched my arm to make sure he had my full attention. "This one's daughter, the Terror, works for you?"

I nodded. "Yes."

"When she was a teenager, she used to lifeguard at the pool on Christian Street . . ."

"Alphonse . . ." Lena's voice carried more than a little warning.

He ignored her and continued. "The Terror, she used to wear this black, one-piece bathing suit, a white blouse tied at the waist and little sandals with flowers between the toes . . ."

"Al . . ."

"In the summer, the men of Christian Street always

found a reason to be out on the stoop at ten in the morning to watch her go by."

"Al . . ."

"Fourteen years old, and she is cussing them like a sailor."

I took a sip of my own wine as Lena spoke. "If you're through with your stories, we're starving."

He looked at me. "You see . . . *Principessa*."

She leaned forward. "What are we having?"

He raised his hands with a flourish. "Pizza Rustica Alphonse."

Lena clapped her hands. "My favorite!"

He downed the rest of his wine, set the glass back on the table with more flourish, and stood. "I stole the recipe from Termini, but he is not here . . ." He disappeared through the kitchen doors, singing "One for My Baby" just under Frank.

I raised my glass, and she touched the rim with hers. "Here's to the lady's revenge and sandals with little flowers between the toes." She smiled and drank. I motioned toward the kitchen where Alphonse was overpowering Sinatra. "He's quite a character."

"My ally."

"He seems to enjoy life."

Her head tilted slightly. "And he makes excuses for people who also make that mistake." The glass lingered there at her lower lip, a movement that echoed Vic's. "When I had the affair, Alphonse let me stay above the restaurant."

"You make it sound like an historic event."

She took a sip. "In our family, it was." She studied me. "I'd imagine you were true."

"True?"

"You know what I mean."

I thought about it, trying to come up with some way of not sounding like a self-righteous prig. "We were always saving for something. I mean I don't think it was that we got along all that great. There were plenty of times we would have called it quits, but it seemed we were always needing something, a new television, a washer and dryer, a car, or for Cady . . . It's amazing what civil service wages can do for fidelity." She laughed, and I studied the pattern of the tablecloth. "I'm not sure how to go about this, but I think we're close enough friends that I have to tell you something." She looked back up at me. "I think I've stumbled onto who it might've been that you had the relationship with."

Her expression changed very slightly, and then she looked at the tablecloth. It was a very long pause, and I was about to say something when she started talking. "I understand Michael threw you out of the hospital?"

"Yep."

"He is healing fast." She held the glass at her lip. "He got a three-day suspension, and it seems to me I should be mad at you about that."

I waited and then spoke very carefully, "As long as that's all you're mad at me about." She raised a perfectly shaped eyebrow as I continued. "It was my plan, but it wasn't my idea." I didn't care for this line of conversation either, so I changed the subject again. "I went to Delaware today. First to sign the Constitution; they have a plaque."

"How was the opera?"

"I think your husband would just as soon I go back to Wyoming."

"I'm sure he would."

I smiled and took another sip of the wine. "Opening night tomorrow?"

"Yes, why?"

I shrugged. "I was looking for a date to take to Henry's opening, but I guess you're otherwise engaged."

She took a long moment to respond, looking at her glass. "Yes."

It was quiet, and I watched her clench her jaw muscles; again she looked like Vic. We listened as Alphonse finished up on a note. "Victor really can sing, but I think I prefer Alphonse; more heartfelt."

"And flat." She laughed a slow laugh that pulled at the top of my chest. "So, if we can't seem to talk about anything else, what's happening with the case?"

"I'm having a beer tonight at O'Neil's with an assistant district attorney. He was a friend of Devon's and was a player in the Roosevelt Boulevard thing."

"Vince Osgood?"

"Yep, I guess it was in all the papers . . ."

"No, just recently there was something."

I let her think while I continued. "Suspended . . ."

She held her hand out to stop me from speaking. "No, this was something that connected with something you said. I've heard those two names mentioned together. Osgood and Conliffe."

"Roosevelt Boulevard . . ."

"No, no, no. It was something else." She continued to think. "I knew I'd heard that young man's name before, but now I can't think where." Alphonse returned with two plates and wrapped flatware, carefully placing them on the table, and poured himself another glass of Chianti. "Alphonse, what do you know about Vince Osgood?"

"The assistant DA on suspension?" He tightened his lips under his mustache. "He would burn his mother to stay warm."

"What about him and Devon Conliffe, the judge's son?"

"What about him?" He took a sip of his wine. "He fell off the bridge; end of story."

"Al . . ."

He looked at me. "You know, I leave you here with this beautiful woman, wine, candlelight . . . And you talk like cops."

Lena set her glass down. "You were a cop."

"Not anymore. You want to talk cop stuff, you talk to your husband; you want to talk women, wine, or song, you talk to me."

She held the glass with both hands and didn't look at him. "Do you still have those friends of yours in the DA's office?"

"No."

Now she looked at him. "Are you going to make me ask Victor?"

He sipped and thought about it, finally sighing. "What do you want to know?"

"There's some kind of connection between Osgood and the Conliffe boy, something I overheard or read somewhere, something recent."

"I'll make a phone call . . . tomorrow, but only on one condition." We waited. "No more cop talk."

I called Henry from O'Neil's. He had a number of ceremonies he wanted to perform in Cady's hospital room and told me he would relieve Michael, and to take the rest of the night off. I told him I wasn't sure I could do that. "Then you have to help."

"I'll help." I could hear him talking to the nurses and wondered about the other patients and the upcoming rituals. "How did the installation at the Academy go?"

"Wonderfully well. They are very accommodating." I thought about the woman with the keys and the security pass. "You are coming to the reception." It was a statement, not a question.

"I can, but somebody's got to stay with Cady."

There was silence on the phone. "She will be better by then." The heat in my face hit like exhaust, and the stinging in my eyes wouldn't go away. Even across the telephone lines, he felt it. "Do me a favor?"

"Yep?"

"Wait until very late. I am not sure that they like pagan ceremonies . . . and bring some eagle feathers." The line went dead.

Ian looked at me as I hung up the phone. "Trouble?"

"Just a little. I have to find some eagle feathers."

He crossed his muscled arms on the bar, the intertwined Celtic snakes writhing up his forearms. "I'll see what I can do."

He probably got stranger requests. I looked around the room and spotted an empty table near the window. The place was crowded, but not as bad as I might have suspected. "Not too busy?"

The Irishman shrugged. "The band cancelled."

"What happened?"

He slid an unasked for Yuengling longneck across the bar to me. "Started drinking too early."

"Irish?"

He smirked. "French, I think."

"Damn French."

"Yah, they'll fuck up the EU, wait and see."

I glanced back at the still-empty table. "I think I'm going to go sit over by the window."

He swallowed a fearful dollop of what the Scots call the creature. "Yer too good to drink at the bar, Sheriff?"

"I have to meet with a lawyer."

"Cady's comin'?"

I took a breath as I stood. "No, and that's something I probably need to . . ." It was then that I noticed Osgood standing at the front door. I raised a hand and got his attention, motioning toward the table in the corner. Ian's looks had sharpened, either at my statement or Osgood's appearance. "I'll have to tell you about it later."

"I'll keep me eyes out fer eagle feathers."

I took my beer and napkin to the table and eased my back against the wall, a good frontier sheriff. "Howdy."

"How are you?"

"I'm good. Can I buy you a drink?"

He took off his suit jacket and hung it carefully on the back of his chair, loosened his tie, and rested his arms on the small table. He nodded before looking around the place. "Why'd you want to meet here? The place is a dump."

I nodded at O'Neil and turned back to Osgood. "Cady lives only about a half a block away."

"Oh." That's all he said.

Ian approached, and I noticed that Osgood didn't bother to look up. "Scotch and water, anything over twelve years old."

Ian looked at him for a second more, then turned and walked away. I watched Osgood. "You two know each other?"

The assistant district attorney shook his head. "Never seen him before." I was pretty sure he hadn't seen him just now either. "How's your daughter doing?"

"She's improving, starting to have involuntary responses." I thought about Henry. "We brought in a specialist."

He nodded. "I hear you're doing a little investigative work?"

I wondered where he had heard it. "Just keeping my hand in on account of Cady, nothing too serious."

He nodded some more. "Watch out for Gowder and Katz." He glanced out the window. "The kike is Internal Affairs and could give a shit and a shake about the truth." He continued to look at the sidewalk outside. "They've been after me for years, and I have no idea why."

Close to ten counts, I figured. "What can you tell me about Devon and Cady?"

"Well . . ." He pulled at the end of his goatee. "I was kind of hoping that we could share information, you know? Help each other out?"

I nodded, all innocence. "You bet."

Ian appeared with the scotch and water and motioned to my untouched beer. "You wan' another?"

"In a bit. Thank you." He nodded and glanced at Osgood, who continued to study the surface of the table. His head came up after Ian had left.

He took a sip of the scotch and rested it back on the paper napkin. "I'm assuming that your focus of interest is the connection between Devon and your daughter?"

"Cady."

He looked at me for a moment longer. "Cady."

"You'd be right."

"There isn't any connection." I looked mildly surprised. "Between what happened to Devon and what happened to your . . . to Cady." He leaned in. "Devon was involved in a lot of shit in which he shouldn't have been involved."

I took a sip of my beer and waited. "He had a little problem, if you know what I mean." He laid a finger alongside one nostril and sniffed. "His difficulties started with this guy, Shankar DuVall, who used to provide Devon's medication for him. They started working on a barter system, you know, medication for legal services rendered."

I thought about the man that I'd tackled at the crack house, the one they called DuVall, but it had to be too much of a coincidence. "What's this guy DuVall look like?"

"Black, tattoos, and one big fucker. Pharmaceuticals and firearms are his thing. Something of an aficionado, I hear."

Not too much of a coincidence as it turns out. And big enough to throw somebody off the BFB, I figured. "So what happened with him and Devon?"

"This ass DuVall and a buddy of his, Billy Carlisle, get caught with eight kilos of designer stuff in a roach-coach at the food distribution center in South Philly. They had this bright idea to sell the stuff like ice cream." He raised a hand, pulling on an imaginary bell. "Ding-ding, get high! They showed pictures of the truck to the jury. There were little kids licking popsicles painted on the sides. You can imagine how that went over." He took another sip of his scotch and shook his head. "Couple of criminal masterminds here. So, anyway . . . DuVall and Carlisle make offers to cooperate with us and the DA picks up the tab on DuVall, leaving Carlisle to dangle, figuring anything Billy-boy knows, he got from Shankar."

I worked on the label of my beer with my thumbnail. "Okay."

"It happens a lot. For a number of these shit bags, cooperating with the authorities means they get a 5k1.1, which means a substantial assistance letter from the prosecuting attorney."

"Cooperation means DuVall avoids the sentencing guidelines and mandatory minimum prison term?"

He held up four fingers. "Four years, three months. Eastern Pennsylvania leads the league with 41.1 percent of the defendants receiving reduced sentencing for playing ball."

"And Carlisle?"

"Nineteen and seven." He exhaled a short laugh. "All for driving an ice cream truck."

"But with enough dope to fill up all the nostrils on Mt. Rushmore." I thought about it. "DuVall got four and three? That seems light."

"He played ball."

I tried to figure a way of introducing the Roosevelt Boulevard incident, but maybe Osgood would bring it up himself. "Where does Devon enter into this?"

"He made a phone call to yours truly, wanting to see if there was anything I could do about Billy Carlisle."

"And was there?"

He shook his head. "Nope." He spread his hands in innocence. "I play by the rules."

In for a penny, in for a pound. "What about Roosevelt Boulevard?"

"What about it?" His voice was stiff.

"I heard some stuff."

His eyes stayed steady. "What'd you hear?"

"I heard you and Devon were involved in a shoot-out up north of here."

He kind of laughed. "What, you got a file?"

I smiled and took another sip of my beer. He watched me, then took another sip of his drink and held it there alongside his head. "That was a Devon deal." He sighed. "It almost lost me my job and may still if those two pricks Katz and Gowder have their way." I tried to decide how much of what he was telling me was untrue. "Devon had a deal with these assholes, and he got scared and asked me to come along."

"So, they weren't chasing you when you came out of your office?"

"No, I made that up, but you gotta admit it sounded better than the two white lawyers going up to Fentonville for a drug deal."

"It does."

"I thought I'd use Devon's connections for a little sting operation I was working on with the narcotics task force. Just laying the groundwork, you know. There wasn't supposed to be a buy, but Devon was hungry, so things fell apart."

"I hear you did some damage to Ramon Diaz with a sawed-off shotgun?"

He set the glass down. "It was him or me."

I had an idea that I had just heard the Osgood mantra and figured I'd just hear the same one if I brought up the small man at the shooting range. "Why has the thought that Devon might have committed suicide been so completely dismissed? I only met him once, but he struck me as a likely candidate."

"I wondered about that myself . . ."

I was warming to the subject. "He was thrown almost twenty feet over the PATCO line to the alley below." I leaned back in my chair and tried to make the facts self-evident. "Unless you had his assistance, I don't know if that's physically possible. I mean I couldn't throw somebody that far."

He lifted his drink and looked at the ice swirling in the amber liquid. "Maybe you could if you were properly motivated." Here's where it was going to get tricky. Osgood was so used to spreading the bull about how tough he was, it was possible he was blind when someone else was doing it. I waited and didn't say anything. He leaned in close. "All I'm saying is that I'd understand how a man could be driven to something hasty, under certain circumstances."

I looked at my beer like a man with something to hide. "Spoken like a true attorney."

His mouth twitched to the side, and I thought I might have overplayed my hand, but he continued following my thread. "That's my job, but I can see how the trash has to be taken out sometimes."

I brought my eyes back up to his. "That's very understanding of you."

"Look . . ." He glanced around, and his voice dropped. "Sheriff, I don't know if you did it and, to be honest, I don't care. There's no way they can mix me up in this, 'cause close to a thousand people can place me at the Painted Bride Art Center's fund-raiser that night." He sighed. "If you did it, happy motoring and God bless."

For the first time that night, I believed him. It didn't mean that he and Devon weren't involved in any number of dirty deals; it just meant that he hadn't personally thrown Conliffe off the bridge. He didn't strike me as a calculating killer. He might be stupid enough to get himself into situations where he had to kill people to get out, but only in the heat of the moment.

Maybe he was happy to believe it was me; it was a mystery solved as far as he was concerned. Whatever his motivation, I had more information to work with and the reputation of a ruthless and avenging father, for whatever good that was.

I was saved from any more questions by Ian's arrival. "Two more?"

I shook my head. "I really have to go."

Osgood threw a twenty onto the table. "This one's mine." He pulled a card from his pocket as he put his jacket back on. "Look, if anything turns up, give me a call." I nodded and took the card like a guilty man. "And if those pricks from IAD start being a problem . . ." He straightened his tie and let that one float as he turned to O'Neil and gestured to the twenty. "That gonna cover it?"

The Irishman studied him. "Sure."

Osgood and I shook hands, and he swaggered his way from the pub. Ian watched along with me as Osgood climbed in the yellow Hummer and was gone.

I swigged the last of my beer and handed it to O'Neil. "Where's the Painted Bride Art Center?"

He gestured with his eyes. "'Bout two blocks from 'ere."

Convenient. I got up. "You two know each other?"

His eyes stayed on the street. "He's been in a couple'a times, with Devon Conliffe, actually." I turned and looked at him. "They had a few heated conversations."

"Have you told the police anything about that?"

He smiled. "Thought that was what I was doing now." He had something behind his back. He deftly swung his arm around and placed it against my chest. It was a beaten up Philadelphia Eagles helmet braced with painted eagle wings on either side. I looked at him, and he smiled. "Close as yer gonna get, Sheriff."

It was still too early to head to the hospital and, after the conversation with Osgood, I figured I needed a little fresh air, so I went up on the bridge. The north side wasn't locked this time, so I could get my first look at the actual crime scene. I looked down on the traffic headed for New Jersey, the taillights of the cars making a random, red-dotted line over the arch of the bridge. I leaned against a large metal bar and watched as a man ran by. He was wearing a reflective vest and was going at a pretty good clip. He glanced at the football helmet dangling from my hand, said "Yo, man, maybe next year," and kept on going.

I reached the general area where Devon had taken the plunge and looked over the edge toward the PATCO line. It would be difficult to throw a man that far. I thought about the man called Shankar DuVall. The guy fit and certainly would have been able to flip Devon like a poker chip. I'd have to see what Katz and Gowder knew.

There were a few vehicles parked along one side of the alley, and I thought it might have been better for Devon if he'd hit one of them instead of the patchwork of concrete, asphalt, and brick below.

A graffiti artist had written ROB LOVES MELISSA on a billboard on top of the building to my right. I thought about the Little Birds and wondered how Melissa was doing these days. I was surely and not so slowly becoming an expert on wounded women.

The building to my left was an old warehouse that looked as if it were being converted into residential loft space. Whoever had picked the spot for Devon's murder had done a pretty good job of finding an area in a city of six and a half million people where nobody would see what happened.

Without the anonymous note that I had received at the hospital, I could have believed a suicide. With all the shit that he and Osgood were involved with and the damage he had done to Cady, who was the one decent thing in his life, I could see the logic of that scenario.

Katz and Gowder had been awfully quick to dismiss the possibility, though, even before I had received the note. Why? And what possible advantage could anyone hope to gain by taking credit for a homicide they didn't commit? And why tell me? Someone didn't want me to investigate this murder and was trying to warn me off. YOU HAVE BEEN DONE A FAVOR, NOW LET IT GO.

I slid my hand along the powder blue railing and felt something under my fingers. I leaned over the edge, far enough to see whatever it was that was taped to the underside of the barrier. The tape and the paper looked fresh, so it had been placed there recently. It was an envelope and, as before, it read SHERIFF.

I'll be damned.

I thought about waiting for fingerprints but, if my pen pal was the one who killed Devon, he wasn't that stupid. I pried a finger under the flap and opened it. It was the same place-card stock, this time with the typewritten message that read GO BACK TO THE INDIAN. Same dropped out spot on the typewritten O.

I stared at it and suddenly felt someone at my side. I started and turned with the football helmet automatically swinging back.

"Whoa, big guy." She was short, dark-haired, and wore a black leather jacket with the collar turned up. A bottle of beer dangled from her hand as she turned and placed both elbows on the railing with utter nonchalance. She took a sip. "Don't do it. Human life is a valuable commodity . . ." She paused for a second. "Ah, fuck it, I can't remember the rest." Vic turned and looked at me, then at the helmet in my hand. "But I can see why you'd want to jump after last season."

# 10

"So, are you trying to fuck my mother?"

I watched the taxi driver's head turn toward us as she finished off the beer and dropped the empty bottle on the floor of the cab. The driver's voice was high and foreign. "Madam?"

"What are you doing here?"

"I'm the emissary from Wyoming; you don't write, you don't call." She propped an elbow on the sill of the open window and pushed her fingers into the black hair. "You didn't answer my question."

The driver's voice rose again. "Missus?"

"Why would you ask that?"

She looked out at the city night speeding by. "I got a flight in earlier and saw the two of you at my Uncle Alphonse's. You looked pretty cozy together so I didn't want to intrude."

"Kind lady?"

I sighed. "Your mother has been a great help."

"You say that like I'm not gonna be."

The driver wasn't giving up. "Madam?"

Vic looked annoyed and glared at him through the rearview mirror. "What!?"

He sounded apologetic. "You cannot leave that beer bottle in the cab."

Vic looked at him for a moment and then picked up the container by sticking an index finger in the opening. "This bottle?" She then slung it from the open window and over the railing into the Schuylkill River. I almost rebroke my nose on the Plexiglas divider when the driver hit the brakes.

It was only a three-block walk the rest of the way to the hospital, and I watched Vic as she soaked up her hometown. "No, I can see that you're going to be a great help." She looked different in the city, as if she were home. She didn't blend in Wyoming, but here it was as if all the pieces fell into place. I had never seen the clothes she was wearing—the black leather jacket, black T-shirt, black slacks, and black Doc Martins. "Does your family know you're here?"

"Only Alphonse. I went in after you guys left."

"How come you didn't come in before?"

She pursed her lips and glanced toward the river. "I like to time my entrances."

The security guards at HUP looked up as we passed by but looked back down as we went up the escalator to the elevators on the mezzanine. Vic stopped and was looking at the note. "It could only mean Henry."

"That's what I thought, but I don't get it."

"Maybe the Indian will." She threw an arm up to hold the automatic doors of the elevator. "You got a key to Cady's place?"

I stood there, unsure. "You're not coming?"

She shook her head. "I don't do this kind of thing well, so I just don't do it."

"Don't you want to say hello to Henry?"

"I'll see him soon enough." It was an awkward moment, but then she smiled and gestured behind me with her chin. "Normally, I'd say let's go get the asshole who did this, but I think somebody beat us to it."

I had to blink to adjust my eyes to the artificial light in the ICU. I could smell burning cedar and sage. The night nurse started to stand but noticed it was me and sat back down. She looked at the helmet in my hand and just smiled. Evidently, Henry had already worked some magic just by getting the clearance that would allow us to perform the ceremony.

He turned and looked at me, registering no surprise when I told him that Vic had arrived. I looked at the intricate arrangement of items in the room. "It is already working."

I handed the Bear the football helmet. "Good thing you didn't need a tomahawk or I would've had to go to Atlanta."

He studied the helmet and the wings with trailing feathers. "This will do."

There was a buffalo skull at Cady's feet with the nose pointed toward her. There were two black stones by her right side on the bed, two red ones on her left, and a red one and black one on the pillow above her head. There was a ceramic bowl that was filled with dirt on one of the carts. Evidently, as a stranger in a strange land, the Bear had great gathering skills.

He put the helmet on one of the monitors, and I watched as he laid sticks on the bed in two parallel lines with each pair of ends joined by a V-shaped connection; it was a *Hetanihya*, or *Hetan*, a man figure. It looked as if the Bear was performing a Cheyenne sweat lodge ceremony but without the sweat or the lodge.

His beaded medicine bag was also draped over the cart; he took his ceremonial pipe, the bowl of which was carved from catlinite into the shape of a buffalo, from it. He fit the buffalo into the stem, filled the pipe, lit it, and then drew a circle around the Hetan with the stem. He puffed on the pipe for a while, then motioned me to the opposite side of the bed and handed it to me. I smoked for what I thought was a commensurate amount of time, then handed it back to him. We went through four bowls of tobacco, and then the Bear scattered sweetgrass and juniper on the stones surrounding Cady. He picked the pipe up and pointed it to the cardinal directions and rested it against the buffalo skull, the stem between the horns. Then Henry took a medicine bundle out of the green velvet bag that he always carried with him—and which, according to him, had saved him from dying of a gut-shot wound deep in a Big-horn Mountain blizzard. He placed the bundle on the pillow by Cady's head and handed me an old turtle rattle that was decorated with teeth and hair and deer toes. I wasn't told to shake the rattle, so I remained still. Henry spoke in a quiet but authoritative voice.

"Spirits, hear me; think especially of me, a miserable man. Those that enter my sweat lodge for safety, going out may they leave behind all that is bad. Take thought of them; that good may come to them, take thought."

He stopped and took a deep breath, and the next part was spoken as if it had just occurred to him. "Let horses of different colors come to them." He nodded toward the west-facing windows and gestured toward the buffalo skull. "Your pipe is filled; come and smoke. When they go out of my sweat lodge, may some good go with them. To the places whence they came, may they all take good luck. May all their relatives receive good; their children let them embrace with joy. Let their way lie along the good road."

The emotion was creeping into his voice. "That our patients may arise with ease, take thought of them; let them once more walk about with joy." His voice caught in his throat, and it was only then that I realized he was speaking English.

"Who are ye that taught this custom? I do not claim to know anything; I am poor; I am far from knowing anything. Old men taught me this way, and if I make a mistake, turn it to good. Everything I ask of you, grant me. *Henahi!*"

I shook the rattle four times, as instructed, and then listened as Henry sang eight songs in Cheyenne. When he finished, he slumped into the chair beside me with his hands trailing to the floor.

I reached out and squeezed his shoulder. "Thank you."

He nodded and smiled knowingly. "It worked."

I looked at him, then at Cady, and back at him. Nothing seemed to have changed. I got up and took a closer look, knowing that Henry didn't make statements like that lightly. I turned back and looked at him. "How can you tell?"

He raised his face, and he continued to smile. "I had a vision."

"Just now?" He shook his head, but the smile remained. He was making me nervous.

"Earlier."

I watched him. "Why are you smiling?"

He laughed. "The vision, you are not going to like it."

I quickly convinced myself that if it were really bad, he wouldn't be smiling. "What?"

"Horses, you will be assisted by horses; powerful horses, paints."

I laughed with him. "I'll take any help I can get."

His face grew serious. "You know the power of this medicine." He stretched his back muscles and looked at me again. "You will be assisted by horses; powerful horses, paints."

"Okay." He seemed satisfied, so I pulled the note from my breast pocket.

He took it and studied it without opening the envelope. "Again?"

I nodded. "At the crime scene on the Benjamin Franklin Bridge, taped to the railing."

He opened the envelope and read the note. "Do you know any other Indians in Philadelphia?"

"No."

He looked at the card again. "Then I do not know . . . Perhaps something to do with the reception?"

"Possibly."

Henry placed the card back and handed it to me. "It will be revealed to you."

I stuffed the tiny envelope in my breast pocket. "Let me guess, by horses."

He shrugged. "That, or by another note."

I decided to sleep in the chair for the rest of the night, sending the Cheyenne Nation to his guest-artist bed. I wished I had my cowboy hat to pull over my eyes, but it was at Cady's. I thought about using the football helmet, but I didn't want to upset the mojo. I borrowed a towel from the night nurse and folded it. I remained like that for a while, staring at the underside of the towel and thinking: GO BACK TO THE INDIAN. Who was involved with all of this who would be sympathetic toward us? Who did we know here? GO BACK TO THE INDIAN; I had, and I didn't know anything more than I had before. Some detective.

I took the towel off and rubbed my eyes. Henry had left

a partial bottle of water on the other chair, so I picked it up, screwed off the top, and chugged what was left. There was a slick portfolio underneath it with a water ring on the cover where the bottle had been. I picked it up and studied the beautifully lit main hall gallery of the Pennsylvania Academy of the Fine Arts. It was the brochure for the Mennonite photo exhibit.

The photograph on the inside cover was of a horse haltered to a broken-down Studebaker pickup. The paint was looking at the camera, and the water bottle that Henry had left on the brochure had wept a perfect circle around its eye. I laughed, remembering Henry's vision, and looked at the text. It was one of the poems that Dena Many Camps had been gracious enough to bestow on the project, and it was elegant and powerful.

> . . . Walks the quiet rushes of the Mni Shoshe, then
> moves north, to higher ground. He motions toward the
> ponies as they rise up
> and release their tears, large drops the size of ripe apples.
> They dance then, as my mother and father shift in sleep,
> dreaming to the rhythm of horses' hooves.

The horse that had been dead for seventy years looked at me, and I wondered if Dena would be at the reception; probably not, as Henry hadn't mentioned that she would be. I could be wrong, but he seemed to talk of her less. I had asked him about the pool tournament in Las Vegas, which she had won, but Henry said she had been seen in the company of a tall, handsome Assiniboine about half his age. The conversation had dwindled from there.

I set the brochure back on the seat, refolded the towel, and replaced it over my eyes, staring at the five words in my head, the warning, the clue, the note passed between the aisles.

I guess I was getting used to the sounds and rhythms of the ICU. I struggled for a while but then tossed myself into a fidgety, ungrateful sleep.

I was still looking at my boots, which floated above the buffalo grass and sage of northern Wyoming. I kicked my feet back and forth and could feel the looseness of my boots on my feet, the air between my socks and the inner-soles. I snuck a glance to my right; the same medicine man was there, and the wind still suspended us above the bluffs at Cat Creek.

We weren't moving but were being held aloft by the current, with our arms outstretched toward the Bighorn Mountains. I could feel the gusts whip my hat away, and I laughed. The medicine man laughed along with me, and I turned my head with the tears streaming from my face, lids clenched with a flattened image of the elderly man who floated beside me. I had to yell over the howling of the wind, but you grow used to such things on the high plains. His head turned toward mine, and I watched as the fringe of his leggings swirled behind him like trailing eddies in the air stream.

He nodded at my one-word question and pointed with his nearest hand, the leathery finger aimed at the canyon below, and they were there: an entire remuda of wild ones, the wind buffeting their manes and tails as they threw the gusts against their broad withers, using the coming storm to their own advantage. The sound of clattering hooves overtook the aching cry of the wind and joined it with a resonance that rose from the stone walls of the canyon. The orange and white pattern of their bodies was like the pattern of the thunderheads that ascended as if they were time-lapse photography, cumulus explosions stronger than technology.

The horses were large and potent, the muscles of their limbs reaching out like the flexing of fingers, gobbling up the distance and reaching out for more. The aged Indian beside me laughed when I glanced back at him, chuckling at their approach.

As they reached the end of the canyon, they climbed the walls with powerful, striking hooves that drove into the rock with sparks of electricity that arched upward, shooting past us and into the clouds. The air was cool with the promise of water, and I could feel my hair standing on end.

They thundered their way up at the same speed that they had entered the canyon, seemingly on a crash course with us. I veered from them and threw myself off balance. I closed one eye like a kid at a Saturday matinee and waited for the impact. The lead mare kicked as though she was ridding herself of an unwanted rider, and the cloud-pattern body twisted. The earth fell away like a flanking strap, and the impact of our collision threw my shoulder down and against her neck as her head stretched upward and the long mane covered my face.

I scrambled to get my fingers into her hair, wrapped an arm around her neck, and dug my legs against her sides. The pressure of her rising body forced the air from my lungs, and it was all I could do to hold on as the backing of the metal star pinned to my jacket drove itself into my chest.

Her hair still covered my face but parted at the rim of the canyon, just enough for me to see that the old man was now astride the broad back of his own cloud pony, his one hand wrapped in the mane of his horse, the other reaching into the billowing expansion above us.

I looked up at the detonation of clouds that seemed like a saturated watercolor. Compacted flares fired deep in the towers of umber, white, and disappearing blue and reflected in the flanks of my paint. Her rhythm was steady and sure and her eyes watched carefully, as if a misplaced hoof would send us plummeting into the distant earth below.

The medicine man's lips moved, and even though his voice was barely a whisper, the sound of his words echoed within the clouds like drums. "This is better, yes?" I stared at him, and it was clear to me he was insane. He laughed. "How can you know the earth if you never see it?"

I looked past his outstretched arm at the glow of the clouds and at one that looked like an eye with a circle around it.

"Mr. Longmire . . . Sheriff?" I opened my eyes, moved the towel, and looked at the hand on my shoulder. It was a man's hand of pretty good size and had a graduation ring on it from the Philadelphia Police Academy. "How ya doin'?"

"Howdy, Michael." He smiled and watched me some more.

"You were snoring."

"Sorry." I looked up at the windows, but they were still black. "What time is it?"

"Little after four. I told Mom I'd take an extra shift, seeing as how I've got time on my hands."

I took a deep breath and looked at the handsome young man with so much of his life ahead of him. "Michael, have you ever heard of a guy by the name of Shankar DuVall?"

He thought about it. "Doesn't ring any bells . . ." He shrugged. "I can ask around."

I nodded. "He might be one of the guys we arrested out on Lancaster Avenue."

"I'll check." He looked at Cady, at the arrangement of the ceremonial pipe, the buffalo skull, and the stones. "Looks like you guys've been busy."

I stood, stretched my arms above my head, and approached the bed with hope ready to curdle at the slightest notice. "I decided to refer to a higher authority."

There was no change, and I could feel my heart cannonballing into my bowels, taking my lungs along for the ride. I took a deep breath and listened to it clatter in my throat like a rattler in shedding season when it is blind, pissed, and strikes out at everything. I heard Michael say something. "I'm sorry, what?"

"You should go home."

I turned and looked at him. "You're right." I then thought about whether I would be giving up Moretti family secrets, finally deciding that I wouldn't. "Your sister's in town."

He looked blank. "Victoria?" His smile returned; he couldn't hold the joke. "I know; I'm the one that called her. I called her day before yesterday." He studied me for a moment. "I didn't think you'd mind, and I thought she'd be a help." I didn't say anything. He continued to smile and shuffled his purple-and-orange-clad feet, still not sure of my response. "She's a good cop."

I finally nodded. "I'm in a position to know that." The kid was a prince.

I started off with a taxi, but my restlessness drove me to abandon it at 20th and Market. I kind of knew where I was and figured if I headed north by northeast, I'd eventually hit Race and take a right. If I got to the river, I'd have gone too far. I watched as a black Expedition stopped at the light and then started up the street. I saw a sign for the Franklin Institute about a block up and decided to continue north for a while.

It must've rained while I was asleep, sometime during my vision, as Henry would have called it. The streets were wet, but it was still the cool of the morning before sunrise, and the halos of the streetlights looked like chain links drifting up the dark city streets. I listened to my boot steps echoing off the tall buildings and gathered wool on the directions our lives take, on the intersections that allowed no U-turn and committed you to your fate. I thought about how I wished there was somewhere I could go and just pay the fine and take my daughter home.

At the corner of Arch, I stopped and looked around. My eye caught some movement behind me, and I turned my head just a little; it was the same black Expedition that I had seen on Market. It sat there at the red light, the reflection of the street lamps making it impossible to see inside. I put my hands in my pockets and acted as though I was deep in thought. It passed me, and I watched the taillights of the vehicle slow and then recede, listening to the radial tires growl as they turned down the deserted street. I took my hands out of my pockets and laughed out loud. What was I thinking? That I was important enough to be followed around the streets of Philadelphia? I shook my head and continued on.

The sun wouldn't be up for a while, so maybe I could grab a couple more hours of sleep before calling Katz and Gowder for a meet. It would be interesting to hear their take on the Vince Osgood Parade of Stars but even more interesting to see their response to Vic. I wondered what Lena's response to Vic would be and wondered if Alphonse had gotten anywhere with Lena's hunch about a different connection between Osgood and Devon.

I was in the middle of all this wondering when I saw the black Expedition again, crossing the street a block ahead. There was a narrow alley to my right, and I ducked in there. I wedged myself in a doorway between a power pole and a utility box alongside the back of a building. I stood there feeling foolish for a few minutes, until I saw the black SUV slowly go up 20th. It looked like a government vehicle, but who would be trailing me in something like that? Osgood? Katz and Gowder? It just didn't make sense, unless they'd come to the conclusion that the notes had made me a viable candidate for being thrown off a bridge next.

I went to the corner and watched as the Expedition turned right a block ahead and, once again, circled around. Whoever they were, they weren't very good at this, which led me to believe they weren't on the job.

I looked back up the alley and started jogging toward 19th. By the time I got to the other end, the Expedition was moving slowly down the street in its attempt to double back. A large Amorosso bread truck pulled up to the light just south, and I pressed myself against the corner of another building. The SUV passed me and stopped behind the truck.

If I was feeling frisky, now was the time.

Approaching unsecured vehicles was how the majority of police officers got killed, but I thundered down the sidewalk, slid to a stop alongside the Ford, and yanked the door open anyway. Before I could say anything, the driver yelled. "Yo, man . . ."

"You tailing me?"

I looked at the tall, lean kid at the wheel. He didn't look

like a cop or a robber. He wore glasses and had long brown hair pulled back in a ponytail and a three-day beard. He looked like a graduate student, and he looked at me like I was crazy. "What?"

I was having the same doubts myself. I held up my hands to show there was no intent. "Sorry, I thought you were following me."

He studied me. "You a cop?"

"Yep." I didn't have to say from where. He nodded and took a breath. I guess I'd almost given him a heart attack. "Sorry."

He didn't move but kept looking at me. "Jesus, man. You scared the shit out of me." He took a deep breath as the bread truck released its air brakes and started around the corner. "I thought you were some kind of carjacker or something."

"No, I just . . . You were driving slowly, and I thought you were following me."

"I was looking for an address, man."

I nodded, feeling the complete fool. "Sorry."

He stuck a hand out and stopped me from closing the door. "Hey, man, do you know where the Municipal Services Building is?"

I shook my head. "No." I started closing the door, but he kept talking.

"I've got this package that has to be delivered by . . ."

I closed the door as he held the FedEx envelope toward me, and it was at the last second that I noticed the ignition switch and the destroyed lock where the Expedition had been hotwired. I clawed at the door, trying to get it back open as he hit the gas, and I slapped at the back of the vehicle's glossy surface.

I watched as he made the mistake of turning left behind

the bread truck that was now halfway down the street and backing into a loading zone with the reverse alarm chirping. I watched as the SUV screeched to a stop at the middle of the block. He hit the horn, but the Amorosso man was having none of it. He locked the air brakes on the big truck and turned on his emergency blinkers, whoever was behind him be damned.

God bless Philly truck drivers.

I pushed off a parked car at the corner and ran for all I was worth, struggling to pull the .45 from the holster at my back. The driver of the Ford continued to blare his horn but, when I was only thirty feet from the SUV, license number 90375, city plates, the reverse lights flicked on.

I slid to a stop in the center of the street in a widespread stance, raised the .45, and yelled. "Sheriff! Freeze!"

He didn't, and I had to decide if a hunch was worth shooting a man, finally deciding that it wasn't. He was still in reverse, but he wasn't going that fast, and I figured, what's the worst that could happen? I jumped up on the back bumper and grabbed the luggage rack as the air left my body on impact. My left hand held the black bar, and I listened as the bracings buckled into the sheet metal of the roof. My feet slipped from the bumper as he accelerated, and I scrambled to get a tiny purchase, trying to not think about what the hell I was doing.

I wasn't going to last long like this, so I raised the butt of the Colt and swung it down on one of the back windows; the glass spider-webbed out to the framework. I could feel the luggage rack starting to go as he hit the brakes at Race and made a right onto Logan Circle. A Japanese compact barely missed us as we made the turn and cut across four lanes.

I brought the butt of the .45 down on the window

again, and this time the glass blew into the interior along with my arm, and I was able to leverage myself up to the armpit into the vehicle.

I pressed my face against the cold metal of the window divider and could feel the glass cutting along my jaw line. "Peace officer! Stop this vehicle now!"

I could see him sawing at the wheel and could feel the pressure of my grip starting to slide me toward the edge of the bumper as he continued to veer around Logan Circle and the Swan Memorial Fountain.

He swerved back toward the outside, deciding to test the waters on the Benjamin Franklin Parkway, but a utility company van cut him off. I took advantage of the slowing velocity to reestablish my grip on the doorway just as the luggage rack pulled completely off the vehicle.

My feet slid on the bumper as I slipped sideways, and I felt my boot hit the surface of the road and pogo with a large hop as I threw my other arm into the back window and scrambled for a grip.

I was to the point of dropping the .45 when my other hand grabbed hold of some small leverage, and it was only when the door I was hanging from made a small jump with a chunklike sound that I realized that it was the interior door handle.

The door swung wide with the momentum of the vehicle, and I was no longer attached. I rolled my back, my head cracked against the concrete sidewalk, and my legs went over my shoulders. I tucked my arms into my chest along with the semiautomatic and hoped that wherever I was rolling nobody would run over me.

I didn't move at first, just watched the black Expedition continue the wrong way down 18th and disappear as I listened to sirens approach like hounds to the hunt.

I tried to focus, but my vision was blurred. My head hurt, and I closed my eyes. I could hear people, so that was a good sign. I opened my eyes and looked up at a gigantic individual with a tricornered hat looking down on me. It was only when I saw it was a statue and that the title on the base had way too many consonants that I collapsed against the cement and tried to breathe.

"Sir?" I felt somebody gently pull at my right shoulder in an attempt to turn me over. "Sir, are you alive?"

I rolled onto my back and watched as whomever it was backed away when they saw the big Colt in my hand. "It's all right . . ." I coughed and cleared my throat, my voice sounding like somebody else's. "I'm a peace officer." The face returned, and I looked at his uniform. "You a cop?"

He shook his head. "I'm the bellman. I been here since the hotel opened, and that was the most dramatic entrance to the Four Seasons I ever seen." I laughed weakly and felt a pull at my abdomen, curled in a little, and returned to my side where it felt better. He kept his hand on my shoulder and talked to me in a soft voice. "Don't you worry, there's help comin', you jus' lie there."

I stared at the traffic and took shallow breaths, absorbing some of the cool from the sidewalk. I felt a little dizzy for a moment, but it passed with the adrenaline discharge, and I stared past the traffic at the fountain at the center of Logan Circle with the swans blowing jets of water thirty feet into the air.

And there it was, the Indian I was meant to go back to.

# 11

"So, you got the license plate number of the truck that hit you?" She sat on the back of the chair with her feet on the seat, the kind of posture that made teachers yell.

It was a cop convention at HUP. They had tried to take me to Hahneman, which was only four blocks from the Four Seasons, but I had told them I'd throw myself from the ambulance if they didn't take me to the same hospital as Cady. After careful consideration and in light of recent events, they took me at my word.

"Like I told the fuzz, city plates, 90375." The stitches at my jawline pulled when I talked. Dr. Rissman was looking at my ear, but he didn't say anything so he must have figured that was old news. I guessed he had come down to take a look at me out of curiosity and that you could pretty much jump in anytime if you were a neurosurgeon.

Vic turned to look at the two detectives as Katz flipped his small notebook closed. "Stolen from the city lot two nights ago."

Gowder looked at Vic, she looked at Katz, and I could tell that they had all three known each other for quite some time. Michael was leaning against a wall, and they had posted a patrolman outside the curtain.

Gowder stepped forward and held up a standard wants-and-warrants vita with a two-by-two photo of William White Eyes. He was slightly heavier, wore no glasses, and the hair was loose. "That's him."

Katz walked over beside Vic and adjusted his glasses, the red dots jockeying for a good seat on his nose. He was a handsome devil, and I could see Lena making the reach. "Released a week ago. After you mentioned him last night, we did a quick look-see. Any idea why he was following you?"

"We cowboys have that problem with Indians, even white ones." Katz gave me a look. "Any word on Shankar DuVall?"

The two detectives turned and looked at Michael, who grinned. "Looks like he was the one that you ran into the other night. Turns out Fraser and the others couldn't retrieve the gun, and he wasn't carrying, so they had to let him go."

"What about his connections with Toy Diaz?"

"We got a hit on an abandoned car in Atlantic City, but no Diaz."

"I think I may have met Toy Diaz last night." They all looked at me as Gowder continued to wait on the phone for the current address of one William White Eyes.

Katz cleared his throat. "Where?"

"At the shooting range; he was with Osgood. At least I think it was him, short guy, Latino, very precise, eyes like a snake?"

The detective nodded his head slowly. "That sounds like him."

Gowder flipped his cell phone closed. "We've got an address."

Vic sipped her coffee. "Asa, why would William White Eyes want to hurt Walt? If he's the one that knocked on the Franklin Institute door, sent Devon to flight school, and wrote the note? We should focus on Toy Diaz."

"Believe me, we are, but maybe the sheriff here was getting too close for comfort."

"He could have run over him twice . . ." I shook my head and raised a single sprained finger. "Excuse me, once."

Katz glanced back at me. "I think White Eyes did a pretty good job on him."

"But he didn't kill him." She hadn't said anything about the note I'd given her, and I thought maybe I wouldn't say anything about it just yet. I reached for the fresh shirt that Vic had brought me from Cady's. She said that she had met her mother there and that Lena was taking care of Dog.

Gowder was watching me. "Where do you think you're going?"

"With you."

He shook his head. "Oh no, you're under house arrest until we get William White Eyes."

I looked at the two of them. "So, the partnership is over?"

Gowder smiled as they left. "Looks that way."

I waited till they were past the curtain. "What if I told you I got another note?" Vic took a sip of her coffee and snorted.

They stopped without turning, stood there for a moment, and then Gowder looked back at Vic, to Katz, and then to me. "Bullshit."

"Vic?"

She took her time taking another sip. "Off the bridge at the crime scene." She pulled the envelope from her pocket and held it up between her index and middle fingers.

I went ahead with putting on my shirt. "I also know where the next one is."

Katz took the envelope, opened it, and read the card. "I don't suppose it occurred to you two to have this dusted?"

"Were there any fingerprints on the other one? Any DNA sample from the envelope?" He didn't answer, and I had mine.

Katz passed the note to Gowder and looked up at me. "Where?"

Vic climbed off her chair and stretched. "Does this mean the partnership's back on?" She stepped over and helped me from the gurney. "So, did my little brother start his crush before or after your daughter was in a coma?"

Bodine Street was in an industrial complex five blocks north of the Benjamin Franklin Bridge. I mentioned to Vic that it was convenient, since she was the only one in the car speaking to me. John Meifert, White Eyes's parole officer, was going to meet us there, which was good, because without the tan sedan parked at the corner we might've never found the place.

He was heavyset with sandy hair and was waiting for us on the sidewalk. He made for the door next to a truck dock. I looked around, but I didn't see anything that would have led me to believe the address was a residence. Meifert shrugged and pushed open a steel door that had a wire-mesh grate over the glass. There was an unused, beat-up counter in an entryway with a scratched Plexiglas divider that led to a freight elevator. We all stepped over the opening between the floors, and Meifert clanged the heavy metal sliding gate that closed from the top and bottom, dropped another safety grating from above, and hit the button to his left.

The whine of the counterweight system and the condition of the cables inspired little confidence, but the battered elevator rose to the sixth, where Meifert aligned the black spraypainted arrows on the gate with the ones on the adjacent bricks. He lifted the safety gate, and we walked out into a large, industrial loft that was surrounded by eighteen-foot glass-paned walls. The floors were hardwood, and there was nothing in the 5,000 square feet except a painted teepee. It was in the center of the space, and its sixteen hand-peeled poles extended upward and into a ventilation cupola.

Everyone, including Meifert, looked surprised. "I take it this is new?"

Nobody said anything but turned and walked toward the structure that would have looked much more at home . . . well, back home. I watched as Gowder unsnapped the holster where his .40 Glock rested.

It was a family-sized teepee with rows of ledger paintings traversing the heavy canvas. It sat there, a domestic island at the center of industrial isolation. As we got closer, I could see that the stake loops were tied off to Velcro straps that had been attached to the wooden floor and that there were buffalo rugs and blankets spilling from the opening even though the flap was secured and tied shut. There was a totem with a mule-deer skull that was painted and wrapped in trade cloth and beads in the Crow style. There were feathers and a fringe of leather draped from the upright pole, which stood in a slot that had been cut in the floor. The place was clean, the floors swept, and the hundreds of windowpanes had been washed and reflected the structure in the middle of the room.

Gowder was in the lead and turned to look back, the empty eye sockets of the antlered skull looking at me over his shoulder. He pointed at the head. "What in the hell is this?"

"A teepee marker." They all looked at me blankly. "It's kind of a combination welcome sign and mailbox."

Everyone else stopped, but I continued to the right, reading the story of the drawings that circled the teepee. The centerline had caught my attention. There were horses with men on them, shooting at each other, not something totally unique to the form, but the details were different than those I was used to seeing. The men on horseback were not red but were white and black. They were not shooting arrows or Sharps but were firing modern weapons; one even wore a 76ers jersey. The uniforms of the white riders and their hats indicated that they were policeman, and the large man falling comically from the back of a horse wore a star on his chest. The centerline had not been finished.

There was a set of paints on the floor, a Dixie cup full of thinner, and a couple of brushes, one of which had paint on it. I stooped and touched the brush, and the bright red pigment was still wet. I looked around and spotted an open window hinged at the top at the back of the loft. "Is that a fire escape?" They all looked at me as I held up a fingertip daubed red. "He was just here."

Gowder was the first to move, quietly slipping the Glock from his holster and heading for the fire escape while gesturing for Katz to take the stairwell. Asa's sidearm appeared in his hand, and they fanned out. Meifert turned and looked at me. "I don't carry."

I caught Vic's attention as she came around the other side and tossed her the .45 from my pancake holster; I wished I were feeling better. I watched as she took the route I would have, the one toward the fire escape. She looked odd with my large-frame Colt in her small hands, but she held it with a confidence born of five years' street duty, all in these very streets.

I watched them, sighed, and continued with my bruised ribs and aluminum-shrouded finger around the teepee. There were more ledger drawings on the backside—one with a man in a suit and tie pushing a red-haired woman from a cliff and then another of the same man falling from what looked like a burial platform: the Devon Conliffe story.

Vic returned with Gowder from the fire escape. He looked at the paints on the floor, kneeled, and tested the brush. Evidently, he didn't trust my analysis. "Careful, or you'll get it on your suit."

He nodded and wiped his fingers on a stained towel that lay on the floor. "Nothing on the roof."

I looked back at Meifert. "If you don't mind my asking, how does a guy like William White Eyes have a place like this?"

"His uncle owned the building and left it to him in a trust."

I straightened up and breathed for a minute. "I take it William comes from money?"

"Quite a bit, actually. The kid had it all, address in Gladwyne, Ivy League advanced degree in chemistry, even a shot at the Olympics in dressage."

Interesting. I turned back to the front and looked at the closed flap. "I assume we are ignoring the fact that we might need a warrant."

Meifert cocked his head. "It's a tent."

We stared at each other for a second, then I glanced over at Vic, tugged at the strips of canvas, and watched as the flaps opened. I looked into the relative darkness of the teepee. "I don't suppose anyone has a flashlight?" They all shook their heads, so I kneeled for a better view. The top flaps were closed, so only a little light made it to the floor. There was stuff in there and the only way I was going to find out what it was was to go in, so I did, warrant be damned.

I was able to keep the finger guard from bumping into anything as I slid into the teepee with my legs trailing behind me. It had occurred to me that William White Eyes might be inside, but I couldn't hear any breathing and made the assumption I was alone.

All I could see were the folds of more buffalo skins and a few Navajo blankets piled in one corner. There was nothing more in there; evidently, William White Eyes was living somewhere else. This place must be a work in progress or just for show, at least for now. I sat there in the muffled silence; I could barely hear the conversation among the three policemen outside. It felt like home, and I closed my eyes for just a moment to block out the talk, the traffic from the streets below, and the thunder of jets overhead.

I thought of the old medicine man that I had seen in my dreams and heard the words that had lifted the two of us above the canyon on the wind that had cleansed and combed the high plains. "How can you know the earth if you do not see her?"

Under the buffalo robes, where the earth would have been if the teepee had been in Wyoming, was a parfleche satchel painted with bright geometric shapes and decorated with horsehair and the tiny cone bells that the Cheyenne call *axaxevo*. I moved back toward the opening so I could see, untied the strips of leather that held the satchel closed, and pulled out two actual ledgers. I opened the top one, and it was a full accounting of some kind of business dealing and was written entirely in a language I recognized but could not read.

I looked up to see Vic's outline in the opening. "No sign of him."

I nodded and took as big a breath as my ribs would allow. "I've got something here." I closed the book and placed it carefully on top of the portfolio. "But I'm not sure exactly what it is."

Once I'd wriggled my way outside, I set the book on my lap and opened it to a random page. Everyone looked, and Vic kneeled in front of me, but Gowder was the first to speak. "What language is that?"

"It's Cheyenne. The teepee design is Assiniboine, that marker is Crow . . . It seems to me that William White Eyes is having trouble deciding what tribe he wants to be when he grows up." I turned a few pages. "He strikes me as a very bright guy."

"First in his class at University of Pennsylvania, majored in mathematics."

Vic was quick with the response. "So, he's a fucking Fortune 500 drug dealer?"

Meifert ignored her. "His father is an investment broker who is listed in *Who's Who*, but his mother died when he was a child—abducted and murdered, strangled up near East Falls in the mid-eighties. The case wasn't ever solved, probably drugs involved."

"What was the mother's name?"

"Candace Carlisle. She . . ."

I interrupted with a question. "Did you just say that his mother's name was Carlisle?" Meifert nodded. I turned to look up at Gowder, who suddenly found the windows of interest. "So, his surname is Carlisle?"

Meifert nodded. "Yeah."

"William Carlisle is Billy Carlisle, who was arrested with Shankar DuVall for trying to sell steamer trunks full of Schedule 1 of the Controlled Substance Act out of the back of an ice cream truck?" I carefully stood, walked over to Gowder, and stepped between him and the windows. "Billy Carlisle, who was in business with Shankar DuVall and Toy Diaz, whose brother was shot by Assistant District Attorney Vince 'Oz' Osgood in the presence of the recently deceased Devon Conliffe?" Gowder still wasn't looking at me. "The same Billy Carlisle who was represented in his pro bono appeals case by my daughter?" I turned, and my voice echoed. "Billy Carlisle is William White Eyes?"

Katz looked at Gowder and finally nodded. "Yes."

I shook my head. "Is there anything else in this little partnership of ours that you're not telling me?"

Gowder looked at Katz. "Devon Conliffe was about to turn state's evidence and implicate Oz, which will take us a little further than the current indictment and suspension."

I stood there for a while, allowing all the lines to connect. "Then it's Osgood."

Gowder shook his head. "Not possible."

"Why the hell not?"

"Because I was with him at the fund-raiser the night Conliffe was killed."

I was fully irritated now. "Then he had it done."

Katz was watching me. "By whom?"

I was yelling now. "Toy Diaz by way of Shankar DuVall, I'd imagine!"

"You don't have to raise your voice." We stood there, looking at each other. "They don't owe him any favors, and they're not on the best of terms anymore."

I stepped toward all of them. The ache in my ribs had receded with the increase of my anger. "Then how about William Carlisle White Eyes?"

Katz adjusted his glasses again. "It occurred to us."

I wondered if I was up to throwing the two of them out the open window. "Partnership's over."

I started lumbering toward the stairwell, with Vic coming up behind me as Katz spoke. "What about the third note?"

Vic called over her shoulder. "If we find it, I'll stop by and personally shove it up your ass."

I only lasted two flights. Vic sat beside me on the flaking gray paint of the tread's metal surface. After catching my breath, I spoke in a low voice. "That was stupid."

She nodded and smiled. "I bet you feel better."

"Not really."

"Look, I know both these guys and, if it means anything, I don't think they took it to heart. Anyway, they're going to want to know about the third note, so I bet you're forgiven by the time we get to the sidewalk."

She was right.

Katz was waiting at the truck dock with his hands in his pockets and the ledgers under one arm. "We need that third note."

I leaned against the concrete shelf with my good side. "Yep, and people in hell need ice water."

He closed his eyes and gave the sun his face. "Nice day for it."

"Where's your playmate?"

"Caught a ride with Meifert; he's decided you don't like him." Katz smiled. "On account of you getting in his face and yelling at him. He's not used to that."

"I'm sorry."

He opened one eye and looked at Vic, who was standing beside me. "Yelling one of those law enforcement techniques you learned out in Wyoming?"

She was now sunbathing as well. "Yeah, that and lunch."

Katz nodded. "Terminal?"

"Yeah."

I hoped it was a location and not a result.


The Reading Terminal Market on 12th and Arch was created in 1892 when the Reading Railroad opened markets below the elevated tracks of the new train shed. It had consistently housed an undetermined amount of aromas since then by creating a gastronomic bazaar conveniently located at street level.

We walked past the Amish baked goods, farm produce, and fresh flowers to a little diner and sat on red leatherette stools at a stainless steel counter. I was in the middle and noticed that neither Vic nor Katz had picked up a menu. A heavyset woman of uncertain age and in oversized overalls set rolled flatware, glasses of ice water, and three cups of coffee in front of us. "What'll it be, hon?"

The wave of nostalgia for the Busy Bee overtook me, and I blurted out the first thing that came to mind. "The usual."

She nodded. Evidently, it was a universal.

Katz slid one of the ledgers onto the counter, opened it, and glanced at the incomprehensible text. "So, you know where we can find an expert on Native American languages?"

I sipped my steaming coffee. "It just so happens . . ." I set it down to cool and took a closer look at the book. "He should be at the Academy; said he had to put the final touches on the exhibit."

"Isn't the reception tonight?"

"Yep." I glanced at Vic. "But don't you have to go to the opera?"

She rolled her eyes. "Puh-lease . . ."

I looked back at Katz. "Henry can translate." I looked at the ledger to give him a little room. "Why didn't you tell me William White Eyes is Billy Carlisle?"

"It's IAD, special prosecutor for the DA's office, and we really weren't able to come forth with any of the information connecting the two."

"Fair enough." I lined up the suspects and started supposing. "Vince Osgood and Toy Diaz are in business."

"It's possible." I looked at him, and he shrugged. "It's likely."

"Devon Conliffe, my daughter's almost-fiancé, was a hophead and a friend of Osgood."

"Yes. And Devon was the money launderer."

I nodded and stared at my coffee. "That makes sense. So, Osgood goes to bat for Shankar DuVall in his official capacity, leaving Carlisle/White Eyes to linger in Graterford."

"Yes."

"I have a question." I placed my hands on the edge of the counter, bumped my finger guard, and felt the vibration all the way up to my elbow. "Who was Shankar DuVall's lawyer?"

Katz thought for a moment. "Not your daughter."

I smiled at him. "I figured there were other lawyers in Philadelphia; I was just wondering who it was?"

"Why?"

I thought about an itch I'd had in my head for the last few days. "I think there are more connections among all these people." Katz scribbled in his pad. "So Carlisle/White Eyes did the cook, DuVall the muscle, Diaz the distribution, and Devon laundered the money while Osgood looked the other way."

"That's the way it's headed."

I thought about the things that weren't adding up. "If Osgood sent Diaz's brother Ramon up the river, why would Toy go into business with him?"

"It was not a happy family; if Oz hadn't gotten rid of Ramon, Toy probably would have."

"How did you find out about the money laundering?"

"We checked the files at Hunt and Driscoll; Devon was channeling large sums of money through clients' accounts, but we're having trouble finding all the numbers. You want to hear the kicker?" I continued looking at him. "They hired him on Osgood's recommendation."

"There's got to be more."

Katz studied me for a moment. "You're thinking that more of these lawyers might be involved?"

"I don't know." I took a sip of my coffee since it had finally cooled enough to drink. "I'm just saying that part of this puzzle is still missing. Some connection is out there; somebody." I thought about it, and it all made sense.

"Didn't Meifert say Carlisle's mother was killed when he was a kid?"

"Yes, it was a well-publicized case." Katz gestured toward Vic. "Her father had that one."

"Can you get me a psychological workup on Carlisle?"

"Absolutely, but why?"

"I think he was the one at the Franklin Institute the night Cady was hurt, and I think he's the one that's been sending me love letters, but I don't think he threw Devon Conliffe off the Benjamin Franklin Bridge."

Katz made a face. "Then why was he following you this morning?"

"Protection."

He made a show of looking at my battered body. "You sure about that?"

I shrugged. "I'm the one that pulled my gun and tried to arrest him."

"So, who's he protecting you from?"

"I don't know; Osgood, maybe Diaz." The food arrived, and the usual turned out to be chicken livers with onions, bacon, and fresh mozzarella. Dorothy would have been pleased. "Billy Carlisle is a Philadelphia drug chemist, but William White Eyes has a romance with the West, a west of which Cady and I may be emblematic." I reached out with my broken finger and gently tapped the leather surface of the ledger. "I think this is going to be a very detailed record of William White Eyes's business dealings with Toy Diaz." I took another bite of the usual. "Anyway, we have to go see an Indian."

Katz picked up his fork and cleaved off a section of his salmon salad. "We need that third note."

I nodded and chewed. "That's why we're going to see the Indian."

The swans and fish the Indians were throttling were still shooting water into the air of Logan Circle when we got there. Katz pulled the unmarked car into a no-parking zone in front of the Four Seasons and cut the engine. As we got out, I waved at the same doorman who had waited with me after I'd been ejected from the back bumper of the Expedition. "Hello, Sheriff."

"Howdy, Lou."

We'd gotten to know each other pretty well while I'd bled on his sidewalk. He came over from his official station and assisted me with the door. "How you feelin'?"

"Fit as a fiddle and ready for love." I reached over the top of the car. "Asa, you still have that photo of Billy Carlisle?"

Katz pulled it from the file on the seat and handed it to me. "Lou, you strike me as a guy who doesn't miss much." I held up the photocopy. "You ever see this guy?" He glanced at the photo. "Some very bad people on both sides of the law are looking for this kid. I'm just trying to bring him in safe."

Lou really looked at the photo this time. "Yeah, I seen him." The old man tipped his hat back and looked over toward the fountain. "'Bout 'n hour ago."

Vic was first. "Are you kidding me?"

"Crossed the street against traffic and sat over by the fountain for a while, then moved on."

"An hour ago?" He smiled at Vic and nodded. She turned back to me. "Why the fuck would he do that?"

I looked at the Logan Circle noble savage in profile. "He changed the note."

I thanked Lou, and Katz gave him a card and told him that if he saw the young man again to give the police a call immediately. We crossed with the traffic and pulled up in front of the Indian that represented the Delaware River. Vic walked a little past us and placed her hands on her hips. "Christ, it does look like Henry."

I sat on the bench. Katz sat beside me, his suit looking better than it would have on a mannequin. "So?"

"I would imagine it's taped to the underside of the seat. Why don't you look?" He stooped down, reached beneath, and pulled something off.

Vic walked back. "Why this bench?"

"It was the one your mother and I sat on after I questioned the guard at the Institute." She nodded and didn't say anything, and I started wondering how far the competitive mother/daughter thing went. "I think he's been following me since I got here, the night Cady was hurt." I looked at Katz. "Aren't you going to dust that?"

He ignored me, thumbed a fingernail under the flap to break the seal, and opened it to reveal the same stock as the others.

I leaned over for a look, but Vic kicked my boot. "You and my mother come to the park a lot?" I raised an eyebrow and kicked her back.

Katz handed me the note. "I'd say your assessment that he changed it after we took the ledgers is correct."

It was typewritten with the same dropout "O." SEE PAGE 72. LOOK WEST, YOU CAN FIGHT CITY HALL.

# 12

Katz said he would catch up with Gowder and then meet me with the ledgers at the Academy later so that Henry could have a look at them. I wanted to get over to the hospital, but it was late in the afternoon and I had run out of time. I needed a shower and could get dressed at Cady's for the reception, thereby killing two magpies with one stone. When Vic and I got there, Lena was gone and so was Dog. There was a note on the counter, along with a roasted chicken and a six-pack of beer in the refrigerator.

Vic sat on the stool. "You don't think we're looking for William White Eyes."

I pulled two of the longnecks from the refrigerator. "No, at least not as a killer."

"Osgood?" I opened both of them and handed one to her.

"I don't think so, but I've been wrong before."

"Diaz?"

I took a sip of my beer. "He's a killer."

"You don't think that he and Osgood could have kissed and made up?"

"Toy Diaz does not strike me as the forgiving type."

She took a sip of her own beer. "The assistant DA could be a pretty convenient partner in crime."

I thought about it. "I think they're in cahoots."

She laughed. "Cahoots, Jesus . . ." She slugged down

the rest of her beer. "It is pretty convenient that Toy Diaz appears to be flying around under the radar, and all the inconvenient people in Osgood's life are meeting with the pavement."

"Including Cady?"

She raised an eyebrow. "Don't tell me it didn't cross your mind."

I shrugged. "Devon was very convincing."

"I would be too if somebody was trying to tear off my head and flush it down a public toilet at Citizens Bank Park."

"I was a little more civilized than that."

She nodded and placed the tip of her tongue at the bottom of a particularly pointed canine tooth. "Yeah, I've seen you in those moods; I bet the meeting was very civilized." She stood and stretched, her black T-shirt rising and exposing the flat, toned muscles of her midriff. I looked away, but I was pretty sure she'd seen me looking. "I need a shower."

"Me too, but you go first."

She had taken the second bedroom upstairs, so I collapsed on the sofa and noticed the blinking light on the answering machine. Vic had stopped on the landing and was looking through the glass of the cupola at the cables that rose from the Benjamin Franklin Bridge. "Cady's not involved with this."

Not for the first time, I studied her profile. "You mean in cahoots?"

She grinned. "Yeah."

I took one of my shallow breaths. It didn't hurt as much. "I think Osgood put the pressure on Devon, and Devon tried to put the pressure on Cady. I think Cady discovered

Devon's laundering scheme through William White Eyes and was going to drop a dime on them. I'm just trying to figure out why she didn't do it."

"You still think Devon hurt Cady."

I nodded and watched her as she stood there looking at the flat light on the powder blue bridge. "I think if it'd been Toy Diaz, we'd have already been to a funeral." I cleared my throat and voiced what had been on my mind since I had heard the message on her cell phone. "How could she let herself get involved in an abusive relationship like that?"

"You mean the daughter you raised?" I didn't say anything. "It can happen to anyone, that's the point." She still looked up at the skyline, and her hands slid across the railing as if she were petting the city. She nodded a sad smile, looked down and watched me for a few moments more, and then disappeared.

I was left with the answering machine. There were people back in Wyoming who were desperate for information about Cady and me. I started to reach across and press the button, but the energy eluded me again. I slumped against the cushions and pulled my hat down, thinking that a short nap might do the trick.

The water began running through the pipes, and it was like rain. I could feel myself drifting off. I sat like that, with my back crooked and my finger guard lying on the back of the couch and thought about what I was going to do about Cady.

The water stopped after a while, and I heard Vic's bare feet padding across the balcony above. I felt myself slipping away but woke a few minutes later because of pressure across both of my thighs. I started to push my hat up, but she took it from me and placed it on her head, an old western tradition. She straddled me with her strong legs and, since the hat was out of the way, I could see that her bathrobe was untied. I could smell the still-wet of her skin, smooth and full.

I started to speak, but she put a finger to my lips and leaned in. "Just shut the fuck up."

She pulled my face forward with the fingers of one hand twisted into the hair at the back of my head, and I buried my face into her breasts as she reached to unbutton my pants. I could feel her taking the majority of her weight up onto her knees as her fingers quickly undid my belt and began working me through the opening in my underwear and jeans. Her fingers felt cool encircled around me, and it was all I could do to restrain myself from climaxing right then.

I could feel her leveraging me, and I slid into her. She gasped and yanked my head back, locking her mouth over mine, her tongue sliding deep between my lips. I could feel her grinding her hips down onto me, the furious quality of hungry passion as if she might swallow me whole.

I thought I heard a noise from behind her, almost as if the door had opened, but ignored it and slipped my hands under the robe, feeling the heat of her body as my fingers slipped beneath her breasts and cupped them. She broke from my mouth and gasped, a guttural growl coming from the back of her throat as she looked down at me and began pulling my face forward again.

I stopped her. "No."

I watched as her nostrils flared and the pebbled surface of her nipples rose and fell inches from my face. "No what?"

"I want to see your face."

Her eyes softened, and she smiled. She pulled my head back, her face a little above mine, and we settled into a rhythm with our eyes locked. I slid myself to the edge of the sofa and for the first time was able to push myself all the way into her. Her eyes flashed again, and her breath caught in her throat as she stayed like that, her grip tightening.

When I was able to think again, I was in the shower trying to wash myself with one hand, the other with a bread bag over it, secured with a rubber band. I couldn't be sure if I was ever going to leave the water; it wasn't safe out there.

Vic must have been reading my mind because, after about fifteen minutes, I became aware of her outline through the opaque surface of the shower door. I turned off the water and stood there, dripping.

"Walt?"

"Yep?"

She waited a moment and then spoke again. "It was just sex."

"Uh huh."

It was a longer pause this time. "You're still who you are, I'm still who I am, and we're still who we are."

"Right."

I watched as she put earrings on and applied lipstick. "The only difference is that we had sex."

"Okay."

She laughed and turned toward the shower. "Are you all right?"

I took a deep breath and winced a little. "Yep." She waited, and I finally heard her let out a long sigh. I wiped the water from my eyes. "Vic?" I stared at the shower control and tried to stay focused. "We can't ever do that again."

She chuckled as she went out, not closing the bathroom door behind her. "Speak for yourself, big guy."

I didn't have any clothes upstairs, so I had to go down with a towel wrapped around my middle. She sat at the counter with another beer and the two-day-old *Daily News* that had the story about Devon Conliffe's death on the front page.

I memorized every detail of her appearance with just one glance: the wife-beater T-shirt; the brown, pebbled leather jacket with studded conchos; the belt with green copper studs; a dark green lace skirt, which stalled out at midcalf; and a pair of clunky-heeled alligator packers.

She had blown her hair dry so that it feathered down and covered her eyebrows, and she wore a turquoise choker and earrings, with my hat sitting ludicrously large on her head. I had known her for three years and, as good as she had always looked, she had never looked this good. "You want your hat back?"

I clutched my towel and pulled my only suit jacket and tie from my bag. "Eventually."

She took a sip of her beer. "You're being weird."

"I'm not."

"You are." She smiled.

"Look . . ." I wondered about what I wanted her looking at. "I've got a lot of things going on in my life, and the last thing we should be . . ."

She cut me off with each word as a statement of its own: "Shut. The. Fuck. Up." She tried to continue, but the urge to laugh was too much. I waited while she laughed at me. "Jesus, Walt, you're acting like some fucking prom queen the morning after."

I stood there in my towel and felt ridiculous.

She got up from the stool and dangled the bottle from her hand like she had on the bridge and walked toward me, slowly. "How about I make it easy for you? We'll just call it rape. I raped you. There. Do you feel better?" She was very close now, and she smelled like our sex, which she hadn't tried to cover up. She gave me a long look from toe to head, where she replaced my hat. "And, if you don't get dressed, I may do it again."

It's hard to scamper in a towel.


Vic said she'd meet me at the Academy with Katz and Gowder and had left me to my own devices and the hospital. We had taken the same cab for a while; Vic's attention stayed out the window as the city rushed by. I kept trying to detect a weirdness in her, but it just wasn't there. It was quite possible that she had more experience than I did. Since the end of her marriage, she'd been briefly involved with a dentist and had had a ferocious weekend with some rodeo cowboy who'd then shown up at the office and been treated to a reenactment of the Battle of Benevento; Ruby and I had desperately tried to pretend that we weren't listening.

"I've only had sex with six women in my entire life." It came out before I had a chance to edit it or make any additions, and I said it like I was talking about heart attacks.

She turned her head and looked at me, with a little bit of sadness. "Oh, Walt . . ."


When I got to the ICU, the head nurse told me they had been trying to call me. Cady had opened her eyes. Michael had been in the room. He was by her bed, standing easily on the one unwounded foot. "How ya doin', Sheriff?"

I looked at her, but her eyes were closed.

"She had them open for about an hour and a half, and she closed them no more than ten minutes ago."

I sat down in the chair by the bed and stared at her motionless face, at the ceremonial Cheyenne trappings still surrounding her, and started to cry. I couldn't stop. All the pent-up emotion of the last week found fissures in my stalwart act and began cracking like ice dropped into hot water. I could feel the strike of tears dripping onto the two-fisted grip of my hands. I wasn't aware of Michael moving, but I felt his hand on my shoulder. The wretched, cynical husk that had written Cady off and had prepared me to let her go was dying. The transition from malice to relief was quick and, when my eyes could refocus, I noticed that I'd crushed the finger brace.

Michael and the nurse kneeled in front of me, both of them looking at the twisted aluminum wrapped around my broken finger. "Doesn't that hurt?"

I tried to catch my breath and noticed that my ribs weren't aching either. I looked past the nurse's head and could see that Cady had opened her eyes again. I smiled. "Not anymore."

Rissman had been called; he had left a message that he wanted to talk with me when I arrived. He was trying to keep my attention as I watched Cady's eyes and counted how long it took her to blink. He said that most comas end with the patients opening their eyes and regaining consciousness, but that 10 percent of those who do fall into the category of Apallic Syndrome and don't respond to environmental stimulus.

I squeezed Cady's hand, but she didn't respond. Her eyes looked into the distance to places I could not see. The color was clear, and the whites as bright as I'd ever seen them.

He said that for her to regain consciousness, both reactivity and perceptivity would have to be present.

I bit my lower lip and could feel the heat returning behind my eyes.

"Do you understand what I'm saying?" He looked at the ceiling, the floor, and my left shoulder.

I looked across the bed at him. "She's going to make it."

He shook his head. "Please don't get your hopes too high. Even in the best of circumstances . . ."

"She's going to make it." I sometimes underestimate the vigor of my statements, and I'd imagine it has to do with having to deal with the law on a continual basis. I rarely let emotion get a strong grip on me or have an influence in my responses, but this was different. I'd been waiting so long for hope that I wasn't letting it slip away. I'd seen what the hopeless approach was like, and I was never going back there again. "She's going to make it."

Rissman said that he was ordering some more tests now that she had opened her eyes and that I had at least a few hours. Michael said he'd be happy to stay and wait for Cady while I went to the reception. I tried not to concentrate on the features he shared with Vic.


"This section tells the story of the Autumn Count; it is a legendary buffalo robe inscribed by Crazy Horse that supposedly had the ability to tell the future." He looked up at us. "I have never heard it mentioned outside the tribal council and certainly never by a white man." He looked back at the ledger and turned the page. "This is the most comprehensive history of the *Notame-ohmeseheestse* I have ever read outside of the reservation." He shook his head. "I would very much like to meet this William White Eyes."

Katz pulled out a chair and sat down across from Henry, while Gowder leaned against the table with his arms folded. Vic stood beside him. "Welcome to the fucking club."

The Academy staff was setting up the finishing touches on the reception that was scheduled to open in less than an hour, and it promised to be quite the wingding. The main hall was festooned with billboard-sized enlargements of the Mennonite Collection, as it was now called, and it was a little odd to have a gigantic Lonnie Little Bird looking at me from behind the table where Henry sat. I could almost hear the "um-hmm, yes, it is so" drifting across the marble-floored hall.

"What about page seventy-two?"

He flipped the pages, placed a hand gently in the corner, and held the book open. "It is a record of business dealings, numbers, but there is a code that I do not understand."

I glanced at Katz, who nodded. "Money laundering accounts."

"So, this ledger possibly gives us the numbered accounts of Toy Diaz's operation?" Katz shrugged, probably weighing the evidentiary value of a prosecuting attorney holding up the ledger in a court of law. "But I guess without William White Eyes's corroboration, these things are pretty much useless?"

Henry looked back at me. "They are incredible works of art."

I reached over and took the ledger from him. "You've

been hanging around in museums too long." I handed the book to Katz, who stacked it on top of the other one. "I guess we need Billy Carlisle."

The detective dropped his head. "I've got a wife and kid who've forgotten what I look like." He scooped up the ledgers, placed them under his arm, and glanced at Gowder. "I'll head back to the Roundhouse and get Meifert on a search for Carlisle. You?"

"I might hang around."

I put my hat back on, and we all stood. I made the general announcement. "Cady's eyes opened."

The Cheyenne Nation was the first to respond, even if his expression stayed the same. "Of course they have." He reached out and thumped both paws on my shoulders. "I wondered why you were acting strangely." I glanced at Vic, who covered her mouth. Henry had followed my look and then added. "We will retire to the hospital after the reception."

"I may not last that long."

He smiled. "I understand. I will meet you there."

Michelle Reddington, the dapper woman with the black dress and security pass, came around the corner from the gift shop and took Henry up the ornate, brass-railed stairs toward the Great Hall, where the majority of the photographs had been hung. He paused at the railing, looked back at me, motioned with his right hand in a fist against his chest, and then pointed his index finger down, the Cheyenne sign-talk for hope/heart.

I smiled back and brought my open right hand within a foot of my face, lowering it down and out to the right with a slight bow: thank you.

Katz and Gowder were equally congratulatory, but I

told them what Rissman had said about being overly optimistic. They agreed that whatever the outcome, Cady's eyes opening was certainly a good sign. Vic stood apart, clutching herself with her arms and smiling; after a moment, she turned and walked away.

Katz excused himself, and suddenly Gowder and I found ourselves looking at each other. "I owe you an apology."

He waved me off. "Forget about it." He gestured toward the bar up on the mezzanine. "C'mon, I'll buy you a drink."

As we were walking up the steps, I noticed that the gates had opened and the lower lobby was filling with well-dressed receptionees. Vic and Katz were carrying on a conversation by the revolving door at the front, and I started wondering what they were talking about—and then wondering why I was wondering. It was about that time that I noticed Vince Osgood and a beautiful young woman handing over their wraps at the coat check. This was beginning to have all the makings of an interesting evening.

Gowder ordered a gin and tonic; I ordered a Yuengling. We wandered up the rest of the stairs and decided to beat the rush to the exhibit. There were about two hundred of the photographs, some in montage, some in their original snapshot format, and some enlarged to the size of doors. Dena Many Camps's poetry was etched across the bottoms and sides of the large ones in a bold italic.

I sipped my beer. "You mind if I ask you a question?"

He studied the photo of the chiefs, who were holding one end of the American flag while some cavalry officers held the other. "Go ahead."

"This case seems pretty important to you and Katz."

"Is that your question?"

I tipped my hat back. "Yep."

He thought about it for a while. "Different reasons; with Katz it's a way of cleaning house. Dirty cops, dirty lawmakers, dirty lawyers bring out the inquisitor in him, and the last thing anyone in Philadelphia ever wants to hear is that Asa Katz wants a sniff of him. He did fourteen years with homicide and they tried to kick him over to cold case, but he took Internal Affairs Division."

"That kind of move can make a man unpopular."

Gowder smiled. "He doesn't care. He never went in for that cult-of-the-cop shit."

"So it's Osgood?"

"For Katz."

I nodded. "He's here."

"Osgood? Yeah, I saw him. Why do you think I stayed?"

I smiled back. "And you?"

He glanced at the picture of Henry's father sitting on the steps with the cat. "You know all these people?"

"Yes."

He nodded and chewed on an ice cube. "You know that crack house you guys took out earlier this week? I was born two blocks away from there."

I studied him carefully. "You mind if I ask you another question?"

"Go ahead."

"You guys were interested in Devon because of the money laundering thing, but who put you onto Cady and me?"

He took a sip of his drink and smiled. "Asa got a phone call from somebody who wanted you looked after."

"Who?" He kept looking at the picture, but the message was loud and clear.

I left him behind and walked along, looking at the familiar photographs. I stalled out at the one of Frank White Shield's wife, who was stringing snap peas on the front porch of their two-room cabin. The photo was compelling, but it was Dena's words that froze me.

> can you hear the sound of old women clacking
> their old tongues to the roofs
> of their mouths in the dust?
> this is prophecy so never
> ask the Indian whether she'd take
> the million dollars or the match.
> gasoline is on the shelf in all our houses.

I hadn't noticed that Vic was standing beside me. "You look nice, Walt." I wasn't sure what to say, so I self-consciously straightened my tie. She made an exasperated sound and reached out to straighten my now crooked tie. "I said you look nice. Stop fidgeting."

"Sorry."

"And stop apologizing."

"Okay." She studied the photograph and was reading Dena's poetry, the point of her nose turned up. I couldn't help but wonder if the world had changed, that things were, indeed, different. "Lucian calls it my union-organizer suit jacket." She wasn't really paying attention to me but was thinking about Dena's words. "You look great, too."

Her head turned back to me. "Thank you."

She smiled, and I smiled back. "Why do I have a feeling that what we did this afternoon was for my benefit?" She didn't say anything, but took a sip of her dirty martini, and I watched the iridescent sparkling in the tarnished gold eye, and was thinking that I was doing exactly what I'd been fighting against for years: falling in love with my deputy.

Someone was standing beside us. It was Osgood and the young woman I'd seen with him in the lobby. "I'm sorry if I'm interrupting."

"Howdy." I stepped back and introduced Vic. The blonde's name was Patricia Fulton, and she was making it abundantly clear that we hillbillies were not the people she had come to meet. He dismissed her to get drinks, which produced volumes of lower lip, but she disappeared.

Osgood gave Vic a strong look, from her turquoise choker to her boots, and I had the urge to toss him off the balcony. "So, you're from Wyoming?"

She finished off her cloudy cocktail and took an olive out that had been impaled by a tiny, plastic sword. "I'm from 9th Street, shitbird, and don't you forget it." She bit the olive, turned, and started for the bar in a calculated retreat.

"Did I say something wrong?"

"No." We both looked after her.

"Is she a Moretti Moretti?"

"I'm afraid so."

He sighed, and his head dropped a little. "Man, I can't catch a break." He noticed my stitches and the finger guard. "What happened to you?"

I shrugged. "I got mugged."

"When?"

"This morning. It's no big deal."

He leaned in closer to me, and his voice dropped. "I have some information for you."

I waited. "Okay . . ."

"Not here." He glanced around. "The bridge. Later?"

I took a moment to respond. "No."

He studied me. "What do you mean, no?"

"I mean no. I've got other things I have to do tonight and running to the other side of town and hanging around on bridges is not one of them. If you've got something to tell me, just tell me."

"It has to do with your daughter."

"Cady. Then I'm interested, but I don't have the time to go anywhere else." I pulled out my pocket watch. "As a matter of fact, I'm only going to be here for about twenty more minutes."

He thought about it. "I'll meet you outside."

"Where?"

"There's an alley behind the building; it turns a corner and there's a loading dock. I'll meet you there in fifteen."

I took a tip from the blonde and tried to look bored. "You bet."

I left him and continued around the gallery, careful to catch Gowder's eye as I got another beer from the bartender and retrieved Vic. "You got your sidearm?"

She looked genuinely shocked. "What?"

"I take that as a no?"

"Yes, that's a no."

I steered her out of the main gallery to the landing as Gowder appeared, and I nodded him toward us. "Osgood just arranged a little meeting with me out back."

His eyes widened. "Put him off, and we'll wire you."

I shook my head. "No, I have every intention of being back at the University of Pennsylvania Hospital within the hour. This case is important, but Cady is more important."

The detective sighed. "How you want to play it?"

"You guys go ahead and get set up. I'll be along in a few minutes. If he sees us together it may not happen." I reached into the pancake holster at my back and handed Vic my .45, which she slipped under her jacket. "It's probably nothing, but the people around this guy have an alarming tendency to turn up dead."

Gowder looked around. "I'll find that woman from the Academy. Maybe there's another way into the alley than the Cherry Street entrance."

Vic looked at me a moment longer then followed him. I stood there and watched as Osgood came down the stairs past me and disappeared into the crowd below; he was talking on his cell phone.

What was it the assistant district attorney had planned? I didn't figure there was any real danger from him, but if Toy Diaz and he were in cahoots, then discretion was the better part of armed backup. And what about Cady? Was it something to do with her connection to William White Eyes? Or was it simply a ruse? Anyway, I had a meet.

There was a general commotion in the lobby. Of all the things I thought I might've seen coming through the brass revolving doors of the Pennsylvania Academy of the Fine Arts, Lena Moretti with Dog on a leash would've probably been the last.

Two security guards, who seemed to be having a hard time keeping up, were following her closely. People were backing away, even though Dog seemed to be in his best form. Evidently the time in Lena's company had done him some good, since he appeared freshly washed and trimmed. She pulled up with the brute and smiled as I got to the bottom of the steps. She was beautiful, flushed, and breathless.

"I brought you your dog."

She reached the leash out to me, and I noticed that it was a black leather one rather than the extension cord we'd been using. I also noticed it matched her outfit, a sleek and sophisticated formfitting black skirt with a black ruffled cardigan over a black knit top. The opera was going to get a run for its money.

"Thank you." Dog sat on my foot.

She studied my face. "I know it's inconvenient, but I didn't have anywhere to keep him tonight." She glanced around the room, and I'm sure she was looking for her daughter.

I thought about the noise I'd heard while Vic and I had been on the sofa. "I, um . . ."

Her eyes flashed back to me. "I'm out tonight, and I wasn't sure if I'd be able to check on him tomorrow, so I thought I'd just bring him over here."

"Thank you." Dog looked up at me, and I tried to think of what to say next, finally settling on the most important thing. "Cady opened her eyes."

She softened and stepped forward, hugging my arm. "I know. Michael called me. It's wonderful." Her genuine happiness cut through the awkwardness. "I have to go. Can't be late for *Rigoletto*."

She gave me a quick peck on the cheek and turned. I watched as the fluted skirt twirled just enough to show a shapely calf, and she disappeared back through the revolving doors. Like mother, like daughter.

Dog looked at me, and I wondered what the hell I was going to do with him. I looked at the two security guards, and the two security guards looked back at me. "Sir, the dog can't stay."

I petted Dog. "That's okay, neither can I."

It had begun raining on Broad Street, a gentle, misting drizzle that glossed the surfaces of the city and diffused the light from the globes above. Even the thunder was gentle in the soft, eastern spring, gently bouncing from the tops of the skyscrapers.

I flipped the collar up on my jacket and pulled my hat down a little as we started around the block; Dog seemed happy to be outside and, truth to be told, I was, too.

I stopped at the corner and looked down the narrow alley. The yellow Hummer was there, and there was an identifying sticker in the window that stated OFFICIAL. There were a few other cars scattered along the building, but the windows were clear of condensation and nobody was in them.

A weirdo wearing sunglasses and a knit cap was smoking a cigarette under the awning of the back door, but I didn't see Osgood. I turned up the alley and walked past an empty Cadillac where the brick pavement turned and ran alongside the building. There was a loading dock, just as he had said, along with a four-story brick warehouse with numerous alcoves that housed windows and doors. There was a chain-link fence at the end of the dock that blocked off the two-foot-wide area between the buildings. I tried to think of a better place for bad things to happen, but the alley was easily the dankest, most forbidding place I'd been in in a long time.

The kid in the knit cap called out to me as I got to the corner. "Hey, mister? You're not supposed to be back here."

I waved him off. "It's okay."

I looked ahead and saw Osgood in a trench coat with his hands in his pockets. His collar was flipped up, too, and he nodded as I looked past him. He didn't make any move to come toward me, so I continued to walk to him, wondering where Vic and Gowder might be, and then Dog paused.

It was at that precise moment that the assistant district attorney's head exploded.

# 13

I watched as the headless body fell forward into the pools of rainwater that had collected on the uneven surface of the brick pavement. It wasn't so much that Osgood's head had exploded as it had vaporized in a crimson mist that had sprayed me along with Dog.

I had ducked and turned my head to the side with the sound, and I was lucky that I had, because deflected 10-gauge pellets smacked against the side of my hat and stung my neck and shoulder. Dog lunged on the leash and barked ferociously as I hung on to the leather strap and yanked him toward me.

There was a familiar roar, and I watched as a slug from my .45 ricocheted off the surface of the narrow passageway between the buildings. Vic stepped from the doorway of the Academy's loading dock and moved swiftly toward the alley in a two-handed stance, firing as she went, while Gowder ran toward the chain-link fence with his .40 at the ready.

I looked up from Osgood's twitching body to the eight-foot barrier with the razor wire strung across the top. I released the leash, and Dog charged toward Vic. I yelled as I started back out of the dead-end alley. "Grab him!"

As I rounded the corner, I took the deepest breath I'd taken since falling onto the street that morning. The pain blurred my vision, and I ran into the kid with the cap, slamming him backward as I stumbled over him and lost my hat. "Yo, man!"

I had regained the sidewalk, and it was a straight shot down Cherry to Broad, but the fifty yards looked like Ten Mile Road. It seemed to take forever, but I turned onto Broad in time to see a large man in a hooded sweatshirt covered with some kind of black rain slicker and with a firearm that looked like one of the old Ithaca Roadblockers sticking out of the unsnapped front; he had just turned the corner at Arch.

I grabbed my side, ran into traffic, and took a diagonal approach that gave me a geometric advantage. I heard brakes squealing as I thundered across Broad and felt the draft of a sedan as it missed me by about a foot. I stumbled a little as I made the median but bulled another car to a full stop on the other side, extended my hands, bounced from the grille, and pivoted across the street as another car swerved and disappeared behind me.

I dodged between two parked cars and turned the corner at Arch as well. People were screaming farther down the block, and a crowd had gathered. "Police! Has anybody seen . . ." About twelve people pointed south. I turned and ran.

He was cutting the corner and taking a left at the next street and was slowing down. For the life of me, I couldn't figure out why he was walking; it was possible that he thought he was clear. I fought the urge to throw up and put my last scrap of energy into the final block.

There was a mob on the sidewalk near the Reading Terminal Market; something must have been going on at the Pennsylvania Convention Center. I looked up through the misting rain and read the moving sign: NATIONAL RIFLE ASSOCIATION NATIONAL CONVENTION.

As Vic would say, fuck me. Maybe I could buy a gun from Charlton Heston.

I tried to see the guy in the gray sweatshirt through the throng; he had seemed pretty tall, so I thought I might have a chance. I started walking toward the large overpass, convinced that he'd gone that way, saw a guy with a hood, but it was the wrong color. I wiped the rain from my face and felt a twinge at my neck; I was bleeding. It wasn't too bad, but I wasn't going to blend in if things got close.

I caught some movement across the street and a little down the block: gray hood. I couldn't see the shotgun; he must've slipped it under the slicker. If it was actually one of the old Ithaca Mag-10s, he'd never have pitched it; it would be too difficult to get another.

I tried to keep up. He was hurrying now, but not so much that I couldn't stay with him. He wasn't going to blend either. He stopped at the next corner, and I panicked for a moment when I thought he was going to hail a taxi; instead, he pulled out a cell phone.

As Vic would say, fuck me again. I had forgotten about Cady's mobile. I reached into my jacket pocket and dialed 911. He jumped the puddle at the curb, careful to hang on to the gun under his coat, crossed the street, and continued down the block as sirens began whistling through the night around us. A dispatcher answered the line. "Nine-one-one."

"This is Sheriff Walt Longmire of Absaroka County, Wyoming. I've got a 10-32 at the southwest corner of Filbert and 11th. I am tailing a homicide suspect who just killed Assistant District Attorney Vince Osgood at the Academy of Fine Arts, and I need assistance."

There was a pause, but not much of one. "Sheriff, that was Filbert and 11th?"

"Roger that. A black male, tall, with a gray, hooded sweatshirt and a long, black rain slicker, headed east at a quick walking pace. The subject is armed with a tactical shotgun."

"Roger that. Can you stay on the line?"

I laughed a short laugh with very little humor in it. "I'd really rather not have this cell phone in my hands when I catch up with him." I started closing the phone as I crossed the street; the man was only about ninety feet ahead and slightly to the left. It was the guy from the crack house, Shanker DuVall.

"Sheriff . . .?"

I closed the phone and stuffed it back in my suit jacket, and silently cursed as he took a left at the next block and disappeared north up 10th. I picked up the pace and saw him slip across a parking lot behind the Greyhound Bus Terminal. I cut across the street at a diagonal, again hoping to gain a little distance.

There were rows of buses, most of them running, and I walked alongside one. DuVall was in front of another row on the opposite side of the lot; he was talking on the cell phone again.

There was a DMZ of about twenty yards that I wouldn't be able to cross without him seeing me. I stopped and started to pull the phone from my pocket when I heard a thumping noise and looked up to see an angry bus driver yelling at me. Even through the windshield and the noise of the diesel, I could hear him plainly. "Hey buddy! You can't be out here!" I motioned for him to keep quiet, but he honked the air horn, and the noise was tremendous. "Buddy, you're not allowed out here!"

There wasn't much choice, so I crossed the lot in the direction that I had last seen DuVall, but he was gone. I glanced between the parked buses and tried not to think about the last time I'd seen most of Vince Osgood.

When I got to the area where the shooter had been standing, I peered around the parked bus and saw nothing but a concrete wall and some weeds. I stooped down, checking to see if I could see any feet, but it was so dark there wasn't any way to tell. I slid along the corrugated side of the big vehicle and wished I had my sidearm.

There was a pole at the end of the row nearest me, but it shed only scattered blocks of light through the bus windows. I wiped the rain off my face again, stepped around a large puddle, turned sideways, and started sliding between the concrete wall and the back of the bus; I figured it was the only direction DuVall could have gone. There was just enough room for me to squeeze after him. Evidently, he hadn't had any trouble, but then he hadn't had any trouble squeezing between two buildings and shooting Osgood either. It was possible that he'd left and that I was alone, playing Greyhound limbo for my own amusement. I tried not to think about the alternative.

I stopped for a second and listened, thinking I heard talking. I listened again, but there was nothing. The driver revved the engine of the bus I was pressed against a few times to get the big motor cleared out; I closed my eyes and held my breath until the cloud of exhaust and soot dissipated. The noise was all-encompassing, and I could see the access doors to the engine rattling as I turned my head and looked down the barrel of an Ithaca Mag-10 Roadblocker shotgun.

I could see only part of his face in the dark and within the shadows of the hood, but I could see his lips moving as his finger tightened around the trigger mechanism.

"What?" Here I was, trapped between a bus and a hard spot, and I couldn't hear the last words I would ever listen to. He paused and then spoke again. His voice was much louder, but I still couldn't make out the words. "What?"

"I said, I was gonna let you live!"

I yelled back. "Thank you."

"But . . ." And he pulled the trigger.

The Ithaca Mag-10 Roadblocker was introduced a few decades back as a tactical 10-gauge designed to stop cars; hence the name Roadblocker. It was expensive, heavy, and carried only three rounds, the idea being that three two-ounce helpings of lead served at just over the sound barrier were enough. However, it had problems that could only be corrected with a longer forcing tube; without the modification, it had a propensity to jam.

And it did.

His eyes widened, and I saw him continue to pull the trigger as I slapped the barrel up; just because it hadn't gone off didn't mean that it still wouldn't.

And it did.

The sound of the buses was bad enough, but the blast from the business end of the 10-gauge shotgun made me hear a high-pitched squeal that felt like a band saw cutting through my brain. I held the barrel above me as the back glass and parts of the bus's aluminum skin skittered down on my face. He tugged at the heated metal of the shotgun, but I yanked, and the weapon came loose, skimmed over me, and clattered onto the ground.

I turned my head, but he was gone. I sidestepped and looked down; he had fallen, and his arm was lodged between the dual wheels of the Greyhound—center shot to the head. I looked up, and Gowder stood about ten yards away in a two-handed stance with his .40 still pointed at the now-dead man.

He looked up at me and said something, but all I could hear was the ringing and all I could do was look back, breathe as deeply as my ribs would allow, and try to stop shaking.

It was a source of great interest to the Philadelphia Police Department and the District Attorney's Office of Southeastern Pennsylvania that Shankar DuVall was leaking onto a stainless-steel table at the city morgue. Gowder said that he got a ride to my call, started walking, and when he saw someone trying to shoot somebody behind the bus, he had taken appropriate, if deadly, action. I was glad that he had, and I reflected that opinion in my formal statement and recorded interview for the investigators.

I looked at the battered tactical shotgun lying on the table between us; it hadn't had an easy life, and I was starting to think that I hadn't either. Gowder was sitting across from me without his gun or his badge. Both of us periodically glanced at the large mirror on the wall under the military clock and wondered who was on the other side. It was 2:33 A.M. I smiled at him and listened to my voice; it sounded as if I were underwater. I could talk, but I still couldn't hear that well. "I'm glad you shot a bad guy, or we'd be here all night."

He smiled and said something.

"What?" He smiled some more and pointed to his own ears. "They say it isn't permanent, that it should get progressively better in the next seventy-two hours, half of which I intend to be asleep." He looked at the surface of the table and probably was seeing all sorts of things that were not there. After a while, I placed a hand out and got his attention, the dark eyes slowly rising to mine. "If you hadn't shot him, I wouldn't be sitting here."

He nodded. After a while, he nodded some more.

They turned us loose; they were through with me, but Gowder would have to sit through another battery of interviews in the morning. By the time we got to the main hallway of the third floor, there was a group waiting for us.

Asa Katz leaned against the wall, and I almost didn't recognize him in tennis shoes, jeans, and a blue windbreaker. Every time I'd seen him, he'd looked like a print ad for *GQ*, but right now he just looked like one tired cop. Vic was also there, still in her clothes from the reception. She looked great and was the only one of us who didn't look exhausted.

Katz spoke to Gowder and then said something to me. "What?"

They spoke among themselves, and then Vic smiled up at me, slipping her arm through mine and leading me down the hallway and into the elevator. She took Cady's cell and called someone as we left the Roundhouse.

She thanked the cops who had given us a ride back to Cady's, unlocked the door, and watched as I walked over to the refrigerator and pulled out a beer; I was feeling a little edgy and thought a nightcap might help. I motioned to Vic and she nodded yes, so I pulled another one from the icebox.

Dog came over for a wag and a pet. I placed the two beers on the counter, sat at one of the stools, and ruffled his ears. My .45 was lying there, along with my hat. I touched the brim and watched as it pivoted on the crown in a lazy circle.

Vic opened the Yuengling longnecks and slid mine toward me. I sighed and smiled at her as she looked back at the door and Dog barked. Maybe it was my ears—most likely it was recent circumstance—but I found my hand on the big Colt as Vic paid the delivery guy and came back with a pizza box. She acted like she hadn't seen my hand on my gun, put the pepperoni with extra cheese and anchovies on half on the table, and retrieved two plates and silverware. She pulled two paper towels from the holder above the sink, handed me one, and said something.

"What?"

She shook her head, opened the box, and placed a slice with anchovies on my plate. I wasn't particularly hungry, but as near as I could remember, I hadn't eaten since lunch. I chewed in a mechanical fashion and sipped my beer.

I tried not to laugh at the situation; here we were with so much to say, and I couldn't hear. I made a conscious effort to not look over to the couch, but something stirred rather deeply in the reptilian coil of my primal nature, and I felt very much like doing it again.

I concentrated on the food instead and finished half of it to Vic's quarter as Dog alternated between us for the crusts. After a while, she stood, saying something with a sense of finality.

"What?"

She placed her hands together, laid them alongside her head, and closed her eyes. I nodded and watched as she stood there for a moment longer, then turned and went up the spiral staircase to the guest bedroom above.

I sat there wondering if I was supposed to follow. I sat there wondering if I wasn't supposed to follow. I sat there wondering.

The answer came to me as I finally noticed the sheets, blanket, and pillow that made up a makeshift bed on the epic sofa. I reached up with the protector on my index finger and used the other digits to feel the gauze padding where the EMTs had patched my neck. I picked up my hat, turning it over and looking at the marks where one of the pellets had raced across the brim and missed my head by a quarter inch.

Cady was lying at the Hospital of the University of Pennsylvania in a coma after having been pushed down the stairs at the Franklin Institute by Devon Conliffe.

Devon Conliffe was dead after being thrown from the Benjamin Franklin Bridge.

Osgood was dead, shot in the head by Shankar DuVall.

Shankar DuVall was dead after being shot by Gowder for trying to kill me behind a Greyhound bus.

That's all I knew.

I turned out the lights, put my hat on since it was easier to wear than to carry, and wondered who was next. I picked up my sidearm, jacking the slide mechanism to make sure that it was empty, glanced up at the balcony, where the light from the guest bedroom was off, and limped over to the sofa. Even after having Vic call and finding there was no change, I wanted to get to the hospital at a reasonable hour in the morning, so I thought that maybe I should try to get to sleep.

My hat seemed out of shape; maybe the shotgun blast had done more damage than I'd thought. I flipped it onto the coffee table and placed my gun under the brim, pulled off my boots, and shrugged off my filthy jacket, shirt, and tie, trying carefully to avoid my numerous and sundry injuries. I stripped off my blood-spattered jeans and collapsed gently onto the sofa with a groan that caused Dog to come over and rest his head on the cushion beside mine. I petted him with the back of my hand and watched as he curled up on the floor, the ever-vigilant protector.

The ambient glow from the bridge cast blue through

the glass of the cupola. The rain had subsided to a soft drizzle that shifted the light from above. There was probably a comforting sound that went along with it, but I couldn't hear it; all I had was the ringing.

Cady's eyes had opened. I thought of going to the hospital now. I wanted to see those clear, cool, gray eyes again. I wanted to watch them blink and know that her fine mind was working in there somewhere, finding its way back, but that was stupid. I was tired, filthy, and couldn't hear.

I pulled the covers up and started to roll over, but my ribs reminded me that I couldn't, and my eyes wouldn't stay closed, so I stared at my hat. It would be a shame if it was ruined—it had gone through so much—but if it no longer fit, it no longer fit. I thought of trying it on again and started to reach for it. The inner band was brown and the lining a shiny rayon red, but something was poking up from the liner that was pointed and white.

"Well, hell." I was still underwater, but I know the words had slipped from my mouth. I blinked and looked again, hoping that perhaps my eyes were playing tricks on me along with my ears, but it was still there. I let sleeping Dog lie and reached over, using my middle and ring fingers to pull the tiny envelope from the battered piece of beaver. The usual typewritten word struck across the crisp stock, and again it read: SHERIFF.

I thumbed open the flap, pulled out the tiny place card, and flipped it over: MEDICINE MAN.

I stared at it, trying to figure out the significance of the two words, but again all I could think of was Henry. He wasn't the only medicine man I knew, but he was definitely the only one I knew in Philadelphia. I thought about the last note. SEE PAGE 72. LOOK WEST, YOU CAN

FIGHT CITY HALL. I assumed that one had to do with the ledgers but, in combination with the earlier note, I wasn't sure.

GO BACK TO THE INDIAN had been a location, and perhaps a portion of the note about CITY HALL was, too; if that was the case, then MEDICINE MAN might also be a location. I thought about the Indian sculpture at Logan Circle and started wondering about Billy White Eyes's fixation with all things native and the public art of the greater Philadelphia region.

I woke up still wondering. When Vic came down the stairs in the morning in an oversized green T-shirt, I had coffee waiting for her.

I slid her the mug; she yawned and perched on a stool. I tried not to notice her legs. "What're you doing up?"

I sipped my own coffee and sat down to look over the collection of books I had scattered over the surface of the counter. "I needed to call the hospital, and I had some thoughts."

She looked at me for a moment. "Your hearing's back?"

I continued to study the open books. "Not completely, but it's a lot better."

I had discovered Cady's library along one of the long walls of the living area. When the law firm in Philadelphia had hired her, she had begun accumulating books on what was to be her adopted city. There were books on its history, its architecture, politics, food, sports and, most important for the moment, its statuary.

"Did you know that Philadelphia has one of the largest collections of public sculpture in the world?"

"So?"

I thought about the prophet having no honor in his

own country and that if you wanted a shitty impression of Philadelphia all you had to do was ask a Philadelphian. I held up the note from the crease of the book. "I got another note last night."

Now she was awake. "Where?"

"I literally pulled it out of my hat." I looked at her. "Who gave it back to you last night?"

She studied the note and glanced up at me, distracted. "The coat check guys. They said that one of the serving staff had picked it up in the alley behind the Academy."

I thought of the dark-haired kid smoking the cigarette. "I'll be damned . . ."

"What?"

I shook my head at my own stupidity. "There was a kid at the back door of the Academy, and I ran into him when I was chasing Shankar DuVall." I looked up at her. "It had to be William White Eyes." I thought back. "He was wearing sunglasses and a cap to disguise himself, but it was the same voice as the one who was driving the SUV, using the same phrase 'hey man' or 'yo man.' Something like that."

"Walt, I would say that a full 70 percent of the residents of Philadelphia use the term 'yo man.'"

I kept my eyes steady with hers. "It was him, and that was also him on the bridge."

"What bridge?"

"When I met you here in Philadelphia."

"All right, just for argument's sake, let's say it was. Why is this kid following you around?"

"I don't know."

"You don't think it's possible that he's involved with this Toy Diaz group and the recently deceased Shankar DuVall?"

"He was, but I don't think he is now, and I don't think

he's a killer. I think he was the cook and the accountant."
She started shaking her head before I could finish. "Look,
the drug business is like any other business; if you don't
keep track of your money, you don't make money."

"Granted."

"If you're running a drug operation, you can't exactly
walk into the office of the nearest CPA. You need somebody good with numbers, somebody you can trust, but
somebody under the radar."

She nodded. "Gladwyne on the Main Line, Ivy League,
Phi Beta Kappa, and Rhodes Scholar William Carlisle."

I refilled my mug and held on to the pot. "But somehow
Billy Carlisle became a loose cannon in the Diaz organi-
zation somewhere around the same time he became
William White Eyes, and I think that happened because
of Cady."

"In the pro bono appeal?"

"Yep."

She smiled. "You think your daughter had a strong
enough moral influence on this guy that it turned him?"

I poured her some more coffee. "You'd be amazed at
the influence a woman can have for good or bad."

She grinned and nodded her head. "Uh huh."

I set the pot back down. "I don't think Billy Carlisle was
that bad of a guy to begin with. I think he made some bad
choices and got involved with some bad people. I think he
got reminded of his conscience in his dealings with Cady,
and I think she became emblematic of something."

Vic nodded and looked down at the collection of books
I had spread across the counter. "What's all this shit,
anyway?"

"Research. The kid's a genius. What's the one thing he
figured I'd eventually pick up on and even be drawn to?"

She looked at the books. "Statues?"

"Indians."

Her eyes widened. "Fuck me."

"The first note wasn't Henry. GO BACK TO THE IN-DIAN was the statue at Logan Circle. I think LOOK WEST, YOU CAN FIGHT CITY HALL means the Indian statues facing west at City Hall." I turned one of the books and shoved it toward her and pointed at the photograph of a Plains medicine man on horseback, his arm raised above his buffalo headdress. "Dauphin at West 33rd Street, east Fairmount Park."

"Medicine man."

I nodded. "I'm headed over to the hospital, but I thought I might stop off at City Hall since it's on the way. The City Hall note came before the medicine man one, and the sequence might be important."

The wedding cake that is the City Hall of Philadelphia was designed to be the tallest building in the world, but by the time it was finished, the Eiffel Tower and the Washington Monument had surpassed it. On four and a half acres of Penn Square, its domed tower tops out just shy of 550 feet to the top of Willy Penn's hat. There are 250 other statues that adorn the interior and exterior of the building to keep him company.

We got out of the cab at the west side of the building and walked across the sidewalk with Dog as though we were approaching some fantastic ship that had been docked at the center of the metropolis.

"I hate this building."

I ignored her and studied the façade. "It's Second Empire, the same as the Louvre."

"It's fruity."

"This is quite possibly the greatest architectural achievement of the late nineteenth century."

I allowed my eye to cast over the dormer pediment figures on the west side of the building and walked a little ahead of Vic as she stopped to buy an Italian ice from one of the vendors that populated the area. Dog strained a little at the leash and attempted to be a part of Vic's transaction, but I gently yanked him back.

It was a beautiful day, and the skies and streets were washed clear with the previous night's storms. I could feel the humidity, and the air felt like the breath of someone close. I dragged Dog along behind me as I angled a little to the left and stood there, studying the dormer caryatids. Above them were two colossal bronzes at the north corners of the tower, twenty-four to twenty-six feet in height: one was an Indian maiden, the other a brave.

I looked at the more than two hundred vertical feet between the statues and me as Vic came over with two cups of Italian ice. "We don't have to climb this ugly fucker, do we?"

"I don't know what we're supposed to do." I took my ice and spooned out a mouthful; it was piña colada, and it was very good. "Is there a tour of the building?"

"Yeah, or at least there used to be."

I clarified my question. "When?"

"When it used to be my division, it was Monday through Friday at 12:30."

"It's Saturday."

"It's Philadelphia; nothing's easy."

I sidled a little more to the left, continuing to study the massive sculptures. "A woman with a child, and a man with a dog." I looked down at Dog, who seemed to be taking an inordinate interest in my ice. "You don't have any notes on you, do you?" He sat in expectation of a treat. I turned back to Vic. "Do you think we're supposed to figure it out from here?"

She shrugged and continued eating her lemon ice. "That hasn't been the case so far."

I went back to ignoring Dog and studied the tower. LOOK WEST, YOU CAN FIGHT CITY HALL. It didn't make sense that William White Eyes would leave a note in a place where we couldn't get it. He hadn't done that before, and I think he was a creature of habit, albeit a creative one. As I finally succumbed and lowered the cup to Dog so that he could lap the remaining syrup at the bottom, I thought I heard somebody say something.

I looked at Vic, who was standing another twelve feet closer to the northwestern corner of the building. "What?"

She stared back at me. "Huh?"

"What'd you just say?"

She looked at me quizzically. "Is your hearing going again?"

I stood there. "Didn't you just say something?"

"No."

This time the voice came from directly behind me. I turned and looked at the grizzled man who owned the Italian ice cart—a stocky balding man with a soiled red apron and striped shirt. "Excuse me?"

He smiled and said it a little louder this time. "Medicine Man."

# 14

He didn't know William White Eyes or Billy Carlisle; he just knew that a guy had paid him twenty bucks to keep an eye out for a large man in a cowboy hat with a dog and when he saw him to say "Medicine Man." He said the guy that had given him the message was tall, skinny, and had been wearing a cap and sunglasses, so he didn't know what color his hair or eyes might've been, but that he was well dressed and had been wearing shiny shoes. He said he always noticed them and that you could tell a lot about a person from their shoes.

He liked my cowboy boots.

He said the guy told him I'd be around yesterday and that he'd tried the two words out on a man that was wearing a cowboy hat but wasn't so big and didn't have a dog. He said the man had looked at him funny, and he figured it was the wrong guy. He said the fella with the twenty had given him the message to pass along yesterday afternoon. He studied me for a while and then wanted to know if he was in trouble. I told him no.

He wanted to know if he got another twenty bucks. I told him no to that, too. He wanted to know whether if he came up with anything else, there might be another twenty in it. I told him I was a police officer and that if he hadn't told me everything, we could continue this conversation at the Roundhouse.

He said he'd told me everything. I asked him if he was sure.

He said he was twenty dollars sure.

The cabbie took the Market Street Bridge, and I looked out at the Schuylkill River and wondered if there were any fish in it. Vic didn't have anything to throw out the window, so I figured we'd make it all the way to the hospital.

"Why would he deliver the message twice, once with the vendor and once in the hat?"

"He didn't think we got it from the vendor, and he was right."

"So, after the hospital, we head up to eastern Fairmount Park with Katz and Gowder?"

I petted Dog and thought about it. "Let them do it."

"Aren't you curious?"

"I'm more concerned about Cady." She nodded, and we rode the rest of the way in silence, but she petted Dog, too.

The detectives were waiting for us outside when we arrived. I asked Gowder about his inquiry. "Postponed till this afternoon."

"What about your badge and gun?"

He smiled the trademark smile. "I've decided to operate on my winning personality and bulletproof spirits."

I glanced at Katz, and he gave me a thumbs up. Vic followed them. "I'm going with them. You don't need me."

I stood there on the sidewalk with the leash in my hand. "Would you do me a favor?" She took Dog.

When I got to Cady's room, Henry was asleep in a chair by the bed with his Phillies cap pulled down over his eyes. Lena looked up from the *Daily News* and held the front page so that I could see a smiling photograph of Vince Osgood when he had a head.

The headline read ASSISTANT DA SLAIN. She raised her eyebrows and spoke quietly. "You're making quite a name for yourself here in the big city."

"I didn't shoot him." I sat in the chair next to her and also spoke sotto voce. "How was the opera?"

"Tame, in comparison." She handed me a cup of coffee from the windowsill, and I took it even though I'd consumed enough of the stuff to tan a buffalo hide. "What happened?"

"It was a lot of running, screaming, and shooting." I looked at Cady. "How is she?"

Lena folded the paper and slid it to the floor beside her chair. "Her eyes were open when Michael and I changed the guard, but she closed them about an hour ago."

"How long have you been here?"

"Since about eight."

"When did the Cheyenne Nation show up?"

"Michael said a little after midnight. He's been asleep since I got here."

She was wearing a floral print sundress and the shapely arch of her foot showed in strapped sandals. She lay back in her chair and stretched her legs. "He's very handsome."

It wasn't hard to imagine Lena as she had been in her mid-thirties any more than it was hard to imagine what Vic would look like in her late fifties; each was a reminder of what could be and what was, with the grip of the past too strong and the grip of the future too frightening.

"Where's the Terror?"

Obviously, she was reading my mind. "I got another note stuffed in my hat after I dropped it last night."

She placed a hand over her eyes and sighed. "Enough of this cloak and dagger stuff." She leaned forward. "I have news for you."

"I'm listening."

"Not that it matters that much now, but Alphonse says Devon Conliffe was turning state's evidence on Vince Osgood."

"I know that."

She looked at me. "How do you know that?"

"Katz and Gowder had to tell me after I found out Billy Carlisle was William White Eyes."

"Who is Billy Carlisle, and, for that matter, William White Eyes?"

I studied her for a long time. "Lena, how come you called Katz and told him to keep an eye on me?"

Her eyes didn't come back to mine, and she sat there quietly with her hands holding on to the paper cup of coffee. "I was worried about you." A little time passed as we looked at each other. She smiled. "Well, I'm not one to pry into police matters for too long." She picked up her purse from the sill, stood, and turned to look at me. "I'm too well trained." She took a pair of sunglasses out and slipped them on. "Do you have plans for dinner?"

"Pardon?"

"Dinner?" She picked up her empty coffee cup and dropped it in the nearby trash can. "Victor and I thought it might be nice to have you and Vic for dinner late-afternoon? We'd be honored if you brought Henry. It'll have to be early, since Victor has another performance tonight. About five? Nothing special, Lena's Risotto a la Marinara Moretti."

I stayed seated and watched her continue to stiffen. "Lena, have I done something to upset you?"

She didn't look at me. "Possibly."

I listened to the flap of the sandals as she disappeared down the corridor of the ICU and wondered if I was developing an unwanted talent for driving women away.

"That was well done."

I turned to look at the Indian as he raised his hat. He studied me as I took the top off the coffee Lena had given me and went ahead with a sip. "You think?"

He adjusted the cap and leaned on the arm of his chair to get a better look at me. "You were using your cop voice. I think that was what pissed her off more than anything."

"Cop voice?"

He nodded. "It is a pedantic tone you use when you are questioning a suspect that . . ."

"All right . . ."

"She has probably heard enough cop voices in her life."

He flexed his neck and moved to the chair Lena had just vacated. I offered him the coffee, and he took a sip. He handed it back to me and noticed my new bandage. "You are hurt again?"

"Yep."

He picked up the paper that Lena had left on the floor. "Would you like to tell me or should I just read about it in the newspaper?"

"Osgood's dead, along with Shankar DuVall." I raised my hands in innocence. "I didn't kill either one of them."

"That is good."

I smiled with him and passed the coffee again. "I got another note . . ."

"I heard. What is your new theory?"

"I think the notes concern themselves with Indian statuary." I pulled one of the books from my backpack and opened it to the photo of the Plains medicine man.

He took the book and cradled it in his hands, and somehow it became more important. His fingers traced down the page. "You think that the preoccupation of William White Eyes with all things Native extends to the art world?"

"Yep."

He took a deep breath and slowly let it out. "I am relinquished of my duties at the Academy and can now assist you full time."

I felt guilty about not having kept him company. "How was the reception? It seemed like a success."

He continued to study the book. "It was."

"How was your speech?"

"Brilliant."

I took another sip of the communal coffee. "You're sounding pedantic."

He nodded and handed the book back to me. "I am now in cop mode."

"You know . . ." He watched me as I watched Cady. "You may be going back to Wyoming alone." He continued studying me as I slipped the book back in the pack.

"That is what you want?"

I shifted in the chair. "I just can't keep you here while I wait for . . ." I could feel the heat rising in my face, so I took a few moments to swallow and let the warmth dissipate. "I don't know when I'm going to be able to go home."

He straightened in his own chair. "Maybe the wait will be shorter than you think." He brought his large hands up and clapped the leather palms together like the report of a rifle with a voice that thundered from the high plains. "Cady!"

I spilled the coffee. The head nurse was standing, but she remained behind the desk; she was probably afraid that the Indian was on the warpath. I turned back toward him with my face set, but when my eyes rested on Cady, hers were open, and they were not staring at the ceiling but at us.

I felt myself rising from my chair and walking toward the bed, and her eyes followed me. I couldn't breathe, and my vision was clouding with the pent emotion of what seemed like a lifetime. I had never seen eyes as beautiful as the ones I was looking into now.

I reached out and took her hand with my battered, finger-guarded paw. "How long have you known?"

He smiled and shook his head at my ignorance. "Just now."

I was standing there looking at him when I thought I felt a mild pressure in my hand that a man without hope would have perceived as a reflex action. I turned and looked at Cady, and her eyes stayed steady with mine. I gently squeezed her hand in return and, once again, ever so gently, she squeezed back. I kneeled down by the bed, the tears stinging. "I see you. I see you, and I felt that just now . . ." I stayed with those eyes, staying with them just as sure as I held on to her hand. "Don't you go away. Don't you ever go away again."

She didn't nod or even move, but I knew she could hear me and understand. I squeezed her hand again, but she didn't squeeze back this time, and that was okay. She was probably tired, and we had a long way to go.

It was Dr. Rissman's day off. Another surgeon from the floor below said that it was a cognitive effect that denoted a reactive concept but not necessarily one of perceptivity. He started to give me the reactivity/perceptivity routine, but I refused delivery and told him "The Greatest Legal Mind of Our Time" was on its way back, so get ready.

The narrow rays of hope I'd been nurturing cracked across the ICU like the sound of Henry's hands, and I sat at the side of Cady's bed for the next hour and forty-three minutes until her eyes closed again.

They wanted to run more tests, and I was the thing that was holding them up. I didn't want to let go and wanted to be there when her eyes opened again, but one of Henry's thunderclap hands rested on my shoulder, and I felt the tug of home from two mountain ranges away.

I brushed the sleeve of my shirt across my face, smearing the residue of sentiment and careful to avoid the parts that were freshly stitched. I laughed.

"What is it?"

I tried stretching my shoulders without pulling at my beat-up, Raggedy Andy head. "I was just thinking that if my face was the first thing I saw when I came to, I might go back to sleep myself."

I looked to see if she would respond when he dragged my hand away, but she didn't. Like Sleeping Beauty, she was enchanted again, and all I could do was wait.

It was a beautiful day, and the warmth of the sun felt good on my back. Henry had picked the Vietnamese stir-fry place near the university for an early lunch, and the food was actually pretty good. The guy had almost dropped his spatula when the Indian ordered in Vietnamese. Since it was a Saturday and the students were otherwise engaged, we occupied one of the picnic tables; my two regular pigeons hopped over and stood beside my boots. I motioned with my plastic spork. "Mutt, Jeff, meet Henry Standing Bear."

Henry nodded at the two freeloaders. "Ha-ho, Mutt and Jeff." Mutt cocked his head at the baritone Cheyenne, but Jeff kept his beady eyes on my fried rice.

I looked toward the façade of Franklin Field and thought about what had happened today. I thought about the chain of violence and death that had been at least momentarily reversed. I thought about acts of kindness and acts of risk that were due a reward.

Henry ate his shrimp with rice and looked at me but didn't say anything. He took a sip of his green tea and studied me with the steady, dark eyes. "What do you think they will find at the medicine man statue?"

I took a deep breath, and it seemed like my ribs didn't hurt as badly. "Now that I've had time to think about it, nothing."

"Nothing?"

"I think William White Eyes was going to be there." I put my paper plate on the ground so that Mutt and Jeff could get a shot at some rice. "He's not going to show for Philadelphia's finest, but he will for us."

He sat the cup down. "This is not over then, is it?"

"He saved Cady." He didn't reply. "You and I both know that if she hadn't gotten medical attention as quickly as she did, she'd be dead." It felt good having some idea of what I was going to do. "He exposed himself, not once but a bunch of times to make sure that we were okay." I used the finger guard to scratch at the stitches at my jaw. "That's just not something I can walk away from."

"Toy Diaz?"

"Has to be. The way I see it, Devon Conliffe tried to put pressure on Cady about the laundering scheme, but when she didn't bite, he was going to turn state's evidence on Osgood. Either Osgood or Diaz got antsy and decided to have Shankar DuVall toss Devon off the Benjamin Franklin Bridge, but then Billy Carlisle became a loose cannon, and everybody decided they couldn't trust anybody."

"You do not think that Shankar DuVall was there at the Academy to kill you?"

"No. It might have been what Diaz told Osgood, or what Osgood planned with him, but I think Diaz had decided that Assistant DA Vince 'Oz' Osgood was not the type to go down with the ship. Besides, DuVall told me himself that he hadn't planned to kill me." I sipped my iced tea. "Now, the only one left with any of the answers is Billy Carlisle, aka William White Eyes."

"So you think it is our responsibility to keep him alive?"

"It's mine."

"Then it is ours."

Our attention was drawn to a sassy brunette who was attempting to walk an oversized dog into the lobby of the University of Pennsylvania Hospital. Henry stuck both fingers in his mouth and whistled with a piercing note that rattled the surrounding windowpanes.

Vic stopped arguing with the security guard, flipped him off, and crossed 34th without looking. Mutt and Jeff scattered in the presence of Dog as Vic sat next to me and took my iced tea. She sat very close. "So, you got any other great ideas?"

"Nothing?"

She held a few ice cubes in her mouth. "Nothing."

"Where are the cops?"

"There was a possible Toy sighting up in Germantown, where a competitor in the highly volatile commerce of grassroots pharmaceutical distribution came down with a critical case of NFP." We continued to look at her. "No fucking pulse."

"Did this competitor fall off a bridge?"

"No bridges big enough in Germantown." She shook

her head and continued crunching the ice between her teeth. "Somebody ran over him with a car. Twice."

Henry and I looked at each other, and then I looked back at Vic. "I want to go up to the Medicine Man and have a look for myself, or have William White Eyes have a look at us." I remembered Lena's invitation as I looked at her. "Your mother and father invited us over for dinner."

Vic choked, picked up the cup again, and began eating more ice. "Yeah, tell 'em I'll pencil 'em in."

Henry watched her for a few moments. "They say chewing ice is a sign of sexual frustration."

Vic slipped her hand on my knee under the table, and I almost jumped off the bench. She continued chewing. "I wouldn't know about that."

"Four hooves down means that the individual died in battle."

I looked at the four bronze horse hooves planted firmly in the granite base. "I thought died in battle was one hoof lifted."

Vic held Dog and input her two cents. "What are two hooves lifted?"

I glanced down at the description in the book. "You mean rearing?"

"Yeah."

I looked around. "Fell off his horse during battle?"

The sloping lawn of this part of Fairmount Park was at odds with the sordid squalor across Ridge Avenue. The row houses on the block were falling apart from the neglect, and the only retail establishment was an after-hours club in what looked to have been a restaurant.

I turned back to the statue and read from the book.

"'Cyrus E. Dallin, 1861–1944.' He was from Utah." The Bear moved a little closer to the statue but seemed distracted and looked at an area to the southwest. "'Famed Native American scholar Francis LaFlesche described the nudity of the holy man typifying the utter helplessness of man in comparison to the strength of the Great Spirit, whose power is symbolized by the horns upon the head of the priest.'"

The Cheyenne Nation walked past me. "Looks like a high five." I glanced up, and it did. "What now?"

"Well, while we're waiting for William White Eyes, we look for a note."

We looked for fifteen minutes. No note. Vic was sitting on the hillside looking at the book of statuary, and Dog had decided to join her. Henry and I were still searching the surrounding trees in hopes that the wind might have caught the note and landed it on a branch but had still found nothing. "It is not here."

"I'm beginning to think you're right."

We walked back over and stood in front of Vic, and Henry asked. "Is this the only Medicine Man?"

She placed a hand across the open page and looked up. "Yes."

I shrugged. "I guess we might as well head back to the hospital."

Henry had parked the Thunderbird across Edgely Street. We made our way to the car when I noticed a tricked-out, fully chromed Escalade bristling with oversized wheels, brush guards, and enough off-road lights to illuminate the Miracle Mile. It was stopped at a discreet distance, and I was thinking about William White Eyes when the tinted windowed vehicle made a casual U-turn and thrummed its way back toward the reservoir and the depths of Fairmount Park.

"If you were an Indian in the city, where would you hide?" I held out my hand to Henry as we watched the Escalade disappear behind the sloping green of Athletic Field. "Gimme your keys."

"Why?"

I started around the car toward the driver's side and tossed the daypack into the backseat, feeling the weight of my .45 inside. "You drive too slow."

He stopped and looked genuinely hurt. "I do not."

"Give them to me!"

He handed me the gold-colored anniversary keys that he had put on the lucky rabbit's foot chain. Vic quickly climbed in the back with Dog, and Henry took shotgun. "Do not wreck Lola."

In the rearview mirror, I watched as Vic put her arm around Dog. "I'll try not to."

I fired up the 430-cubic-inch police interceptor and began intercepting. Fortunately, we were parked in the right direction, so I gunned her and quickly motored across the hill, following the only road the Cadillac could have taken. At Fountain Green Drive we had to make a decision. Vic hung over the seat and pointed left. "Stay on the reservoir road. He'll either double back or continue the loop back up 33rd."

She was right. We turned the corner in time to see a black Escalade continuing north on the four-lane. I made a turn on a late yellow, drifted to the right, and pulled in behind a delivery van in the slow lane. Back at Dauphin he stopped at the light, and we slowed behind the truck, but the light changed too quickly. "Damn."

Henry's eyes stayed on the black SUV. "What?"

"If he'd stopped at the light a little longer, I was going to get out."

"Yes, that worked so well last time . . ."

Vic was still hanging between the seats as I pulled around the step-van and accelerated. The Cadillac made a left without hitting the turn signal, then a hard right on Strawberry Drive. "I don't suppose either of you got the license number yet?"

I hung back at the turn, but it's hard to go unnoticed when you are a powder blue vintage convertible with a cowboy, an Indian, a brunette, and a dog inside. He had steadily accelerated as we approached the light at Strawberry Mansion Bridge, and by the time he got to the intersection, he was running a straight sixty. Fortunately, the light was green, and we shot onto the ramp of the bridge about ninety feet behind him, barely missing a bicyclist who shook his fist at us.

The fifty-year-old steering on the big Bird felt a little loose as we dropped over the Schuylkill Expressway and watched as the Caddy continued to gain speed but easily make the corner at Greenland Drive. I hit the brakes a little as I turned the wheel, powered through the curve, and flattened the accelerator to the floor as the bulk of the cast-iron engine exploded internally, shooting us up the tree-lined thoroughfare at eighty.

I noticed that Vic had pulled my .45 from the pack. "There's a stop sign up here!"

I saw the Escalade blow through the sign with a squealing right and continue up the next street at full throttle. I looked over my left shoulder but couldn't see anything but the forest for the trees. We were committed, and I only hoped that our luck would hold as I kept the pedal to the classic metal.

I had guessed we'd pushed our luck about as far as it would go when I saw the brand-spanking-new Grand Cherokee pulling the two-bay horse trailer just as we got to Chamounix Drive. I cut the wheel, and we dropped off the road, easily outrunning the laboring Jeep and jumping the street. We missed an oncoming Volvo station wagon in the other lane, slid into the gravel approach to the stables, and clipped the sign as everybody blew their horns. I saw the Jeep turn into the stables as we renegotiated the asphalt and straightened into our lane. I looked down the road ahead of us but could see nothing.

"I cannot believe you just dented Lola."

I ignored him and slowed, asking over my shoulder. "Where does this go?"

She slid the mechanism back on the semiautomatic. "It connects with Conshohocken Avenue, turning back where we came from, or down Falls Road and the expressway."

I yelled over the engine and wind noise. "Which way would you go?"

"Expressway!"

We rounded the corner, drove behind a large mansion, and suddenly the point became moot. There were large sawhorses across the road that effectively blocked entry and declared in large black and orange letters, ROAD CLOSED DUE TO CONSTRUCTION.

I hit the brakes, and we all looked at each other. Vic gestured with her chin. "Go on ahead around the circle and back down."

I followed her directions and continued around and back onto the drive, where we could see straight down Chamounix. There was no Escalade. She gestured to the right, where an unlabeled road disappeared into the trees. "There."

I made the turn and hit the throttle again. "Where does it go?"

"Nowhere. It dead-ends in about a quarter mile."

I made a sweeping turn and looked down at a pastoral idyll. I could see the Cadillac backing up with the beginning of a three-point turn at the end of the road. I hit the gas and barreled down the two-lane drive with no name, rapidly coming up on the black Caddy. He finished the turn and whipped the big vehicle straight at us. My nerve stayed steady as we approached each other at a climbing sixty.

Henry grabbed the dash. "What if it is not William White Eyes?"

Almost in answer, I felt and saw two things: the tinted side window on the Caddy was down and something was being thrust between the side-view mirror and the windshield. At the same time, I felt Vic rise and shoot just as the tick-tock compressed fire of a fully automatic weapon blistered the surface of the road in front of us and ripped its way up the front of the Thunderbird.

I veered to the right as the windshield exploded, and I tried to yank Vic down by her leather jacket. The return fire of the big Colt had struck home, and I watched as the heavy slugs bit into the hood, windshield, and door of the Escalade as it rushed by us and glanced off the side of the T-bird.

I hit the brakes and turned the wheel, stretching our momentum into a sliding turn, but at least two of the tires were flat, and we warbled to a stop; the Escalade was about fifty yards back down the road. I threw the door open and pushed off from the side of the car. I'm not sure what I thought I was going to do without a sidearm, but I figured I'd think of something when I got there. I heard Dog barking and coming up fast behind me.

In the reflection of the Cadillac's side mirror I could see someone frantically attempting to do something and desperately hoped that he wasn't about to reload. I got about halfway there when Dog overtook me, and I yelled at him to come.

The man in the Cadillac turned, roared the motor, sprayed grass and turf as he reached the curve, and was gone. I slowed to a stop and stood there in the middle of the road with the spent shells of the 9 mm scattered across the pavement. I made a few silent vows to myself as my jaw muscles clenched and stretched at the sutures.

Toy Diaz. Had to be.

I placed my hands on my knees and attempted to catch my breath as Dog came over and stuck his nose in my face. My sides were killing me as I made the slow walk back to the T-Bird. I was dizzy, and I was sweating, and it seemed very hot as I looked up at the big convertible, which was stretched across the road. Henry was in the back, and I picked up my pace. There was blood on the white leather of the cavernous seat, a lot of blood.

Henry had pulled her down and had cradled her head while applying pressure to the wound with his shirt. One of the slugs from the assault rifle had caught her in the side, just under the arm at the oblique muscles. It was hard to say where else the slug had gone. I leaned in and looked at her tarnished gold eyes, which were already glazing with shock. She raised a blood-coated hand and smiled. "Stop being weird."

# 15

It was as bad as it looked and maybe a little worse. The 9 mm slug had taken a hard left where her love handle would have been if she'd had one, and a second had clipped her just above the collarbone and had taken a bit of the shoulder blade with it. My attempts at filling the available beds at the Hospital of the University of Pennsylvania had not gone unnoticed, and Rissman had asked if I wanted all my people in one wing. I noted that it'd be convenient.

I called the Moretti family, although Vic had told me not to, and sat down in the hallway to await the onslaught. Chavez had taken our statements; he said that Asa Katz would be here momentarily but that Gowder was still being queried about the Shankar DuVall shooting.

"How's that going?"

He shrugged and slipped the papers into his aluminum clipboard. "I'd put it down as a service to society, but you never know."

Henry said he had a few loose ends to tie up and that he'd be back in a couple of hours. I apologized for getting dents and bullet holes in Lola, but he didn't say anything. He took Dog, and I figured I was in deep trouble.

I went up to Cady's to wait for Vic to get out of surgery and found Jo Fitzpatrick sitting in a chair by my daughter's bed. Jo was incognito in jeans, a worn pair of rough-out boots, and a weathered Carhartt coat that looked familiar. They were deep in the throes of a one-sided conversation concerning the case of the Atlantic City company that had attempted to do a little under-the-table trading. Evidently the case had been transferred to Jo, and she was getting Cady up to speed, even if all my daughter could do was look at her while she talked and occasionally squeeze her hand. It was hard to breathe when I went into that room.

"What happened to you?"

I had a tendency to forget what I looked like as of late. "I thought I might blend in better if I had a few more bandages." She looked at me doubtfully as I stepped to the other side of the bed and reached out to hold Cady's other hand. "How is she?" Cady squeezed back, and I watched as her eyes slowly tracked from Jo to me. I sighed and listened to my breath rattle as she squeezed my hand again.

"She's looking much better, don't you think?"

"Yep."

She waited a few moments before speaking again. "I had a little time this morning and thought I'd come over and help out."

"Thank you." I kept my eyes on Cady's, but hers had closed. I gently slipped my hand away. "Jo, do you mind if I ask you a question?"

It was a slow response. "I guess not."

"What would you say your firm's position is toward Cady?"

"I'm not sure I understand."

I swallowed. "I'm thinking of taking her back to Wyoming and, without the ability to consult with her in all this . . ."

She stepped a little forward and into my line of sight, and I could see from the general attitude of her body that she was more relaxed. "Cady is one of the best lawyers in the firm." Her voice broke a little, and I could hear the wind outside the windows and in between her words. "David Calder, the senior partner, called me up to his office yesterday morning to make sure that we were doing everything we could for her." When I glanced over, tears were on her face. "He said that no matter what it took, and no matter how long it took, we were to be committed to Cady's recovery and her continued position in the firm."

I nodded and looked back at my daughter. "Then I think we're going to go back home."

"To Wyoming?" She sounded a little relieved.

"As soon as she can." I squeezed Cady's hand again, but she was asleep. "I've got a few things to attend to and so does she." I smiled and looked at the young lawyer on the other side of the bed. "Can I ask you another question?"

She smiled back and wiped her face. "Sure."

I waited. "Who assigns the pro bono cases at the firm?"

She coughed and swallowed, wiped her eyes some more, and then cleared her throat, gesturing with her hand to explain the time it took to respond. "That would be me."

I nodded. "You."

"Yes."

I nodded some more. "So, you assigned William White Eyes to Cady?"

She stayed steady. "Yes."

"Jo . . ." I smiled again, just to let her know I wasn't going to jump over the bed and handcuff her, and went and sat in one of the chairs beside the window. I thought that maybe if I sat down it would be easier for her. I picked up the book on the public art of Philadelphia. She didn't move, and her back was to me. "The way I figure it, Osgood pressured Devon . . ."

"I told them to not let Cady find out about any of this stuff."

I kept looking at the book. It was an old trick, but she didn't fall for it and stayed as she was. "Well, it looks like you were right." I waited, but she stayed silent. I flipped through the book to the section on northwest Fairmount Park. "Where's Riley Elizabeth?"

At that, she turned and looked at me. "What?"

"I was wondering where your daughter is?" I studied the book as she crossed to the other chair, sat, and folded her hands in her lap.

"My mother is taking care of her." She turned her head and looked out the window.

I took a deep breath and let out with a heavy exhale, attempting some comic relief but probably sounding more like a tire going flat. "William White Eyes wasn't supposed to get out."

"No."

I looked at Cady. "Leave it to 'The Greatest Legal Mind of Our Time' to mess up the appeal." I laughed, and Jo turned to look at me. Her hair hung back on her shoulder, providing a stark contrast to the cream-colored luster of her skin. I smiled at her. "You want to hear something funny?" She waited. "I partially believe you." I thought about it. "It's pretty obvious that when Billy Carlisle went native he became a problem, but when he met Cady, he took Devon and Vince Osgood into the liability column with him. I might be a problem for Diaz, but nothing on the level of Devon Conliffe, Vince Osgood, and, worse yet, the now named William White Eyes." I continued to look at Cady and interrogate Jo Fitzpatrick. "Did you know that Osgood was in business with Toy Diaz and Shankar DuVall?"

"No."

I went back to the book and read about a statue near the Rex Avenue Bridge on Forbidden Drive, of all places. She didn't say anything more. "What more do you know about William White Eyes?"

"Nothing."

She had waited just a moment too long, so I gave her one more opportunity. "You're sure?" I listened as the severity of all the things I had told her settled like a sedimentary layer of criminal activity, making us both feel unclean. Her lips trembled and her mouth opened, but it took a long time for no words to come out. I looked at the waning afternoon sun as she quietly picked up her things and left.

I studied Cady and sighed, thinking about the photograph in her office of her and Jo. "The tiniest reason I have for wanting you back is so you can help me figure out all of this."

Katz was coming out of the elevator when I got to it, so he did an about-face and followed me in as I pushed the button and stuffed the book on Philadelphia statuary under my arm.

"You might want to skip the third floor."

"I take it the entire Moretti family is in attendance?"

"En tutti."

He adjusted the glasses on his nose with an index finger. He looked at me for a while longer, but I continued to stare at the numbers as the elevator slowly descended to three. "So, it was Toy Diaz?"

"Yes."

I felt suddenly tired. "Let me guess; the Escalade was stolen."

"Off a lot in Wynnewood."

"Where's that?"

He was distracted and looking at his notes. "The Main Line; Toy has expensive tastes."

"Is that near the area of the Medicine Man statue?"

"Not particularly." He looked up at me. "You have a theory?"

I thought about it. "Not anymore."

"Tell me anyway."

"We know that Diaz is looking for William White Eyes."

"Yes."

"With all the notes, it's pretty obvious that White Eyes was tailing me for Cady's sake, but with Osgood dead I think he realized that he was the one who needed protection and so has come to the conclusion that we're the only thing standing between him and a Salvadorian necktie."

"Okay."

"The Indian statues are the key, and the trick is knowing which one is next."

He closed his notebook and grimaced, leaning against the elevator wall. "That may be a little difficult."

"Maybe not; there's only one left." I opened the book from Cady's library and held it for him to see as the door to the third floor opened.

Lena was standing alone in the hallway as we stepped out of the elevator. I handed Katz the book and reached an arm out to her. She looked up and smiled sadly. She didn't take my hand. "I hear she's doing all right?"

"Yes, thank God." Her smile weakened. "She was asking for you, so you better go in."

I stood there, glancing down at my scuffed-up boots. "I'm sorry."

I listened to her take a deep breath and watched as she folded her arms across her chest and looked past me. "Hello, Asa. You might want to stay out here with me." There was no edge in her voice, just fatigue. I glanced back at Katz, who quietly closed the book, looked at her through the split lenses, and put a hand out to touch hers.

I stood there for a moment more and then continued down the hallway. I opened the door and stepped into the room. Vic the Father and a group of young men were gathered around the bed; there was a younger version of Victor, a variation on Alphonse, one that didn't look like anybody in the family that I knew, and Michael, who glanced up and smiled.

"How ya doin', Sheriff?"

"I'm okay. Thank you, Michael."

She was watching me, but they had her trussed up pretty good, so I felt confident in going the rest of the way into the room. I looked at her father and brothers, then back to Vic, who smiled and raised her hand to me. "Where the fuck have you been?"

By the time Asa and I got outside, Henry was valet parking a dark green, one-ton duelie, fortified with grille guards and an extensive roll bar and fifth wheel. He took the keys back from the valet guy when he saw us.

I gestured toward the giant vehicle. "What is this?"

"We needed a rental car."

I looked at the behemoth. "Why didn't you just get a Bluebird bus?"

"If you are going to drive like Patton, then we need a tank." He waved at Katz and then walked around as I went to the passenger-side door. "Besides, I am thinking that we may have to haul something."

"Where did you rent this?"

He smiled across the broad scoop that straddled the hood. "I did not rent it, your insurance did."

Great.

I stopped and invited Katz along, but he said he'd check in with Gowder at the inquest and meet us at the Valley Green Inn at the Wissahickon ravine in Fairmount Park at six. He handed me back the book.

I climbed in and shut the door; it sounded like a vault closing. I reached back and scratched behind Dog's ear, then turned and fastened my seat belt. Henry studied me; I knew I'd fooled everybody up to now, but he knew me too well, perhaps better than I knew myself, and was unlikely to let my mood go without comment. "Uh-oh."

"Drive."

The uh-oh was all I got. He hit the starter, and the truck clattered to life. "I have been in touch with the Delaware Indian Association, and they . . ."

"The what?"

He turned and looked at me, better than matching my stone face. "The Delaware Indian Association."

"What the hell is that?"

"It is a rural institute for the advancement of Indian resources in an urban environment. I spoke with a nice young woman there, a Felicia Sparrowhawk, who said that the last contact they had with William White Eyes was when they arranged for a part-time job for him at the Chamounix Stables in . . ."

"Fairmount Park."

"Yes." He navigated the on-ramp for the Schuylkill Expressway alongside 30th Street Station and joined the traffic headed west. "It was a probation program between prison stints."

"That would fit for numerous reasons."

"Yes." I watched as he glided the big, more-than-utility vehicle through traffic like a tiger shark swimming lazily through a school of smaller fish. "There is a contact at the stables, but Ms. Sparrowhawk didn't have her name. She thought, by the sound of things, that there might have been something more there than an employer/employee relationship."

I nodded and watched the traffic skitter out of his way; Henry drove smoothly, if slowly, navigating to the exit at the right. I thought of a Gladwyne cowgirl, and how it was all too convenient. "I already know who it is."

He glanced at me and then nodded. "As do I, but there is more." He slipped a hand in the inside pocket of his black leather blazer and handed me another note, identical to the ones we had received before. "I returned to the Medicine Man, in hopes that with Toý Diaz even momentarily inconvenienced, William White Eyes may have returned with a note."

I opened the tiny envelope and read BIG CHIEF.

"You know where this is?" I opened the book in my lap so that he could see the illustration at the upper lefthand corner.

He glanced down and nodded. "Close?"

"Very."

"Tonight?"

"Yep."

"How is Vic?"

"Good." I had done pretty well up until now, but I could feel the numbness returning to my face and the stillness to my hands. I slowly unwrapped the bandages from my left, bent the aluminum protector back from my index finger, and dropped it on the floor of the big truck.

He glanced over. "What are you doing?"

"Trigger finger."

"You are right-handed."

I watched the trees. "I want both."

---

He took the exit, and we drove the same ravines that we had earlier. "The woman teaches horseback riding to urban underprivileged children on Saturday afternoons."

I nodded. "The Saint of Fairmount Park."

He shook his head and studied me, his eyes pleading with me to behave. "Maybe it would be best if you were to wait in the truck, since you are angry with the world?"

I folded my arms and looked out the side window at all of the trees. In Wyoming, the silver-green aspens would be in leaf, quivering in the breeze like pinwheels. "I'm not mad at the world. I'm angry with William White Eyes for taking us on this wild goose chase, but the distiller's choice, single-cask, limited edition, pissed-off I am holding in reserve is for Toy Diaz."

"Let us try and remember that, shall we?" He pulled into the Chamounix Stables, and we both looked at the sign I had knocked over earlier, still lying in the barrow ditch.

When we got out of the truck, Dog followed, and Henry and I put the sign back against the pristine and manicured garden that led alongside the path to the stables a short walk away.

We each propped a boot on the first rung of the corral, leaned our folded arms across the top of the fence like bookends, and watched as a girl in pigtails who looked like she was in grade school made a strained and determined attempt at keeping her tiny bottom on a Western saddle. A young woman in her early thirties held the lead and twitched the bay's flanks, keeping the fat mare moving at a regulated pace. The horsewoman looked as though she would have been more at home in Wyoming, and just looking at her brought a longing in my chest. She wore a battered, black quarter horse 60 hat, and a thick brunette braid uncoiled down the back of her sand-colored Carhartt barn coat. When she turned I could see a jacquard silk scarf at her neck, the denim, snap-front shirt, Western belt, and shotgun chaps.

Jo Fitzpatrick.

I felt a little of the preparatory anger fade with the blue of her eyes as she glanced at Henry and me. On the next go-round, she tilted her head and nodded toward the stables. "I'll be done in just a minute."

We returned to the main path and entered the barn through a large opening pointed toward the road. It was a pretty good-sized place, with two dozen stalls running the length of the slate flooring. There were about a dozen horse heads that turned and looked at us as we entered, one nickering loudly from only a few stalls down.

Dog and I tagged along behind the Bear as he went straight to the animal that had spoken to him, a large paint, patchworked like clouds of cream in iced coffee. I pulled up short and looked at the animal, Dog stopping alongside. The big girl swung her head from Henry and looked directly at me, letting loose with a lung-vibrating whinny. Henry followed the horse's gaze and smiled. "She knows you."

"Uh huh."

"Come say hello."

I walked toward her; the small, brass nameplate read CREAMPUFF. She looked exactly like the paint in my dreams. She stuck a prehensile and exploratory nose toward me, and I could see her powerful withers as the large brown eyes blinked. I reached a hand out, palm down, and let her sniff me, rubbing her lips on my knuckles. I pushed a forelock from her face, and Dog nudged my pant leg: jealous.

Henry had walked to the center of the stables to another opening at the side that led toward the corral where we had first seen Jo. There was a large tack shed adjacent to the passageway and next door, a makeshift office. I stopped petting the mare and walked to the doorway as Henry and Dog continued toward the corral. Dog stopped to look back at me when he realized that I was not following. The paint whinnied again, and I looked at her.

Henry spoke. "What?"

"Wait a minute." I entered the office and pulled the latest note from William White Eyes out of my pocket, extracted it from the envelope, and threaded it into the mechanical typewriter that squatted on the plywood desk.

I struck the O key; it had the dropout.

I stood there, until I could hear a horse approaching at a relaxed pace on the stables' slate floor. I slowly stuffed the card and envelope back in my pocket and followed after Henry and Dog. Jo Fitzpatrick was leading the little girl in from the corral. She nodded at Henry as he looked at the smiling child, riding tall in the saddle; she and Henry were eye to eye.

"I hope we did not cut your ride short?"

"You did." The little girl nodded, and her pigtails bounced up and down.

"She'd stay out there all day if I let her." Jo glanced at the aspiring equestrian. "She likes the riding part, but not the work afterward part."

Henry rumbled back. "Who does?"

Joanne led the horse past Henry around a corner and to the left. We followed them to the last stall, and I watched as Henry lifted the little girl from the saddle and placed her on the ground as Jo unhooked the cinch and removed the saddle, placing it on a stand in the walkway. The Bear put his hands on his knees and looked at the child as she spoke to him.

"Are you an Indian?"

He raised a palm to her and spoke with all the seriousness of a Senate subcommittee. "How."

She giggled and pointed toward me. "Is he a cowboy?"

The Bear regarded me. "Sort of."

The little girl motioned toward the horse. "This is Thunderbolt."

Henry nodded and glanced at the overweight mare with an appraising eye. "Looks fast."

She nodded enthusiastically. "He is."

"She." Jo removed the bridle and the blanket and dragged a set of steps beside the horse, now munching noisily on a feeder full of alfalfa cubes. She handed a couple of brushes to the girl. "Get to work, Juanita."

She led us toward the tack room/office but changed her mind and took us out toward the corral. "It's so nice; I hate to be inside on a day like today."

"I agree."

I glanced back into the stables. "Is she going to be all right in there alone?"

Jo snorted a short laugh, the first sign of humor I'd seen in her today. "Unless Thunderbolt eats her."

We pulled up at the fence, and she hooked a boot heel in the lowest rung, trailed her arms across the top, and looked at the two of us. She seemed more relaxed than in the firm's offices or in Cady's hospital room, our presence notwithstanding, so I decided just to ask what I had suspected. "Osgood is the father of your child?"

She stayed looking at me. "Was." I nodded, but it took

her a while to get going. "He wasn't a bad guy, not in the beginning." I nodded some more and looked at my boots. "Needless to say, it didn't work out. He provided monetary support, but that was about it." She pushed her hat back and pulled at a wayward lock behind her ear. "Oz found out about Devon's drug problem and, when he left our firm, he got him the position with Hunt and Driscoll, essentially blackmailing Devon into money laundering. Devon was always delicate but, with the escalated drug use, he was threatening to cave on the whole deal. I'm sure that Oz didn't kill Devon himself, but I'm just as sure that he had it done."

I looked at the beautiful young woman and thought of her beautiful young child, and I made the mental note that the damage would stop here, but I needed information. "William White Eyes. I don't have time for any more fictions; if you care about keeping him alive, you need to tell me everything you know. Now." I fished the note from my pocket and held it up.

She looked at it and looked away, the tears collecting at the corners of her eyes. "Jesus . . ."

"He's staying here?"

She finally spoke again. "Off and on. There's a gardener's shed on the trail."

I stuffed the note back in my pocket. "Is he there now?"

"No."

I let it settle for a moment. "That was a pretty quick answer."

She shrugged and looked resigned. "You're welcome to look, but there's nothing up there. He borrowed a horse this morning and said that he wouldn't be back." She turned away again.

I looked at Henry. "A horse?"

"Yes."

That was a twist I hadn't counted on, William White Eyes riding off into the Fairmount Park sunset. "He didn't say where he was going?"

"No."

I stood there and watched as the tumblers fell into place. "You're both from Gladwyne."

She exhaled a soft breath of amusement. "We grew up across the street from each other."

Katz and Gowder were seated at a table on the Valley Green Inn's porch, which was located in yet another part of Fairmount Park, and were sipping iced tea as Henry and I walked up the steps and sat in the two empty seats next to the detectives. "How'd the inquest go?"

Gowder smiled and raised his glass. "Exonerated." He pulled back his suit jacket, revealing both the badge at his belt and the .40 at his armpit.

"Congratulations. I would've hated for you to lose your job by saving my life."

Katz had a large map of Fairmount Park laid out on the table, and I had my book with the photograph. Gowder leaned in and looked at the red spot where Katz now pointed. "This is our boy, huh?"

"Just below Rex Avenue."

I looked at the map. "The next road north?"

"Yes, but it's not as easy as that. There are access points here at Valley Green, Rex, Thomas Mill Road, and Wises Mill Road on the other side."

I studied the light green section of the map where Wissahickon Creek curled its way north and west. "What's this dotted line along the creek?"

Katz adjusted his glasses and placed his chin on his fist. "That's Forbidden Drive."

I examined the relatively innocent-looking road. "Why Forbidden Drive?"

Gowder and he both looked at me like I was an idiot. Katz spoke slowly, just to make sure I got it. "Because you're Forbidden to Drive on it."

"Oh."

Henry and I looked at each other; we were thinking the same thing.

# 16

The Indian chief Tedyuscung was neither a chief nor an Indian, but he sat as a memorial to the Lenape who first occupied the area anyway. This particular rendition of Chief Tedyuscung was actually the third to occupy the rock overlooking Wissahickon Creek. He was over fifteen feet tall, with a hand at his brow to shield the sun so that he could watch the departure of his people who had seen the white man's writing on the wall and had moved to Pennsylvania's Wyoming Valley, of all places. His nose was broken and his peace pipe was missing, but the nobility of royalty was still there. Lesser beings had made their pathetic bids for immortality by scratching their initials in his sides, but he forever looks west and does not move. I took a tip from his book, and neither did I.

I had picked a small outcropping of rocks to the west of the chief and was huddled at the base of a black oak with the rain dripping off my hat and into my lap. The showers had started around ten thirty and continued to drench the place for the next hour and a half. I had confiscated a hunting poncho from Cady's place, one that I had given her years ago, and it was doing a pretty good job of keeping me dry except for my boots, which were beginning to squeak whenever I moved my toes.

It was dark, but I could still make out the profile of the big chief, and it wasn't hard to see Henry in him, just as I'd seen my friend in the Indian statue at Logan Circle.

The giant Indian was looking toward me but beyond to a place where I hoped to return. I watched as the sheets of rain fell between us, and I allowed my eyes to adjust for the thousandth time to the momentary blindness caused by the brief flashes of lightning and my ears to recover yet again from the thunder.

The outcropping provided a clear view of the area, of the trail leading up from below, the cut-off to the statue, and Tedyuscung himself. Other than the leaves, which blustered with the periodic wind, the only movement had been when I had stretched my legs from underneath the poncho more than an hour earlier, an event I had now convinced myself had blown my concealed observation.

I had been here for four hours, but William White Eyes or, more importantly, Toy Diaz, may have been here for five.

I thought about the course of events that had led me to wait for an informant and a killer in this small, tree-shrouded ravine in Fairmount Park as it crept up on midnight. Other than the obvious obligations of the law and its enforcement, I was here because I was attempting to save William White Eyes's life in repayment for his saving Cady. I was here because of Jo Fitzpatrick and Riley, and because of the two men sitting in a Fairmount Park Services truck parked at the barricade near Valley Green Avenue, one of whom had saved my life in a bus station only two nights before. And I was here because of Toy Diaz and what he had done to Cady, Vic, Osgood, and Devon.

Somewhere in the distance, the synchronic circles of our pasts had tripped a domino, and the steady whirr had grown till it now drowned with the roar of contingency. I knew he would show as surely as the dark rain was falling around me, just as my aching legs knew they would receive no quick relief.

I listened as the unsteady clop of horse's hooves made their way up the broken trail behind me. At first I thought it must be Henry, who had grown tired of waiting, but the Bear's patience could rival that of the marble chief, so I assumed it was finally William White Eyes. The sound was faint at first but slowly grew with each step until the horse stopped on the trail to my left, only a dozen feet away.

I listened as his mount situated a hoof forward for an even plant and expulsed a deep exhale into the moist, cool air. The vapor from its breath clouded for a moment in my peripheral vision and then misted in long trails with the prevailing eastward wind.

I had shallowed my breathing so that it didn't show in the cold of the spring storm and, with the appearance of the horseman, I was lucky I remembered to breathe at all. I listened as his weight shifted on the horse's back and looked at him as he searched the surrounding area. After a moment, he nudged the bay forward, and they continued around the appropriately shaped horseshoe corner of the trail and approached the Indian statue. William White Eyes wasn't wearing a poncho or a jacket; he was naked, except for a loincloth that appeared to be perilously attached around his hips, and his body, as well as that of his horse, was painted with the multicolored geometric patterns and red streaks of a Dog Soldier.

William glowed in the limited light of the hillside, and if Toy Diaz was out there, there was no way he could miss him. I watched as the pale young man, who was decorated for battle, stopped, pivoted, and looked around; he didn't see me.

It was possible that Diaz was not there, that the evening would end with me convincing William White Eyes to fill in all the gaps in the story and with the police rounding up Toy Diaz in a nonviolent interaction, so that I could take my daughter, my friend, my deputy, and my dog and go home to Wyoming. It was possible, but not likely.

Diaz had displayed a knack for cleaning up the loose ends of his operations by the most expedient and merciless means. You didn't get where he got by sending thank-you cards; you got there by being the biggest, meanest son-of-a-bitch in the Valley of the Shadow of Death, or on Forbidden Drive, as the case may be.

William rose, threw a leg off, and started to slide to the ground on the opposite side of the horse. I scanned the hillside but nothing moved. I could continue waiting, but I needed to get him out of here.

I stood on stiff legs and teetered there for a moment; William had stopped his dismount and stayed on the horse; he was still looking at the statue. I couldn't lose him this time. I stood there, sure that the crunching of my knees and the rustling of the stiff, plastic poncho would turn his attention toward me, but the constant washing sound of the rain against the trees must have drowned me out. The horse had heard me and was looking directly where I stood, his far eye circled with red paint. I waited, scanning the hill to see if there might be any other response from anywhere else.

Nothing.

I took half a step to the edge of the rock ledge and looked at him. I was now a good fifty feet distant, and I didn't want to spook him; he was on horseback, and I'd never catch him. "William?" He turned in the saddle, and

I could see the line of his profile in the flash of lightning to my right. "It's Walt."

This time he heard me. "Sheriff?"

"Yep." I stood there waiting as he turned the gelding toward me.

"I guess you got my note?"

"I did."

He looked around. "You're alone?"

I cocked my head. "Pretty much."

He nodded and even in the distance, I could see him gnawing on his lip. "Devon hurt her."

"I know." I circled around in the direction he'd taken to get to the statue. "And I owe you an awfully big favor for getting help."

He laid the reins to one side as the horse turned toward the trail. "I didn't kill him."

I waited. "I know that, too."

The horse shifted his weight, so I stopped. He watched me for a moment and then asked, "How is she?"

"Improving." I started to take another step and then thought better of it. "Her eyes are open, and she's responding."

He nodded and shifted the reins. "That's good news." I waited as he watched me. "I guess this all seems kind of weird to you, huh?"

I figured, why lie? "A little." I gambled on another step and, in three more, I could block his retreat to the path, at least as well as a man afoot can block a man on horseback.

He cleared his throat. "I'm more at home here in the park than in the city."

"I was hoping that would be the case."

He shifted his weight on the gelding as it planted a hoof in anticipation, the circled eye still on me. If William

White Eyes didn't know what I was doing, the horse did. "I don't know how much you know about me."

"Quite a bit, actually."

He nodded and looked down at his hands. "Cady told you?"

"No, I've made a case study of you lately."

He nodded some more. "I wasn't sure what I should do next, but I thought you might have some ideas."

"Well, the cops want you, but they don't want to kill you." I took another step. "It seems to me you've got an awful lot of information they need."

"Toy Diaz's account numbers."

"Yep." I took the final step, William watching as I stood at the trail. He turned the bay toward the stone stairs and retainer wall where I could look him in the eye. "I'm not sure if Mr. Diaz is around, but I wouldn't be surprised. We need to get you out of here."

"I'm the safest I could be, here."

"No, you're not." I looked around, acutely aware that we were not out of the proverbial woods. "I think they've been all over this park looking for you. I think the sooner we join my friends at the bottom of the hill the better." I stepped back to block him from taking the trail behind us and gestured to the path below. I stepped around the bay and looked up at him. "I'll go first; just in case." I cleared the .45 from the poncho and looked ahead, where I hoped, if there was trouble, was the direction from which it would come.

We zigged the first part and had just begun our zag when I thought I saw movement at the next curve. I stopped and studied the shadows of the trees in the black of the rain-soaked ravine, raised my arm, and stopped the horse on the rounded stones of the trail. "Whoa . . ." The bay halted and let out with a sigh that pressed hot breath on the exposed back of my neck.

I had just about convinced myself that it was nothing when I thought I heard a sound like something moving. It was not discernable, just a sound that sounded different from the rest. I waited and then motioned for William to stay put.

I eased down the path with the big Colt pointed in the direction of the movement and sound. Henry wouldn't have left his position at the base of the hill, and the police were all stationed at the vehicle entrances of Wissahickon Park.

I slipped a little on one of the larger rocks and caught myself before I landed on my ass or shot myself in the foot. I waited and then carefully approached what still looked like a tree. It was a tree.

I shrugged and turned back, walking with the .45 to my side. There was no reason for me to climb the hill again, so I motioned for William to come down. He nudged the horse in response, and we were lucky he did, because that's when the first series of shots ripped through the woods like the tearing of the muscles in your chest.

The muzzle flash came from the trees above. Toy Diaz must have followed us. He made the mistake most civilians make with an automatic weapon—his shots were high and climbed—and, once again, if William White Eyes didn't know what to do, the bay did; it ran like hell and straight toward me.

I threw myself to the right and landed against one of the retainer walls as the bay passed me, with William unhurt and holding on to the horse's mane and riding low against his withers. Another volley from the automatic dotted an unconnected blaze after him, kicking rock shards and sparks as it went. I rolled up on one shoulder and fired four rounds into the darkness behind us. There were no answering shots.

Nothing.

I stood and listened and hoped that William and his horse had arrived at the bottom where Henry could corral them. I kept the .45 pointed up the hill and hustled into the type of situation I despised.

I ran up the path to the spot where I thought the shooter must have been. There were shell casings scattered across the trail and a muddy slick where someone had slipped and fallen. There was a dark liquid on the rocks. I smeared it with my hand and held it to my nose: blood.

I looked up and down, still seeing nothing. I was at the end of a turn and I couldn't see to the next segment of the trail through the foliage, but I knew it was there. Taking the direct route was a calculated risk, but the only hope I had was to cut the distance to William White Eyes before Diaz cut that same distance. I thundered over the hill and threw my arms up to block at least some of the branches from blinding me as I went, half-running, half-falling with all my momentum. I was top-heavy and could feel the weight of my upper body and arms pulling me forward so I flipped the safety back on the Colt before I toppled onto the path below.

I struggled to my side, lifted up on one arm, and watched as a dark figure turned the corner ahead of me and disappeared. I could hear the clatter of horse's hooves on the trail below; I was still a distant third.

I heaved myself up and stumbled forward in another straight-line attempt at interception, feeling as if I'd run the gauntlet of tribal initiation. I finally gave up on protecting my face and pummeled my way forward like some refrigerator catapulting its way down the hillside after being thrown from above. I raised my head but couldn't see anything.

The sounds of the chase were still below me. The cutback was not as lengthy this time, and I was able to arrive at the ditch alongside the main trail as Henry charged from the rock-walled path to the left; he was on one of the paints and was holding the reins of the bigger of the two horses for me.

"Where are they?!"

"They did not come this way." He wheeled his horse toward the bridge farther down the hill. Mine balked and crow-hopped toward Henry as I holstered the .45 and attempted to get a hand on the horn, but the Bear held the leather straps steady as I mounted.

In the best of situations, I am only a competent horseman and, after being beaten half to death by every tree in eastern Pennsylvania, I was lucky I even knew which way to face. Henry was already gone, and I felt the lurch of gathered horse muscles as the big mare shot from under me and surged toward the arch of the stone bridge. I grasped my hands around the leads and bounced forward, almost coming unseated at the first strike of her gallop. She was very fast, and she seemed to know where we were going. I assumed she would follow Henry, and the only thing I needed to do was remain neutral and allow her to take us where we needed to go.

Hi-yo, Creampuff.

The trail split in two directions on the other side of the bridge; the Bear had reined in his mount and was standing in the stirrups; he looked west and then east as my paint slid to a stop alongside him. I settled my rear into the seat and tucked my heels down for a better ride. "Well, hell . . ."

He actually smiled as he turned his paint to the left, and they blew down the incline to the east, easy in the saddle and melding together in a rhythm of man and horse. Creampuff started to follow him, but I wrapped the reins and veered her to the right. I broke west and thundered down the ramp to Forbidden Drive as the rain continued to pummel me. The big paint's gallop was steady and, after I got centered, I could see further down the trail to the periodic illumination of the dusk-to-dawn lamps, which were momentarily faked to darkness by the flashes of lightning.

I dug in my heels and allowed the mare to have her head; in an instant I was around the far turn. I heard the terrible sound of the automatic again, like fibers being torn in cloth.

I could feel Creampuff reaching out and grabbing the rough surface of the path and throwing it behind us. I leaned with her and missed a sign by inches, almost spilling the two of us on the rain-slick trail. Just around the corner, I could see that something was down and that Toy Diaz was warily approaching it. It was a horse, kicking and screaming in the pathway, with William White Eyes trapped underneath.

The drug dealer could not catch a galloping horse, but the 9 mm had.

The fickle streetlights chose that moment to burst into full illumination, and there was a sharpness to the edges of everything, a glistening, as Diaz stood to the side of the fallen horse, careful to stay clear of its kicking legs. My paint's mean streak and mine kicked in in a last-second attempt to save William's life, and I felt the surge as Diaz lifted his arm.

It's possible that he was so concentrated on the action that he didn't hear me or that the echo of thunder in the ravine had deafened us all. Either way, by the time he heard us, it was too late. The big paint didn't slow; she didn't veer or misdirect her momentum. She simply ran right over Toy Diaz.

He must have pulled the trigger on impact, but the rounds flailed emptily into the hillside to the left. There was a momentary muffling of the horse's hooves, and her balance shifted just a little as I reined in and veered from the injured horse lying on the gravel.

I thought I would come unseated when the paint reared and pivoted to the left. She stiffened her legs and backed away from the smell of blood and the screaming of the other horse. She wanted nothing to do with the scene in front of us and backed away into the trees along the creek bank.

She reared again, and this time I wasn't as lucky. I fell against the saplings that lined the Wissahickon as she went over backward, slipping on the wet gravel and falling to the side. I clawed my way to the left as she slid right and rolled. We both made it to the flat area of the trail at the same time, whereupon she turned left and disappeared away from the vehicle approaching from the direction we'd been heading, its revolving yellow emergencies strobe-lighting the shiny surface of the pebbled path.

I pulled the .45 from the small of my back and clicked off the safety.

Diaz had been thrown to the side of the trail; he still lay there, face down and unmoving. The shoebox-shaped automatic was there as well, where the horse and I had struck him, far out of reach even for a whole man.

I approached carefully with the Colt pointed at his

head. He didn't move, so I kneeled beside him, and placed my fingers along his wrist. There was a pulse.

His clothes were soaked from fording the stream, and he wore a hooded black leather jacket that was water-logged and must've weighed a ton. I put his hand back on the pavement and lowered myself enough to look at his face. He was, indeed, the small man I'd seen with Osgood at the shooting range. He might have been handsome then, but he had struck the pavement like a cue ball, and his head seemed lopsided under the hood of his coat. The leather was torn at the shoulder, and he was bleeding from a spot where one of my .45s had clipped him, near a gauze bandage at his throat where Vic must've gotten him before.

He opened his eyes and blinked but said nothing as I watched him. My voice came out in a heavy rasp. "Don't move."

I felt the blood rushing to my head and the throb of my own pulse as a large, white truck pulled up. The door read FAIRMOUNT PARK COMMISSION, but the two men who got out weren't carrying rakes.

"Are you all right?" I stared at the little red dots. "Sher-iff, you all right?"

I converted the chill in my back to a nod. "Yep."

Katz looked past me, and Gowder continued on to Toy Diaz. I stumbled a little as I walked away, stopped, and just stood there, breathing and fighting the nausea that rose in the back of my throat. I became aware of a noise in front of me and a screaming that wasn't human.

William White Eyes had disengaged himself, pushing with his good leg, and had dragged himself to a shallow ditch; he was covered in dirt and leaves. His eyes were large as he struggled to rise up on one elbow but, even from a few yards away, I could see that something was broken in him. He slumped back against the ground, groaned, and looked at me as the screaming continued.

I stared at his pale, white body in the stark illumination of the street lamps that had pulsed on again and noticed how all the different colors of his war paint now looked black. I went over and kneeled beside him. "You okay?"

His voice wheezed with effort. "No."

I kept quiet and held on to him till the EMTs arrived and took over.

I walked back up to the path where the gelding still kicked weakly. I kneeled again and placed a hand on the bay's neck beside the Cheyenne medicine sign for wind. The horse attempted to raise its head but let out a rattling gasp and resettled. I counted at least five bullets in the poor animal. My father was a blacksmith and had told me when I was a little boy that the beasts of the field didn't feel pain the way we humans did. I remember not believing him then, and I still didn't.

I could hear the steady clop of hooves on the pathway stones as Henry rode up from behind and, from the sound, I could tell that he had captured my mount. More vehicles arrived, adding blue and red to the already abundant yellow that ran between the trees. I'm sure if it had been daylight, I would have been able to look back up the ravine and seen Chief Tedyuscung with his hand over his brow, looking west, at the mess of things in general. The screaming continued along with the sirens, and something was going to have to pay; that's the way it always was, and it was usually the innocent.

I was cold, and my legs complained at carrying my weight. My eyes didn't seem to want to focus as I pushed my hat back and felt the trapped rain run down my back.

I looked at my hands and watched them shake, and a chill ran through me. I placed my hand back on the bay's neck to steady him and, looking into the eye with the circle around it, spoke to him softly. "Easy . . . Easy boy . . ."

A weight hung in my chest and, before my eyes could completely blur, I raised the Colt and fired.

# EPILOGUE

Two weeks, and I still had the screaming in my head.

I tossed a few more crumbs from my bagel to Mutt and Jeff, who were looking a little thicker than their hundred or so compatriots scattered across the roach-coach area of the Hospital of the University of Pennsylvania. I guess they felt like they'd found good pasture and saw no reason to move on. It was slow going with the finger brace Rissman had put back on me. My ribs still groused every time I took a breath, but everything still hurt a little, so I just ignored it all.

"Are you going to answer my question?"

I looked up and again thought about how much she looked like her daughter. I thought about how seeing women in floral-print summer dresses gave me hope about things in general, and I thought about what she knew, which was probably more than I wanted to admit. "I'm sorry."

Lena took a sip of the coffee she had brought with her. "Toy Diaz?"

"He's a little worse for wear. He's going to have a supervised rehabilitation at Graterford, and it promises to be lengthy since he no longer has his friends in the district attorney's office."

"What about the young woman?"

"Jo Fitzpatrick?"

"Yes."

I tossed the pigeons more crumbs. "By the letter of the law, she didn't do anything wrong." I reached over and picked up the cup of coffee she'd brought for me; it was finally cool enough to drink. "Maybe it just seems like enough people have been punished for this mess. Every mistake she made was because she cared about people or because she cared about her child." Lena nodded, but I don't think her old-world sense of justice was satisfied. I sipped my coffee as she and Mutt and Jeff watched. "I don't know." I slapped my hand on the backpack, containing all my homework from Detectives North. "If Katz and Gowder want to pursue it . . ." I let it trail off, just as I had the investigation.

"I hear William turned state's evidence?"

"Yep, it was as I'd suspected. Vince Osgood and Toy Diaz headed up the operation and, when Billy Carlisle became a bit of a problem, Osgood decided to streamline the operation by retiring him to Graterford. The wildcard was the unscheduled release of William White Eyes. That set a power play into motion between Osgood and Diaz, which meant that one of them had to die." She looked at me over the rim of her coffee cup, the ginger of her eyes in full bloom. "Diaz needed a soldier, and Shankar DuVall fit the bill. The official Academy of the Fine Arts plan was to kill Osgood; DuVall just didn't count on Gowder or Vic."

"Or you." She finished her coffee and decided to give law enforcement a rest. "The Indian abducted my daughter today?"

Vic had been recuperating at Cady's, while I had been spending most of my time at the hospital with my daughter. "Henry said something about Pine Street. Since they're driving back, I think they were taking Dog and going antiquing."

She nodded but couldn't resist more questions. "So the lawyer connection was through Devon Conliffe, and he was responsible for the money laundering?"

I tossed some more bagel to the pigeons. "The tripping point was Cady; she wouldn't play."

"And so Diaz had DuVall throw Devon off the Ben Franklin Bridge?"

"Yep. As Alphonse said, Devon was preparing to turn state's evidence. When Osgood and Diaz found out their boy had all the fortitude of a cheap lawn chair, they decided to start doing a little housecleaning. At least that's what William White Eyes said."

She stretched her legs out and crossed them at the ankles. "How does he know?"

"He was there."

She turned to look at me. "William was on the bridge?"

"Yep. He was tailing Devon to make sure he didn't go back to hurt Cady any more." I thought about it. "I don't think he knew Diaz was going to have Shankar DuVall kill Devon but, when he did, I think it might have sealed the deal on his wavering allegiances."

She watched me, and I watched Mutt and Jeff. "So, was there anybody in this case that didn't deserve to die?"

"Yep." I didn't say anything more but just sat there thinking of a large brown eye with a painted circle around it.

Lena let go of my arm when we got to the hospital valet parking kiosk and swung around to look at me. The dark luster of her hair shone blue in the morning sun, and I noticed that her smile had the same lupine slant as Vic's. The Moretti women smiled like they were going to eat you, and you'd like it. "Dinner? I know a place for pizza."

"I bet you do."

"Bring Henry and the Terror. Michael says he'll stay with Cady."

"I think that might be turning into a situation."

She nodded. "I think you're right."

She examined my finger brace and gently stroked a valentine-red nail across the bruised flesh. I waited a while before I spoke again. "It was you who opened the door at Cady's when . . . Before the reception, I mean." Her head slipped to one side and she looked up at me through her lashes, her eyes sharp for only a moment.

"I'm sure I have no idea what you mean."

She saw the Thunderbird pull up before I did, and that most likely explained what happened next. She stepped in close, rose up on tiptoes, and placed a very gentle kiss on my lips. I might've leaned in a little after her, but she gave me my hand back and turned to walk past the powder blue convertible like a panther in floral print.

Vic was studying her mother very closely as she passed, the summer dress swaying provocatively in time with the slap of sandals against her naked heels. "Mother . . ."

Lena paused at the back seat for only a moment to scratch under Dog's chin. "Victoria . . ."

I walked over and leaned against the chrome frame of the windshield as all the males in the vicinity watched Lena disappear down the sidewalk and into the crowd.

Vic poked me in my still-sore ribs. "What? Are we fucking interrupting something here?"

It took me a while to think of anything safe to say. "I thought you guys were antiquing."

She raised an eyebrow. "Looks like you were, too."

Henry interrupted, before it could get any uglier. "It is our last day, and I have not seen the Liberty Bell."

I nodded and looked down at Vic's arm, which was still

in the sling. "It's cracked, but like most broken things, it's worth keeping." She looked up at me and smiled. I glanced at Henry. "Headed back early tomorrow morning?"

"Yes." He looked back at the beast. "Are you sure you do not want me to take Dog?"

"No, I might need him, and he's good company." I studied the streamlined flanks of the Thunderbird, admiring the work of the South Philly body shop. "You gonna be all right driving back by yourself?"

He smiled. "Yes. I am meeting my brother in Chicago."

I stood there, more than a little surprised. "Lee?"

"Yes."

I knew that the two had spoken only once in the last fifteen years, and only a handful of sentences at that. "I thought you guys didn't talk?"

He nodded. "I thought it was time we started." A moment passed. "Dena is in Rapid, so I may stop and see her, too."

I continued to watch him, but he didn't say anything else, and I could feel those slender strings thread their way down the Rocky Mountains, across the plains, over the Appalachians, finally coming to rest in attachments, here, in Philadelphia. I pulled the backpack further up on my shoulder and looked down at Vic. "What about you?"

"I've got a flight to Billings this afternoon. Chuck Frymyer's picking me up."

"Who?"

"Frymyer, the deputy you hired for Powder Junction?" I nodded some more, and they both watched me very carefully. "What do you want me to tell the county and Kyle Straub?"

There was everything to say, but no way to say it. "Tell them that I'll be coming home, eventually."

She exhaled a quick laugh. "They won't like the sound of that."

I cleared my throat and got off Henry's fender, allowing two fingers, including the one in the finger guard, to rest on the side mirror. "Well . . . Tell them I'm slow, but eventual."

She continued to smile and gently enclosed my fingers with hers. "That, I know."


Cady was no longer in the ICU but had been downgraded to a regular room on Vic's old floor. Dr. Rissman was standing at the nurse's station when the elevator doors opened. "Those cops were here, looking for you again." He adjusted his glasses. "But I think it was a social call."

I stopped and put my hands in my pockets. "They know where to find me." He looked at the floor, the wall, and finally at my left shoulder. I thought about how irritating I had found the trademark behavior when I'd met the man and how it endeared him to me now. Lightning rods didn't look you in the eye. "I want to thank you for all you've done."

"I didn't do that much."

"Excuse me, but that's crap. Besides all the manual labor, you gave me hope and that gave her hope." Finally, he looked directly in my eyes and smiled.

Michael was sitting by the bed reading the sports page of the *Philadelphia Inquirer* out loud. He was back on regular duty and was wearing his uniform. "How ya doin', Sheriff?"

"They still punishing you with third watch?" His eyes were tired, and he really didn't have to answer. "So, you got out of having dinner with us tonight."

He nodded and folded up the newspaper. "I told Mom I'd stay here, but you get everybody else."

"Who's 'everybody'?"

"Mom, Al, Tony, Vic the Father, Vic the Son, and Vic the Holy Terror."

A tiny terror of its own ran through me. "I just saw her downstairs, and she said she was flying out this afternoon."

He nodded and stretched his back. "I guess she found a way out of it, too." He stood, squared his shoulders, and placed his cap back on his head. "I guess it's just you and the family."

"Sounds interesting."

He laughed. "It's always that." He tucked the paper under his arm and covered a yawn with his hand. "I'm going home to take a nap; see you here around seven?"

He turned back to Cady, squeezed her hand, and left.

I sat in his chair, pulling it a little closer to the bed. I covered my face with my hands and again listened to the screaming that now resonated like the strings in a piano. I listened to their vibrations, to the chords and the melody that connected all of us. I thought about Henry's brother, Lee, about Dena. I thought about Vic, about her family. I thought about Cady.

I pulled her book from the backpack, from its spot between the printed dossiers and depositions Gowder and Katz said I had to read through before my meeting with the district attorney's office and the fifth district court. I leaned forward with my elbows on my knees and her book in my hands. Like a lot of things in my life, I'd just about worn it out, but it was worn out with love, and that's the best kind of worn-out there is. Maybe we're like all those used cars, broken hand tools, articles of old clothing, scratched record albums, and dog-eared books. Maybe there really isn't any such thing as mortality; that life simply wears us out with love.

It took a while for my eyes to focus, but when they did, the words were familiar. " 'Long, long ago, there was a king and queen . . .' " I felt a squeeze on my hand but tried to keep my attention on the page. " '. . . who didn't have any children.' "

"Da-ddy . . .?"

I continued reading. " 'One day the queen was visited by a wise fairy . . .' " My eyes blurred like they always did, and I watched as the drops hit the wrinkled page where they had struck so many times before.

"Da-ddy . . ."

Her voice was not strong, and Rissman said the pronunciation will continue to get better. We had a legion of hours in rehabilitation ahead of us, but if she continued to improve at the rate she had so far, the neurosurgeon said I might be able to take her back to Wyoming next month. I continued reading. " ' . . . who told her, you will have a lovely baby girl.' "

"Da-ddy . . . ish okay."

I look up at the clear and beautiful gray eyes, at the winning smile of youthful invincibility, at someone far more courageous and determined than I, and sometimes I make it through the entire story.

But most of the time, I don't.

Craig Johnson's fourth novel
featuring Sheriff Walt Longmire
is also available.

Read on for the first chapter of . . .

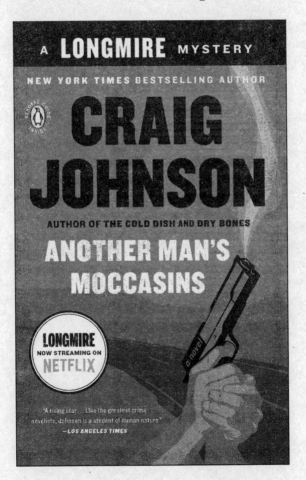

# 1

"Two more."

Cady looked at me but didn't say anything.

It had been like this for the last week. We'd reached a plateau, and she was satisfied with the progress she'd made. I wasn't. The physical therapist at University of Pennsylvania Hospital in Philadelphia had warned me that this might happen. It wasn't that my daughter was weak or lazy; it was far worse than that—she was bored.

"Two more?"

"I heard you. . . ." She plucked at her shorts and avoided my eyes. "Your voice; it carries."

I placed an elbow on my knee, chin on fist, sat farther back on the sit-up bench, and glanced around. We weren't alone. There was a kid in a Durant Quarterback Club T-shirt who was trying to bulk up his 145-pound frame at one of the Universal machines. I'm not sure why he was up here—there were no televisions, and it wasn't as fancy as the main gym downstairs. I understood all the machines up here—you didn't have to plug any of them in—but I wondered about him; it could be that he was here because of Cady.

"Two more."

"Piss off."

The kid snickered, and I looked at him. I glanced back at my daughter. This was good; anger sometimes got her to finish up, even if it cost me the luxury of conversation for the rest of the evening. It didn't matter tonight; she had a dinner date and then had to be home for an important phone call. I had zip. I had all the time in the world.

She had cut her auburn hair short to match the spot where they had made the U-shaped incision that had allowed her swelling brain to survive. Only a small scar was visible at the hairline. She was beautiful, and the pain in the ass was that she knew it.

It got her pretty much whatever she wanted. Beauty was life's E-ZPass. I was lucky I got to ride on the shoulder.

"Two more?"

She picked up her water bottle and squeezed out a gulp, leveling the cool eyes back on me. We sat there looking at each other, both of us dressed in gray. She stretched a finger out and pulled the band of my T-shirt down, grazing a fingernail on my exposed collarbone. "That one?"

Just because she was beautiful didn't mean she wasn't smart. Diversion was another of her tactics. I had enough scars to divert the entire First Division. She had known this scar and had seen it on numerous occasions. Her question was a symptom of the memory loss that Dr. Rissman had mentioned.

She continued to poke my shoulder with the finger. "That one."

"Two more."

"That one?"

Cady never gave up.

It was a family trait, and in our tiny family, stories were the coinage of choice, a bartering in the aesthetic of information and the athletics of emotion, so I answered her. "Tet."

She set her water bottle down on the rubber-padded floor. "When?"

"Before you were born."

She lowered her head and looked at me through her lashes, one cheek pulled up in a half smile. "Things happened before I was born?"

"Well, nothing really important."

She took a deep breath, gripped the sides of the bench, and put all her effort into straightening the lever action of thirty pounds at her legs. Slowly, the weights lifted to the limit of the movement and then, just as slowly, dropped back. After a moment, she caught her breath. "Marine inspector, right?"

I nodded. "Yep."

"Why Marines?"

"It was Vietnam, and I was gonna be drafted, so it was a choice." I was consistently amazed at what her damaged brain chose to remember.

"What was Vietnam like?"

"Confusing, but I got to meet Martha Raye."

Unsatisfied with my response, she continued to study my scar. "You don't have any tattoos."

"No." I sighed, just to let her know that her tactics weren't working.

"I have a tattoo."

"You have two." I cleared my throat in an attempt to end the conversation. She pulled up the cap sleeve of her Philadelphia City Sports T-shirt, exposing the faded, Cheyenne turtle totem on her shoulder. She was probably unaware that she'd been having treatments to have it removed; it had been the ex-boyfriend's idea, all before the accident. "The other one's on your butt, but we don't have to look for it now."

The kid snickered again. I turned and stared at him with a little more emphasis this time.

"Bear was in Vietnam with you, right?"

She was smiling as I turned back to her. All the women in my life smiled when they talked about Henry Standing Bear. It was a bit annoying, but Henry was my best and lifelong friend, so I got over it. He owned the Red Pony, a bar on the edge of the Northern Cheyenne Reservation, only a mile from my cabin, and he was the one who was taking Cady to dinner. I wasn't invited. He and my daughter were in cahoots. They had pretty much been in cahoots since she had been born.

"Henry was in-country, Special Operations Group; we didn't serve together."

"What was he like back then?"

I thought about it. "He's mellowed, a little." It was a frightening thought. "Two more?"

Her gray eyes flashed. "One more."

I smiled. "One more."

Cady's slender hands returned to the sides of the bench, and I watched as the toned legs once again levitated and lowered the thirty pounds. I waited a moment, then lumbered up and placed a kiss at the horseshoe-shaped scar and helped her stand. The physical progress was moving ahead swimmingly, mostly due to the advantages of her stellar conditioning and youth, but the afternoon workouts took their toll, and she was usually a little unsteady by the time we finished.

I held her hand and picked up her water and tried not to concentrate on the fact that my daughter had been a fast-track, hotshot lawyer back in Philly only two months earlier and that now she was here in Wyoming and was trying to remember that she had tattoos and how to walk without assistance.

We made our way toward the stairwell and the downstairs showers. As we passed the kid at the machine, he looked at Cady admiringly and then at me. "Hey, Sheriff?"

I paused for a moment and steadied Cady on my arm. "Yep?"

"J.P. said you once bench-pressed six plates."

I continued looking down at him. "What?"

He gestured toward the steel plates on the rack at the wall. "Jerry Pilch? The football coach? He said senior year, before you went to USC, you bench-pressed six plates." He continued to stare at me. "That's over three hundred pounds."

"Yep, well." I winked. "Jerry's always had a tendency to exaggerate."

"I thought so."

I nodded to the kid and helped Cady down the steps. It'd been eight plates, actually, but that had been a long time ago.

My shower was less complicated than Cady's, so I usually got out before her and waited on the bench beside the Clear Creek bridge. I placed my summer-wear palm-leaf hat on my head, slipped on my ten-year-old Ray-Bans, and shrugged the workout bag's strap farther onto my shoulder so that it didn't press my Absaroka County sheriff's star into my chest. I pushed open the glass door and stepped into the perfect fading glory of a high-plains summer afternoon. It was vacation season, creeping up on rodeo weekend, and the streets were full of people from somewhere else.

I took a left and started toward the bridge and the

bench. I sat next to the large man with the ponytail and placed the gym bag between us. "How come I wasn't invited to dinner?"

The Cheyenne Nation kept his head tilted back, eyes closed, taking in the last warmth of the afternoon sun. "We have discussed this."

"It's Saturday night, and I don't have anything to do."

"You will find something." He took a deep breath, the only sign that he wasn't made of wood and selling cigars. "Where is Vic?"

"Firearms recertification in Douglas."

"Damn."

I thought about my scary undersheriff from Philadelphia; how she could outshoot, outdrink, and outswear every cop I knew, and how she was now representing the county at the Wyoming Law Enforcement Academy. I was unsure if that was a positive thing. "Yep, not a safe weekend to be in Douglas."

He nodded, almost imperceptibly. "How is all that going?"

I took a moment to discern what "all that" might mean. "I'm not really sure." He raised an eyelid and studied me in a myopic fashion. "We seem to be having a problem getting in sync." The eyelid closed, and we sat there as a silence passed. "Where are you going to dinner?"

"I am not going to tell you."

"C'mon."

His face remained impassive. "We have discussed this."

We had—it was true. The Bear had expressed the opinion that for both of our mental healths, it might be best if Cady and I didn't spend every waking hour in each other's company. It was difficult, but I was going to have to let her out of my sight sometime. "In town or over in Sheridan?"

"I am not going to tell you."

I was disconcerted by the flash of a camera and turned to see a woman from somewhere else smile and continue down the sidewalk toward the Busy Bee Café, where I would likely be having my dinner, alone. I turned to look at Henry Standing Bear's striking profile. "You should sit with me more often; I'm photogenic."

"They were taking photographs with a greater frequency before you arrived."

I ignored him. "She's allergic to plums."

"Yes."

"I'm not sure if she'll remember that."

"I do."

"No alcohol."

"Yes."

I thought about that advisory and came clean. "I let her have a glass of red wine last weekend."

"I know."

I turned and looked at him. "She told you?"

"Yes."

Cahoots. I had a jealous inkling that the Bear was making more progress in drawing all of Cady back to us than I was.

I stretched my legs and crossed my boots; they were still badly in need of a little attention. I adjusted my gun belt so that the hammer of my .45 wasn't digging into my side. "We still on for the Rotary thing on Friday?"

"Yes."

Rotary was sponsoring a debate between me and prosecuting attorney Kyle Straub; we were the two candidates for the position of Absaroka County sheriff. After five elections and twenty-four sworn years, I usually did pretty well at debates but felt a little hometown support might be handy, so I had asked Henry to come. "Think of it as a public service—most Rotarians have never even met a Native American."

That finally got the one eye to open again, and he turned toward me. "Would you like me to wear a feather?"

"No, I'll just introduce you as an Injun."

Cady placed her hand on my shoulder and leaned over to allow the Cheyenne Nation to bestow a kiss on her cheek. She was wearing blue jeans and a tank top with, I was pleased to see, the fringed, concho-studded leather jacket I'd bought for her years ago. It could still turn brisk on July nights along the foothills of the Bighorn Mountains.

She jostled the hat on my head and dropped her gym bag on top of mine. She turned to Henry. "Ready?"

He opened his other eye. "Ready."

He rose effortlessly, and I thought if I got it in quick that maybe I'd get an answer. "Where you going?"

She smiled as the Bear came around the back of the bench and took her elbow. "I'm not allowed to tell you."

Cady's current love interest, Vic's younger brother, was supposed to be flying in from Philadelphia on Tuesday for a Wild West vacation. I still hadn't gotten a straight answer as to with whom he was staying. "Don't forget that Michael is calling."

She shook her head as they walked past me, pausing to lift my hat and plant a kiss on the crown of my head. "I know when he's calling, Daddy. I'll be home long before then." She shoved my hat down, hard.

I readjusted and watched as they crossed the sidewalk, where Henry helped her into Lola, his powder-blue '59 T-Bird convertible. The damage I'd done to the classic automobile was completely invisible due to the craftsmanship of the body men in South Philly, and I watched as the Wyoming sun glistened on the Thunderbird's flanks. I had a moment of hope that they wouldn't get going when the starter continued to grind, but the aged Y-Block caught and blew a slight fantail of carbon into the street. He slipped her into gear, and they were gone.

As usual, I got the gym bags, and he got the girl.

I considered my options. There was the plastic-wrapped burrito at the Kum-and-Go, the stuffed peppers at the Durant Home for Assisted Living, a potpie from the kitchenette back at the jail, or the Busy Bee Café. I gathered up my collection of bags and hustled across the bridge over Clear Creek before Dorothy Caldwell changed her mind and turned the sign, written in cursive, hanging on her door.

"Not the usual?"

"No."

She poured my iced tea and looked at me, fist on hip. "You didn't like it last time?"

I struggled to remember but gave up. "I don't remember what it was last time."

"Is Cady's condition contagious?"

I ignored the comment and tried to decide what to order. "I'm feeling experimental. Are you still offering your Weekend Cuisines of the World?" It was an attempt on her part to broaden the culinary experience of our little corner of the high plains.

"I am."

"Where, in the world, are we?"

"Vietnam."

It didn't take me long to respond. "I'll pass."

"It's really good."

I weaved my fingers and rested my elbows on the counter. "What is it?"

"Chicken with lemongrass." She continued to look at me.

"Henry's dish?"

"That's where I got the recipe."

I withered under her continued gaze. "All right."

She busied herself in the preparation of the entree, and I sipped my tea. I glanced around at the five other people in the homey café but didn't recognize anyone. I must have been thirsty from watching Cady work out, because a third of the glass was gone in two gulps. I set it back on the Formica, and Dorothy refilled it immediately. "You don't talk about it much."

"What?"

"The war."

I nodded as she put the tan plastic pitcher on the counter next to me. I turned my glass in the circular imprint of its condensation. "It's funny, but it came up earlier this afternoon." I met her eyes under the silver hair. "Cady asked about the scar on my collarbone, the one from Tet."

She nodded slightly. "Surely she's seen that before?"

"Yep."

Dorothy took a deep breath. "It's okay, she's doing better every day." She reached out and squeezed my shoulder just at said scar. "But, be careful...." She looked concerned.

I looked up at her. "Why?"

"Visitations like those tend to come in threes."

I watched as she took the tea and refilled some of the other customers. I thought about Vietnam, thought about the smell, the heat, and the dead.

## Tan Son Nhut, Vietnam: 1967

I had flown in with them.

A spec 4 on the helicopter ride had asked where I was going and watched as I'd tried not to throw up on the dead that were stacked in the cargo area of the Huey. I wasn't sick because of the bodies; I'd seen a lot of those. I just didn't like helicopters. The men had been in a mortared helicopter that had been waved off to an area outside the defense perimeter—firebase support in the DMZ for Khe Sanh. They were wrapped in plastic ponchos because the army had run out of body bags. They had run out of food, ammo, and medicine, too—the dead were one of the few things of which there always seemed to be plenty. The young corpsman smiled at me, his thin lips grinning like a death's head, and told me not to worry. He said that if I got hurt, they could have me in a base-camp hospital in twenty minutes, critical and they would have me in Yokosuka, Japan, in twelve hours. He had gestured to the plastic-wrapped bundles behind him. Like them, who gives a shit.

Later, I studied the chromate green interior of the Quonset hut as a lean air force investigative operations officer squinted up at me through his thick glasses and the sweat. He was studying my utility cap, so I yanked it off my head and returned to attention. I was sweating, too. Specifically, we were there to win over hearts and minds, but mostly what we did was sweat. I had been fighting the feeling that, since arriving in Vietnam coming up on six months earlier, I was melting.

He made me wait the commensurate amount of time to let me know that I had performed a breach of military decorum with my cover and that the major was not pleased. "What the hell am I supposed to do with you?"

The majority of the humidity in my body was draining between my shoulder blades and soaking the waistband of my fatigues. "Not sure, sir."

"What the hell is a MOS 0111?"

"Marine police, sir. Investigator."

He continued to shake his head. "Yeah. I got the directive from MAF. Your papers cleared the provost marshal at Chu Lai, so I guess battalion headquarters has decided that you're my problem now." He looked up at me. He had the look, the look I'd seen a thousand times in the short period I'd been in-country. He was old—an age that had snuck up on him in the place that would stay with him for the rest of his life. The event had him, the war was his religion, and his youth was gone with his eyes. "Marine inspector?"

I remained silent and focused on the corrugated wall in an attempt not to stare at the photo of DeDe Lind, *Playboy*'s Miss August 1967, that was hung there.

It was December.

The major looked back at my duty papers, rustling them in disbelief. "Inspect? Hell, I didn't even know you jarheads could read." He flipped the page, and I figured the real trouble was about to begin. His eyes came up slowly. "English major?"

"Ball, sir." I'd found it best to downplay higher education in the armed forces, and football was always a quick and successful diversionary tactic.

He blinked behind the glasses and frowned an acceptance that I might not be the complete wastrel he'd first imagined. "What'd you play?"

"Offensive tackle, sir."

"The trenches? Outstanding. I played a little in high school." With a leather helmet, I figured. "Is that right, sir?"

"Halfback."

"Yes, sir." Backup, no doubt.

He studied my papers some more. "I didn't play much." I didn't know what to say to that, so I just stood there with my mouth shut, another method I'd learned in dealing with military hierarchy. "Look, somebody owes somebody a favor and that's why you're here." He leaned back in his green metallic chair, which almost matched the chromate walls, and finally remembered that I was still at attention. "At ease." He dropped my papers and concentrated on me as I took a quarter step to the side and placed my hands behind my back. I was still holding my hat. "We've got a little drug smuggling problem on the base, but nothing big. We've already got some very good men working on the situation. I'm only guessing, but I'd say the provost marshal wants one of his brand-new MOS 0111s to get his feet wet."

He continued to consider me, and I guessed that he wanted a response. "Yes, sir."

"Why mother-green-and-her-mean-machine can't police her own messes, of which there are plenty, is a mystery to me, but you're here and we'll just have to make the best of things." He glanced back at the papers on his desk. "You are new, and it won't take long for everyone to figure out why you're here. So the best thing you can do is keep your mouth shut and do what you're told. You got me?"

"Yes, sir."

"All of the work you've done in the past has been under the direct supervision of navy investigators; now, however, you will be working with air force security personnel and central intelligence detachment, who, I am sure, you will find infinitely more capable than the swabos."

"Yes, sir."

"I'm putting you with Mendoza, who is our own 377th, and Baranski of Central Intelligence Division. They've been working the case for about five weeks, and you will provide the muscle."

"Yes, sir." If he belched, I was going to yes-sir it.

"They're first louies, and you will follow every order they give you. Understood?"

"Yes, sir."

"They're class of '66." He slipped my papers back in the folder and handed them to me. "That means there's one of you butter bars left; gives great hope to the war effort."

"Yes, sir."

"Dismissed."

When I got to the outer office and handed my folder to the airman, there were two first lieutenants leaning against the doorway. One was short and dark; the other was a tall bon vivant with an Errol Flynn mustache. The tall one had blond hair, air-force-blue eyes, and army fatigues. He stuck his hand out, and I shook it, taking in the casual, self-assured swagger of a man very content with himself. "You our new pet Marine?"

"Yep."

He lit a Camel cigarette and swiveled his head to look at his partner, who now extended his hand. I shook his as well. He spoke with a strong Texas accent. "Mendoza. This here is Baranski."

I had already read their names above their right pockets, just as I was sure they'd already read mine, but it was now a different protocol. I slipped my hat back on. "Longmire."

"Sheriff Longmire?"

I turned and looked up at Rosey Wayman, one of the few females in the Wyoming Highway Patrol. She'd been transferred up from the Elk Mountain detachment about six months ago and had been causing quite a stir here in the Bighorns. "Well, if it isn't the sweetheart of I-two-five." I watched as the trademark grin showed bright white teeth, and her blue eyes sparked.

Maybe my evening was looking up. I wondered when Vic would be back.

"I'm sorry to bother you, Walt, but we got a call in, and Ruby said this would be where you were."

"What've we got?"

"Some ranchers found a body down on Lone Bear Road near Route 249."

Maybe my evening wasn't looking up.

That was near Powder Junction. It was July, and it didn't take much deduction to figure out why the locals were out on that desolate part of the county road system. "Swathers or balers?"

"Balers. They supposedly swathed last week."

No square hectare of grass went unshorn in a Wyoming summer. The Department of Transportation usually subcontracted the cutting of grass along its motorways to the lowest-bidding local ranchers, which allowed the state grass to become a private commodity commonly known as beer-can hay.

I poked a thumb toward the blond patrolperson as Dorothy returned with the dish full of chicken and lemongrass. "Can I get that to go?"

No matter what aspect of law enforcement with which you might be involved, there's always one job you dread. I'm sure at the more complicated venues it's the terrorists, it's serial killers, or it's gang-related, but for the western sheriff it's always been the body dump. To the north, Sheridan County has two unsolved, and Natrona County to the south has five; up until twenty-eight minutes ago, we'd had none. There you stand by some numbered roadway with a victim, no ID, no crime scene, no suspects, nothing.

I got out of Rosey's cruiser and nodded to Chuck Frymyer and Double Tough, my two deputies from the southern part of the county. "Walt. She's down over the hill."

We headed toward the giant balers at the edge of a large culvert. Lieutenant Cox, the highway patrol division commander, was standing halfway down the hill toward the barrow ditch with two more of his men, still writing in their duty books. It was near their highway, but it was my county. "Hey, Karl."

"Walt." He nodded at one of the pieces of equipment where two elderly cowboys sat, one in a beaten straw hat and the other wearing a Rocking D Ranch ball cap. "You know these gentlemen?"

"Yep." The two got up when they noticed me. Den and James Dunnigan were a couple of hardscrabble ranchers from out near Bailey. James was a little wifty, and Den was just plain mean. "How you doin', James?"

Den squinted and started in. "We swathed two days ago, and she wasn't here...."

James cut him off. "Hey, Walt."

"What'a we got?" I figured the HPs had already gotten a statement from them, but I thought I'd give the brothers another shot at the story before we went any further.

"Already told 'em." Den gestured toward the HPs. It had probably been a long day, it was late on a Saturday afternoon, and he evidently felt they had been detained long enough.

"Tell me." I remained conversational but made sure it wasn't a question. Frymyer had his notebook out and was scribbling.

James continued in a soft voice and did his best to focus on the conversation at hand. "We was balin' and come up onto her."

"What'd you do?"

He shrugged. "Shut 'er down and called 911."

"Go near the body?"

"Nope, I didn't."

"You're sure?"

"Yep."

I glanced at Den, who was blinking too much. "Den?"

He shrugged. "I went over to the edge of the culvert and yelled at her." He blinked again. "I thought she might be asleep. Then I saw she wasn't breathin'."

I had Den show me the exact route that he had taken, and then I retreated to the top of the culvert with my two deputies, where it was unlikely anybody had been. I squatted down in a hunter's crouch and listened as Cox dismissed the Dunnigan brothers.

I turned to Chuck. "You know how to open a baler?"

The sandy Vandyke smiled back. "Born to it."

"Go crack that one open and check the contents and then split the last two bales northbound. If she was walking or running from somebody, then she might've dropped her purse or something along the way." Frymyer paused for a moment, and I looked at him. "You need help?"

He glanced back at the one-ton bales. "Yes."

I looked at Double Tough, and he started off with Chuck.

There was still a lot of light—it was like that in the summer this far north—and you could plainly see where the young woman had played out the last moments of her life. She was provocatively dressed, inappropriate for the surroundings. She had on a short skirt, a pink halter top, and no shoes. Her long, dark hair was tangled with the grasses; it had been blown by the ever prevalent Wyoming wind, and you could see her delicate bone structure. The eyes were closed, and you might've thought she was asleep but for the blue coloring in her face and a swollen eye, and the fact that, from the angle, it was apparent that her neck had been broken.

I listened as Cox came up and squatted down beside me. "You losing weight?"

"Yep, I'm in the gym with Cady every day."

He nodded. "How's she doing?"

"She's good, Karl. Thank you for asking. Hey, speaking of Cady, could I get you to have Rosey call into our dispatch and ask them to tell her I won't be coming home tonight?"

"You bet." He tipped his campaign hat back. "DCI's on the way. I think you got the wicked witch of the west herself." I nodded. T. J. Sherwin was always looking for a reason to come up to the mountains in the summertime. The division lieutenant plucked a piece of the prairie and placed the harvested end in his mouth. "We checked all the way back to Casper, Walt, but no abandoned vehicles." He glanced after my deputies. "Your guys gonna check the baler?"

"Yep."

"Good. My guys wouldn't know which end to look in." He studied the body of the dead girl and then looked up at me. "I've got men checking all the Chinese restaurants in Sheridan, Casper, and Gillette to see if anybody's missing...."

"Don't bother." I ran my hand over my face. "She's Vietnamese."

## A PENGUIN READERS GUIDE TO

# KINDNESS GOES UNPUNISHED

Craig Johnson

# An Introduction to
## *Kindness Goes Unpunished*

*Kindness Goes Unpunished* begins with Walt Longmire reading a fairy tale to a class of skeptical kindergarteners. "My daddy says you're a butt hole" (page 1), one of the children offers. Another child blurts out that his daddy "smokes his medicine" (page 3). Walt finds himself uncharacteristically flustered and overmatched by the five-year-olds as his storytelling skills falter. But this rather benign predicament is only a prelude to much worse troubles that lie ahead.

When Walt journeys with his friend Henry Standing Bear from the familiar ground of Absaroka County, Wyoming, to Philadelphia, he anticipates nothing more taxing than attending a gallery opening for Henry's prize collection of Indian photographs and a visit with his daughter, Cady. But a vicious attack on Cady leaves her near death and embroils Walt in an investigation that casts suspicion on Cady's boyfriend and fellow lawyer, Devon Conliffe, and Assistant District Attorney Vince Osgood, as well as drug dealer Toy Diaz and the brutal Shankar Duvall. As Walt moves back and forth between staying at Cady's bedside and searching frantically for the man who hurt her, he is drawn deeper and deeper into big-city drug crime and a political cover-up. Along the way, a series of mysterious notes left for him suggest someone is watching, anticipating, and perhaps guiding his every move. But is it the killer or someone trying to help? And why do so many people who might be able to answer Walt's questions keep turning up dead?

Within this narrative frame, *Kindness Goes Unpunished* offers fans of Walt Longmire all the dry wit, cultural sophistication, and cowboy toughness they have come to expect from the Wyoming sheriff. But it is also very much a novel about the bonds of family and friendship, and the necessity of hope for navigating life's violent contingencies. Walt knows the odds of his daughter surviving a coma are long and that the odds of emerging from it fully intact are even longer. How to maintain hope in the face of such uncertainty—and in the midst of the violence and corruption he finds in Philadelphia—is the central theme of this fast-paced thriller. And while Walt's skills as a storyteller may have failed him in the classroom, they keep the narrative of *Kindness Goes Unpunished* taut and unpredictable, and his skills as a detective never falter.

# A CONVERSATION WITH
# CRAIG JOHNSON

*Why did you choose* Kindness Goes Unpunished *for your title?*

It's no secret that I like using phrases for my titles that might have a double or deeper meaning. This one came from the former *Philadelphia Inquirer* editorialist Steve Lopez. "Philadelphia, land of giants, where no act of kindness goes unpunished." I think it speaks to the fact that some of the best actions in our lives are the most misunderstood, and for Walt, Philadelphia and the East can be a contrary environment outside his experience or jurisdiction. A stranger in a strange land, his emotional state concerning his daughter lures him into a dangerous place where he feels as if he has to make up the rules and mete out punishment. In law enforcement or life, that's a desperate place to be.

*Family seems particularly important in* Kindness Goes Unpunished—*the bond between Walt and Cady but also between members of the Moretti family—and there is a degree of tenderness in your novel not found in many mysteries. Did you set out to make family a central concern of the novel or did it emerge as you told the story?*

The importance of relationships is central to the story and to Walt's life. Although the image of the vengeful loner is pretty iconic to the American West, it is not in my novels. Walt's strengths lie in his connections to his family, his friends, and the people of the community. In the stark background of the high plains, the society of mankind becomes more evident, but it doesn't mean that it's any less essential on Broad Street. Family makes you tender, makes you confront your own humanity on an elevated scale; makes you deal with society, justice, honor, integrity—and that's all before leaving the breakfast table in the morning. I think it was Sam Peckinpah who said it best: *You need to enter your house justified.*

*The importance of hope also runs throughout the novel. Why did you decide to make hope such a powerful force in* Kindness Goes Unpunished?

I'm not all that interested in the acts of violence that people perpetrate upon each other, but I am interested in the aftereffects of those acts. I've dealt with the aftermath of those dark moments, and that's the part that has resonance for me. The positive aspects of the human condition can be tenuous in those times, but they are all we have to keep us going. Intrinsic to a "murder mystery" are the less than desirable traits of human interaction, but I think we, as writers, are also faced with conveying the good. We need to keep a positive outlook on humanity when faced with it at its worst. Hope, faith, and charity are damned important in keeping that humanity, even if those acts of kindness are punished. Just ask somebody when the chips are down. Without hope, well, there isn't much of a future.

*Why did you choose Philadelphia as the setting for the novel rather than the familiar terrain of Wyoming?*

I like the cheese steaks from George's on 9th Street in the Italian Market. Just kidding, even though I've been known to eat three a day. Seriously, I met my wife there. I love Philadelphia, and think it sometimes gets overlooked as one of the grand cities of the United States. So when I was casting about for a city that Cady might live in, Vic might've come from, and a place to which Walt would have a connection, Philadelphia became an obvious choice. That, and I have two daughters and a granddaughter there. Also, I wanted to take Walt out of his element and not have the novel seem like a bad episode of *McCloud*. (Sorry, Dennis.) There were things I wanted to explore outside of Absaroka County, so that I could learn and convey more about Wyoming, the West, and Walt in contrast.

*This is your third Walt Longmire novel. Are you discovering more about Walt as you write about him from one novel to the next? Has he changed since you began writing about him?*

Oh, God, yes. Any time you take on a series in first-person present tense, you're going to have to get to know that character damn well. I think it's also more than pretty important that Walt and all the continuing characters in the books grow and change; it's important to the readers and to me. When I first introduced Walt Longmire he was in the throes of an elongated depression, but in dealing with the complications of the case that is solved in *The Cold*

*Dish*, and by facing his problems, he started coming around. He surprises me every day, and I figure that's a good thing because if he's surprising me, he might just be surprising the reader, and that's part of my job.

*What motivates you as a mystery writer—the issue of crime and the criminal mind, the deductive reasoning of detective work, the larger social problems that crime so often reveals?*

All of the above, but the seminal motivation is definitely social problems. People always ask where I get my ideas, but just from the limited view I have of society, I get more ideas than I'll ever have time to write. I subscribe to the *Wall Street Journal, New York Times, Washington Post, Philadelphia Inquirer,* and *Los Angeles Times* either in print or online, and the news from these sources is enough to make me want to climb up in the trees and start screaming, but it's that irritation that motivates me for the long haul. Injustice is the burr under my saddle blanket, and it has become Walt's as well.

*What mystery writers have most influenced your own work?*

Shakespeare, Chekhov, Dickens, Steinbeck, Harper Lee . . . Go ahead, tell me that they aren't mystery writers. I dare you. Walter Van Tilburg Clark, Dorothy M. Johnson, Wallace Stegner, M. F. K. Fisher, Larry McMurtry, James Lee Burke, Tony Hillerman, James Crumley, Elmore Leonard, and George MacDonald

Fraser. Some of them are mystery writers, some are Western writers, some are both, some are neither. I don't like to classify as to genre, I guess. Poetry is important to the process; I learned that from my buddy Mark Spragg. I read a lot while writing and poetry is like jet fuel—Wendell Berry, Yeats, Rudyard Kipling, just to name a few. I was fortunate enough to use the work of another good friend, Mandy Smoker, in the novel—you want to know how smart this cowboy writer is? Smart enough to not try and write Indian poetry.

*No doubt your readers are eager for the next novel and particularly curious about how the relationship between Vic and Walt will develop. Can you give us an insight and possibly a hint about what's next?*

Kiss and tell, huh? Umm . . . no. Well, I can talk about what it was I was attempting to do, but I'm not giving out with any forecast. I think the development of an event in the relationship became a foregone conclusion for a lot of readers, and the question was how long I was going to stretch it out. I'm nothing if not reactionary—in the Oxford English Dictionary way—so I opted for what seemed a natural conclusion, sooner rather than later. The motivational factors were there, whether they were love, sympathy, mother/daughter competition, or just plain lust, and the sex was indicative in its spontaneity. As stated before, I never think that the act itself is as important as the aftermath. Isn't that always the case? It's going to complicate things, but then why shouldn't it? The layers of complexity in the character's lives are the lifeblood of the series. Look for clues in how the characters deal with what has happened. Walt reacts with the more stereotypical female emotions of regret, concern, and connection, while Vic takes the more masculine response by looking at it as "just sex" (page 210). There's a lot of generational stuff going on there, as well as gender. Will either or both of them get their hearts broken, live happily ever after, will these responses remain the same, or will they change and grow with the characters? I guess we'll have to wait and see.

# Questions for Discussion

1. What makes Sheriff Walt Longmire such an engaging character? What are his most appealing qualities? In what ways does he differ from other sleuths?

2. *Kindness Goes Unpunished* begins with Walt trying—and mostly failing—to tell a story to some kindergarteners. "I'm not sure when it was that my storytelling abilities began to atrophy," he says, "but it must have been somewhere between *Sesame Street* and *The Electric Company*" (page 2). What storytelling skills does Walt display as the narrator of the novel? What is distinctive and compelling about the way he narrates *this* story?

3. What does the opening scene reveal about Walt, about how he is regarded in Absaroka County, and about some of the problems that community faces? Why would Craig Johnson begin the novel in this way?

4. Henry Standing Bear is convinced that the healing ceremony he performs for Cady brings her back from her coma. In what ways does this suggest a fundamentally different approach to healing than standard Western medical practice? Why does Henry

feel it is important for Cady to "hear" them speaking even while she is in a coma?

5. Dr. Rissman tells Walt not to get his hopes too high for his daughter's recovery. But Walt knows that hope is essential. "I'd seen what the hopeless approach was like, and I was never going back there again" (pages 214). In what ways is the novel as a whole about the importance of hope?

6. What enables Walt, with help from Vic and Henry, to unravel the mystery behind the murders in Philadelphia? What special knowledge does he bring to the case? Would ordinary Philadelphia detectives have been able to solve it?

7. How does Sheriff Longmire regard Philadelphia and Philadelphians? How is he regarded in the city? What cultural contrasts does Johnson develop over the course of the novel?

8. Look closely at how Walt Longmire questions people. By what means is he able to detect whether or not they are telling the truth?

9. *Kindness Goes Unpunished* features some very strong women characters—Lena Moretti and her daughter,

Vic Moretti, as well as Cady Longmire who, even though she is incapacitated for most of the action, is still a powerful presence in the novel. What makes these women so forceful? How do they deal with the men in their lives?

10. How did you feel about the passion ignited between Vic and Walt? What was the spark that set it off? How do you imagine their relationship will unfold?

## ALSO AVAILABLE

# Land of Wolves

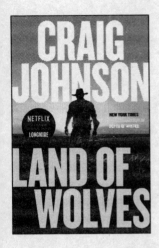

When an itinerant shepherd is found dead in the woods, the circumstances suggest suicide —but the shepherd worked for a powerful family of Basque ranchers with a history of violence. It isn't long before Longmire is pulled into an intricate investigation of a possible murder, all while a renegade wolf roams the Bighorn Mountains. Longmire must identify the true predator before it's too late.

"A taut, engrossing thriller from one of the most exciting voices in the genre." —*Newsweek*

VIKING             PENGUIN BOOKS

Ready to find your next great read? Let us help. Visit prh.com/nextread

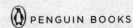